My
Other
Heart

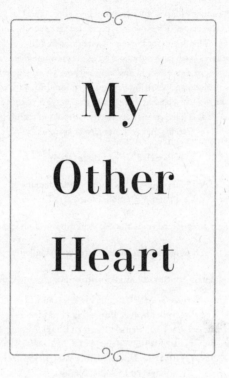

My
Other
Heart

Emma Nanami Strenner

PAMELA DORMAN BOOKS • VIKING

VIKING
An imprint of Penguin Random House LLC
1745 Broadway, New York, NY 10019
penguinrandomhouse.com

A Pamela Dorman Book/Viking

The PGD colophon is a registered trademark of
Penguin Random House LLC.

VIKING is a registered trademark of Penguin Random House LLC.

Designed by Cassandra Garruzzo Mueller

LIBRARY OF CONGRESS CATALOGING-IN-PUBLICATION DATA

Names: Strenner, Emma Nanami, author.
Title: My other heart / Emma Nanami Strenner.
Description: New York: Pamela Dorman Books/Viking, 2025.
Identifiers: LCCN 2024055029 (print) | LCCN 2024055030 (ebook) |
ISBN 9780593831014 (hardcover) | ISBN 9780593831021 (ebook)
Subjects: LCGFT: Novels.
Classification: LCC PR6119.T7426 M9 2025 (print) |
LCC PR6119.T7426 (ebook) | DDC 823/.92—dc23/eng/20241202
LC record available at https://lccn.loc.gov/2024055029
LC ebook record available at https://lccn.loc.gov/2024055030

First published in hardcover in Great Britain by Hutchinson Heinemann, an
imprint of Penguin Random House Ltd., London, in 2025.
First United States edition published by Pamela Dorman Books, 2025.

Printed in the United States of America
1st Printing

The authorized representative in the EU for product safety and compliance is
Penguin Random House Ireland, Morrison Chambers, 32 Nassau Street,
Dublin D02 YH68, Ireland, https://eu-contact.penguin.ie.

For Maya

My
Other
Heart

PROLOGUE

~ഉ~

Mimi

Philadelphia International Airport, 10:15 a.m., May 18, 1998

Mimi Truang did not yet know that her baby was gone. She sat back and closed her eyes, coffee in hand. It was still some time before they could board the connecting flight to Newark for their journey home to Saigon. Packing up last night had been difficult; Ngan had refused to sleep.

She'd finally succumbed as they'd approached the airport on the bus, closing her eyes and dropping like a heavy sack of rice on Mimi's lap at eight minutes past six that morning, exactly one hundred and four minutes after they had boarded the bus. Mimi's arm had lost all feeling as she held on to her child, trying not to drop her as a wave of fatigue dragged her along. It had taken a lot of energy to divert her daughter while she was awake. A one-year-old who had only just learned to walk wanted to explore everything. The old ladies seated across the aisle began the trip cooing over the cute, chubby baby. But after an hour, they started to tut at the crying. When Mimi's things fell from her bag into the aisle as she tried to find something to distract Ngan, she was met with a curt *Ma'am, we need to keep the aisle clear, people might trip, okay? DO YOU UNDER-STAND WHAT I'M SAYING?* Strangers always seemed to speak slower and louder when they got annoyed with her.

Check-in was equally hard. *Ma'am, please watch your child,* the man behind the counter had said, examining their passport photographs as Ngan slipped off the ledge of the conveyor belt that weighed her bags. Mimi tried to distract her, encouraged her to wave the bags goodbye, but the baby wanted to follow. The man behind the desk had the uncomfortable look young people got around an infant or an old person: embarrassment at the lack of self-consciousness. It was the thing that parents loved most in their children in infancy and loathed most in their elderly parents.

MIMI WRAPPED HER arms around herself; muscle memory had taught her to make herself small and inconspicuous. The smell of weak American coffee floated up from the Styrofoam cup in her hand. She would never get used to this. When she first joined her sister, Cam, in Philadelphia two years before, they walked along Arch Street, outside Reading Terminal Market, sipping coffee in the brisk autumn air. *Dirt water,* they called the coffee. They guffawed and hooted at their joke. *Two cups of dirt water, please.* But when they became too loud, enjoying themselves too much, the sneers and looks would begin. So their jokes were kept private, spoken within their own four walls. Soon she'd be back home. *Café Sua Da* would be waiting. No more need for hushed voices. She sipped her dirt water and winced. As if in agreement, her daughter giggled from her "hiding place" beneath her seat, and Mimi felt small sticky fingers squeeze her ankles.

The hot liquid ran down her throat. There was still a day's traveling left before they would land on Vietnamese soil. Ngan's whining interrupted her thoughts, and she shuffled through her handbag and pulled out a cracker. Mimi leaned down and offered it into the space beneath her seat. Her daughter's plump hand took it quickly, and there was silence from her again. Now only the ambient noise of the airport and the muffled announcements interrupted her every thought. She patted her pocket to check for their passports and her remaining money and mentally subtracted the dollar fifty she'd spent on the coffee and milk. The oily smell of fast food lingered in the air. Next time she would remember to sit farther away from the restaurants. She looked at the grime and dirt on the floor and thought about Ngan's hands touching everything then going into her mouth. Mimi pulled a tissue from her pocket, already soiled, and grabbed at Ngan's hands to wipe them. But Ngan pulled away quickly.

Mimi could never get used to the air in America: its taste, its smell, the way it felt on her skin. The cold was in her bones all the time, and the food gave her constipation or the opposite. America had been a storm in her stomach from the moment she arrived. She had never found peace. The shouting and the cursing she could tolerate; she rarely understood what was being said anyway. People said *fuck* a lot. And she couldn't understand why the fucking had to involve mothers. But the food offended her most. Bread like she'd never known. She missed the perfect crispness of a *banh mi* and the soft clouds of white dough inside it, the heady fragrance of the mint and coriander and chili in the air—the sweet saltiness of pork and rich pâté. Instead, there was only dirty oil and flaccid bread, noodles that were, in fact, not at all what they claimed to be. She wanted to take her child and get out of this place where she could not be understood, or considered, but always discarded instead. Her invisibility was a noose around her neck that tightened every day. Even now, as the time to leave edged closer, and Mimi's heart flipped at the thought of putting this fetid land behind her, people would look at her for only a millisecond before dismissal. She didn't count.

Mimi reached down to place her cup on the floor but changed her mind as she remembered that Ngan's little hands would seek out the hot liquid. Instead, she got up and put the cup on the table two seats away. She sat down again and reached between her feet, her arms stretching under her. She didn't want to get on her knees, the floors were filthy, but she had accepted when they traveled that Ngan wouldn't understand this. She would wipe her down later in the bathroom, and rinse her arms. Americans and their poor hygiene, she thought. The stench of bleach was everywhere, but there was always an underlayer of filth. Nobody mopped their floors properly here. Cam's landlord used to walk through their apartment with his shoes on, traipsing the dirt from the filthy streets across her clean floors.

Mimi waved her arms side to side, windshield wipers searching for her daughter's fleshy arm or leg. Mimi's armpits hurt from the awkward motion, so she got down onto her knees to pull Ngan out from under the seat.

Her child was gone.

Act One

CHAPTER ONE

～✦～

Kit

Philadelphia, April 2015

S o where are you from?" the Uber driver asked.

The cloying scent from the Black Ice air freshener sat in the back of Kit's throat. She could see the hairs coming out of his ears. She glanced at her watch.

"Here, I'm from Philly," she replied. Kit Herzog knew what he really wanted to know.

He looked at her in the rearview mirror. Their eyes met, then he set his gaze back on the road. There was another odor beneath the freshener: dirty hair or skin. She kept her hands on her lap, not wanting to touch any of the surfaces. A new song started to play on the radio.

"You know this tune?"

She nodded. "Teardrops" by Womack & Womack; her mother played it in the kitchen sometimes. She started to see signs for Roxborough. Not far to go now.

"Great song." He hummed.

She would be late for Sabrina, but at least Sabrina's mother would be out. Mrs. Chen worked a Saturday job and Sabrina was always at home alone.

"So hon, are you from Philly? You look, uh, I don't know, like there's somethin' else in there. Like, where are you *from* from, you know?"

Kit was asked this almost every time she met an adult outside of her family circle. Mr. Fischer, the new History teacher, got straight to the point at the beginning of the semester. "What is your ethnicity exactly, dear? Pan-Asian is it? Hawaiian? South American?" He had a habit of putting her on the spot, and she dreaded his class.

Her skin bristled at the thought that the ambiguity of her complexion and eye shape should become an open invitation for questioning. Cece Daley, with her long legs, platinum-blond hair, and cheerleading squad accolades would never be asked to explain her origins. "Daddy's from California and Mom is from Ambler, right here in Pennsylvania," she would probably say, unprompted. Kit had seen Cece in the Home Depot on weekends, calling her father "Daddy."

"So? What is it?" he persisted.

"What is what, Sir?" she asked, her voice sharp.

"What is your background, hon?"

There was no reason for her to hold this back. She could put him out of his misery in a few words. But she thought, Why should she explain? She was still stewing over the fight with her mother that morning, and the kiss with Dave in the basement the night before, and how he had said: "Hey, we're still keeping this between us, okay?" She wanted to get to the safety of Sabrina's bedroom. She wanted one of those jasmine teas Sabrina always made. They would watch a movie, talk late into the night—just the two of them, so they could really talk, unlike at her house on Gravers Lane, where she was always listening for the creaking floorboards announcing her mother's arrival.

"If you don't mind my asking, of course."

She thought, *Actually, I mind very much.*

"I'm adopted," she replied quietly.

⁓

"Tupperware . . . when I grow up, Kit, I'm going to invest in Tupperware." Sabrina sighed as she looked into the fridge. She stacked and unstacked plastic containers. "We have so many empty butter containers for leftovers. Does your mom do this? Probably not, I guess. I mean, look at this one. One dumpling. Why didn't someone just eat it? And Tupperware is cheap. You can go to Walmart and buy like a dozen sets for nothing." She shook her head, replaced the top of the butter container, and put it back in the fridge. "Oh! I found them," she said, her voice singing in happiness as she brought out a plate with a picture of penguins dancing on an iceberg. No dish in their home was the same, unlike Kit's house, where everything was a full set from Crate & Barrel.

"You gotta try these, they're so good." Sabrina placed the plate, which held two cakes, between them. The top of the pastry was carved with intricate ridges in the shape of a goat.

"Did your mom make these?" Kit asked, holding one carefully, cradling it in the cup of her hand like a small bird.

"Course not. We bought them in Chinatown."

"Your mom makes things sometimes. Those cute flowers out of the vegetables and stuff? She could have made it." Kit felt the heat rise to her face.

"I guess. These are mooncakes, my mom buys extra for the year on discount—she doesn't believe in sell-by dates. They're still good to eat though."

9

When she put the cake back down on the plate, Kit noticed that the edge of its soft casing had a dent. She felt her mouth curling down at the thought of an old cake, long past is expiry date. Sabrina returned with a knife to cut it in half.

"What's so great about this cake?"

"They're just totally different. Not like anything you get here, you know?"

"I don't get it," Kit muttered. But her friend hadn't heard her, and she wasn't appreciating the personal sacrifice Kit made to be there: the cab driver and his questions, the stench of Black Ice still on her clothes. She glanced at her phone; there were no messages from Dave.

Sabrina cut the mooncake in half, revealing the shiny, perfectly preserved shape of a heart layered in pink, yellow, and orange-red bean paste.

"Isn't it beautiful?"

Kit shrugged.

Sabrina pushed the plate over to her, offering her the first taste. Kit's mother had brought her up well; she should have eaten the first mouthful with relish and complimented her host. But she couldn't remember these lessons in that moment.

"I hate that red bean shit," Kit said.

Sabrina's features clouded with hurt. She looked like a girl in a manga comic book, a close-up of her face in the picture box with giant weepy eyes and a wobbly line for tears on the way.

"Don't have it, then," Sabrina retorted and forked a big portion into her mouth. The piece was too big, and Kit could see that Sabrina's pleasure had floated away like a child's bubble that had burst.

The meaningless hurt caused over a mooncake.

Kit looked at it and thought how she actually did want to try it, she wanted to taste something sweet. But this had always been their dynamic—Sabrina, the chirpy mouse who would edge too close to Kit's lair, where she would snap and snarl as Sabrina limped away. This was her nature against Sabrina's soft, accepting ways. She thought of the books she'd seen on her mother's bedside table, like *Nature vs. Nurture: The New Way to Parent*. Sabrina said that she was always taught by her mother, Lee Lee, to avoid taking risks at all costs and respect her elders. There was no other way in the Chen household; everything came back to these two rules. But Kit found other ways, and sometimes wondered why Sabrina didn't try to as well, even if the freedoms in her home were different. Maybe it was as simple as that, that her parents never enforced the same rules that Sabrina had to live by. Or maybe it just wasn't in Kit's nature to do as she was told.

"What's up with you? You're in a terrible mood," Sabrina asked, her tone cautious, as she poured their tea.

"Yeah, family lunch at the Harrisons' was annoying. Dave was there." Kit wanted to say more, about how he had asked to meet her the night before and they had fooled around in his den while his parents were out. But the words wouldn't come. Sabrina's kindness in spite of her own snappy remarks left her feeling guilty.

"You wanna talk about it?" Sabrina asked, pushing a steaming mug toward her. "I know you guys have some kind of understanding or whatever, but I'm here, I'm a good listener."

The balled-up jasmine leaves began to unfurl in the hot water.

"You think Dave is a racist?" Kit asked suddenly, dipping her finger into the liquid.

"What?"

"Nothing, never mind."

"I don't think so, Kit. I mean, he's dated different girls. He's in my political science class, and he's a liberal," Sabrina said.

"Yeah, I guess. I just don't understand why he is so weird about *us*, you know?"

Kit saw Sabrina searching for the right words to respond.

"I'm like the last person who understands guys. I kissed Seth Hartmann three times before I dumped him, and like, we were hardly even boyfriend and girlfriend . . ." Sabrina's voice trailed off.

"I know, I know. But hey, this is your summer, right? And then we have college. We are going to *live!*" Kit forced a false cheeriness to her voice, but underneath she wanted to cry.

"Do you think so? I really hope so. I'm so ready for high school to be over," she replied in almost a whisper.

For the first time in weeks Kit shifted her gaze away from her problems with Dave and noticed that Sabrina looked tired. Something was weighing on her friend. She tried to remember what Sabrina usually did on weekends, but she realized with some surprise that she always assumed her friend was studying or waiting for Kit to invite her over. It never occurred to Kit that Sabrina's life extended beyond her blue row house, her studies, and Kit herself. She looked around the kitchen and saw Sabrina's Dell laptop nestled and shut on top of the side counter. The stickers on the cover had started to fade. The pile of *kawaii* Japanese corgis looking over their backsides now looked like a fluffy cloud, but the Keith Haring dancing figures and the "So Fetch" and "Hacker Inside" stickers still retained their original colors. Kit remembered how happy Sabrina had been when Kit had brought them back for her from her vacation to San Francisco the year before.

"What's up, Rina?"

As Sabrina looked up at Kit, an expression of surprise passed behind her friend's eyes.

"Oh, I'm just trying to work through some stuff, you know, end-of-year things."

"Talk to me." Kit leaned forward. She remembered how her mother would do this when she wanted to encourage her to open up, and Kit congratulated herself for being so sensitive to her friend's needs.

Sabrina took a breath and closed her eyes for a moment, as though she were about to jump into a cold pool.

"I'm trying to figure out how I can get to China before college. I want to go visit my family. Or at least see this place I'm supposedly from."

This wasn't what Kit had expected to hear. It took her a moment to take it in, until thought after thought tumbled out, one after the other.

"What do you mean? Like this year? For real?"

"Well, yeah, I mean I gotta do it soon. I haven't really talked to my mom about it yet. You know how she can be. I've been saving up money from tutoring and babysitting jobs. I think I'm going to have enough by the end of July."

Kit nodded. She did know how Sabrina's mom could be. Kit's usual exasperation with her own mother would disappear the moment she saw Lee Lee Chen with Sabrina, enforcing her rigid rules that often made no sense to Kit at all. It was in these moments that she allowed herself to be grateful for her adoption by a nice, liberal, upper-middle-class Pennsylvania family. The kind of parents who would let her stay out late because her friends were. The kind of parents who congratulated her for simply trying even though she achieved mediocre grades and showed no real promise in sport. *You got your dad's hand-eye coordination, that's for sure,* her father joked. She was relieved that they allowed her to experiment with her clothes when she started to care about how she was dressed, and even helped her shorten the hem of her school uniform skirt. She was thankful that they bought her a cell phone at almost the exact same time that all her other classmates got them. Sabrina was never given such freedoms.

And somewhere deep in the recesses of Kit's mind were thoughts that never passed her lips. She was happy that her life was nothing like

Sabrina's. She didn't dare consider how it might be to be raised by a mother like Lee Lee Chen. She thought of all the parties Sabrina had missed because her mother did not believe in socializing outside of school hours, or the times that a trend for a certain water bottle or backpack had swept through the girls in her class and Sabrina had looked on, with the same old items she had started school with that year.

Don't you ever just want to say no? Kit wanted to ask Sabrina, but she knew her friend well enough to know she never would. They were built differently.

"If I save and work these summer jobs for the first month, and get going with the passport application, I might be able to visit for two weeks in August. Just before college starts. Even if I don't manage to go to Mom's exact birthplace, I could see some of China. I could see the land, listen to the people. Travel, finally. You know what I mean?"

"Why do you want to go so much though? Like, do you even know the people you'd have to stay with? And what if you hate it there? And you're on your own?" The moment Kit said it, she felt foolish.

"I guess that's the whole point. I don't know anything about what to expect. That's the part that's exciting to me. It's about knowing where you're from. Where you belong. *You* know what that feels like, of all people."

The silence dragged on for a moment too long. Kit wasn't sure how to respond to that.

⁓

There was a constant struggle within Kit: her need for control, to always have exactly what she wanted, battled against the kindness she also

14

wanted to give. Most of the time it was easy, because Sabrina was the people pleaser. They had been friends in kindergarten, first and second grades, and then they stopped talking. Kit couldn't remember why, but something had shifted in her circle of friends. If she really examined it, she would come to realize that her mother had nudged her toward their family friends and their children. *Their* friends, who lived in *their* neighborhood. But Kit wouldn't realize this until much later in her life.

Sabrina referred to the years that Kit and Sabrina were no longer friends as "when you were in the group." Kit barely thought of Sabrina at all during this time. She had not deliberately broken away. In fact, her memories of those years were like any eight-year-old's: the spotlight was on herself. Her mother had organized her social life with the care expected of a Chestnut Hill Academy parent. Kit went on playdates at large mock-period houses after school. She carpooled with Casey and her sisters to ice-skating in the afternoons and attended birthday parties. During the time she wasn't friends with Sabrina, her world existed purely within a five-mile radius of Germantown Avenue, the main boulevard that ran through her leafy, well-heeled suburb of Philadelphia. Kit's life was a rhythmic composition through the seasons: summers eating ice creams the size of her head at Bredenbeck's after camp, pumpkin picking at Maple Acres Farm, choosing Christmas trees with her father, Terry, behind the Saturday market, and Easter egg hunts at the country club. In the summer, they rented houses next to her parents' friends down the shore with activities packed into each day, so Kit was never bored. That is why she never thought of Sabrina during those years—there wasn't time.

WHEN KIT TURNED nine, there were three unbearable weeks of school when she cried every day in the car and begged her mother to let her stay home. There was a trio of notoriously cruel girls who were a few years older than her, and she had somehow come into their line of fire. Overnight it became Kit's turn to be their source of amusement. During a freezing February morning, the name-calling began. "Kit Herzog has got tiny eyes. Kit Herzog has a mustache of blackheads. Kit Herzog has such gross dark hairy legs. She's a tarantula from the jungle." Her eyes were not slanted, nor did she have a mustache of blackheads or hairy legs. In fact, she was remarkably less hairy than the girls calling out to tease her, which seemed to her the greatest injustice of all. When Kit was younger, she had a tendency to attract attention. Unlike Sabrina, she was loud, and until these taunts began, she was unfazed by older children—if they were game, she would play or talk with them. Sabrina, on the other hand, maintained a well-practiced invisibility that kept her out of trouble, making her body as small as it could be, folding into herself, disappearing into a crowd. Kit's voice carried across a room or a playground, and she was always conspicuous to both new friends and enemies.

During those weeks when she was the target of the mean older girls, Kit's eyes were red from the panic every morning of what she faced at school. *Please please don't make me go to school today*, she begged Sally. The three older girls stood in the corner beside the library when she walked in. They all had the same mousy hair, freckles scattered across their noses, they could have been siblings, wearing the same hoodies from J.Crew in red, with mittens hanging out of their sleeves. She searched for the teacher, a point of safety. The clock showed another four minutes before Mr. Greenhill would come out and tell them all to go to class. But it was too late, they'd seen her.

"Hey, look who it is," they started. "I could see her mustache from the other side of the room."

Kit dipped her face into her fleece collar.

"Ewww, yeah I can see it, even though she's trying to hide her face from us."

The librarian, Mrs. Bleecker, walked past, and they all chorused their good mornings with playful smiles stamped across their mouths. *Good morning, Mrs. Bleecker.*

Kit's stomach lurched.

They started to walk toward her, she tried to edge closer to Mrs. Bleecker, and suddenly, she felt a weight crash against her, her backpack pushing her forward, four or five steps out of control before she regained her balance. She looked behind her to see Sabrina staring at her wide-eyed, as if to say *keep moving.* And all Kit could remember after that was getting away from the girls and sitting down at the desk beside Sabrina's, relief settling over her. Even when Kit had been in "in the group" and distant from Sabrina, there was never a moment when she couldn't reach out and find Sabrina there if she wanted to, and she always did.

CHAPTER TWO

Kit

Chestnut Hill, April 2015

That day with the mooncake, which was the last time Kit slept at Sabrina's house, though neither of them knew it then, Kit was preoccupied by her friend's significant plans for summer, and moreover, by the fact that she had made no such plans for herself. As always, she relied on the safety net of her parents' annual rental of a beach house. Dave's family, the Harrisons, would rent the house next door. She would go to parties down the shore with the same people from the year before and the year before that. Her parents accepted that Sabrina would stay with them at the beach house for a few days every summer. Back at home in Philly, Kit would sunbathe at the country club pool when temperatures soared, and when she felt like company she'd invite Sabrina to join her. But now, Kit was overcome by an impulse to leave Chestnut Hill as soon as possible. And preferably before her friend, because she always did everything first.

What Kit couldn't tell her mother or Sabrina was that the most pressing reason she had to travel after graduation was to get away from Dave

Harrison. When Sabrina revealed her plan to go to China for the summer, within a matter of hours Kit decided that she too would leave for her own adventure, as though she had come up with the idea herself.

As the end of high school drew near, everything in Chestnut Hill was a searing reminder that her heart had been brutally discarded and she had no way to mend it unless she could be somewhere where *he* wasn't. The final semester of high school had been weighed down by the clandestine embraces and heated kissing in corners of houses out of anyone's sight, followed by his distance from her in public. Most days, her eyes flickered over the length of the hallways, searching for his silhouette, waiting for him to acknowledge her. She never learned from the pain she felt as he looked through her. She just continued to hope that one day he'd be different.

THE NEXT WEEKEND, Kit was lying on her bed daydreaming. She'd spent the last week creating a full picture in her head of what her own adventure abroad would look like. She heard her mother's footsteps passing down the hallway and called out to her. Sally stood in the doorway with a vase of wilting flowers. Kit never called for her mother.

"Mom," Kit said, turning onto her back and shuffling herself up to sit against the headboard of the bed. "I think I want to travel."

She watched her mother's expression, a rearrangement of thoughts for a moment. Kit had expected a different response, enthusiastic support for her declaration. It occurred to her that she should have waited a day or two to bring this up; they had put their family dog down that morning, and though Kit had felt sad momentarily, Tripper had been her mother's dog, not hers. But her self-reprimand evaporated as she rationalized, *She needs to know as soon as possible. Flights need to be paid for, and where was she going to stay in Tokyo anyway?* Kit started to imagine herself checking into a hotel on her own, pulling a suitcase along to the check-in desk and waving her parents' "emergencies only" credit card at the receptionist. She wanted to laugh aloud at the image she'd built in her mind, as though she were playing house at the Please Touch Museum.

"Sure, of course you do," Sally answered, fixing her expression, which did little to hide her surprise.

"No, you don't understand. I want to travel *this summer*. Like in the next couple of months. To Japan. I know my ethnic heritage has always been a little blurry, but you know how I've always had this really strong pull to Japan, right? Sabrina and I were talking about our Asian heritage. I think it would be good before college starts to have a better sense of my identity? Don't you agree, Mom?"

Her mother stared at her. Kit noticed a redness around the edges of her green-gray eyes from the tears she'd shed earlier over Tripper. Kit didn't really see her mother cry, she only heard her behind the closed doors of her bedroom sometimes.

Kit stared back at her, unable to control her smug expression as she felt a surge of pleasure from the delivery of her words. The satisfaction of stating the importance of her beliefs, the phrase *sense of identity*, felt good coming out of her mouth.

"I . . . what?" Sally asked, looking for her words.

"Mom, you don't need to answer now. I just needed to ask you, okay?" Kit said.

Kit felt she had truly done a good deed: thoughtfully giving her mother advance notice. And she smiled at the fuzzy internal glow of her mature generosity.

"Kit, this is not the time," was all her mother said finally.

"Mom," she groaned, knowing that the more she pushed, the better the chance her mother would acquiesce. But for now, Sally had shut her down.

"What is it, Kit?"

Kit looked up, hostility starting to build.

"I'm sorry about Tripper, Mom. I am. Maybe I shouldn't have asked right now. But I think this is important too." She waited for the recognition of her empathy, the olive branch extended.

Instead, Sally walked away, and Kit felt a hot anger spread inside of her, right up to the roots of her hair.

"Where are you going?"

Her mother continued down the hall to her bedroom, and Kit sank down and screamed into her pillow.

She rolled over and stared at the ceiling, but her fury dissolved quickly. Kit's life suddenly seemed ignited with possibility.

She relished the thought of sharing the news at school the next day: how she had planned to go to Japan to find her roots. It had always been Japan to her, after all. Finding her roots and finding her birth parents were two very different things, and the former was far easier to stomach, with less possibility for unwelcome surprises.

—⁓—

In the eighth grade, Kit had decided that her birth mother *had* to be Japanese. It took almost no time for her self-declared origin story to become the truth in her mind and others', because it was never questioned. Nobody would question the adopted mixed-race girl with white parents.

Why shouldn't she be Japanese if she willed it to be so? The boys in her class were going through a Nintendo anime game phase. The female characters were drawn with long legs, short skirts, and big brown eyes with floppy fringes. One day Todd Peterson announced after a soccer game that Kit's lookalike was one of the characters in a game they played. The other boys gathered around his phone and looked up at her and back, and they hooted and laughed at the resemblance.

"Hey! Come see this, Kit. It's you," he called as he waved the phone at her.

She stood, welded to the ground. A quick internal fight over whether she should ignore him or not took place. She hesitated and then walked over slowly. The heat rose up her neck and to her cheeks. She tugged at the neck of her T-shirt. She peered over Todd's shoulder as he zoomed into the image. The girl did look like her. She could see the resemblance. Kit's skin tone was a shade or two darker, but the heart shape of her face, the light brown specks in her eyes, and the way the bangs she had been growing out fell just over her eyebrows were like her. In that instant she decided she would keep her bangs and told herself to remind her mother to book a hair appointment.

Her chest filled with pride, and she felt a rush of happiness at all the eyes on her. She felt like the heat of the afternoon sun was warming her through the windows, just like a dog might be lying blissfully in the glow of the sunshine.

"Yeah, man, this is you. So weird! Even your hair." Todd pulled at her ponytail.

From that moment, Kit decided she *was* a little Japanese. And over the years, the fictional narrative became a reality. In her mind, her birth mother also had the large shiny brown anime eyes. The mother she imagined would have worn a kimono on New Year's Day, and sometimes Kit would scroll through her Instagram feed to look at the Japanese mothers who posted elaborate lunchboxes, rice balls with cute googly eyes and octopus sausages that were both appealing and repulsive at the same time. She followed her favorite stars and influencers, and when they posted from Tokyo, she would like the images. Her mother bought her a vintage travel poster of springtime in Tokyo, and she had it framed on her wall. As the years went by, the frame became dusty and hung askew, and eventually most of the image was covered by other moments in her life she wanted to display more. Photographs of her and Sabrina, a Valentine's Day card from the tenth grade that she was convinced Dave had left in her locker. But somewhere back in the same recess of her mind where she was grateful for her white adoptive parents, she believed she might really be Japanese.

As Kit had expected, four weeks before the end of high school, her parents gave in and gave her a graduation present: a plane ticket to Tokyo. Sally called her old family friend Rick Buchanan, and it was agreed that Kit would stay with him and his family in Tokyo for the better part of the summer. Rick's two children were about Kit's age, a boy and a girl, and he held a senior position as a diplomat. Kit's comforts would be taken care of in every way that was within a mother's control.

It seemed the perfect arrangement, but Kit still wanted to apply her own conditions. *Am I going to be chaperoned all the time, Mom? It's important to me that I am independent, you know. Especially before college starts.*

In truth, Kit felt some relief knowing that her mother was watching over her, because venturing so far from home scared her. Leaving her hometown, the familiarity of the same street she'd lived on her whole life, going so far away from her anchor points was terrifying. A controlled freedom was what Kit craved. Freedom that wasn't too extreme or daring, with the soft landing of her mother's touch.

She was thrilled at the thought of sharing her plans to travel with

Dave. What better way was there for her to tell him that his silence over the phone and at school was hardly noticed, than her bold decision to travel to the other side of the world. *Her* trip. She would explain to him in detail the long journey, the jet lag, and the mystery of a completely different land. When the Harrisons came over to watch the game that weekend, what would have been an awkward afternoon of Dave and Kit deliberately avoiding each other's gaze suddenly gave her the hope of shifting the power paradigm between them.

"Kit has decided she is going to have an adventure this summer in Tokyo." As her mother announced her news, she flushed with self-satisfaction but still found herself avoiding Dave's gaze.

Kit shrugged. "I figure, this is a good time, you know? Before college." She surprised herself with her feigned nonchalance while her heart raced, hoping that Dave would pick up on the implication that it was *her* trip, to be taken on *her* initiative.

Mrs. Harrison gasped with delight. "Wow, Kit, this is so exciting! Honey, remember I told you about our friend from high school who is a diplomat? His name is Rick and his gorgeous wife is Yuriko," she said to Dave, who wasn't listening to his mother but grunted in acknowledgment. "Oh, and do you remember, Sal? When he introduced her to us? She was like a little doll just sitting there."

"I wrote to Rick," Sally told her.

Dave looked up from his phone. "How long you going for?" he asked before returning to his text message.

Kit wondered who he was messaging.

"Six weeks. That's quite awhile, isn't it, sweetie?" Sally said, answering Dave's question for her.

He looked up again. Kit searched his face for signs of a reaction, but after their eyes met for a moment, he looked at his phone again.

"Yeah, it's basically the whole summer."

Dave heard her. She knew him well enough now to see the impact of her words. He put his phone down, closing the screen so she couldn't see what he had been doing.

~ ❧ ~

A year ago, Kit had sat on the beach, shoulders pink with sunburn as Dave stood over her, his shadow stretching out along the sand. *Hey, come down to Troy's party later?* His voice made it sound like it wasn't really a question.

That night, as they sat on the sand watching the orange flames of the bonfire, her leg fell against his, and he didn't move. She wanted to look up at him, to see any expression in his face that might give away his feelings, Instead, she studied the parts of him that she could take in up close. She studied his legs, the golden-blond hairs, and his hands. She liked Dave's hands. His nails were always clean and short. She had noticed this about him long before he'd started to make her heart soar. Hygiene and pride in appearance: Kit cared about these things. For the rest of her life she always noticed men's nails. And if their nails were too long, unclean, she would instantly strike them from her mind.

When he stood up and reached for her hand, she let him take it, and he led her down the beach. She only realized after they had walked for five minutes in silence, her hand in his, that she had left her sandals by the bonfire.

He draped his arm around her neck, and she felt herself lean into the side of his body, until he stopped suddenly and turned quickly. They were face-to-face, and she could feel his breath on her lips. It wasn't what she had thought it would be. The kiss. She had expected tenderness and feeling; she wanted words from him, but instead he said nothing. His tongue stabbed at hers, her mouth awkwardly open, feeling too wet, as he rubbed his hands over the small of her back, and then around to the bare skin of her stomach. When he stopped and came up for breath, she stepped back to search his eyes, but found nothing.

~ ⚬ ~

CHAPTER THREE

Mimi

Philadelphia to Ho Chi Minh City, June 1998

There was little that Mimi could remember clearly in the time after she lost Ngan: the days morphed into weeks, months even. First, she was swept into a pitch-black hole of terror, and then she was thrust into the depths of ice-cold water, a ghoulish riptide taking her further and further away from her Ngan. There were no tears, instead she felt a choking in her whole body, a persistent ache that held back the tears that would fill the ocean between her Vietnam and America. She was flooded with images of Ngan: a newborn, her paw-like hand clutching the fabric of Mimi's T-shirt. Sometimes Mimi had wanted to shake it away. But she loved her, how she loved her. Sure, during that journey to the airport, Mimi had lost her patience when Ngan tried to wander out into the aisle of the bus. But Ngan knew her mother loved her. A child knows how much a mother loves them.

Even in that moment just before she was gone, Mimi told Ngan how much she loved her. "Good girl, smart girl," Mimi had said as she smiled and gently tried to reach below. And then she had searched beneath her seat, and the cavernous emptiness of that space swallowed her up.

"Ngan!" she had shouted.

Mimi felt herself being sucked into a well. She kept shouting into the crowd, into the space between the ceiling and the heads of people walking past her. She screamed at the blank faces that stared at her as they pushed their luggage slowly in front of her.

But Ngan did not come.

The things a person is self-conscious about disappear when desperation takes over. The rolls on your stomach you were so worried about against the waistline of your trousers, an ill-fitting shirt, the bags under your eyes. When the anguish comes, you just don't care. You don't care about the sound of your voice that's decibels above everything, and the people who stare wide-eyed at you like you are a wild animal. You don't care about the guttural savage cry that emerges from the depths of your breaking heart as you try to grasp for something that is gone, that has disappeared.

"Ma'am, you need to control yourself." A man, who looked like a pink pig with sprouting orange hair, mouthed slowly.

A sound came from Mimi, from deep inside the well of her being. She didn't recognize it as her own. The realization that she couldn't find the words, that the language she had a shaky grasp of got her nowhere. She couldn't communicate her despair to anyone—it only pierced her insides and brought forth the animal from her depths.

"Ma'am," he continued, but his silhouette blurred around the edges. She couldn't make out the things in front of her. Someone was holding her arms behind her, thick sweaty hands squeezing her until she felt her arms might snap. Mimi's mind raced through thick matter, she couldn't see clearly nor could any word in any language other than her own form on her lips. She was pushed into a room with harsh fluorescent lighting;

she needed to squint to focus. The strength left her body, and she felt herself become limp. She whimpered and felt tears and mucus running down her face. Her shirt had opened, her faded bra exposed for everyone to see, but her arms were pinned behind her, and she was helpless.

The conversations that took place around her sounded muffled. She couldn't catch the words, though she tried so hard to concentrate. "Documentation." "Boarding." "Police." That was all she heard. Nobody came for Mimi that day. Nobody helped. Too much time was passing. She wanted them to search the terminal sooner, every plane earlier, every parked vehicle and every suitcase should have been searched. But nobody came in time. She saw no search party. And nobody was brought to the room with the blinding lights to speak to Mimi in her native tongue. Instead, she sat and waited. As the minutes passed and she could feel Ngan getting further away, Mimi's whimpers turned into wails again. It was all too late.

When her sobbing finally became too loud, she felt a sting against her arm, the painful piercing of a needle through her flesh, and soon her eyes drooped. She fought it, fought with everything left inside of her. Then the world went black.

After Mimi was sent home to Vietnam, after she woke up on a plane with her arms tied to the chair, after she sat in transit beside security guards in countries she didn't know, who would not look at her. She begged the officials in Tan Son Nhat to let her board another plane, but she was treated like a criminal. Finally she returned to Cam, who'd gone back to Saigon six months before her, and she laid in the bed her sister had made for her on the floor. In her fits of sleeplessness and swirling grief, she heard her sister talking to her husband through the thin walls of the next room.

"What if she's wanted by the authorities?"

"What are you talking about? If anything they are the ones who need to be held accountable. A child is missing and they did nothing." Cam's voice was rising.

"You are naive if you think that will ever happen. We have nothing."

WE HAVE NOTHING. Mimi knew it was true, there was nothing she could do, but she would not accept it. Every waking moment held the deep fog of her loss, and when the air cleared briefly, the darkness returned, like a night that would never end.

Mimi would never get over that day. And it wasn't because she was sedated and found herself flying over the Pacific back to Saigon without her child. No, she would never get over that day because she had been powerless, which forever altered how she saw herself. And because she had, ever since, been weeping from a private faucet inside her, unable to keep her thoughts from the pink smiling pig man with sprouting orange hair who told her to control herself as she wept for her baby and begged for help.

She lay in the darkened corner of Cam and Duong's rooms in District 9 of Saigon for days. She woke up each morning with her head throbbing, her thoughts slowed by desperation, frightened to open her eyes and face reality. Her Ngan was gone. Sometimes her sister would draw open the curtains and Mimi would squint her eyes shut: *too bright*. When Cam would spoon food into her mouth, she felt the suffocating urge to cry. She would lie back down, replaying the moments in the airport, every day an emphasis on a different detail, how the men in uniform spoke to her, how the empty space beneath her seat had felt as she waved her arms around, how the fast-food shop in front of her smelled.

Everything had closed in on her. She was drowning, lost in this savage fog of pain. Drawn between her and what had happened was a sliver, a thin red line of what she should feel and do. But she could not move. Her heart had been crushed inside of her chest.

CHAPTER FOUR

Sabrina

Philadelphia, May 2015

Things had changed between the two girls. Kit became more guarded. She rushed home at the end of day, no longer waiting for Sabrina by her locker, and she stopped talking about whatever had been happening between her and Dave. But if Sabrina had to pinpoint the moment the air between them started to swell, it was the moment Kit had announced that she would be traveling too, over the summer. It wasn't just a regular vacation that Kit was going on, it was her own version of Sabrina's trip: a rite of passage, self-discovery in the distant country she was meant to be from.

"So my mom has organized this whole thing in Japan for me. I guess we have these family friends there. I'm going to do something different this summer, before college." Kit had said it so fast that if Sabrina hadn't been listening she would have missed it. They were walking along the edge of the soccer fields after school on a Friday afternoon.

"Wait, so you're going to Japan? When did you decide to do this?"

A mixture of emotions passed through Sabrina. She was jealous, curious, and angry. A rage started to run through her like a fire catching on kindling.

Kit shrugged. "I don't know, I think I told you, right after we talked about the summer." She played with the chewing gum packet in her fingertips.

"Did you? I can't remember that. But wow, this is all happening so soon. Like you just wanted to go . . . and then you just, go?"

"I guess, yeah. Hey, do you want to have dinner at mine tonight? My mom said you can come over, we can order in?"

And so Kit would go to Japan—her parents would pay for all of it. Kit had asked for something, and her parents gave it to her. Sometimes Sabrina allowed herself to imagine what that must feel like—to want something and be able to have it immediately. But then, Sabrina reminded herself that she didn't understand the inner workings of Kit's feelings. Kit would be going to a place that *could* be her birth mother's origin, and move a little closer to knowing where she was from, to understanding her identity. And for this, Sabrina always forgave her friend, even when jealousy threatened to eat her up.

If Sabrina hadn't been so distracted by her college applications, she might have been more angry at Kit. But her gaze had settled elsewhere. That night she lay in her bed, after applying her face cream and closing her laptop. Lee Lee was already asleep, and she could hear her soft snores through the corridor. Sabrina had taken to wearing earplugs at night to block out the sound, which had started to bother her. Once Lee Lee's breathing settled, Sabrina reached under her mattress and pulled out the envelope she had retrieved from the mailbox when she got home. She ran her finger over the college name and read it again. PROMPT ACTION REQUIRED. She slowly pulled the envelope open and took another breath before unfolding the letter. It was thin. Thin was never good news.

Perhaps it was better this way, she thought. If she didn't have the place, there was less to lose.

Dear Sabrina,

Congratulations! The committee has reviewed your application and we are happy to offer you admission for the Class of 2019. Prince-ton received a record of more than 17,000 applications this year, and your accomplishments, extracurricular activities, and personal qualities stood out among a strong pool.

She couldn't read the rest of the letter, her hands were shaking too much. She would need financial aid, and she was afraid she would not be granted any. Sabrina decided to tell her mother later, once she had the offers and the money in place; she would fill all the forms in as Lee Lee, she wouldn't say anything until she had all the information. What would Lee Lee do with her in another state? Even if it was just over the river in New Jersey? She carefully closed the letter and put it under her mattress again. Suddenly Kit's news of her trip to Tokyo didn't bother her so much.

⁓

"Americans love to tell you what nothing town they're from. The towns they spent their whole lives trying to get away from and then deserted the moment they were old enough to leave. Why do I need to know if somebody comes from Michigan and it rains there for five months every

year? Why? What is so interesting about that for me? It's always an unin-
teresting fact they want to tell you. The weather, some boring baseball
player who was from there." Lee Lee complained as she sat back in her
La-Z-Boy in front of the TV. She rubbed her feet together, then crossed
her ankles. She threaded a needle and began to mend a hole in her favorite green dress. It was a murky, deep green. Sabrina wished she would
throw it away. She had worn it last to the parent-teacher conference,
paired with a pale lilac blazer, and Kit had said, *Wasn't your Mom wearing that at the church barbecue last weekend?*

She wanted to believe that Kit didn't mean it unkindly, but lately Kit
had been angry. In fact, Kit had been angry for almost an entire school
semester for reasons she had not shared with Sabrina. Kit had always
dominated their relationship and liked to be in the driver's seat. Decisions on what they would do over the weekend, which coffee shop they'd
hang out in, and what movie they'd go and see always fell to Kit. And
Sabrina was happy to let her decide. Because in Sabrina's life, there were
plenty of other things that required decision-making. She welcomed the
space to be led instead.

Lee Lee was overbearing in many ways, but nothing could really be
done in their household without Sabrina. It fell to Sabrina to deal with
the school communications. It fell to her to pay the bills. If the house had
a leak or a damaged window, it fell to her to speak with the landlord and
arrange for someone to fix it. She didn't know what it felt like to know
that a home was forever. This was the seventh home she had lived in with
Lee Lee. And she was now poised and ready for a sudden announcement
from their landlord that they had to move out. She adapted fast.

Sabrina was good with computers and numbers, and Lee Lee would
stand over her mesmerized as she would type their monthly budget into
a spreadsheet. When money became tight at the end of the month, Sa-

brina reallocated their funds in just a few swift movements of her mouse. The gas in the car would only be filled half or quarter. They would postpone dentist appointments and endure the pain a little longer when the balance got low. Lee Lee was capable of doing this alone, but she took comfort from her daughter sharing these decisions. Sabrina's days were full of decisions—decisions other teenagers who attended her high school didn't have to make. When it came to deciding where she would drink coffee or what movie she would see, she was happy to defer to Kit, who didn't know the extent of Sabrina's responsibilities at home. Kit never looked out beyond the realm of her own existence, and Sabrina never asked her to.

Kit's anger that year, though, had unsettled their friendship's neatly formed pathways. Sabrina didn't really understand how the girls at school became consumed with rage toward their parents. She had seen Casey Steinham scream at her father in the parking lot. Sabrina wondered, if her father had been in her life at all, whether she would ever feel so angry she would make a scene of this kind. She couldn't imagine such a thing, namely because she couldn't even picture the man who was her father. In turn she never felt sad or missed him, and it was easy to accept that it was only her and Lee Lee, because it was all she knew. Whenever she asked her mother, she said, "Not now, *xiao haizi*, I cannot talk about such things."

SABRINA DREADED SUNDAYS because Sunday was church day. Lee Lee had decided that the best way to create *guanxi* was to be a good churchgoer. Sabrina stood beside her mother, whose voice rose higher and higher during the hymns, until she reached a new octave Sabrina had never heard before. She suspected her mother enjoyed the singing, and she noticed how the members of the congregation greeted Lee Lee with gentle familiarity. Sabrina knew her mother would never say it, but she enjoyed being part of this American church, and that she was invited back time and time again.

It happened during one of her visits to Lee Lee's favorite church, the Episcopalian Church of Chestnut Hill. *The building is most churchish for the most serious of Christians*, she exclaimed. One morning, at choir rehearsal, Lee Lee met Sally Herzog for the first time.

"Hi there, Sabrina," Sally had called out.

"Oh, hi, Mrs. Herzog," she replied.

"Are you here for choir practice?"

Sabrina nodded. She could hear the rustling of her mother's bag stop, the sound of her standing up right behind her. *Don't come over, don't come over*, Sabrina said to herself in an inaudible whisper.

"Ah, so you are Katherine's mother? Yes?" Lee Lee asked.

"Mrs. Chen. I'm so pleased to meet you," Sally said, her hand extended, eyes downcast.

She had seen that expression on Sally's face before. It was the same one she had when she talked to Kit and Sabrina's PE teacher during parent-teacher conferences.

"Your daughter Katherine is very charming. Sabrina and her have become very good friends," Lee Lee said, shaking her hand for too long. *Let go, let go.*

"Yes, Kit talks about Sabrina all the time at home," Sally replied. "We must have you both over one of these days. We would love to get to know you better."

Sabrina could see the lies coming out of Sally Herzog's mouth, forming clouds of air in the entrance where the biting cold from outside seeped inside, fading as the words lost their meaning. Dragon's breath.

"Yes, we would like this. When shall we do it?" Lee Lee pressed on.

"You know, I have got to look at my calendar. I will call you or get a note through Kit to you. It was so nice to meet you, Mrs. Chen."

Sabrina breathed. They would part, and it would be forgotten.

"Mrs. Herzog," Lee Lee persisted.

"Sally, please."

"Sally. I will call you. For the girls. We can meet—I have no husband, sometimes it's good for us mothers to come together. This is what you do here, isn't it? The children play, and the mothers, we can do something."

"Oh, I'm sorry . . . I didn't know you were alone . . . I mean . . ." Sally stuttered. Sabrina thought, *Yes you did.*

"No, no sorry. No need. This is life sometimes."

The interaction was in painful slow motion to Sabrina.

"Yes, sure. I'd love that, Mrs. Chen," Sally said as she started to move away.

Sabrina willed the interaction to be over fast; she hated to see people lie, especially to her mother. And she knew there would be an onslaught of questions from Lee Lee about the Herzog family on the way home in the car.

~∞~

No matter how bad a day Sabrina had, or how frustrated she was with her mother, Lee Lee's cooking was a fast-acting balm. Lee Lee Chen's passion *was* cooking. Sabrina loved to watch her face when she sliced through garlic, ginger, and spring onions with a giant cleaver. This familiar action filled Sabrina with a feeling she couldn't name. Was it pride, love, home, belonging? The wok that Lee Lee shook over the open flame still made Sabrina nervous, but in her seventeen years, not once had she ever seen Lee Lee burn herself. Her favorite dishes were the ones that her mother loaded with chili. She loved the heat and how it reached the back of her throat, and she had to suck in an extra breath to cool her mouth down. She loved Lee Lee's homemade pickled cucumber salad with its tart vinegar and fresh, tiny, savage red chilis, the clean smell of which would fill the room. Her favorite dish was the bright chicken and garlic chunks with green chilis and peppercorns she spooned over her glistening white rice. Radiant, ostentatious, morning glory stems bunched neatly as they were cut and served into three sections on the plate. None of Lee Lee's cutlery and dishes matched, but Sabrina saw an elegance in the pink and orange plates. She saw their elaborate patterns.

When her mother was finished serving the food, Lee Lee pulled up a chair and watched her daughter with a crooked smile.

"Eat, eat," she said "Oh, I loved *Lazi Ji* when I was little too. This is my own mama's recipe . . ."

"Tell me about her, Mama." Sabrina asked. All Sabrina knew was that her grandmother had died when she was nine. Sabrina remembered the exact week because it was the only time her mother had lain in her bed with the curtains drawn for six days. Sabrina was afraid, and hungry, and ate only peanut butter sandwiches that week. She'd always asked her mother to make her peanut butter sandwiches like the other kids, and now that the time had finally come for her to eat them, she hated the taste. She missed her mother's rice, her mother's fruit and eggs, she missed her mother's hands busily preparing food on the narrow kitchen countertop. When the six days passed, Lee Lee appeared in Sabrina's doorway early one morning and offered to drive her to school. It was the best morning.

But whenever Sabrina tried to ask after her grandmother, Lee Lee always had the same answer, just like she did for her father, "Not now, *xiao haizi*, I can't talk about such things." One day Sabrina would try to understand all the pain her mother felt about her past and the pieces of Sabrina's life that were missing.

CHAPTER FIVE

Kit

Chestnut Hill, May 2015

I'm not going away this summer anymore," Sabrina announced to Kit one morning as they were changing for gym.

There was no "hey" or any familiar greeting between them when Sabrina walked into the girls' changing room. The familiar, repulsive smell of old sweat and damp towels hung in the air, mixed with the bleach that had been mopped across the floors.

Sabrina blurted out her news to Kit with what would have appeared to anyone else as apathy. But Kit knew her friend better than that.

Sabrina adjusted her hair in the changing-room mirror. Her cheeks were flushed and her mouth a flat, rigid line.

Five other girls in their senior year had just left in a cloud of body spray, throwing paper towels stained with cheap makeup into the trash can.

"What are you talking about? The trip?" asked Kit.

"Yeah, it's off."

Kit glanced at Sabrina sideways in the mirror. She couldn't name what she was feeling—guilt, pity? She suddenly found it difficult to swallow—an awkward lump forming in her throat—the kind she felt when she tried to lie to her parents. Kit had wanted to travel and the arrangements were made within a week. Sabrina had saved for the better part of a year and now the entire trip was off.

"What happened?" Her voice came out in a whisper, surprising her.

"What do they call it when there's an event that nobody can control? Like, nobody's to blame? They put it in contracts and stuff. A force majeure."

"What do you mean?"

"An act of god, a natural disaster, circumstances beyond our control." Sabrina sighed heavily.

A feeling of defensiveness crept up on Kit, on hearing impatience in Sabrina's voice at Kit's lack of understanding—a feeling she knew she had to push down because her friend was hurting.

It didn't occur to her that there were plenty of things that Sabrina had no understanding of. How to order an Uber. Because she always took the bus. How to sign the chit at the country club, since no one there pays in cash. It didn't occur to Kit in that moment that this life-changing trip Sabrina had planned would be a first of so many things, including boarding an airplane for the first time in her life.

"A major pipe burst in our bathroom. Our landlord is away over the summer. He's not responding to us. We needed to get it fixed, and I had to pay out with the money I saved. So now I can't book the flight. There goes my trip."

Kit took in a sharp breath. She didn't know what to say. The air between them stood still and Kit felt anger toward Sabrina and herself for the silence. It was entirely true that Kit had the money to travel and Sabrina did not. It made up the very fabric of what separated them, a thick seam that always kept them apart. Kit remained here, and Sabrina over there. Still, she wished that Sabrina had not had her dreams dashed before she herself had boarded the plane and had to feel the bitter self-loathing. It was like a grief she'd never known, for everything she had and everything that Sabrina did not.

"It's okay, Kit," Sabrina finally said and walked out.

CHAPTER SIX

Sabrina

Philadelphia, May 2015

On her way out of the Asian American Immigration Coalition office on Vine Street, Sabrina squinted at the afternoon sunbeams that blurred her vision. She walked, her feet moved one step in front of the other down the hot sidewalks. Car horns sounded impatiently in the slow-moving traffic. A courier on a bicycle, who stood upright on the pedals, shouted at pedestrians, *Move your bodies!* She recalled how she loved and hated downtown Philly. The dirt landed on her skin, a film of black soot from the exhausts of tired, trawling cabs and garbage trucks. She loved the scruffy streets in Center City. Even the magnificence of the city hall spires was edged with unlovable side streets littered with unhoused men and women panhandling, and young boys in baggy tank tops and low-slung jeans who paced up and down as if to say *What can I get for you today?* She passed row houses that looked like they had been stuck together haphazardly. When the streets started getting gentrified, she saw lofty brownstones. She imagined the polished wooden floors she'd seen at Kit's house. In the winter months, when the

Herzogs turned on the underfloor heat, Sabrina and Kit would lie down on the floor and laugh as they pretended to make snow angels. *I'm never getting up.* They shrieked and giggled. When Mr. and Mrs. Herzog were there, she never knew quite how she was expected to behave. Did she need a coaster for her drinks? The kitchen island had marble finishing and separate sinks—one for washing up and one for prep—so which sink should she wash her hands in? How should she stack the dishwasher after they'd eaten? Her worst evenings were when Mr. and Mrs. Herzog invited her to join them for dinner to do "small plates," where they shared dishes, and she felt frozen to her seat and waited to be offered a spoonful of different dips and tried to eat with a smile on her face.

In Sabrina's mind, these fancy houses bore *some* resemblance to Kit's house, although Kit's house was a sprawling suburban home compared to these narrower city townhouses. But these brownstones and Kit's house on Gravers Lane had walls so thick you couldn't hear your neighbors sneeze, unlike the flimsy walls of her own home. Sabrina imagined the elaborate blooms of flowers from the garden or an expensive local florist's arrangements in every room; she thought about the heated floors and cool silent, air-conditioning that didn't shake the room as it revved up like it did at hers. At Kit's house, Mrs. Herzog tended to a patch of vegetables that Mr. Herzog had built a protective fence around, and sometimes they sat eating croissants in the breakfast alcove overlooking the backyard. Sabrina was mesmerized by the blue jays and northern cardinals that came and feasted at the bird feeder. The thought that her mother would enjoy that sight always passed through her mind when she sat there watching the colorful birds fly in and out of the garden. Lee Lee loved birds—she always said that their freedom had no end.

The couches in Kit's house, and there were several—in the great room, as Mr. Herzog referred to it, and the TV room—were so enormous that Sabrina was swallowed up by the plush upholstery when she sat down for movie nights. She loved to rub her hand up and down the armrest and look at the changing texture of the forest-green velvet. In the winter months, Sabrina had loved to go over for sleepovers, especially if Mr. and Mrs. Herzog were out and they left the fireplace on. Kit brought blankets, and they sat in front of the TV, her whole face flushed by the heat radiating from the hearth as she pretended to watch whatever show Kit had chosen, staring into the flames that cracked and spat out sparks against the fireguard. She loved how her clothes would smell of burning wood afterward as she stepped out into the icy winter air.

SABRINA WALKED THE length of Vine Street. In the distance, she saw the neat rectangular silhouette of the Franklin Institute, where the length of the Schuylkill River in the distance expanded to the west, and she remembered how her mother would take her to sit on the steps and watch people walking by in the spring.

They sat outside because Lee Lee refused to pay the entrance fee. It was only when Sabrina went for her first sleepover at Kit's that she went inside the Institute and walked through the giant model heart installation she'd heard the other children at school talk about. Kit had run through the main exhibition, calling *This way, Rina!* But Sabrina wanted to slow down, to run her hands over the uneven walls and imagine she was really inside a beating heart in someone's body. It was a boring outing for Kit, who had complained in the car to Mrs. Herzog that they had only just visited last month, and that she wanted to go to the Philadelphia Zoo instead for cotton candy. But Sabrina's eyes were greedy, and she took in everything. Kit rushed her through the Electricity Exhibit, where children lined up to spark their own circuit boards. Sabrina hadn't had her turn, but Kit wanted to leave, so they left. Kit had seen it all before, and Sabrina knew she had to fall into her friend's rhythm or she wouldn't be asked over again. For a moment in that museum, Sabrina wished that Kit did not exist and that she were there alone. But by the time they licked the edges of their ice cream sundaes outside, she had forgotten this and looked, eyes filled with admiration again, toward her friend.

UNLIKE THE CLOSED gated driveways of Chestnut Hill that told anyone on the outside to *Keep Out*—the straight lines of Center City Philly gave Sabrina comfort. There was an equality here. She felt an entitlement seep into her, as though she could take a risk on anything as much as the next person. She was not expected yet to stay within her box, because everything was up for grabs. Nobody knew her, there were no invisible lines. It could have been the chaos that emerged in unexpected places from street to street: one minute she was walking through a financial district and surrounded by men in suits on their cell phones, the next she saw overflowing trash cans and lines outside the PECO Building, made up of people mostly asking for their electricity to be turned back on in spite of defaulting on payments. She had stood in this very line with Lee Lee for the same reason. The low-rises that clustered around the Comcast Center and skyscrapers respected one another's vistas. Back in Chestnut Hill, at school, there were invisible lines everywhere: between Kit and her, between Lee Lee and Sally Herzog and all the other mothers and daughters at CHA.

Sabrina often wondered what lay beyond state lines, in a way that Kit would never understand. The world was always there for Kit to take, but for Sabrina, within the boundaries of her home and high school, she waited to be asked and never stepped out of the place she was assigned. The Delaware River to the east was too far for her—beyond the boundaries of her familiar, sometimes claustrophobic hometown. And yet, she felt hopeful here in the city, miles away from school and Kit. There was something in the grime that reminded her that things happened here, no matter where you came from, no matter how little you had, that something was afoot even though it could be dangerous. No matter how much she felt, she stood still, waiting, looking upon the horizon for something to happen to her.

～✺～

When Sabrina realized she was no longer going to China, she applied to work at the country club. She would be paid double what she had earned at Mrs. Moskovitz's café in Roxborough the previous summer, and the job became more appealing with Kit away all summer.

"You'll see, my *xiao haizi*, you'll make more use of your summer holidays right here at home than Katerin all the way over there doing whatever she is doing. Nothing serious, nothing useful."

"That's not the point, Mom." She huffed and regretted it the moment she saw her mother's eyes flick to her face.

"We have the life we have. We have to make the sacrifices. Another trip will come," Lee Lee said.

Sabrina said nothing. She knew better than to argue with Lee Lee about the injustice of having to give up her hard-earned savings for a household emergency. Every paycheck that Lee Lee ever made went to their household emergencies and non-emergencies, this was just life. At least, that is what Lee Lee would have said in response.

AT THE BEGINNING of senior year she had decided that she would take an internship along with other summer jobs before any hopes of travel had taken shape. She had gingerly pushed the door open to the college counselor's office for their first meeting. Mr. Jenkins was a short, wiry man with skin that was the shade of yellow chalk, and while his arms and legs were thin, his stomach protruded over his belt like a watermelon. She noticed his college diplomas on his wall: St. Austin's University and DeVry University in Illinois. Behind him were family photographs: A wedding photograph of a younger, strawberry-blond version of the man sitting before her, dressed in a pale blue tuxedo beside an unsmiling woman. His three children, miniature versions of their parents, with flaming red hair and the same translucent, pale skin.

"You know, Miss Chen, I've been looking at your transcripts. It would really help if you had a cause to fight for," he said without introducing himself or looking at her at all. "The low-income students I've got into Ivy Leagues, the top tier, Harvard, Princeton, Stanford, and Yale, they all had a cause to get passionate about, you know? I mean, of course, CHA *is* a public school, so this is great for us in terms of quotas, but don't take this the wrong way, Ms. . . . ." He paused to look up her name on her file. "Chen . . . Is that Chinese?"

She tried to answer, but he continued.

"Asian kids with good grades are a dime a dozen. I think this is a great opportunity for you to explore your own ethnicity and use your disadvantage to your advantage. If you don't mind me saying so."

She did mind.

"You must have faced some kind of racial discrimination in your time growing up here. We're not an especially diverse community, here in Chestnut Hill."

Sabrina stared at him as he spoke.

"It would be better, of course, if you were from a less affluent country like a Cambodia or a Vietnam, maybe. China is considered more developed and desirable now, but we can work with this. It helps, of course, that you are from a single-parent household," he muttered as he flicked through her transcripts.

"Your grades are good—but that's to be expected, under the circumstances."

"The circumstances?"

He peered over his glasses to look at her and then pulled them off. His eyes narrowed and traveled over her in a way that made her feel like a meal he took a particular dislike to.

"Your circumstances. You are from a low-income family unlike many of your peers here. Based on my years advising our high school graduates, with your ethnic and cultural upbringing, I assume you are hardworking and high achieving. Don't tell me Mrs. Chen isn't on you at home to bring back excellence with every report card?"

"Well," Sabrina said. An almost whisper, "She has high expectations."

"Yes, in my experience this is typical of lower-income Chinese culture parents."

Mr. Jenkins pushed his glasses back up the bridge of his nose. Sabrina wanted to look away, but her eyes stayed on his nose. *Low income. Minority culture.* Her mother would have sniffed at this and called it a duty. *Hard work is not a choice. These children in your school, they proudly say they go to this public school but treat it like a castle. They don't know what it is to have nothing. To have no choices. They have something to fall back on. They can indulge in arts, sports, music, and the theater because they have the money to. Their parents will always give in to them, saying it's letting the children have the freedom to choose for themselves, but this is only what you say when you have money. You have a duty to me, your family. I gave you this chance. You have to take it and do something with it. Or you will work at a restaurant, a kiosk, like all the others. Like me.*

"Ms. Eva Kim will be expecting you downtown at the Asian American Immigration Coalition for your summer internship. She helps the Asian immigrant community in Pennsylvania with civil rights issues, navigating financial aid, a lot of things that you might find yourself feeling passionate about . . . given your background. She has worked with some of our Asian American students before. She's a . . ." He paused. "A real character, shall we say. Okay, Ms. Chen. Goodbye." He passed her a piece of paper and didn't look up at her as he waved her toward the door.

⁓∽⁓

"Don't slam the door," a gruff voice called out, a voice that sounded like it had been roughened by cigarettes and shouting.

Sabrina looked around, but she couldn't see anybody in the poorly lit office. A small window looked out over the low-rise redbrick vista of the Temple University campus two blocks west. The bell tower loomed in the distance. Dust motes floated in the air in front of the window.

A woman came out of a back room; she was not who Sabrina had expected to meet. A small, muscular body wearing a plain black dress with sleeves, her hair cut with a severe fringe that sat in a rigid straight line over her brows. Her age was impossible to guess. Her eyes were bright behind her black-rimmed glasses, and for a moment Sabrina felt like the woman was looking right through her, as though she could see right into Sabrina's thoughts.

"You're here for the internship starting next month, right? Sit, sit . . ." She waved her hand to the chair in front of her desk. "I'll be right with you."

Sabrina sat on the edge of the seat, her knees pushed together, and she straightened the fabric of her blue cotton dress over her thighs. She glanced at the college diplomas from Princeton and Penn State on the walls, which hung askew. On the desk was a clear pink plastic Nalgene flask with brown tea leaves that floated in the water. It had turned a murky tone that looked like a puddle of dirty water. She wondered if it was the same chrysanthemum tea her mother drank for her digestion.

"That prick Jenkins sent you down to me, is that right? Asians fighting *Asian* causes? Did he say something like that to you?"

Sabrina tried to croak a response. Her breath was stuck on *Mr. Jenkins, the prick.*

"He's a self-important dickhead, and no better place for him to reassert his misplaced beliefs than in the guidance counselor's office in a high school in one of the whitest townships in Philadelphia."

"I . . ."

"It's okay, I know you agree. I can tell in your eyes you do. You have good transcripts, Chen. What brings you here?"

"Well, Mr. Jenkins suggested . . ."

"You don't need to be sheepish. He might have suggested it, but you didn't have to come all the way out here. Something in you compelled you to come down. What is it? Microracism in trig? Are you an outcast? What about your parents? Have you seen them endure Asian hate? Talk to me, girl."

When Eva Kim spoke, the air in the room stood still and grew electric. Sabrina felt as though she were suddenly awake. After years of slumber in a dark cave, she finally saw there was an opening that she could walk through, and the light was blinding.

"I guess . . ."

"Go on." Eva took her glasses off, sat down in her seat, and stared, but there was warmth in her eyes.

"I'm tired of being invisible."

"You're put aside, are you? In class? Socially?"

"Yes, people expect me to be a certain way and there's a suffocating cloak over me, I can't explain it."

"You're doing a good job of it so far. Keep trying. You seem like some-one who's good with words." Nobody had said this to her before. Sabrina knew she was good with words too.

"I'm sick of being the smart Asian kid. Of being the girl most likely to be a math professor when I hate math. Maybe I want to explore the arts, or be an actress, a writer, to have a voice. I'm tired of sitting in the shad-ows. I'm tired of waiting. Because it's all I do—politely, quietly, I wait."

The silence in the air was charged.

"Good answer."

"It was?"

"Sharpen those elbows, girl, I'm gonna teach you how to push your way to the front of the line this summer."

Sabrina felt the edges of her mouth form a smile, and it came from her insides. Her heart prepared to take flight.

"But first I'm sending you out to get some coffee, and then I'm going to talk you through what we are going to do here."

"Where's the nearest coffee shop?" Sabrina said, standing. Her skirt was creased, and she knocked a pile of folders to the floor.

"You'll find one," Eva said with a hint of a smile and passed her a $10 bill.

Sabrina felt her feet carry her down the hallway fast. Her legs and body trotted confidently ahead while her head tried to catch up, like a child pulling a balloon. What had just happened in that small dusty room?

CHAPTER SEVEN

Sabrina

Chestnut Hill, May 2015

Every Tuesday of her senior year, Sabrina would wake and feel a cold dread descend over her as she remembered she had drama class. Mrs. Saunders was a free-spirited "luvvie," a word she'd recently read in a British newspaper that she used only in her internal monologues. Mrs. Saunders wore elaborate print dresses with ruffled sleeves and an unapologetic sheepskin coat that flew open like a cape behind her in winter. She had disobedient strawberry-blond curls and fine, delicate ankles. Once, she bumped into Mrs. Saunders in the local farmers market; she was holding an armful of blue hydrangeas. She told Sabrina she loved to put a stem in each room of her house.

Sabrina wanted more than anything for Mrs. Saunders to see *and* ignore her simultaneously. She was terrified of the day she might decide to push Sabrina to *let out her wild side.* The class was always invited to sit cross-legged on the floor for five minutes, before they began any of the curriculum, to do deep belly breaths, which Mrs. Saunders claimed would release any neural tension and help open up the authentic inner voice. Sabrina's greatest terror, though, was anticipation of Improv Day. Mrs. Saunders never gave any warning. You could walk in, and she would suddenly say, "Kids, let's set our inner selves free. It's Improv Day." Mrs. Saunders had the nose of a bloodhound for identifying emotional trigger points that would bring forth *a great scene.* Her eyes would scan the faces in the room. Sabrina had seen several students lose themselves completely, and this terrified Sabrina—that she might unravel in the same unsightly, public way. Mrs. Saunders, though, was very popular among the students. There was a long-standing rumor that she had once dated the actor Hugh Grant in London when she was touring with a company that put on an Arthur Miller play in the West End, though Sabrina suspected this to be wholly made up, maybe even by Mrs. Saunders herself.

Kit liked Mrs. Saunders, and Sabrina knew this was mainly due to Mrs. Saunders's preference for pretty girls. She would sometimes congratulate Kit's scenes with a *Just lovely, my dear, what a charming thing you are.* And like a dog that had been praised for bringing back a ball, Kit would sit a little more upright, with a happy little wriggle of her chin.

ONE WEEK IN May, the summer temperatures started to soar, the sprinklers ran over the school fields every morning, and the students rushed from class to class in shorts and a lightness in their feet. After their deep belly breathing, she felt Mrs. Saunders's eyes on her. And the words she had dreaded all morning, *Let's improvise,* ricocheted off the walls.

"Sabrina Chen, we haven't seen you up here before. Come join me."

A ferocious heat rose to the surface of Sabrina's skin. She paused, hoping she had misheard, and looked round to Kit, who was busy checking her cell phone.

Sabrina walked slowly. Her feet felt like they were sticking to the ground. She heard a cough from the back row and murmurs among some of the students. Otherwise, the room felt cool from the blast of air-conditioning that had been running all morning. She stood beside Mrs. Saunders and felt like she was sinking into quicksand. She could barely make out the faces of the students sitting in the front row.

"I want you to start with this line—"

"Wait, who else is going to join me?" Sabrina looked around her, into the wings and then back at the audience. But nobody came.

"Oh, honey, this is your moment. Let's try a little monologuing today."

"I'm not sure, Mrs. Saunders . . ."

"Come on, Miss Chen, give it a try, this is a no-judgment zone. Give it a whirl. It's just a few minutes of your life."

Sabrina took a breath.

"That's it, take a deep breath, my dear, you can do it. Now then, here's the starting point. *Mother always says* . . ."

Sabrina could see Kit's face. She grimaced as she slunk deeper into her chair.

She tried to say the words, but her voice was small.

"My mother always says . . . um, my mother always says . . ."

"Go on, dear, start with a truth. *Sometimes a truth is all it takes.*" Mrs. Saunders's hand squeezed her own and it felt warm and dry against Sabrina's cold fingers. She stepped back into the shadows. And then Sabrina was alone.

Sabrina took a deep breath, felt her belly expand, and exhaled.

"My mother always says, we need to work hard." Her hands shook, but she reminded herself to focus on something beyond the faces before her, just as Mrs. Saunders always suggested for stage fright. Then the words came to her. And for once, she allowed them to leave her mouth before she could turn them over to check them again and again.

"My mother always says that the world owes us nothing. But she doesn't say it like I just said it, in an indifferent kind of way. *Sabrina, you work hard, okay? You work harder than everyone. We have nothing compared to them. You have nothing. You remember. You work until your fingers bleed.*

"I can see you guys don't know how to respond to that. It's uncomfortable, the unheard voice of an angry Chinese mother who wants to live vicariously through you. But this is the ambient noise in my house. Only it's not coming from some integrated sound system in the walls like in your houses. It's in human form and right up in your face. This close." She held her palm up in front of her nose.

"Yeah, that's my mom. Success is big in my house. But success has many forms. I guess beating the person who has more than us defines success in its purest form for her. It's getting the best grades. All the time. I can't lie. She wants to see you all fail. You, and you, and you." Sabrina pointed at random silhouettes before her. "And for me to succeed. She will relish your shortcomings and see them as mere steps for me to grind my foot on while I climb this metaphorical ladder she has in her mind. She wants me to beat you."

There was laughter. She didn't know if it was at her expense, a mockery, or if she had struck a chord.

"And most people here do have more, right? I don't mean it in a 'poor me' way. I mean it as fact. It's the way of the world; we can't all have the same. And there's something about knowing where I am that I've always liked. There's a cleanness to it. A purity. Maybe that's some kind of brainwashing from my mom too. Like there's no gray with her. She just says exactly what is happening in her mind and it probably leaves her mouth before the thought is even fully formed. Yeah, there's purity in that."

Sabrina paused. The silence in the room enveloped her. She heard nothing but her own breathing as she awoke in her surroundings again. She could see Mrs. Saunders nodding in the front row. Her hands were clasped together, and her eyes were shiny. *Keep going*, she mouthed. Sabrina felt herself stand taller.

"My mother always says that birds are her favorite because they don't stay in one place too long. They don't linger by staying still. But I think no animals do that, right? Maybe a seal, I dunno. But the bird thing—she loves Japanese paintings of birds, drawn with a fine brush. Those super-detailed paintings where you can see every single stroke on the page. She loves those. She says that birds stay for a moment, so if you really pay attention, you can catch them in their beauty. They'll let you enjoy them. And then they're gone. It's funny how she likes those Japanese paintings though. She loves the cranes, those long-legged birds, they're so elegant. They always remind me of the makeup worn by the geishas—you know, the white skin and the blood-red lips. Those cranes and the puff of red on their heads. I saw a documentary once and the ladies kind of glide, they walk so delicately down the streets in Kyoto. It's kind of funny how that's what she is obsessed with. It's all hi-tech there, and cool subcultures in Japan, right? All those futuristic neon lights. I look at pictures of those crossings and cool girls in the parks that are all famous and it's like a wonderland. One day I might go there." Sabrina paused, and she kept her eyes up, she didn't look at where she knew Kit was sitting.

"But yeah, my mom and Japan. It's like she hate-loves it. Because it's the opposite of her. It's all refinement, and nothing is stuck together with tape like everything is in our house. In the hierarchy of fancy Asia, Japan and Korea are right up there, and then China is kind of like a gray area, right, because yeah, Shanghai and Beijing are all the new Sleeping Tigers and all, but in the countryside we have less than nothing. And I say *we*, but I've never been there, and I don't even know if I went whether I'd belong there or not. And the truth is that my mom is from the least fancy place possible. They didn't have a television growing up, they didn't have a radio. They had nothing. Sometimes they could barely afford to eat rice, and that's like the cheapest thing you can eat in the world, right? That's her origin story, but she collects pictures of these aristocratic elegant birds from a country that is all about refinement and elegance and subtleties. Like, she'll find one on the internet and ask me to print it and be all like, *Sabrina, you see, this tiny feather? How do they paint that?* One day I'll take my mom to see those cranes in real life. We'll go to the snowy place in Hokkaido, where you can see them do those beautiful courtship dances, their thin legs jumping up off the white powder and nodding their heads to each other. I know she'll complain about the cold. *Why did you bring me here, Sabrina? You know I hate the cold. I don't even like the Japanese.* Yeah, she doesn't like the Japanese. That's for another day. And there is nobody more outspoken and less subtle than my mom."

She could hear soft breathing from the seats in front of her. Mrs. Saunders gestured again for her to go on.

"My mother always says that the world is full of surprising moments. And that living in America is full of opportunities. We just have to have the vision to see them. She says it like, you either got the goods to see this or not. She has, that's for sure. She knows when she has a shot at something, and she takes it. It's probably the thing I kind of love about her most. Even though I've never told her this. We are not the kind of family that talks about love. I don't think I've ever told her I love her. She hasn't told me either. But that's okay. Love has many forms, right? What are the five love languages?" She lifted her fingers to count them herself. "Acts of service . . . nope. Quality time . . . no again. Receiving gifts . . . nope, nope. Words of affirmation . . . not from my mom. Physical touch . . . yeah, that's a no. But my mom's love language might be in the form of a *baozi*. You know what a *baozi* is? It's a fluffy, delicious bit of pure white Chinese bread filled with sweet, savory filling. And they're steamed and cooked to total perfection and more delicious than anything I know. And my mom makes the best. If I had to sum up my childhood and comfort in one single word, it's the hot steaming beauty of a perfectly formed *baozi*. So I guess that's my mom's gift to me. Because I know she's tired, she's worked a long-ass twelve-hour day, and sometimes she still comes home and cooks up a storm. And a *baozi* takes work. She's gotta knead that dough, and then cook and chop up the pork or vegetables or chicken or whatever is inside, and find a way to perfectly steam the bread and filling. It's an art. But she does all that. And then she watches as I chew on that puffy cloud of deliciousness, and I can feel the love with each bite. It's right there, getting into the very marrow of me. She says that watching me enjoy her cooking makes *eating the bitterness* of hard work and life worthwhile. All that goodness, all that nourishment—that's love right there."

Sabrina finished talking. Kit stared at her, her mouth hung open slightly. She'd never seen this expression on her before. It looked like envy. The rest of the class were clapping and hooting. She felt the light weight of Mrs. Saunders's hand on her shoulder. And then she saw another pair of eyes that she was pretty sure had never really looked at her before. They were Dave Harrison's.

CHAPTER EIGHT

Sabrina

Philadelphia, June 2015

Lee Lee's impression of Kit was formed in elementary school, and it never changed. She hated the sight of small children crying and throwing tantrums in public. *Americans are so indulgent, loud, look at me,* she would snap, the center of her lips pinched down, as though the most sour lemon had found its way into her mouth. To Sabrina's mother, the constant need for self-expression was one of the worst qualities of their adopted home. *This would never happen in China. A person must learn to endure.*

The first time Lee Lee saw Kit was in pre-K, when she threw herself down on the school playground, arms thumping and legs kicking. Sally Herzog insisted they needed to go home, but Kit simply refused, wailing that she was going to stay.

"No, go home yourself!" she shrieked at Sally, whose face had turned a deep scarlet. Lee Lee's lips pinched tighter as she watched the exchange. This was an expression Sabrina would always picture when she thought of her mother. Years later, when she herself became a mother, she fixed her own face if she thought she might mimic the same bitter expression.

"This is terrible behavior from a child. Sabrina, this brings shame to a family." Lee Lee tutted as she turned out of the school car park, on a rare afternoon that she collected her daughter at the end of the day.

"Everyone does it, all the kids," Sabrina muttered. Lee Lee nodded and put her foot on the accelerator.

"Not us. We are respectful to parents. And we do not draw attention to ourselves like that," she said, waiting for her daughter's agreement.

This was the first time Sabrina realized that her mother wasn't the same as the other mothers. She watched as her mother kept her eyes firmly on the road ahead of her, in spite of the static traffic jam.

"Mrs. Ward says it's important to express yourself; she says this is how we can understand one another's feelings better," Sabrina said.

"That just sounds like an excuse to be dramatic and over the top with your feelings. Don't listen to Mrs. Ward."

"But she's my teacher, Mama," Sabrina said, her eyes widening.

"You listen to her when she teaches you reading, writing, mathematics. That's enough. But you remember that is not how I've brought you up."

Sabrina realized that Kit would never be tested in the same way, although she too was *not an American*, not wholly anyway. Something in the tone of her skin, the ways her eyes were wider, almond shaped with that double eyelid and light brown hair. She would never understand what it was to be put in a box and shoved aside. Kit would live her life with one foot in one world and the other free to roam where she pleased.

The boundaries of Sabrina's existence were clear. She would not go to expensive summer camps or drive a Jeep with the hood down through the cobbled streets of Chestnut Hill. She might go to the shore if the Herzogs extended an invitation, but usually she was working over the summer. Sabrina learned to look on at her friend's world without resentment. The way a dog knew to wait outside a store, she was never invited in unless someone had left the door open accidentally.

THOUGH SHE NEVER begrudged Kit's privilege, her looks, or her pseudo-popularity, she did envy one thing: her origin story. This was how Kit referred to it, a precious tale to share with the chosen few, her unique badge of mystery. The girl who was left and then found. Kit's story took on a legendary status when they started their freshman year in high school. They walked through the heavy wooden doors to the Upper School building on the first day of school, and Sabrina heard the mumblings. *That's the girl who was adopted.* And with each step they took further down the hallway, the story became more fantastical. *They found her on their doorstep. Her mom was a Japanese hostess. She was a model who got pregnant with some guy and couldn't go home. She'd been through four different homes before they found her the place with the Herzogs.*

Kit's expression was flat during those first weeks of high school. She kept her eyes ahead of her, on nothing in particular. Sabrina always thought her cheekbones looked more prominent, her eyes wider than the other girls, to Sabrina Kit was poetic even. Sabrina watched with admiration as Kit's lack of reaction only increased her mystery and allure, especially to the sophomore and junior boys. As though Kit were always destined to play this role of a mysterious new arrival, even though she had been there all along. Soon people stopped talking about her murky origin story and instead it was how much she looked like an actress in the latest Netflix series. Kit's flattened expression morphed slowly into a smile that started to twitch at her lips. Only Sabrina saw it.

Kit's self-assurance ebbed and flowed like the water in the Delaware River. The winters of her self-doubt would freeze over, and it fell to Sabrina to thaw out its edges. But when it swelled over its banks, Sabrina had to run for cover and wait for the flood to subside.

That fall of freshman year, Sabrina looked at Dave Harrison as though she were seeing him for the first time. He had always been in their classes, and part of Kit's family circle, but now he stood in the hallway, his shoulders broader than they were before the summer began. He carried his backpack slung over his gray varsity sweatshirt, and his hair looked like it had been brushed to the side with purpose. Dave didn't have the same movie star looks as his older brother, Brad, but his eyes were softer. When they walked past him, his eyes lingered on Kit, taking inventory of her. Sabrina felt pain and longing fill up her entire being, right up to her throat. She watched his gaze, her feet becoming heavier as she walked beside her friend. She watched his eyes follow Kit, and she felt the beginnings of a crack start to take shape inside her.

—∽—

The summer before senior year began, Sabrina joined Kit down at the shore for a week. It had taken her almost an entire semester to persuade her mother to allow her to go. Sabrina kept hearing the Herzogs say to every family friend they invited over to their beach house that it was the hottest July for ten years. She sat beside Kit quietly, waiting for the thundering beat in her chest to subside before she could open her mouth to join in the dining-table conversation. Kit was relaxed and sat with her foot raised up on the seat of her chair, occasionally scolded by Mrs. Herzog for bad table manners. Sabrina took care to keep her knees together, and chew with her mouth closed, heeding every instruction she had heard Mrs. Herzog make at the dining table over the years.

When the Harrisons arrived for the final three days of Sabrina's stay, the thought of mealtimes filled Sabrina with a heavy dread all day. Brad always sat beside Kit—the unspoken rule that the two eldest in the families should sit beside each other regardless of the age gap. Sabrina did not say one word during the meals. Nobody noticed. She pushed the flaccid string beans around her plate, she took small, lackluster bites of her hamburger, her corn was untouched. She watched as the brothers ate two hamburgers each and fought over the last servings of baked potatoes. Brad teased Kit, and Sabrina noticed that sometimes Kit's arm leaned against Brad's, or their knees would touch as they sat side by side. Dave's brother was the kind of popular older boy who intimidated Sabrina so deeply she found herself shrinking into whatever surface her back was against. Kit, on the other hand, took his taunts with a smile and flirted back furiously in a way Sabrina didn't recognize.

Dave, too, became smaller around his brother. Brad's voice drowned out Dave's, but Sabrina heard every word that Dave said. The adults had begun to slur their words around the table, their voices rising with every glass of wine they drank. Sabrina thought to herself that nobody had asked her a single question. She had lost track of how long it had been since she had spoken. Dave ignored his brother and turned to her.

What are you taking for AP next year? And her heart fluttered furiously.

She felt something stuck in her throat as she tried to summon up her voice. But Dave kept asking more questions, questions that weren't just a way for him to talk about himself.

"WHAT WAS UP with you at dinner?" Kit asked as they sat together alone on the porch later, eating ice cream sandwiches. It was the Harrison boys' turn to wash up after the meal.

"Nothing, why?"

"You were so quiet. You hardly said a word, just whatever you and Dave were whispering about. Is it Brad?" She nudged Sabrina with her shoulder. And Sabrina felt her face flush up to the roots of her hair.

"My god, no way."

"Really? Doesn't look like no way to me." Kit smirked.

"He's way better looking than Dave, in my opinion," Sabrina offered.

"Do you . . . you know, like him?"

Kit shrugged and looked away. Sabrina listened to the hooting inside and wondered what made Kit so visible to every boy they met while Sabrina felt like a blank silhouette, a shadow that she merely filled, behind her friend.

The following night they were invited to a party. Sabrina stayed behind to talk to Lee Lee; she had promised to call that night. She agreed to meet Kit for sundaes on the waterfront before going to the party together. *To line our stomachs,* Kit had said.

"I don't want you drinking, Sabrina, remember you're a good girl."

"Yes, Mom." She knew how hard it was for Lee Lee to allow her to go.

"Remember your manners, and you text me. Have you said thank you to the Herzogs today? Did they like the dumplings I made?"

Sabrina had thrown the dumplings away before arriving at the Herzog house.

"They did, Mom, they loved them. Mrs. Herzog said to say thanks."

"I knew they would. I took out the chilis. What are you doing there every day?"

"We go to the beach, we play board games. Just regular stuff, Mom."

"Okay, you're using that hat and the swimsuit I bought you? Make sure you don't sit in the sun."

Sabrina looked at the white line her watch strap had left on her wrist from that afternoon.

"I'll try."

"You will get dark and your skin won't be so beautiful."

"Yes, Mom. How was your day anyway? Are you okay?"

The internet is not working again. What do I do?

Who do I call if the air conditioning isn't working again? Can you do it from there?

Have you paid the gas bill?

❧

Sabrina arrived at the party alone. Dance music pulsed through the walls. Bass rumbled through the wooden floors that were sticky with beer and wine. She paused in the doorway and stared at the kitchen counter, covered in half-empty bottles of liquor and the triangle of beer pong cups that sat forgotten. Her sight adjusted to the dimness. She almost didn't see Kit, whose eyes were bloodshot. The alcohol had loosened her movements, her hips swayed, and her shoulder tilted to one side, leaning up against Brad's. She stood beside a group of senior boys Sabrina had never spoken to but watched from afar in the high school cafeteria, being careful to avoid walking past their table. Sabrina searched the room for Dave but couldn't find him. When she approached Kit, she saw a half bottle of wine dangling from her hand. Kit lost her footing for a moment as she saw Sabrina.

"Rina!" she said. "I didn't know if you were gonna make it. You been so long, baby."

"What are *you* doing here? You were supposed to meet me an hour ago. I've been waiting for you." Sabrina said the words fast, through her teeth, but low enough that nobody else could hear.

"I came early with Brad, I didn't realize. I thought I messaged you. Ooops, I'm sorry. Have a drink with meeee," she said, knocking her shoulder into Sabrina's. She could smell the wine, and the smell of sweet vape smoke drifted toward her from the group standing beside Kit.

"You didn't reply to any of my messages." She hated the sound of her voice as she complained.

When Kit pulled her cell phone from her pocket, it fell to the ground, and Sabrina kneeled down to pick it up.

"Oops, thank you, my BFF," she slurred. "Yeah, I see you texted me a buncha times. I didn't hear it."

Brad draped his arm around Kit's neck but faced his friends. Sabrina scanned the room for Dave again.

"Come on, Rina, let me pour you a cup." Kit broke away from Brad and hooked her arm through Sabrina's, pouring wine from her bottle into a red party cup.

Sabrina gulped down the sour, warm wine. She wanted to shudder, but she held her breath and offered the cup again to be filled.

"That a girl," Kit said, pouring more wine.

By the time the alcohol unknotted the tension in Sabrina's body, Kit had wandered back to Brad. Sabrina walked across the sticky floor, still searching for Dave. It was her first real high school party, but she already felt like she had outgrown it. She hadn't even had her first joint or thrashed around on the dance floor. She had never been a part of these moments—and suddenly she didn't care about missing out on them.

She found him sitting alone on the stoop of the house, holding a cigarette between his thumb and index finger.

"You smoke?" he asked, holding the cigarette up to her. She shook her head.

"Suit yourself," he mumbled and stared out at the people passing by the front of the house.

Sabrina searched for something to say, something that might make him look at her. Nothing came, and she coughed on her own spit as she breathed in too quickly. Dave offered her his bottle of water, and she took a long sip. She expected to taste the cigarette, but there was nothing, just the smooth plastic spout of the water bottle, and it occurred to her how their lips met in that moment, though she knew he wouldn't think of her at all.

THE FOLLOWING DAY, Sabrina and Kit went to the beach after eating peanut butter and jelly sandwiches in silence in the kitchen. They laid out on their towels. Sabrina always worried about the sand and the mess it would make on the Herzogs' white Turkish towels.

"You're so fussy," Kit muttered, and Sabrina watched as Kit's sandy feet left streaks across the fabric. The sand made Sabrina's skin itch. She wiped her feet again.

"So last night, Dave and I kind of started this thing," Kit said, reclining, her eyes concealed by her sunglasses.

"Last night?" A cascade of images from the house party ran through her mind. *When? Did she sneak out? Why didn't I notice? I thought it was Brad she liked, not Dave.* How did so many things happen last night that Sabrina missed? She thought she had been there with everyone all along.

Sabrina had hardly spoken to Dave during senior year. In fact, she had given up altogether on having any connection with him until a few weeks before graduation, when he appeared before her in the library. The sound of a chair being pulled up at her table interrupted her thoughts, and there he was.

"Hey. What you working on?"

Dave sat across from her and leaned over the pile of books. *Advanced Spanish Grammar*, Steinbeck's *The Grapes of Wrath*, Faulkner's *As I Lay Dying*, and Flannery O'Connor's short stories.

"A paper I have for AP class." Her words left her mouth slowly, and she felt herself lean backward and her cheeks began to flush as she looked at him.

"What's it on?" He peered at her open folder, her neat, small writing annotating the handouts.

"We did a whole thing on these authors. It's kind of an interesting class actually."

"Right." He spun his pen on the table and took out a MacBook Air. "You know, I wish I'd taken that class. I didn't realize until it was too late I'm really into these writers."

"You are?"

"You sound surprised."

"Well, yeah, I am. I didn't know you were into English lit."

"I am. I wanna be a writer one day," he said.

She looked at him and nodded but couldn't think of anything to say. She wondered if Kit knew this about Dave.

"You're gonna sit here?" she asked, scanning the room, looking for Kit.

"You were saving it for someone?"

"No, not really . . ."

"Cool." He put his headphones on and opened up his book. She stared at him for a moment, her mouth slightly open, searching for something else to say, but her mind went blank with the thrill of his presence.

For the rest of that period, she could not concentrate on her paper. Instead, she thought about how her hair smelled. And whether he had sat there to enlist her help with his assignments. She had to fight the urge to ask; she wanted to feel the warmth of his approval on her skin. And then she thought of what Kit would say had she walked in at that very moment. The rest of the day passed in a blur, and Sabrina was relieved not to see Kit at all. She rushed a message to her, to say she had to head home to help her mother, an excuse that always passed unquestioned. What Sabrina didn't expect was the exhaustion that overcame her that night. And now this boy, whom she had watched carefully from the sidelines, this boy who had ignored her for the last twelve years, this boy who was like an actor on the stage, acting alongside her friend, the main characters, suddenly looked out at her in the audience, and she felt the heat of the spotlight on her.

Until this day, senior year had been a year of waiting for Sabrina. A year of wishing the time away so that her life could begin in college with new friends, new teachers, new neighbors, in an environment where she wasn't burdened with how everyone else saw her: an Asian immigrant's daughter, AP class nerd, low-income household, a latchkey kid, Kit Herzog's sidekick. Senior year had been about patiently plowing forward with her studies, keeping her grades sky-high so the world might open up. She couldn't wait to leave, for the rest of her life to start. She had not cared nor known about anything she might have missed during her final year in high school.

Then, that afternoon with Dave in the library, as though a warm breeze blew in through the window and shook the musty papers that lay before her: the wind changed. She had wanted the year to end fast so she could reinvent herself, but suddenly she was overcome by a painful urge to be present. She was not ready for her future yet. She wasn't ready for Princeton yet either. She wanted to stop time and stay right there, in Chestnut Hill Academy, and have a high school moment.

Hours later, Sabrina sat awake, leaning over the schoolwork spread out on her bed. Her neck ached as she wrote notes in the margins of the Steinbeck novel she had already read. She realized that her fingers turned the pages of the book that Dave had thumbed through earlier, and a thrill rushed through her, followed by a shudder at the realization that Kit felt this every time she was with him. She wanted to feel it too.

CHAPTER NINE

Kit

Philadelphia International Airport, June 2015

The fact that the flight was so long had not occurred to Kit until she stood behind her father, hoisting her huge black case with a white ribbon tied on the handle (*for easy identification on the carousel*, Terry had said). She would arrive in Japan a full day later, and the distance between her and her family, her house, her bedroom, even Sabrina, suddenly felt vast.

The thought of everything continuing as usual once she had gone left her simultaneously comforted and troubled. Her perfect little life moving forward without her. It was unimaginable.

She was anxious to get away from her parents quickly.

"Are you sure, honey, that you don't want to do this unaccompanied minor thing?"

"Sal, it's too late for that—the airlines need notice for these things. You can't just do it as we check in."

Sally brushed her husband's obstacles away as though they were flies buzzing around her face.

"I can figure it out, Mom. I'm eighteen. It's a short layover in Newark. I can always ask someone if I need help. Everyone speaks English." Kit forced a smile, though she was starting to question her ability to do all of this independently. She was going to college in the fall, she could handle a trip alone. There was a niggling feeling at the back of Kit's mind that she had chosen Penn because it was close enough to home. She could go back any time she wanted. She pushed the thought away immediately.

She could see Sally's eyes starting to glisten, as though tears would come at any moment.

"You didn't want Sabrina to join us to see you off? I thought she might come to the airport," Sally asked.

Kit hadn't told her mother about the burst pipe at the Chen household. She hadn't told her mother that Sabrina was no longer going anywhere for the summer, but instead working two jobs. She hadn't told her either that when Sabrina had asked about her trip, Kit had felt it necessary to keep her answers brief and change the subject quickly. She knew her mother would take pride in her consideration of her less-fortunate friend's summer plans being dashed by—what was it that Sabrina had called it—a force majeure. She thought about the phrase again, and knew she would use it in the future. But for now, she felt satisfaction when she thought of how understanding her expression was the last time she saw Sabrina. She was lucky that her family could send her to Tokyo for the summer. It was not her fault that Sabrina's could not.

Kit had other things on her mind. She was wearing a brand-new outfit. Sneakers she had carefully picked out for her trip, new sandals packed in her suitcase, and high-waisted jean shorts that she would wear with her cropped T-shirts. She had put a new case on her phone and the Kanken backpack she carried was carefully packed with her iPad, Kindle, and toiletries for the flight. She couldn't wait to get through security to buy herself an iced coffee, a Venti Iced Coffee, that would make her mother raise her eyebrows immediately and say *You're not going to sleep tonight if you drink all of that, honey.* But Kit could do as she pleased, because she was not going to be supervised. This new thrill of independence rushed through her. She would be a different person. The kind of person people looked at with admiration, thinking how young and adventurous she was, marching through the airport to board a flight to a faraway country. *Sir, is this the way to the gates?* she would ask a security guard.

She felt Sally's gaze linger on her with sadness. She hugged her parents goodbye, pulling away as she started to feel a homesickness she wasn't prepared for. She turned quickly and walked through the bag check without looking back at them.

CHAPTER TEN

Sabrina

Philadelphia, June 2015

Sabrina remained annoyed with Lee Lee after she paid for the burst pipe with her money for her China trip. Though in truth, this seemed to open a gateway for resentments that had successfully been buried over the years.

The day Kit left, Sabrina woke up with a gloominess that quickly transformed into sulking. She wore a pout that she could not remove from her face and she knew her mother would not be able to ignore.

"Why you care what Katerin does? She has a different family, different life. You are you. And for her, maybe it's more important she knows where she is from. She has white parents, she doesn't know how it is to be Asian. Poor kid. Must be so confused." She had started to refer to children as "kids" only in the last four months, since starting her cleaning job downtown at the South Philadelphia public school. The agency that had placed her in her previous cleaning job had suddenly closed down. But Lee Lee was happy in her new job at the school. *No mice like the offices,* she announced after her first week there.

"I guess I don't think of Kit as Asian."

"That's the problem." Her mother slapped her own leg. A shine formed over Lee Lee's eyes, and her tiny, nimble fingers gripped harder on the edges of the plastic bag she folded into a meticulous triangle before placing it into a shoe box beside the sink. Sabrina thought about how she had never once reached for any of those plastic bags, ever. "This is why she needs to go back to Asia even more. She doesn't feel Asian. She doesn't *think* Asian. But she *is* Asian. She doesn't know who she is."

"I'm not sure I feel that Asian, really." Sabrina sighed. She regretted the words the moment they left her mouth. Lee Lee stared at her and put the next triangle down. They were getting smaller and smaller, the edges tighter.

"You do. I have brought you up so you do. You understand about duty. Your school is full of spoiled kids, but you are *my* child. You know you must respect, you know about the shame of not being dutiful and respectful. You do your homework, you wash the dishes, you make your bed, you *obey*. I know children your age can be naughty, the girls around you in your American school especially. But you're a good girl, my Sabrina. Yes, girls like Katerin, Western mixed girls like her especially, believe they're special. We always say they get the good genes. They believe they have something different to everyone else. That they're *unique*." Lee Lee crossed her fingers as she made quotation marks and wiggled her fingers up and down, a habit Sabrina and Kit had once teased her about years ago, which only led to Sabrina enduring three days of silent treatment from Lee Lee, disrespecting her mother in public.

"I know, I know, you have never been to China," Lee Lee continued, in an animated conversation with herself now. "And in many ways you are American too, something I will never be. But you *understand*. This is why it is so good you are the way you are, my girl. And you will have greatness, great chances that I never had. If you keep being good, you will have it all."

Sabrina said nothing, she knew her mother was waiting for her to nod. *If you keep being good.*

"The thing about Katerin, you will see. Later in her future, she will be so confused. She won't know where she belongs. Is she white? No. Is she Asian? Why is nobody treating them special when they become older and middle-aged and no longer look so charming. It's different for you, Sabrina. You know who you are. Your character is strong. Because the home is strong, and your heart is strong."

Sabrina knew this too. Sometimes she felt a surge of happiness under her mother's eye, her approving nod as Sabrina set out and achieved everything she was expected to. But she simultaneously hated this part about herself: the unquestioning obedience.

SABRINA'S SULKING OVER Kit's departure lasted just a morning, and by the following day she felt brighter, as a rush of freedom that was new, a jittery adrenaline ran through her body. She had her offer under her mattress for the Ivy League school she had always dreamed of going to, and she might see Dave at the country club when she began her shifts. Sabrina jumped down the final three steps into the kitchen and helped her mother unload the weekly bag of expired groceries onto the table. Lee Lee peeled away the brown outer leaves of the spring onions and muttered under her breath, "Americans so wasteful—look at this, perfectly good, fresh inside, like new."

"I don't know, Mom, this looks like it's done," Sabrina said, pointing at the sprigs that had turned brown.

"Yes, but you're still saving when you get the expired stuff nobody wants. There is goodness there. No matter what it looks like on the outside. Don't forget that."

"I guess . . . but isn't that a waste too? To force yourself to cook with everything and then possibly leave that food to go bad?"

"To have an abundance is never bad, Sabrina."

Sabrina turned her cell phone camera onto herself to check her mascara. There was a small smudge of inky black at the outer edge of her eye. She licked the edge of her finger and tried to wipe it away.

"Sabrina," Lee Lee said sharply. "What is wrong with you?"

"Nothing." Sabrina glanced at her reflection again. The smudge was gone. "I'm getting ready for my shift at the country club, then downtown."

"Are you wearing makeup? What is that around your eyes?" Lee Lee's voice had sharpened.

"No, I rubbed it off, was just playing around." Sabrina turned away from her mother.

"You are distracted since you have these jobs. Make sure you get your focus back before college, my girl," Lee Lee said.

"I will, Mom, don't worry. I just need to go send an email before my shift," she said as she rushed up to her bedroom, checking her phone. Was she hoping for a message from Dave or Kit? She didn't know who she was waiting for exactly, but there was nothing.

⁓

Soon after graduation and Kit leaving, Sabrina settled into her summer routine. She split her days between the country club and the Coalition office. She walked down to the country club from the bus station every morning, listening to music. She blasted Fleetwood Mac's "The Chain" and loved the freedom of nobody knowing how loud her music played, or how old the songs were that she listened to.

As the last guitar chords faded, she paused the song and took her headphones out before she walked through the staff doors at the club. She always arrived early. Lee Lee said this was a sign of valuing the time of others, and if she wanted to get far in life, that was the first step.

Mornings at the club were always reserved for the older members who exercised before their working day began. The fury of the sun was still dormant. Instead, there was a golden blanket over the tennis lawns as a single groundsman pushed a roller along the edges of the grass tennis courts. She listened for the sprinklers in the distance that swayed over the golf course. A lone F-150 drove past her, and she watched the swallows diving in the shape of the number eight through the clear, cloudless sky.

Sabrina had hoped to see Dave Harrison at the club, but eight shifts had passed already and there was no sign of him. She knew he was a member and played tennis, because of all the times she and Kit had walked past the grass courts last summer to catch a glimpse of him.

Sabrina settled into her routine quickly. After she set all the tables for the summer camp kids, she arranged the refreshment counter for the adults in meticulous order: tea bags and coffee capsules in lines according to color. By ten, the first wave of campers came in from their tennis clinics, their sweaty, dirty hands messing up the surfaces, fingerprints smudging the shiny countertops. She waited until the last kid left and then polished everything again with Windex and paper towels. Some middle schoolers, who should have known better, left juice cartons and empty packets of chips and granola bars strewn across the tables. By the end of the first week, Sabrina knew which kids cleared up after themselves and which ones didn't. Every day she absorbed something new in the behavior of these rich kids: the cliques that quickly formed during these breaks; the turns of phrase *I was legit over it, so thirsty*; to the roughhousing between the boys that swung between aggression and affection. A slap across the groin led to hysterical laughter. The persistent taunting was bullying really, but somehow it also translated to male bonding. She couldn't understand it herself, she never had when she saw it in the school corridors either, but she accepted its place within the walls of the club-house.

Playing in the background on the mounted plasma televisions were tennis matches taking place somewhere else in the world. Sabrina was strangely mesmerized by the sound of the players grunting as they hit, bestial, but cathartic. She wondered what it must feel like to pelt the ball the way they did. The battle between the two men was hypnotic, rushing between painted white lines, the flex of the muscle sinew in their legs. She stared at the slow-motion playbacks on the screen and the subsequent final rulings of In or Out. The tournament was taking place in Europe somewhere, and she could hear the voices of the umpires, calling for the crowd to quiet down.

She heard Dave before she saw him.

"Hey, Thompson, pick up your trash, you animal."

He was behind her, and she could tell from his voice that he was on the other side of the room, but Sabrina's body tensed, knowing he was there. She looked down at her polo shirt, and rubbed the apple juice stain that she couldn't remove last night. Like the girls she'd seen earlier, she wanted to brush her hair back with her hand, glance at him over her shoulder, and smile, but instead, she kept her head down. She knew a part of her wanted to stay busy, for him to pass through the clubhouse and not even realize that she was there.

"Sabrina Chen," he said.

She turned quickly and felt the end of her ponytail get stuck on the side of her face. She brushed it away.

"Oh hey." She felt herself color as she ran her hands over the front of her shorts.

"You got a job here for the summer?"

"Yeah, saving money for college."

"Oh yeah? Doesn't it make you sick to your stomach seeing all of us CHA Country Club brats at our leisure?"

Us. Our. He surprised her, and she felt like she had been slapped in the face. She had expectations of him, of course, but not for such self-awareness. Was he putting it on for her? Was the shame of his privilege real? She looked at his neck color a shade of pinky-red as he spoke, and his eyes searched hers. What was he looking for? Reassurance?

"Not too sick," she replied. The words had left her mouth before she could think.

"You like tennis?" he asked.

Sabrina had heard of Wimbledon but knew nothing of tennis beyond what she caught on television. She knew that Serena Williams was a big deal, she had heard of Federer and Nadal, but that was the extent of her knowledge. She didn't understand how a game was scored, nor did she know what made one player good and another one bad.

"I don't really know much about it, but I like what I've been watching today."

"This is one of the big grand slams. I went to the US Open with Dad last year. It's pretty awesome. I like tennis."

"Yeah, I figured." Sabrina looked at his tennis shoes, scuffed, with the laces loose and undone.

"Has Kit left now?" He didn't look at her as he asked.

"We keep missing each other, but yeah, she's in Tokyo now or on her way, I think. She's going to have an amazing trip."

"Yeah. So it looks like everyone's taken off for the summer."

More silence, and she felt the internal tug of wanting to stay but wanting the conversation to end.

"Well, I gotta go so . . ." Sabrina said, stepping away from him. The toe of her sneaker squeaked against the tiles.

"Hey, so Wimbledon starts soon. We can watch the highlights. I can show you how to score a game if you like. I'll call you, Chen, that okay?"

He hadn't waited for her response. He had assumed she would just say yes, and he was right.

—✺—

"So we never talked about why you didn't take this vacation, kid," Eva said as she typed furiously on her keyboard, not looking at Sabrina as she spoke.

She tapped the keys with a staccato strike, and Sabrina noticed that every period she would press with her index finger, as if she were striking a typewriter. *Next!*

"We had a situation at home. I had to use the money I saved for my ticket."

Eva looked up for a moment, then pulled at her bottom lip, deep in thought. Sabrina later came to recognize this gesture—it meant Eva wanted a cigarette.

"What happened? What was the situation?"

"We had a burst pipe that flooded our bathroom, and caused a ton of damage to our ceiling, and well, I needed to pay for it."

Eva stopped typing and shifted her chair to face Sabrina.

"Landlord?"

"He's away. And he's kinda difficult, and we needed to get it fixed right away. It was damage control."

"Your mother didn't have the cash to fix this thing? Pay a plumber?"

"My mom is a janitor, Eva. She earns too little. We literally live from paycheck to paycheck. And I had this chunk saved up for my trip to China. A ton of babysitting and tutoring I did throughout the year."

"Riiight . . ."

Sabrina had a sense of unease as she tried to read the air in the room. The longer Eva seemed to chew the inside of her mouth, the faster Sabrina's pulse quickened.

"When did this happen?"

"Just before prom."

"Prom? Oh gross. Tell me please you'd rather put your head in a vise than that sickening bullshit."

Sabrina shook her head and grinned. "The vise, every time."

"That's my girl." Eva laughed. "So tell me, do you have a Chinese passport? American passport?"

"Yes. I mean, I think so."

Eva raised her eyebrows at her, and Sabrina started to feel queasy.

"You *think* so?"

"My mom was dealing with that part."

The silence stretched between them, and Sabrina felt the dawning of a truth she had been avoiding for as long as she could remember. Apparently, Eva Kim already knew it.

Sabrina stood up and her chair made a screeching noise on the floor. She walked to a filing cabinet and pretended to look for something.

"It's a damn shame, this unforeseen event. I don't know what to call it," Eva said.

"Yes. That's what it was." Sabrina shrugged, but her eyes were starting to well up. "A force majeure," she whispered.

"Well, let's call it providence. You never would have come to me if that shitty pipe hadn't burst in your bathroom."

LATER THAT DAY, as the sun started to set over the city's skyline, Sabrina sat on the bus to Manayunk, leaning her head on the scratched window.

> DAVE: Hey Chen, are you free tomorrow afternoon?

She started to type, then deleted her message. Her heart raced.

She was working with Eva Kim the next day. With one sentence, her summer could change. Could she say yes?

> SABRINA: Hey, I'm working downtown at the Coalition
> tomorrow until around 4:30.

What had changed since Kit had gone away? Or was that the very thing that had changed? Perhaps he was just filling the time, and she was the only one still in Chestnut Hill for the summer.

> DAVE: Coalition?

Sabrina forced herself to put her phone down before she began to type a response.

Earlier that day, Eva Kim had told her how she had kept a lawyer waiting for seven weeks before drafting a reply on behalf of her client once. *There's real power in silence sometimes, kid. As long as you use it at the right time. It's kind of like the idea of not caring, right? Suddenly you've got nothing to lose. Silence will turn some people into total maniacs, so use it when the moment's right. You hear me?*

Five minutes later, she saw he was still online. Maybe he was waiting for her, and she finally began to type.

SABRINA: The Asian American Immigration Coalition. I'm
    doing an internship there this summer.
DAVE: Cool. So come over to mine after. We can hang out.

Hang out . . . there it was, she would be alone with him. Again, he didn't ask. It occurred to her that the Harrisons were not accustomed to asking or waiting for a response. She ran her finger over the screen of her phone and studied his messages again. She pictured him moving on to messaging someone else. She was just one of many on his chat list. But for Sabrina, there was nobody else.

CHAPTER ELEVEN

Sabrina

Philadelphia, July 2015

Y ou look different today, Chen," Eva Kim said as Sabrina
walked into the office carrying iced coffees for both of them.
She was due to *hang out* with Dave later. "You got a hot date?"
Sabrina felt her face flush.

"I don't," she replied too fast.

"Someone you want to impress, then?" As she spoke, Eva Kim continued to trawl through her document with a yellow highlighter, never looking up.

Sabrina said nothing and hoped the questioning would pass. It did.
And she felt a gratitude to Eva Kim for reading her, for seeing what she
was willing to say and what she was not.

SABRINA'S CAPTIVATION WITH Eva Kim grew stronger every moment
she spent with her. Instead of rushing out the door at the end of every
afternoon, she lost track of time until the summer sun started to dip.

She began to realize that Eva Kim's office was a finely tuned chaotic web of order: papers scattered over every surface, binders stuffed with letters, pink folders covered in coffee stains. Sabrina constantly felt the need to tidy the office, yet it was as though this tangled mess were a carefully constructed maze of clues that all played a vital role in whatever cases Eva was working on at that moment.

Sabrina watched from the only seat in the office that was not taken by a big pile of books and binders. The seat had become her desk. The back of the chair had a large crack that ran down the middle, which sometimes dug into her shoulder blade.

"So you didn't think about applying to any colleges besides Penn State?"

Sabrina shrugged and shook her head.

"That is not a proper response, Chen. Did you?"

Sabrina stared at her hands for a moment and then looked up.

"There was one more, yes."

"An Ivy?"

Sabrina nodded, and Eva Kim nodded in response.

The car horns down on the street were muffled by the window as one driver continued pounding the horn for what felt like minutes.

"Well, I need to look into it more, but I *believe* I'm probably more likely to get a full ride to Penn State than Princeton. Just from the sheer competition alone. It's amazing I have the offer, but the financial aid is hard to get. It feels impossible."

"Nothing is impossible. Pray tell, how was this news received at your prestigious fancy-pants high school?"

"CHA is public, Ms. Kim."

"You're shittin' me."

"Oh yeah, it's a public school with ninety-eight percent higher-income attendees."

A silence fell between them, and Sabrina watched the expression on Eva Kim's face change. She stared into space ahead of her and began to shake her head, then she typed furiously onto her computer. She paused and looked up at Sabrina.

"Yep, you're right. How could I have forgotten this. Those motherfuckers . . ."

Sabrina still felt shocked when Eva Kim swore.

"What do you mean? Who? Who are the mother . . ."

"I mean those fucking privileged assholes have leveraged all their social, snotty contacts to bring in all the top-notch private-school teachers and donations from that white, privileged cobblestone Chestnut Hill community to make a public school have all the frills of a private elite school while ticking off the public school checklist. It's the ultimate flex of those with money making the system work for them. All their rich snotty friends moved into the district, so those who are really in need of a public education are priced out, and voila, they've basically created a private school under the guise of it being *public*. They've pumped up the school with donations from wealthy parents so they don't have the fees but all the extras in this one school for their already privileged kids. You understand what I'm saying?"

"I think so?"

"I think you do. It's basically benefits for all the people who have plenty already, and the kids who actually need the donations, and the help, and the input, they get pushed aside."

Sabrina took a deep breath. Everything Eva Kim said was true, she just hadn't looked at it face on until now. And the unfairness of it.

"And your trip? Your mom was fixing it, was she? She made quotation marks in the air when she said the word *fixing*. "Getting her old contacts across the river to get the documents together for you so you could travel in and out?"

"I couldn't say for sure, but I guess so. I didn't really have any other way of . . ."

Eva nodded and abandoned the topic completely, and Sabrina was so grateful again that Eva understood her without her having to say the words that were so painful to get out. That Eva Kim knew when to leave Sabrina alone.

It wasn't until this moment that Sabrina started to consider the extent of the injustice of it—the complete imbalance she witnessed but didn't fully understand. She always felt like she was intruding in a place where she didn't quite belong. She felt a cloak of invisibility cover her as she boarded the school bus while others drove away in SUVs. She felt embarrassed every time Lee Lee arrived at a parent-teacher event wearing the same faded green housedress with the hem frayed from too many washes, while the other mothers wore expensive dresses and designer handbags slung over their shoulders. It was understood that most of her peers would attend any college they liked. Every morning she walked into the school foyer to see the names of the Harrisons and Herzogs etched into the marble wall in order of their generous donations.

Show-offs, Lee Lee mumbled.

It was the first time that Sabrina had ever talked about her status with anyone, and something inside her heart felt unlocked.

The Harrisons lived in a four-story brownstone east of Rittenhouse Square in the Society Hill district. Sabrina heard no traffic as she walked down the shaded street lined with swaying cherry blossom trees heavily laden with leaves. Dave opened the door to her with a smile she had only seen a handful of times before. The heavy door closed behind her, and beyond the stone steps and doorway, she found herself in a black-and-white marble entrance hall looking at her reflection in an enormous Art Deco mirror with a sizable globe-shaped glass light installation that she later heard Mrs. Harrison describe as "midcentury." Further down the hallway, she could see a massive kitchen with a powder-pink marble island and baby-blue velvet upholstered stools lined up alongside it.

The hallway had a faint scent of figs mixed with a heady floral fragrance from the large display of lilies on a round glass table. Unlike Sabrina's house, there was no line of pegs for her to hang her bag or jacket by the front door. She stood awkwardly as Dave said, "Hey, Chen," and gestured for her to follow. *Should she take her shoes off? Where should she put her bag?*

She started to untie her Converse.

"Hey, don't worry about that. You want a cold drink? Looks hot out there."

The cool air-conditioning hit her as she followed him to the kitchen.

"Uh, sure. What have you got?"

"Everything."

She imagined what that would look like.

THE DEN WAS darker, and Sabrina's eyes took a moment to adjust. There was a whiff of laundry detergent in the air, the scent she recognized from passing Dave in the school hallways. For a moment, she imagined burying her nose into Dave's back, between his shoulder blades, and inhaling. Then she thought of Kit doing that very thing, and her throat closed up. She forced herself to black out the image, like the curtains they pulled on airplanes to separate first class from everyone else.

"So what's going on with you, Chen?" Dave sat down on the couch and tipped his head toward the seat, inviting her to join him.

Sabrina shrugged, her mind racing to find a quick quip.

"How's this internship going? What are you doing there?"

"It's uh . . . kind of basic stuff, like filing, but I get to help this woman, she's interesting, kinda weird, and kinda awesome. She helps Asian immigrants who have no rights. She works with them and represents them in court, helps them to get basic health care, gives those who are struggling a voice, I guess is what she would say."

"What's her name?"

"Eva Kim. Her name is Eva Kim."

"You like her?"

Sabrina paused, and she felt her heart fill up for a moment at the thought of Eva.

"I really do. She's super tough, and foulmouthed, and she gets shit done."

Dave's eyes widened. "That's the first time I ever heard *you* swear."

"Yeah?"

"It suits you."

"DAVID! ARE YOU HERE?" Footsteps interrupted them, the loud clip-clop of high heels on wooden floorboards.

"Yep, I'm down here."

"Did you not get my messages? I need you to let me know if you're coming to the Agarwals for dinner tonight. Rita needs numbers. Oh hello there."

Mrs. Harrison swept into the room, a cloud of perfume following her.

"Hello, Mrs. Harrison." Sabrina stood up quickly and bowed slightly, a gesture she immediately regretted.

"Oh, hi, love, how *are* you? I didn't know you had company, David." Mrs. Harrison's eyes scanned Sabrina and rested on the country club logo on the left side of her polo shirt.

"I love this country club merch you're wearing—David, we have to get some too." She had moved so close that Sabrina could see where Mrs. Harrison had drawn between the fine hairs of her brows.

"Yeah, Sabrina came over after work. We're just hanging out. Might catch a movie. So I won't be coming tonight, Mom, sorry." He shrugged and pulled his cell phone out.

"Sure. Make yourself at home, Sabrina."

"Thank you. You have a beautiful home, Mrs. Harrison," Sabrina said quietly.

"Oh, that's sweet. Thank you. I do miss our big place in Chestnut Hill, but this little spot suits us so much better now that Brad's at college, and Dave is leaving us soon too." She waved her arm into the air.

"Mom, do you need anything else?" Dave asked.

"No, my darling, no. Otherwise, if you need anything, check in with Jona, okay? And have fun! Nice to see you again, honey," she said as she clip-clopped back up the stairs.

"Who's Jona?"

"Oh, she's our housekeeper."

"Riiiight . . ." Sabrina walked around the room and started to examine the collage of photographs on the pinboards. Some were of Brad's friends and girlfriends. She noticed there weren't as many of Dave's. In one, taken in front of the Colosseum in Rome, his brother's arm was thrown around his neck, but Dave's eyes always gave him away, those mournful eyes that looked out at the camera lens, his body leaning away from his brother's.

"You think I'm a brat?"

"Well, I knew you guys were rich," Sabrina said, gesturing around her.

Dave laughed, "Brutal . . . but yes, my parents are, and objectively speaking, I am a brat. What does your house look like?"

"We live pretty simply," she replied quietly.

"As in, our house feels like excessive or something?" He gestured with his arm toward the PlayStation and enormous TV.

"Americans are so wasteful. My mom's favorite subject."

"Your mom says that?"

"Yeah, all the time."

"Well, we are. I mean, she would hate my mom. If the food is past its expiration date, even if it's still good, it goes in the trash."

Sabrina said nothing and thought about what her mother would do if she saw the Harrison's house. She imagined her mother's eyes would be like saucers as they looked around the carefully curated artwork, the ornaments deliberately displayed. A bowl of lemons on the kitchen counter. *What do they need so many lemons for?* This was a different world from Sabrina's, a way of living the Chens did not understand. It didn't even compare to Kit's house. Everything about Dave's home made Sabrina feel like she should be thanking Mrs. Harrison for allowing her inside.

"Yeah, it's different in our house," she said.

Act Two

CHAPTER TWELVE

Sally

Chestnut Hill, July 2015

The hyacinths were starting to turn. This was the time of year when Terry would start to cut them back, but Sally wished he would leave them alone for longer. The regal flowers seemed to transform overnight, and she always found herself in mourning for their lost beauty. But she could also see that the aging hyacinths were equally beautiful in their decay, if not more so. Their ethereal, papery, fine petals became transparent, like a fairy's wing. This year she wanted to see the whole garden covered in these elderly blooms, in all their quiet glory. *We're still here*, they said.

Sally Herzog thought of her daughter, Kit, at almost every moment. She had not known this type of obsessive distraction since she was a teenager in the throes of first love. The irony that it was probably over Rick Buchanan back when she was younger, Kit's host in Tokyo. They had all been a little bit in love with him in those days. The last moment she'd seen Kit was as she passed through security at Philadelphia International Airport to board her flight to Newark, on her way to Tokyo.

Her daughter never looked back.

Sally hoped Kit had been struck by the sudden sadness of parting from her. Any other explanation might break her heart completely.

She had read a few months ago that one of the telltale signs of anxiety was asking "what if." *What if the plane crashes? What if she is kidnapped? What if someone drugs her? What if a car hits her in Tokyo and I never find out? What if she is so happy she never returns?*

There was a permanent fear that lived in the back of Sally's mind and heart that one day Kit would discover her true heritage, seek out her birth mother, find her place in the world, and never return to her. Or that Kit's abandonment by her birth mother would cause so much pain that Sally would not be able to soothe her child, to make it better. Sally also worried that Kit's growing sense of displacement wasn't just regular teenage turmoil but permanent damage caused by Sally. What if it was her anxiety and the parental rules she felt she had to impose on a child that she sometimes couldn't make sense of? She looked at the clock; it was 5:32. Terry was away for the week in Delaware. She poured herself a gin and tonic, more gin than tonic, and then wandered up the stairs, where she could hear the silence of the rooms, the absence of Kit, no tip-tap of Tripper's feet. She felt a cavernous hole in her heart left by her beautiful, magnificently stupid vizsla, and by her absent daughter. How lonely she felt as she walked around the empty rooms of her house.

She looked at the photographs of Kit on the gallery wall she had painstakingly put up six months ago when she was redecorating the reception room. Kit was five years old in one picture—a family portrait taken out in the Wissahickon Valley Park. Kit had been difficult that day. Weekends were hard back then. Kit came home exhausted from stepping in line at school all week and needed to shuck the day off like a dog shaking away river water. Whenever she had the chance she wanted to rush into the wilderness, freely, but Sally shouted for her to return.

Terry had no patience at the time and only changed gears to become a better father much later. But all the early years, the toddler's irrational tantrums, the boundary testing, this all fell to Sally. *I'm just not a small kid kind of dad,* he explained at dinner parties. Instead, his theory was, if it's difficult, throw money at it, which most of the time she appreciated. It was easier that way. She could hire a sitter when she needed a break, she could always go for a hair appointment or to the gym. They enrolled Kit in every extracurricular activity so it didn't constantly fall to Sally to entertain her. Since Terry didn't want to do the heavy lifting, she never had to justify the choices she made when it came to outsourcing.

Terry was tall and slim in the photograph hanging in their reception room. He was thirty-seven years old back then, still bearing a resemblance to the man she first met, a playful gentleness lingering around his smile and eyes.

She had been pretty when they'd met in the mid-1990s. She was in her twenties, slim, with sun-kissed shoulders, her freckles scattered over her nose. People would call her "doe-eyed." The world seemed much larger to Sally back then. Terry had pursued her with patience, and after they were married, they bought the house on Gravers Lane. It was while doing yard work, during their second month there, that she met Mrs. Reynolds. The lady had lived on their street all her life, her children and her grandchildren too. "This is as close to Eden as you'll get," she said. Terry had beamed with pride, but Sally nodded and smiled at the neighbor, her eyes widening behind her sunglasses. A chill ran through her. She pressed it down, so deep it rarely bubbled back up. This was her life now. This was all her life would ever be.

Sally had once had lofty hopes for her future; she had wanted to be a professional volleyball player, she had wanted to work in advertising, she had wanted to move to Europe. But Terry started up his law practice in Flourtown, just three miles northwest, and once they bought the house, they were bedded in. Then suddenly, like the hyacinths, she saw herself in the mirror. *This is my face now.*

When they finally decided they wanted children, the trappings of suburban life in Pennsylvania became less of a burden. Her thoughts, her will, her emotions, everything was channeled into getting pregnant. Their friends turned up to parties with rosy flushed faces, gently cradling their flat stomachs, declaring in hushed voices that they were just seven weeks along, that they weren't going to find out what they were having. *It's one of life's last real mysteries, don't you think?*

Elizabeth McKay, married to Terry's best friend from high school, stood proudly beside Sally at a Fourth of July barbecue. Her thick middle jutted out to announce that she was pregnant and that everyone could relax, Jim wasn't shooting blanks. With every announcement, Sally felt a little smaller, she felt the crooks at the edge of her face sinking down. Every month, when she felt herself bloating and mood swings descending, there would be a small spark of hope. The years of trying, countless doctors, and carefully scheduled nights of sex with Terry meant that something between them died. She read every book, marked calendars, ate pineapples in winter, took folic acid supplements the size of grapes, lay with her legs raised up against the wall while Terry snored beside her. Sometimes she was exhausted and longed to shower away the semen and sweat that stayed there between her legs, but she waited patiently. Twenty minutes, the doctor had said. Eventually, they gave up after nine years of trying. The McKay baby was now a surly eight-year-old boy, and their other friends were on baby two, three, four, even five.

The adoption pamphlets lay on the dining-room table. She left them there until, finally, Terry took them away. The snow had fallen heavily across the gardens that winter. The white blankets over the lawn and driveway muffled the sound of passing cars.

Terry poured himself a coffee as she sat at the breakfast bar reading the *Chestnut Hill Reporter*. He stood in front of the refrigerator, searching for milk. She saw the carton right there from where she sat. He could never see what was right in front of him.

"I sent the papers in. So let's see." He didn't look at her as he said it.

Her eyes began to fill with tears, but she sat still. "Terry," she said.

"Let's see, love. Let's see."

Two years and twenty-four days passed, and Kit came into their lives. She was fourteen months old, and they had to adjust to telling age by months instead of years. Sally had known moments of fear in her life: when she almost crashed her car in high school during a snowstorm; when she had been in a bar in the city late one night and a man started to follow her down the street; when she had lost her virginity; when her father had been diagnosed with colon cancer and died two years later. The first day Kit wandered into her house, with an unsteady step padding from room to room, Sally was paralyzed with a terrifying fear she'd never known. It seeped into the deepest well inside her, tainting the water forever. There was so much to lose now.

Images of what her daughter could be doing on the other side of the world played through Sally's mind. She wanted to be the type of mother who was free and trusting. This had always been her intention, and she knew that by the time Kit reached adolescence, her daughter would want to know more about her biological mother. Or not. Because Kit always surprised her. Sally was still teaching herself to avoid expectations. The gin and tonic she drank while wandering around her empty house had kicked in now, and she barely startled when the shrill phone rang in her pocket. It was her daughter.

"How was the flight, honey?" She wondered if she was slurring her words.

"It was so long, Mom. But it was fine. I slept when it was nighttime in Tokyo like you said to."

"How are things there? Did Rick and Yuriko meet you at the airport okay?" Her words felt like they were coming out in slow motion.

"Yeah, Mr. Buchanan was there with their driver. Mom, they have a driver! Did I wake you?"

"Oh no, no." She *was* slow. "Did you eat? Are you eating Japanese food?"

"Yeah, a little. It was good. You would love it."

Sally smiled. You would love it.

"Have you given them the thank-you gift?"

"Yeah, right away. And they've given me a whole floor, with a bathroom and everything. You didn't tell me he was an ambassador." *She had.* "They call the house the Ambassador's Residence. Doesn't that sound cool? Or was it the Ambassador's house . . . I can't remember. I haven't met Ryo, Ree-yo, am not sure I'm saying this right, or Amy yet. But I think one of them is starting college and the other has another year of high school to go? Is that right?" Sally wasn't sure.

Kit's voice was breathy with excitement, the way it would be when she won a soccer game at school, or her grades had been better than she had expected. Until just a few years ago, she could talk to her daughter for hours. And then when Kit turned fifteen, it came to an abrupt halt, and now, Sally was starving. But like cool water running down her throat, she could hear that enthusiasm vibrating through her phone. She heard it sometimes when Kit spoke to Sabrina.

"I can't wait to hear all about it, honey."

"It's like a movie set, the skyscrapers, lights, highways that run through the city. And then like a cute little old temple. But it's super clean too. Not like Philly."

"Just make sure you're being careful, okay? Safe."

"Oh that's another thing, Mr. Buchanan was telling me that basically there is almost like no crime at all in Tokyo. Like, it's one of the safest cities in the world."

"Well, still, that doesn't mean you don't have to be careful, right? You're still a beautiful young woman in a city you don't know. So just make sure you're cautious."

"I know, I know." Her breath had slowed down, she was no longer listening. "Anyway, I better go. I love you. Tell Dad I love him too. I'll probably just message you, okay? Easier than calling with the time difference."

"Well, I don't mind, you can call anytime, sweetie, I love you so . . ." But Kit had already hung up.

Sally stood for a little longer, looking at the home screen of her cell phone, a picture of Kit smiling in her graduation gown, taken just a few weeks ago.

She felt an overwhelming sadness in that moment, but instead of crying she walked to the refrigerator and made herself a cheese sandwich. She bit into the grainy bread Terry insisted on buying and thought about how she missed the spongy texture of a regular white loaf. It had been months since she had last eaten bread, let alone a sandwich. She continued wandering around the empty house and laughed as she trailed the crumbs behind her. *Look at me. I'm ridiculous*, she thought to herself.

The next day, Sally had a headache that throbbed in such a dull, nagging way she regretted the second gin and tonic she made herself and wondered if Kit had noticed her tipsiness when they spoke last night.

A photo came in from Kit, a plate of raw fish and sushi that turned her stomach, with the caption "Lunch!" She looked up her daughter's Instagram account to find she had posted the same caption as she did in her message, and something in Sally smarted, a pain that was sudden and stinging. She tried to reassure herself that at least Kit had taken the trouble to send her the message, which separated her from the friends who followed her account.

Terry video-called, and she reluctantly answered.

"You okay, love? You look a little tired," he said, the angle of the phone tilted, catching half of his face and shoulder.

"I'm fine. Just couldn't sleep."

"Maybe take a nap," he offered. "I have that case to close today, so I might be back later than I had hoped. You go ahead without me tonight with dinner and everything," he said. "I'll let you know later whether I'll be back tonight or tomorrow."

She wanted him to share more about his work, but she knew that he never did because his assumption was that she was uninterested with the ins and outs of his challenges. So long as she could stay on Gravers Lane in the house they had, as close to Eden as they could get, drive the Volvo, have lunch with her friends, play some tennis, it was enough for Sally. At least that was what Terry assumed.

She knew that in her husband's eyes her life was so comfortably arranged that she *could* lie down in the middle of the day, just to recover from a sleepless night, and nothing would be lost, nothing was at stake, nothing compromised. Nobody needed her to be anywhere, nor needed anything from her.

Another message came through. "There's a party tonight at the Residence. Having a great time!"

Sally felt her stomach plummet. The idea of Kit with Rick and his wife, Yuriko, had been theory until now, and even then, they were far enough away from her, but the thought of Kit, with her voice a little too loud, her overconfidence when she felt uncomfortable (her daughter could even be a little too forthright), and her Americanisms chafed her in a way she had never known before. Sally wondered what Rick and Yuriko would make of Kit. She wondered if they ever thought of her.

CHAPTER THIRTEEN

~∘~

Mimi

October 2002–December 2004, Saigon

Mimi could never leave Ho Chi Minh City. She remained there, in case by some wild twist of fate her daughter would retrace her mother's journey back. This fragmented thread of hope knotted around her, and she stayed put, four years later, six years later, and so many more still. If she stayed, maybe somehow Ngan would return to her—like a homing pigeon.

Meanwhile Mimi's sister, Cam, moved to Da Nang once she married. Her husband wanted to live by the sea.

"Every day I'm surrounded by insects crawling everywhere, worms, beetles, I can feel them on me at night." She moaned to Mimi on the phone, "Why a fish bait store? Why couldn't he start a jewelry shop, clothes, or something like that? Even a fruit stall would have been better."

"I bet you eat the best fish in town though," Mimi tried to say.

"I would be happy to never eat fish again. Did you call that woman at the hotel?"

"Not yet."

"You better. You can get yourself a job. If it's anything like the hotels here, these foreigners will pay big tips, you'll be able to get yourself some land in no time. And I know, you are not thinking of this, after America, after Ngan. But maybe you will meet someone again too, start over."

Mimi was silent. The loss of her child in America lived in a separate space of pain, where nothing fit within its jagged edges, not the death of her father during the war, or Ngan's father abandoning her almost immediately after she fell pregnant. Everything that mattered to her was lost that day in the Philadelphia airport.

"Anyway, you better call that woman. I have to go."

Mimi didn't mention to Cam how thin she had become or about the argument she'd had with their aunt, who had told her she was depressing the customers, that her aunt's children were starting to get anxious around her, and that there was no work left for her at the laundry service anymore. She needed to find another place to live. So Mimi had no choice. She called the *Thien Duong*, the Paradise Hotel, and said she would take any job they offered.

And they did offer her a job that paid more money than she had ever earned before. She started working as a chambermaid. They said she wasn't presentable enough to greet the guests. So she began to clean. Every day, she arrived early to work, took her trolley and knocked gently on the guest-room doors before letting herself in. After a few months of working in the rooms, sifting through other people's dirty sheets and laundry, she found tips left for her on the bedside tables, just like Cam had said. Sometimes it was almost a week's salary. When the restaurant staff were let go for stealing bottles of wine from the cellar, Mimi was called in to serve, and she collected more tips then. "You are more presentable now," she was told.

She worked ceaselessly every day, smiling at the guests who looked tentatively at her in the hallways; some of the bolder ones, usually men in bright shirts unbuttoned too low, would shout out *Xin chao*, pressing their hands flat together in front of their chests and bowing. She nodded her head in recognition of their efforts, smiling to herself. These big white men, Mimi began to learn, didn't greet her with any intention of interacting. It was for them to feel better about themselves, that they spoke to the help, that they smiled and acted gracious to the hired hands who cleaned their soiled bedding and wiped their bathrooms clean of their human waste. She saw from the lift in their shoulders and their smiles that they felt pleased with themselves. She wondered what they saw when she passed them, if they would even know the difference between her face and the girl who worked behind the desk if they weren't dressed in different uniforms.

Sometimes, the American guests would shout *Goooood morning, Vietnam* somewhere in the hotel, usually by the pool, where they clutched bottled beers as they lay back on their towels, bellies hairy and bursting from the fabric of their shorts. Cam and Mimi had watched that film in Philadelphia and laughed at the sight of the girls all dressed in white *ao dais*. "These stupid Americans think we are dressed for *Tet* every day of the year. What about when we go to the market? Clean the house? They think we're wandering around in white clothes, with all the dust, mud, and rain? Where are the ponchos? The aprons?" They laughed at the beginning of the film before they began to see the death, and then they had to turn it off. Mimi held Ngan in her arms that night, singing softly and wishing that Ngan would never know what it was to be hungry or afraid. Mimi smiled as she passed the men in the hallways and thought how nice it must be for them to only see what they wanted.

The weight of her needing to return to America was always present. It stayed there inside her, a permanent pull at her insides. Mimi's soul had shattered, and the remaining shards dug deep into her heart, where scar tissue enveloped it to keep what was left from disintegrating. She existed, nothing more. Her skin was dry, her eyes bloodshot, her spirit faded. Most days, she stared into the space before her. When anyone asked her what she was looking at, she said she didn't know.

⁓

By the time that Ngan would have been six years old, Mimi had changed jobs several times. She now worked as a helper in private households for expat families. Every morning she drove through the busy side roads of District 2. She had finally saved enough money to buy a motorcycle and drove it to the river daily to watch the murky brown water flow past. Green snakes would swim upstream and disappear into the floating shrubbery. Otters slipped into the water from the jungle banks, snatching fish from the bottom of the riverbed, emerging out of the water's surface with sleek wet heads and jet-black eyes, bringing the fish up to their sharp fangs and ripping their heads off. She watched their incisors rip into the flesh, blood soaking their whiskers, and then the fish's body would be tossed back, worthless to them. She couldn't eat fish anymore and decided then that she didn't like the otters.

Another time, she saw a dead human body float past, and she vomited on the banks. The gray, swollen corpse brought up a stench, and unspeakable images of her Ngan passed through her mind. But most of the time, she just watched the movement of the water, the artery that ran through her city, feeding it, taking from its people when the rains came, giving back less and less as the construction and development increased. She watched new buildings rising around her, past and beyond the orange rooftops of typical Saigon houses and the rocks at the bottom of the well she had been sitting on for years. She could see the light again, and it breathed life into her, the darkness a little less black every day.

~

On the day that Mimi and Toan's story began, she arrived early to work, her belly full from a steaming bowl of *Pho Ga* from the nearby stall rumored to be the best in the district. *You're too scrawny, make sure you eat all the chicken skin. I'll give you extra*, the woman ladling the bowls said. The edges of Mimi's mouth were still burned from the sliced chili she'd piled onto the herbs. There was an unusual wind, the palms swaying noisily as if to complain that they should be left to their own devices and that these gusts were too rough.

A group of European tourists had been staying at the hotel; she thought they might be Italian. Among them, a small-boned woman with a beaklike nose and multiple piercings in her ears had been sick for almost a week. Each day that Mimi returned to service her room, the girl's face was more gaunt, and wet, dirty towels were passed to her with a request for more. Mimi wanted to ask her what she had eaten, whether she had been drinking the water, but she couldn't get the words out of her mouth. Instead, she passed the towels in silence. She left extra bottles of water and a coconut she had cut and put a straw through on the third day, when the girl looked especially bad. Everything was supposed to be logged and charged to the room, but instead, Mimi had knocked on the door, left a tray, and waited to see the girl emerge before quickly walking away to her other jobs. On the sixth day, Mimi went up to clean the room and knocked with the four fresh towels ready to pass through the door.

117

Nobody answered, and she stood waiting for some time before letting herself in.

She found the room deserted. A sadness swept over her. She liked looking after the girl with the earrings. She felt there should have been a goodbye, to acknowledge the significance of their connection, however minor. They would never see each other again. She looked around the room, touched the cabinet, where the drawers had all been left open. Mimi put the air-conditioning on high to clear the air, even though the hotel management told her not to, to save on electricity. Beside the table, she found two five hundred thousand dong notes and a message scribbled in English on the pad. *Thank you for looking after me.* A smile crept up to her mouth. She folded the notes and placed them neatly inside the waist of her skirt. That would cover the month's rent, maybe two. All for a few extra towels.

She scrubbed the surfaces, sprayed every corner and patch of floor, got down on her knees to wipe away every stain, picked up every hair. The lemon-scented bleach cleared her sinuses. She left the taps running, and steam came in through the bathroom as the water roared at searing hot temperatures. She soaked the cloths in the sink, her hands burned for a moment when she squeezed them and hung them up to dry. She wiped the mirrors and windows. She preferred the finish of vinegar and water on the surfaces. She stripped the sheets, made crisp folds into the edges of the beds. She looked over the room at the neat lines of the bedding, the gleaming side tables, and smelled laundry powder and cleaning products. For a moment she let the happiness envelop her as she sprayed the air with mosquito deterrent.

The extra money, the bowl of *pho* that morning, had put a spring in her step as she walked down to the supply room and put away her trolley, slotting it neatly into its numbered space. The other housekeeping girls kept their distance from her when she passed them in the hallway. She noticed they had stopped whispering years ago, but they still didn't look her in the eye. She wandered out of the entrance, reading her cell phone messages from Cam, when someone ran into her. His weight pushed her forward, and his hand caught her arm before she lost her footing.

The air had been knocked out of Mimi's body. She hung in midair before scrambling onto her feet, realizing the man's hand still gripped her forearm. She pulled away and looked back to see his round flat face and a nose that was too small for it. He looked her over, and she started to walk away.

"Look where you're going," she snapped, although she had been the one who hadn't looked where she were going.

She felt his eyes on her as she walked away but refused to turn back.

TOAN LIKED TO say it was love at first stumble. People never asked how they met, but Toan always told them how he crashed into a distracted Mimi one sunny November day at the Paradise, and his life changed forever.

Oh, it took you so long to even smile at me, he reminded her years later. *At first, I thought you were beautiful but without a nice face. You know the kind of women I mean. Some girls are beautiful, but you don't see any kindness. And when you finally laughed, I realized you were not beautiful but had a kind face. You have a very nice face. Which is much better in a wife.*

The day after the stumble, Mimi observed him for the first time. He had a bounce in his step, a broad smile that swept up his face and creased his eyes and nose, taking over every part of him. In Mimi's opinion, being a driver was not an especially ambitious profession, but if they were lucky enough to have a foreign employer, it at least meant a regular income. To her, running your own business was the ideal, though her sister's husband had tarnished this image with the rotten stench of fish bait that

Cam described. A man living in a fancy compound in Thao Dien, whose name she couldn't recall, had begun a coffee chain, and now he was one of the wealthiest men in Asia, the only Vietnamese on that list. A master of oneself. That was the Vietnamese dream.

Parked along the street outside the Paradise Hotel were lines of Toyota Land Cruisers. The more industrious drivers cleaned and polished the cars—she noticed Toan did this. Others napped for hours with their feet sticking out of the window, occasionally emerging to sit on their foldaway stools and read the newspaper. Mimi wondered how they could bear it, to always be at the mercy of someone else's clock. She at least knew the hours she was required to work. She knew when to arrive and when she could leave. There was a small freedom in that.

In those days, Mimi believed the need to sleep and rest bore down into the very essence of being Vietnamese. Everyone seemed to wake early, worked from the first light of day, filled their bellies at lunch, and as the heat rose and rose, a nap was expected. Sleeping bodies could be found all over the city, in hammocks hung between lampposts, or trees, in the back of trucks, or even on construction sites. A worker might place a cardboard sheet down as a makeshift bed in the coolest place they could find for a snatched moment of rest. Yet something in Mimi's Americanization meant that she viewed it as laziness. How would you make it in this world when you were sleeping through the middle of the day? Toan, she saw, was someone who didn't sleep either. He was always busy, washing his car with pride as the sun's rays hit its gleaming surface.

That afternoon she watched him from the window of a room she was cleaning. He wore sunglasses as he sat on his folding stool beside his parking spot, and she wrote him off as ridiculous. How could a man in service to another consider his appearance so much that he would spend time looking in the mirror to try on sunglasses, she thought. Months later, she learned that they were given to him by his last boss, an Englishman who had only worked in Saigon for a year but had no family and treated Toan like a friend.

WHEN SHE FINISHED her shift that day, she walked out of the staff entrance and found him standing across the road. She knew he was there for her, but she ignored him, her eyes fixed firmly ahead. She put her hand to her waistband, and felt the folded paper still there. He leaped across the busy street, his hand expertly held up to tell the motorbikes to move around him as though he accompanied a foreign dignitary across the road.

"Are you all right?"

"Fine, thank you," she said quickly.

"I just didn't want you to hit your face, that was all."

"I didn't. Thank you." She quickened her pace.

"I'm Toan . . ." he called after her.

No man Mimi had depended on had ever turned out to be reliable. She was suspicious, dismissive even. But Toan was insistent. Every day he waited for her, standing in front of the Paradise. He would walk beside her, matching her pace, footsteps in unison toward her bike, and then he'd watch her disappear into the dusty pink light of the evening streets.

He pressed her to smile, pressed her to eat more, and insisted he walk her to her bike when her shifts ran too late. One evening he wasn't there because he had to take his boss to the airport, and she felt her shoulders drop.

Six weeks into their courtship, she decided it was time to tell him about Ngan.

"I suppose you've heard the rumors about me," she said as they walked down the riverbank.

"That you are a lovely woman seeking a husband, someone like me?" He smiled and nudged her with his shoulder.

"About what happened to my child. And the man who left me, unmarried and pregnant in America. I'm damaged goods."

"I see nothing damaged here," he said and took her hand.

She let him hold it.

"We have all suffered in this country, all of us have lost and felt pain. But to lose a child is something I cannot imagine."

She knew he had questions. But he never asked her why nobody had helped her that day at the airport. Whether she ever found out if Ngan was dead or alive. And how she could return home and know her child was still there? He didn't know yet that they had sedated her to board her on the plane after seventy-six hours of sitting in their immigration office and accusing her of trying to regain entry into the country illegally. He didn't know that every day she tirelessly went through every American newspaper that was thrown away in the hotel garbage to see if she could find anything about a lost child, nor that she still woke up screaming at night because of the unspeakable nightmares she would have about her Ngan, imagining her limp body lying somewhere in a forgotten wood outside of Philadelphia. She still remembered her own silent screams as she was dragged away. Mimi was too tired to explain any of it.

They watched the river moving faster now. Evening had arrived, and the air cooled, large collections of leaves and river weeds floated by. They sky was pink over the Mekong. Toan picked up a stone from the ground.

"If I get this in that cluster of weeds there, you'll have dinner with me next week."

Mimi nodded and stared out at the cluster. He threw it in silence, and it landed short.

"Best out of three?" he asked.

CHAPTER FOURTEEN

Kit

Tokyo, July 2015

From the moment Kit landed in Tokyo, she was hungry. Her stomach grumbled at everything she saw: the convenience stores with rice balls, an endless array of iced coffees, machines dispensing soft serves and multicolored snacks. She passed shops with sliding doors that revealed counters with people sitting in neat rows, eating bowls of savory noodles, the smell of meat grilling floating out into the street. It could have been the jet lag, but the hunger wasn't just in her stomach; it was in her eyes. The buildings were vast and lower than she had expected, unfamiliar. The facades came alive with bright lights and screens, the buildings curved in ways she'd never seen, and highways snaked through the city.

Kit felt like she towered over people in the street, but nobody turned to look at her; nobody asked her where she was from. She wondered whether it was acceptance or the anonymity of this sprawling city, so far from the familiarity of home. The sound of the trains and traffic enveloped her gently. The arms of the sprawling city embraced her in its thronging silence. She wanted to examine everything up close, smell and touch it all. She wanted to run her hands along the ridges of the lanterns that hung just at her eyeline as she walked down the narrow streets. She wanted to search for the city's secrets. Her ears rang with pleasure at the sound of the rhythmic ebb and flow of a language she couldn't wrap her tongue around, not even a few of the words, a song with notes she couldn't reach.

On her first day, she rushed out to explore. Mrs. Buchanan had given her a detailed list of trains to take in order to get home afterward, and a card with their address written down if she got really stuck. Later, the midday sun burned down on her shoulders, but she continued to walk through the city. Kit stopped outside a *Neko* café and looked through the window. She'd seen these places on Instagram. Cafés with cats that wandered around and relished attention from the customers. She didn't like cats, and she watched as three high school girls in sailor uniforms giggled over their iced coffees while a fat cross-eyed ragdoll flopped around on their laps, leaving swirls of hair over the navy fabric of their skirts. The hair on their clothes made her feel a little sick. A slim tabby in the window looked out at Kit with disdain. Further down the street, a group of mothers sat on a small bench outside a soft-serve stall, licking green matcha ice creams as they rocked their babies in their carriers. Every time they laughed, they covered their mouths in a gesture tinged with embarrassment.

She walked for hours. Kit wanted to see everything. There was no plan, she just had to take it all in—nobody was going to call her and check on her whereabouts. She was completely left to her own agenda, and it was intoxicating. Then, her calves started to ache. She wished she had worn sandals instead of her sweaty sneakers. There was a thin veil of dirt over her skin. She could smell it. But it was nothing like the grime she felt in Philly. She followed her map back toward the Buchanans' home in 1-Chome, passing the Imperial Palace moat and then going straight toward Shinjuku. She got a second wind and kept going. The vast crossing and train lines seemed to spread around her as she arrived at Shinjuku's main pedestrian crossing, facing the massive station. She headed down a side street and suddenly found herself standing among bars with shutters closed and neon signs outside yet to be lit for the evening patrons. A red-and-pink sign outside one of the tiny doorways said: SHORT TIME: 2,000 YEN. The brazen illicitness of the sign seemed to be whispering loudly.

Everything suddenly looked seedy and dirty around her, and she wondered what it was like at night, whether these side streets were still deserted, as the people who booked the rooms by the hour covertly headed up the dark stairways. Something moved behind the trash cans, and she quickened her pace; she hurried back toward the main roads leading to the central station depot.

She stopped in front of a row of vending machines, lights flashing, offering iced coffee, hot coffee, lemon drinks, peach drinks, and Coke. She took a picture and posted it, then slotted the coins in and chose a slim can of Coke Light. She saw her reflection in the glass, her hair light against the jet-black hair of the people passing behind her. She felt enormous beside the Japanese people crossing the roads, especially the women, a full head taller than them. She clutched the icy can and followed the signs for her platform. She had never seen such crowds of people. In New York, yes, in Times Square, but this was different; everywhere she looked there were throngs of people. Occasionally she would notice another *gai-jin*, a foreigner, and feel a strange comfort in seeing someone else who didn't quite fit in.

The train carriage was almost empty. She looked out the window and stared at the metropolis: bumper-to-bumper traffic and crowds trickled along outside. The light was magnificent in the late afternoon, as billboards were illuminated and the reflective windows of office buildings glittered as if to show themselves off to her. She watched the tiny figures of people move in and out through the roads. She stared as she passed the multiple traffic lights, highways, and bridges that all intersected somehow like the most exquisite twisted metal across the vista of the city. The sun was orange here in Tokyo, shining down from the deep blue summer sky, and everything it touched eventually became pink and soft. She was suddenly overwhelmed with joy, and her eyes welled up with tears. Her soul felt quiet, her mind silent except for the words *I'm here*. She wouldn't experience that feeling again, of arriving and being entirely out of herself and her body, because afterward it would be as though she had always known how it felt to be in Tokyo.

The sunburn from three days of sightseeing made the temperature in her body rise from the inside out. She had ended up at the Asakusa shrine at midday and dawdled over the stalls and then the *omikuji*. Her post had gotten 117 Likes, and Dave had put a pair of clapping hands beneath the picture. That night she fell down the rabbit hole of his Instagram and Snapchat, taking screenshots and zooming in on his pictures. Before she left, they didn't even speak about college or what had passed between them. He had just said *Have a great time* as he dropped her back at her house. There was no end because, if she was really honest to herself, there had been no beginning or middle between her and Dave Harrison.

But Kit forgot about Dave the moment she set eyes on Ryo Buchanan. She had lost track of time and forgotten her hosts were having a party that night when she had returned to the Residence after a day of sightseeing. She arrived to the house lit with pretty lights and humming inside from the chatter among the guests. Panic descended on her as she stood at the entrance and looked down at her dusty shoes, filthy against the glistening shine of the marble floors. Kit had also forgotten that Ryo and Amy, their children, were back from their respective trips.

When she saw Ryo for the first time, he was standing in the middle of the cocktail party talking to three middle-aged men. One of them had their hand on his shoulder, and his silhouette was like an infrared figure in a film—with a heat that drew her to him even when she tried to look away.

Mr. Buchanan brought his son to her before she could rush up the stairs to change her dirty clothes from the day out in the city. Ryo greeted Kit with a familiarity she didn't know how to handle.

"You're both the same age," Rick said as he steered his son toward Kit. "This is Sally Herzog's daughter, Katherine, remember I told you she was staying with us."

"Kit . . ." she whispered, but her own name was caught in her throat.

"Welcome to Tokyo," Ryo said and kissed her on both cheeks like she'd seen French people do. More heat. She could smell his soap. The scent was something she recognized, but it smelled better here, coming off his skin under the black ceiling fans that whirred above her and the muted hum of the conversations around them.

"I hope you had a good day around the city. Tokyo can be a little overwhelming at first. But Ryo can show you around—he knows all the hidden spots around this town." Rick winked at his son.

"I sure do. Wait, I have to get something for Mom, I'll be right back for you, Katherine," he said and hopped back into the crowd. When he moved she felt like he leaped—as though simply walking was too ordinary for him. She watched him and realized her mouth was hanging open.

She suspected Ryo was less a boy, almost a man. He had the kind of triangular, broad-chested body that narrowed at the waist, with skin the shade of tawny gold, and he filled his clothes as though they had been made for him. She knew right away he was neither American nor Japanese, but somewhere on a different plane she might have recognized a little in herself.

He did return.

"What can I get you to drink? I knew you were staying with us, but I guess my folks were distracted by this party and forgot to remind me when you were arriving. Are you all settled up in the guest room?"

"Yeah, it's great up there. I feel bad, I forgot about this party. Your mom mentioned it to me this morning and I just lost track of time in town," she said.

Kit rubbed the skin on her chest and wondered if she could take a cold beer from one of the girls passing drinks trays around the room. Ryo stood before her and she felt like he took up the entire room, and suddenly, her entire universe. He pushed back his thick dark hair, watching her with a smile that seemed to know more about everything than she did. She wanted to notice things about him that made him less perfect. Maybe he wore too much gel in his hair, maybe there was something affected about him, maybe he was a poser. But his hair was soft, just washed, he wore shorts and walked barefoot through the house. If anything, he was as underdressed for the party as she was. He was wearing a white shirt, and suddenly white shirts were her favorite thing for any boy to wear. She stared at him and committed everything about him to memory. He greeted adults in a way she hadn't yet learned to, meeting their eye, an affectionate embrace as though they were old friends, equals even, and this made her feel a vast expanse separated her from the world he seemed so comfortable in.

"These things can be kinda boring, don't you think?" he whispered. Kit felt his shoulder brush against hers.

"Well, I can't say I've been to a lot of them." Kit surprised herself with her candid honesty, but seconds later she hated the sound of her own voice.

"What do you think so far?" he asked. Kit didn't dare look at him as she stood beside him.

"Definitely not like the parties my parents throw back home."

"And that's Philadelphia, right? I heard you're starting Penn this fall? I'm headed to Berkeley."

The Buchanans had spoken about her before she arrived. Maybe they'd spoken about her since she'd arrived too. Having not cared too much about the impression she made, she suddenly realized she cared very much.

"Hey, you want a sharpener? A day of sightseeing can really take it out of you." He smiled, and she noticed he had dimples. "It's my pick-me-up when I have to go out and I'm tired."

Kit didn't know what was being offered to her, and she felt herself tensing through her legs and up to her ears. Her life in Chestnut Hill so far had been free of peer pressure, largely due to the safe protective force of her friendship with Sabrina and nonrelationship with Dave Harrison. She followed Ryo to the kitchen, where trays of hors d'oeuvres and drinks had been left out for the servers to take.

"Here, hold these for me." He passed her two tumblers from the freezer. Her fingers created little circles on the frosted glass. "My pops is obsessed with frosted glasses. I'm starting to get it now though."

He took a bottle of Patrón Silver tequila from the back of the freezer and she watched him pour the thick liquid into the glasses and squeeze in fresh lime.

"This might just make the party a bit more interesting." He winked and passed her a glass.

Kit looked at the shot and a small breath of relief escaped her mouth. This was a real drink, the kind people drank in penthouse apartments in the city. Not the kind of drinks she'd had under the bleachers at school, or at Casey Steinham's house parties when her parents were away.

"Are you okay?" he asked.

"I didn't know what kind of sharpener you were talking about." Kit laughed and put the glass to her mouth.

"Oh really?" Ryo looked at her with an amused glint behind the eyes.

"Oh no. I'm not into drugs and stuff. I just, well . . ."

"You just didn't know whether I would be."

A silence fell between them and they both started to laugh. They finished their drinks, then Ryo heard his mother call for him and brought Kit back to the party. "I'll come find you later. Welcome Katherine . . . Kit."

She watched him disappear through the crowd toward his mother. Kit felt like she was watching him in slow motion.

Out beyond the grand reception room and through the wide doors that had been opened up for the party, she could see an American flag waving over the pristine lawn. It looked strange and out of place. Kit looked around the room again, her body warm and fuzzy from the drink. She rubbed her arm. There would be a streak of red skin now from the friction. She stopped in front of a cluster of photographs on a baby grand piano, all in glistening silver frames. She touched the edge of a frame and saw the fog of her finger make a halo, then disappear, leaving a smudge mark.

The photograph was of Rick and Yuriko Buchanan, standing beside the Clintons. Rick was a handsome dad. There was a picture of Ryo and his sister in traditional Japanese kimonos outside a temple. A high school graduation portrait of Ryo. Yuriko's modeling pictures from the 1970s were displayed in a perfect line, and Kit thought of the photo on the wall back home, of Sally smiling with her lacrosse team from high school. Something pulled at her throat.

"You wanna beer or wine, Katherine? Kit, is it?" Amy Buchanan, Ryo's younger sister, was standing beside her.

"Kit, call me Kit. I, uh, I'm not sure. You're Amy, right?"

Amy ignored Kit's question and any introduction.

"You don't drink?"

For a moment, Kit tried to translate Amy's tone. Her accent fell somewhere between American and European, and she sounded different from her brother and father. There was a clipped ending to her words, the way she would expect a British person to speak, embedded into her American accent. She couldn't tell by her tone whether Amy was judging her or if it was just how the words came out of her mouth.

"I do. I just, I guess I don't know if I feel like it right now. And, you know, I'm staying at your parents', so I don't know how they feel about drinking. It's kind of different back home." Why was she speaking so much? Kit realized she could feel that tequila now.

"Your parents or like generally in America? Where are you from again?" Amy didn't wait for Kit to answer. "Because my mom can be a total bitch about things, but she is kind of relaxed about a little drink at a party, especially when it's not a sit-down thing." Amy talked fast, and Kit realized quickly that if she hesitated, Amy would fill the silent space. She didn't know whether she found Amy rude or refreshing.

"Wait here, okay?"

Kit watched Amy move as fast as she spoke. Amy's glass, set down on a sideboard, dripped heavily with condensation, and Kit quickly put a coaster underneath it. Amy's skin was pale compared to Ryo's. They didn't look similar to her at first, but there was something in how they carried themselves that said they were from the same world. Amy had freckles scattered over her nose that matched her light auburn hair. It was pulled up into a top knot, and it was hard to tell what its natural color was.

She returned with two glasses of white wine. "It's cool," she said, triumphant, and handed Kit the drink.

"Are you sure?"

"Oh totally. If my parents are cool with me drinking they're cool with you. Relax, you're our guest."

"Right, as long as you're sure." Kit looked around but neither Rick nor Yuriko looked her way.

"Dad said he knows your mom too. They were at high school or neighbors or something."

"That's right, I think they grew up together or something. Do you know my mom?" Kit asked, hoping Amy would say she did.

"I don't know. I meet so many of my parents' friends and work people, it's hard to keep track."

They sipped their wine, Amy's glass already almost empty while Kit tried to hide the urge to wince as the sour liquid hit the inside of her mouth.

"Hey, did you bring your suit? We can go swim. I think Ryo and his friends are going to the pool soon, so we can bail on this lame party. I'll get one of the girls to bring a tray of drinks down. Come on." Amy grabbed Kit's hand, and her palms started to sweat. There wasn't enough time for Kit to respond or react, Amy was already pulling her away. She tried to wriggle her hand away from Amy's grip, but it only made Amy hold on tighter.

Kit wished she could change. Her high-waisted denim cut-off shorts were sticky around her lower back, and her J.Crew T-shirt made her feel so ordinary. Amy wore a baby-doll dress that skimmed her midthighs when it fell, but as she ran down the lawn, the hem floated up, and Kit saw her lacy neon pink underwear. She caught a glimpse of Yuriko's face in the background, lips pursed. For a moment, she looked like the Dover sole her mother bought from the market on Saturdays. *I've been sole searching*, Sally would giggle, and Kit always rolled her eyes.

Amy's legs were long and thin, and she wore nothing on her feet. She hopped through the grass, while Kit tripped clumsily in her Vans. She awkwardly tried to stop herself from treading on Amy's toes.

At the bottom of the lawn that sloped down at the end was a small outhouse that had white walls and lounge chairs folded up against it. Kit could see the piles of stacked cushions that would have been put away at the end of the day, the way they were at the country club back home. The far side of the pool was lined with a wall of bamboo plants that formed a fence and Kit could see the lights in the water. She thought it looked cold, and noticed how the sound of the party had become muffled and distant.

"I didn't bring a suit, but it's cool, I can hang out by the pool instead, seriously."

"I have your size, don't worry. I keep a bunch of bikinis down at the pool house."

Kit went into the pool house to change, her stomach churning at the thought of borrowing a bikini from Amy. She listened for voices outside by the pool and silently prayed that Ryo and his friends would stay away until she was fully immersed in the water. She heard a loud splash and started to feel dread in her gut, and needed the bathroom suddenly. She felt uncomfortable in Amy's black bikini; she longed for her favorite Adidas one-piece she used for her swim meets. Kit stared at her reflection in the bathroom mirror, at the pale skin of her stomach, where the waistline of her jeans had left a mark. The buzz of her fancy chilled tequila and white wine was wearing off. She tried to push down the slight swell of her belly into the line of the bikini bottoms. She wrapped herself in a towel and walked out to find Amy waiting outside the pool house. Ryo and his friends sat on the other side of the swimming pool. Where were his friends earlier? Had they just arrived?

"Let's see," Amy said, tugging at the towel, and Kit opened it fast and closed it again. She saw Ryo glance up at her, and her face flushed, heat rising through her neck and cheeks. "Okay, I hardly got a look, but so cute. You have such a good figure, and the boobs. I'm flat as a pancake." She looked down and tugged at her bikini as if to show her. Amy's familiarity was strangely flattering; Kit felt like she was accepted, but she wished she wouldn't touch her so much. Kit never hugged Sabrina, and rarely her own mother.

"I feel a bit exposed." Kit held the towel over her chest, hating the sound of her voice as she trailed behind Amy.

"No, you look so cute. Come on, let's go swim." Kit followed Amy, who walked along the side of the pool in her tiny bikini in front of everyone, though nobody looked. Kit was relieved that the swimming pool was some distance from the main house and the formal party. She flung her towel aside and sat on the edge of the pool and eased herself in. Amy was shouting something in Japanese to Ryo, who smiled at her and turned back to his friends. The water cooled Kit down instantly.

"How long are you in Tokyo for?" Amy asked, sitting on the side of the pool and dangling her legs in the water. Kit noticed her toes were painted red.

"I love your pedicure."

"Oh thanks. It's from the best place in Harajuku. It's classy enough that even my mom likes it. Like amazing Japanese nail artists, not one of those dodgy nail bars with like illegal Vietnamese girls—I read this article about it. I'll take you next week if you like." Kit rubbed her feet together underwater.

"I'm here for the summer, well, six weeks. Until August."

"And then college? Where are you going again? Are you excited, my god, I'm so excited to be done with high school soon. Just like the freedom, and the guys at college, new friends."

"Yeah, totally. I'm going to Penn. I'm not sure yet what I'm going to major in. I wanted to travel a bit before school started, so I came here."

The pretense of her independence felt good coming out of her mouth. *I wanted to travel. I came here alone.* As though she had dreamed up the trip on her own, booked her tickets alone, and, having her own money, took sole responsibility for herself. The same way she would walk into Target with her handbag in third grade, clutching the pocket money she'd saved from setting the table or helping her dad clean the car. Nobody here knew any better. This was her story. Kit had chosen to travel alone.

"You're *ha-fu?*" Amy asked.

"Ha-fu?"

"You never heard that? It's when you're half Japanese, like one parent is Japanese and the other isn't. You look like you're mixed something, like us."

The way Amy said it, it was completely different from any other time Kit had been asked the loaded question *Where are you from from though.* It wasn't an awkward obstacle that stood in the room, to be avoided or dealt with head-on. She felt it all the more today after walking around Tokyo, where she felt deeply foreign, a clear *gai-jin.* Instead, Amy was actually asking if she was like them, if she was one of them. And nobody had ever asked Kit this question before.

"I am. I guess I am *ha-fu,*" Kit replied quietly.

"Cool," Amy said and dove into the water, splashing Kit in the face.

She watched Amy swim to the other side of the pool, and for a moment, time stopped. She felt like she had been falling from a great height for years and finally landed on a pillow. Relief swept over her as she realized that nobody wanted her to explain. Nobody asked her where she was *really* from. *Ha-fu* was enough. She belonged.

CHAPTER FIFTEEN

Sally

Philadelphia, November 1993

The first time that Rick Buchanan brought his Japanese wife back to Chestnut Hill to meet his family, it had caused a ripple so discreet that it was hardly noticeable at first. Sally, Rick, and Judy Harrison (née Thompson) had grown up on the same street. They had gone to the same high school and even college. After graduation, Sally went on to get a job in Center City. Judy moved to New York and returned to Philadelphia several years later when she became pregnant. Only Rick actually left. He went to Washington, joined the diplomatic service, and never returned, not even to the house he had bought on Germantown Avenue. He never lived in Chestnut Hill again.

A fine bond of memories and history remained among the three of them, though the thread had begun to fray over the years. It started when Judy met her husband, Jason Harrison, who came from old Philadelphia money and grew up on the Main Line, in Villanova. His parents had a house with a Louis XIV room and chandeliers shipped in from Venice. Their wedding reception was at The Plaza in New York, and Judy's junior executive position at Vera Wang meant she got her wedding and bridesmaids' gowns at a steal. Sally had hated her dress, it ballooned out from her rib cage and did nothing for her figure. The bridesmaids who were taller than the bride were forced to wear flat shoes. After the wedding, they moved back to Philadelphia and bought a brownstone in Society Hill. Jason continued to climb the ladder at Goldman Sachs, and he commuted up to New York and kept a pied-à-terre in midtown.

The first Thanksgiving after Judy and Jason's wedding Rick returned from his first assignment in Japan to introduce Yuriko, a petite, dark-haired, grave-faced Japanese woman, to his family. They had been married in Japan, and only her family had attended the ceremony. Sally didn't know what had happened between Rick and his parents, or what had stopped them from going to the wedding—it surely wasn't the cost. But Rick never explained, and she never asked.

Sally invited the newlyweds for dinner during their stay, and she watched Yuriko arrive from her living room window. She didn't know what she was expecting to see. Yes, Yuriko's skin was porcelain white, she had large eyes, long, flat dark lashes, and a tiny frame, but she wasn't the woman Sally had expected to walk alongside Rick. Sally didn't know who she was expecting to walk through the door that day, but the woman she met was quiet, serious, and unlike anyone she had ever met before. She also stood beside Rick with a self-assurance that was unshaken. This was the man she belonged with.

Judy joined Sally at the window and gasped, "Oh my god, she's like a little doll. How cute."

She rushed past Sally to greet Yuriko outside.

"You are just beautiful, Yooo-ree-ko. Am I saying it right?" Judy looked up to Rick for assurance.

"Yu-li-ko. It's lovely to meet you, Sally," she replied in perfect English.

"Oh my, your English is just wonderful. I'm Judy, by the way, not Sally." She corrected her loudly and slowed her words.

"Oh, I'm so sorry," Yuriko replied, bowing her head.

"Yu-li-ko, this is our host today, our Sal." Judy threw her arm around Sally and felt her shoulders tense.

Sally had so many questions for Rick. How had they met? How did they communicate? Had Yuriko always wanted to marry an American? Had Yuriko worn a kimono at the wedding? What did her family think? And most of all, why hadn't it been her? But she could never ask the last question. Instead, she watched Yuriko's polite, stiff smile and barely detectable nod, every time Judy pawed her and called her adorable.

At the dining table, Yuriko sat with her hands neatly in her lap, her body tucked into a small tidy space. Her voice was barely audible, so Sally had to lean closer to her to hear what she said. She only spoke when she was addressed and never tried to dominate the conversation. When she laughed, she covered her mouth with a pressed ivory handkerchief. Sally assumed Yuriko's teeth were crooked or discolored, but when she finally caught a glimpse as she placed a small piece of beef Wellington into her mouth she noticed they were little, neat, and white. Sally felt cumbersome and too big beside her. Her wrists were almost double the size of Yuriko's. Her hair was unruly with curls while Yuriko had a glossy sheen on her poker-straight hair that reflected the light of the room.

After they left, Sally's husband, Terry, said, "She's built like a child, I don't know. Don't you think it's a bit weird? I mean, think of them together in bed? She barely has breasts." Sally was annoyed that Terry had been thinking of Yuriko's breasts. In truth, it surprised her too that Rick had chosen *her*. He had been the most enigmatic of the three as well as "the most likely to succeed." Everyone had been a little in love with him. She had a moment of regret when she learned he had married. Now she knew who he had chosen—this quiet, petite, bird of a woman who spoke their language as though she were trying an unfamiliar food for the first time, with caution. Did Yuriko ever challenge him? she wondered. But Sally didn't know if she would have been able to challenge Rick either.

The day after the dinner, Rick and Sally walked over the sodden grounds of the Wissahickon. A wisp of frost in the air filled her nostrils.

"Can I ask you something that you might find a little blunt?" she asked Rick.

"Shoot," he replied, a passive smile on his lips that gave nothing away.

"Do you guys ever fight?"

"Yuriko and I?"

Sally nodded.

"Yeah we do, but not a lot. Sometimes in Japanese, actually. I'm trying to learn the language, the culture. She is trying to understand my ways too. We are from two very different worlds, but we find our way."

"It all sounds very romantic. A love without borders, something like that. I only ask because life can be tricky—and well . . . like I'm learning, marriage and friendships, and family, require a whole bunch of complicated, difficult conversations. You know?"

"I think I know what you're trying to say. But you think my life isn't real? It's not all romance and love against the odds, you know? Do you think the silent judgment I get from my parents when I bring my wife home isn't something Yuriko and I discuss openly when we're alone?" he said heatedly. "You think my dad, whose father fought in the Pacific, isn't full of judgment about me marrying a Japanese woman? Everyone has a view on whether we can make it work or not. It's not the same as if you and I had gotten together or any other relationship. We're always on the outside, and that's fine. But I also hate that she has to experience that. We talk about real things, Sal, we find a way." Speckles of spit flew out of his mouth, and Sally felt her cheeks flush.

"I'm sorry, I had no idea it was so hard, that you have to deal with that . . . lack of acceptance. We should be past that by now. It's the nineties."

"Why would you? You're married to a nice white kid from Montgomery County."

Silence fell between them, the crunch of leaves beneath their feet the only noise for some time.

"I didn't mean to snap. It hasn't been an easy trip home, that's all," he said as they reached the gates that opened up onto the road.

"I get it. Well, maybe I don't. How is her family?"

"The total opposite. They are so proud that she's married a diplomat. It's such a quiet culture, so restrained, and people are so polite, at least I've found it that way. It's unexpected given our histories. But you know, there's always an underlying tension too. I'm always going to be the foreigner she married. I will miss cues, and we don't realize how loud we are as Americans, because Japan is so . . . *silent*. I don't know if I'm making sense but, there are a lot of things unsaid, you feel it in the air, but for the most part her family are kind, they welcome me."

Sally looked at him, his handsome well-formed nose, the plentiful dark hair that fell about his eyes and that he pushed back when he spoke. She had always thought he looked like JFK Jr. She imagined the children he would have with Yuriko, and without thinking, said, "You're going to have the most beautiful children."

He laughed. "People keep saying this to me. Why is everyone imagining our kids? It's weird, right? Like just because we'll have mixed-race kids, I'm suddenly aware of so much more. And aware that I actually *haven't* been aware of what other people go through. Other people who don't look like us."

"I never thought about it."

"I know, Sal, me neither. Not until I met Yuriko."

By the end of Rick and Yuriko's visit to Chestnut Hill, everyone had heard about Rick's exotic Japanese wife. The tiny, five-foot, four-inch frame of this woman was discussed by everyone from the blue-rinse crowd at McNally's Tavern on the Hill to the farmers market down on Mermaid Lane.

Did you hear? Rick Buchanan has married a geisha.

No, no, his Japanese-language exchange student.

I heard she's pregnant.

Actually, they're doing it for a green card. She's really landed on her feet with that one. They must be in some kind of financial trouble.

No matter how many times Sally would set the story straight, fueled by her newly enforced loyalty to Rick and Yuriko's struggles, the people of Chestnut Hill wanted to believe that Rick Buchanan, the 1983 quarterback, most likely to succeed of his class, had married a geisha. Some of them, in the deep recesses of the bars at night, once the alcohol had fortified their nerves, suggested she had been a hostess. But to Sally, Yuriko was a sacred spirit-like figure—she represented adventure and a life far beyond Eden, her small life in Chestnut Hill, and anything she dared consider for herself.

~⌒~

CHAPTER SIXTEEN

Kit

Tokyo, July 2015

After the party, Kit didn't see Amy and Ryo again for several days, but Kit was fixated on the Buchanan children. Amy's bedroom door remained closed until the afternoons, as she usually got home late and emerged even later in the day. Ryo had set off right after the party on a hiking trip with a friend from California around the Nakasendo trail.

By the time Kit woke up each morning, Mr. Buchanan was either walking out the door or had already left for work in the embassy building on the compound. Yuriko was usually in her office trilling down the phone in Japanese. Kit didn't understand a word of this melodic language, but she recognized the difference in tone and octaves when Yuriko was speaking into a handset and when she was addressing someone in person. She hosted parties, flower arrangement classes, and coffee mornings for the American Japanese Society, and was always heading out to lunch.

The Buchanans were busy and lived very separate lives. They expected Kit to be the same way.

This was after all what she had wanted: to be independent and seek out this culture she was so convinced she was from. Only none of it so far was how she imagined. She didn't look at the Japanese women walking past her on the streets and wonder if they were her birth mother. She felt so dramatically different from them that there was no way that she could be theirs and they could be hers. Sally and her freckled, pale complexion and strawberry-blond hair made far more sense to Kit than these raven-haired women she saw in this new city.

She found herself skipping the landmarks she wanted to see and instead found herself traipsing from store to store trying to dress how she imagined a girl who Ryo might date would dress. One afternoon Kit was alone in the house. Everyone was out: Ryo and Amy especially ran full social schedules, she realized. Kit lost three hours scrolling through her Snapchat and Instagram, constantly refreshing to see if one of them had sent a request to follow her. Kit longed to be around them again, to soak up their essence into her own. She spoke to herself in the bathroom as she dressed in the late mornings, trying on Amy's pronunciation of words like *water* and *straw*, elongating the *a* sound. She suddenly wanted to be a part of what was proclaimed to be *mixed something*. When Amy did send a request to follow her on Instagram, she felt the need to pull back on her posts and curate them better. She had requested to follow Amy back, and lay on her bed, scrolling through Amy's feed when a WhatsApp message appeared on her phone. She sat up, worried for a moment that Amy would know she was looking at her whimsical posts.

> AMY: Hey, you wanna come out tomorrow? Some of us are going out to Roppongi. Come along? xx
> AMY: P.S. I'm not being ridiculously lazy, I'm just over at the American club meeting a friend. See you later X

She examined the kisses at the end of the messages. She wanted to ask who "some of us" were, but she waited and continued to scroll through Amy's feed. She looked at a photo of Ryo, which Amy had captioned "My Rock." She looked at photos of white sand beaches with sunsets hovering over the horizon, Amy's caption reading "Golden Paths only" beneath, and a photo where she leapt in a star shape on a boat in the black string bikini she had lent Kit the day before, with a shooting star emoji. Most of the time, Amy's chin tilted up, a knowing edge to her smile. The captions of some photos were in Japanese instead of English, with the same generous dose of emojis of shooting stars. In some, she was strumming a guitar and singing in a voice that Kit found unremarkable. She tried to find Ryo, but his account was private, with just the silhouette of his face against a sunset.

The next day, Kit wandered through the paths surrounding the Imperial Gardens in the morning. She had planned to take a train to Hakone alone and try to catch a glimpse of Mount Fuji. She had woken up in time, but something had welded her to her bed. To catch the train up to Hakone in time, she would have had to get up at six, leave the Residence by seven. But by eight, she was still lying in her bed staring at the ceiling and intermittently picking up her cell phone.

When evening arrived, Kit waited in the hallway for Amy. She examined the family portrait on the wall. It looked like it had been taken several years ago. Yuriko stood upright, her smile stiff with eyes opened wide. Rick had a hand on her shoulder, giving the portrait a formal feeling, and Ryo stood on her other side. Amy was barely adolescent. She wore her hair in a long braid that hung over one shoulder, tied with a ribbon. Her dress matched Yuriko's navy wrap dress, and she sat with her feet to the side, ankles crossed, in ballet slippers.

Kit suddenly became aware of a presence and saw Amy watching her from around the corner. For a second, their eyes met before Amy jumped out, skipping to stand beside Kit.

"Hey! Sorry, did you wait long? I told Linda just to let you come on up," she said and looped her arm through Kit's and guided her to her bedroom.

Kit was suddenly aware that she was outside Ryo's bedroom, the door ajar, the bottom of a neatly made bed visible from the hallway. A bathroom connected Ryo's and Amy's bedrooms. The primary bedroom door was also open; there was a dressing table with expensive-looking bottles in a cluster on a marble tray.

"So tonight we are going to hang with some of my and Ryo's friends, okay? Then I have go to meet a friend, so you can either join me or stay with Ryo and his gang. Up to you."

"Oh, sure. Are you meeting up with your boyfriend? Do you have a boyfriend?" Kit asked, her mind on Ryo. She didn't know that he had returned from his trip and that she would be seeing him.

Amy shrugged as she sat cross-legged on the floor on a yoga mat, the back of her black lace bra showing as she leaned forward in her cropped T-shirt. Kit tried to imagine being so nonchalant about a boy.

"How long have you lived here? It's so organized in here." Kit ran her hand over the shelf on the wall with books lined up carefully in height order.

"I can't take credit for that. We have Linda. We move every four, five years so I never feel quite settled into my space. I guess your house is all homey. How long have you lived there for?"

"Oh, well, it's the only house I've ever lived in."

"Whoa!" Amy stopped to look up at her, taking this in. "I can't imagine that."

"Yep, since I first got to my parents' house, I guess."

"That's a weird way of saying you were born there." Amy laughed.

"Oh no," Kit said, and then she realized that Amy was the first person in years who didn't know that she was adopted. "I'm adopted, so I guess, when I got to my parents' house from the orphanage or wherever."

Amy stared at Kit, her mouth open. "*You're adopted,*" she said slowly and sighed. "So, your mom is what, Japanese, like my mom? No, she must be American, white American like my dad? Because our parents knew each other, right? Almost everyone my dad ever introduced me to from Philadelphia is white. And I mean, like, *white-white.* Whereas in college, he curated a more diverse friendship group, you know?"

"That's right," Kit replied. She had never heard anybody refer to friendships as something that were curated. She felt Amy's eyes on her. Looking at her face, she could almost see Amy choosing which parts of Kit's story she deemed important and which she could disregard.

"So you never met your real parents? You don't know their story?" Amy finally asked.

Kit examined her nails as Amy spoke. *Real parents.* Then she said, "No, but now that I'm eighteen I'm legally entitled to look into it. But I think because they have never been part of my life, there has to be a reason for that. It was a closed adoption. So they wanted to stay anonymous." She didn't know yet why she wasn't telling Amy what little she knew about her birth mother. Kit's palms started to sweat. Amy suddenly hopped up from the mat and turned toward her closet.

"I think that's amazing, your self-control. I mean, I couldn't leave something like that alone. It's like too tempting. How can you not know? If you want, I can help you look into that. I mean, I'm sure my dad and his government stuff might be helpful there. Maybe it can open some doors or something. Think on it, honey," she said and moved to the closet.

"Thanks, I mean, I think aside from finding out some parts of their appearance, education, family background, I'm not like, entitled to find out their names and stuff. Unless I hire some private intermediary, and I don't have that kind of money . . ."

Amy stopped for a moment and took in a sharp breath. Kit watched her turn the words over in her mind. Waiting.

"So what do you know about your parents?"

"Not much. Only that I had an Asian mother. Most likely Japanese," she quickly added.

"So you don't know if, say, they put you up for adoption before or after you were born?"

"No."

"Or if, like, your birth mom was in a really bad financial situation or not. Or if you have like a brother or sister?"

"No," Kit replied, her voice almost a whisper.

It had been years since Kit thought about her birth mother's motivations for putting her up for adoption. There was a part of her brain she didn't venture into, thoughts that would make her heart constrict and feel an anger and shame she didn't know how to hold. She had always assumed that the choice was simple: the Herzogs could give her a better life, they were better equipped to raise her, and the adoption had been a selfless act by her birth mother.

"Huh," Amy said, and then turned on her heel back toward her closet to pull out clothes.

The topic was closed.

⁓

After her fourteenth birthday, Kit was allowed to stay home alone while her parents went out for dinner with friends. One night she sat on the couch and scrolled through the internet to study paparazzi photographs of a famous actor and actress who had adopted children from all over the world. She examined the way the little girl from Ethiopia held her Caucasian mother's hand, and the Cambodian boy skipped beside his Caucasian father, and the smiles on their faces. An impulse took over her, and she ran across the house to her father's office. The top drawer of his desk was usually locked, but Kit knew where all the emergency keys were kept. Her mother had made a big deal about trusting her when she had turned fifteen and gave her a tour around the house to show her where every spare key was kept. Kit groaned and rolled her eyes. *Why do I need to know how to stop the water, Mom? I'll just call Dad.*

She unlocked the drawer and looked in the A folder for adoption. Nothing. Then K for Katherine. Finally, right in the back under W were her adoption documents. Inside a worn-out brown manila envelope with a green county stamp from Pennsylvania Courts was a certificate that stated her legal status as a dependent and child to Sally and Terence Herzog. There were bills to the adoption agency and a lawyer who had prepared the paperwork. Then, one piece of paper with the words "nonidentifying information."

She stared at the words.

Age: 28
Height: 168 cm
Level of Education: Unknown
Religion: N/A
Ethnic Features: Asian
Originates from: Unspecified
Health: Good
Other Children: Unknown

That was the first time a terrible thought rushed through her mind—were there other children? Did she have siblings? Was she the only one who wasn't kept by her real mother? Was there something about her that had repelled her birth mother so much she didn't want her? She pushed the thoughts away and buried the file back in that drawer with the documents and locked it away. *I will not go there.* She repeated. Again and again.

⁓ᴑ⁓

A few days after looking at the documents, Kit asked Sally, "Did my birth mom ever get in touch? Did she ever ask about me?" She watched her mother from the breakfast nook in the kitchen. The blue tits were feasting at the feeder in the garden. The leaves had started to change color. Just that morning, a groundhog had crawled out from under the toolshed. Fall was on its way. Her mother was making pancakes and slicing strawberries. Kit had asked not to have fruit, but her mom insisted. *You have got to take a bit of yin with the yang, honey. Or is it ying and yang? I never know. We should look that up.*

When Kit had said "birth mom," her mother's hands had stopped in midair for a fraction of a second. Only a person who really knew her would have seen it. Kit saw it.

"No, honey, she never got in touch."

A question answered simply with no emotion. At the time, Kit felt angry at her mother for her response. She wanted a softer explanation. The words felt too hard, too direct. Kit looked at her mother's face and tears threatened to fall.

"But even if she did, Dad and I wouldn't just let her see you like that—you know that, don't you? We would have to discuss it carefully as a family. And decide what was best."

"Why? Why couldn't she see me if she wanted? I'm her daughter," Kit said.

Her mother put the knife down and placed both hands on the counter.

"Katherine, you are *our* daughter. All I know about your birth mother was that she loved you enough to know that she wanted a better life for you. That's all the information I have. It was a closed adoption. Remember we've talked about this before? We have to respect their wishes, and there is little we can do about how they wanted it to be. You remember the terms of a closed adoption, right?"

"Kind of," she muttered.

"It means that the people involved chose not to share their identity. It means that we are not entitled to know the woman who gave birth to you."

"So I can never find out?"

"I don't think so, honey. Of course, when you're a legal adult, there are options, and we certainly won't stand in your way if you want to pursue that. But that is some time away."

Kit watched her mother with a wary eye. This was where the conversation was supposed to stop, but she couldn't leave it alone.

"I saw a movie where a girl finds her birth mom and she becomes part of her family, almost like a sort of long-lost aunt or something."

Her mother's mouth became a straight line. She took a deep breath, and Kit saw her chest puff up and then deflate as the sound of her sigh warned Kit she was close to the edge now.

"Honey, that's a movie. Real life is different."

"But how do you know that won't be how it is for me?"

"I don't. But what I do know is that we want the best for you. And while you are a minor, we will make damn sure we make the right choices for you, our daughter. And protect you in every way we can." Her mother took another deep breath and walked out of the kitchen. Kit waited, but the bowl of pancake mix and strawberries were left there, and her mother didn't return.

There were many things she pushed, boundaries she tested—she liked to play at the edge of her parents' patience to see how far she could go. And usually, she won. She was stubborn and deftly navigated the lines drawn and stretched them out over time. But when it came to her birth mother, she didn't push. Something stopped her.

Instead, she thought about it with no limitations. Sometimes she would lie awake at night and fall into a dream where she pictured a woman in a printed dress, with shiny jet-black hair and narrow shoulders, hands placed together in front of her, looking at Kit with a serene smile.

She became obsessed with films and shows about adoption. Then she wrote a secret list of facts and stories about any adopted actors and actresses. As though there were an invisible thread that bound her to them. This thing connected them uniquely, in a way that nobody else could understand. Only Sabrina knew about this list.

When her parents went out one weekend, Sabrina and Kit huddled under a blanket in the living room to watch Hallmark movies about adopted children. They always had a happy outcome: an adopted child escaped a life of misery and deprivation to be with her newfound family. A montage of happy laughter and hugs with the new family would follow. But in Kit's mind, her birth mother was an enigma she built up— a silhouette that appeared in her dreams, a faraway figure who lured her in.

. . .

Amy's phone started to ring. She lifted her finger to Kit and mouthed, *Just give me a minute,* and walked out of her room. Kit looked around at the bedroom. There were photographs of large groups of friends on skis gathered on a mountain, the girls holding up peace signs with their fingers, their heads tilted toward one another. Amy's closet was heaving with clothes, some were scattered over the floor, spillover. Kit stood and entered the bathroom, where she looked at the two sinks side by side. Amy's was messy: open palettes of eye shadow with grubby applicators strewn around the surface. There was a smell of perfume that she recognized from the Duty Free in Newark. She looked at Ryo's side of the bathroom. It was neat, a clear line between the two siblings. His electric toothbrush stood on its charger so it would never run out of battery. He had floss beside his toothpaste. And a plain moisturizer, one bottle of aftershave.

Kit leaned over the sink to examine her pores and took out the foundation compact she had in her pocket. The door opened from Ryo's side of the bathroom. He stopped in the doorway and looked startled to see her there. She stood upright at the sight of him, her index finger in midair.

"Oh hey," he said. Kit wondered if he would close the door and excuse himself, but he didn't leave. Instead he stepped over the threshold of the doorway.

"Hey," she replied. Kit felt the heat rise to her cheeks as surprise and delight at his presence bubbled up inside of her.

"Do you mind?" he pointed to the sink.

"No, sure."

She looked back at herself in the mirror and tried to remember what she was doing.

He started to run the water in the sink, and she watched him take the soap in his hands. There was a surgical precision to how he carefully ran the bar between his fingers, the lather neat and white over his knuckles and fingernails. She flicked her eyes down at his hands. She loved his hands. There was no hint of any clumsiness in his movements. She thought that he must be deliberate in everything he did, and looked at the tooth-brush in its charger again.

She touched the skin under her eyes; he looked at her reflection in the mirror. She watched him fold the towel again and hang it carefully, tak-ing longer than she imagined he usually would. He turned to her and smiled, and left. He left the door ajar, and she could hear him fall onto his bed, and the deep breath he inhaled and then let out.

When Kit walked back into Amy's room, she was pulling a dress out of her closet.

"So yeah, I'm meeting this guy tonight—a new guy, a bit older. I met him online on this app. So many cool guys who aren't in high school, you know? I'll probably just meet him after hanging with you guys for a bit. Let's find you something to wear," Amy said, unaware of Kit's flushed complexion.

Amy held a dress up against Kit, who was standing against the wall, her thoughts not yet caught up with Amy's. Amy explained to Kit that she was an old soul, which was why friends came to her for advice. Kit wondered whether people asked for it or Amy simply offered it. There was a lilt to the way she spoke, which sounded like questions were not welcome, and her advice was sacred. It struck Kit that Amy couldn't de-cide whether she wanted to act older or younger. She flipped between a terrifying maturity and a strange childishness that made Kit want to protect her. When she explained things about Tokyo or her dad's job and how "things worked in Japan," she took on a teacherly expression that looked as though she were saying *Kit, I'll show you the way.*

"This will look so good on you. The guys will go crazy. Oh my god, I never even asked you if you had a boyfriend."

Kit stood and arranged her body behind Amy's dress. She looked at herself in the mirror. The neckline was so low she wouldn't be able to wear a bra with it. She wondered for a moment what Dave would have said if he had seen her in it. She changed in the bathroom and peered at the trays of eyes shadows and lipsticks on the shelf. Kit pulled out her own small makeup bag and applied her eye shadow with her finger. She looked at the smudge on her eyelids and it looked clumsy to her. She wanted to wipe it away.

"Gorgeous," Amy said and moved away from the mirror for Kit to see.

In the mirror, Kit saw a girl who might holiday on yachts, travel to Europe, speak another language, maybe French, greet people with air kisses, and order cocktails. She did not look like Kit Herzog from Chestnut Hill, who had slept in the same bedroom for the last seventeen years of her life. This was someone else.

～∽～

"Mona says the first time is the worst," Amy explained to Kit at a booth table in Bar Zero Zero. It was hard to hear what she was saying over the loud music. The dense cigarette smoke dulled her senses.

"My friend Mona has met so many guys online like this." Amy waved her phone at Kit. "She's over there." Amy gestured with the two fingers that held a cigarette between them and then straightened up, waved to Mona, and suddenly looked like a little girl, waving from the rear window at the car behind. Amy's friend Mona, who they met up with at the bar, was accompanied by a short man with blond hair that flopped to the side. Kit guessed he must have been almost thirty, if not more. Amy had transformed herself: thick smudgy dark kohl liner over a smoky purple eye shadow that made the green speckles in her irises look like the jade bangle on her wrist. Amy's skin was pale in the flashing lights of the bar, her veins visible as they ran down her arms like blue ravines.

Kit thought Mona was the more beautiful of all of them. She stood taller than Amy, her long limbs moving with a languid assurance. Her almost black eyes and hair, the petite diamond piercing in her nostril, and her feline eyes were striking. Kit wondered why Mona didn't draw the same overt looks that Amy did from the men in the bar. She wondered if it was the visceral naivete of Amy that made her so intriguing.

"I really hated the idea of meeting someone like this, you know— someone I hadn't even met in the flesh before," Amy said, her eyes darting around the room. "But the fact is, it's how everyone is doing it out in the real world, right? And it sure beats dating those high school losers." She shuddered and then laughed, a loud, mouth-open laugh that sounded hollow. "I mean, don't get me wrong, I got catfished a couple times. And there were some sleazy-looking guys too, who sent all kinds of weird messages. But Sean is super nice and respectful. He's a music teacher. Not like these guys you see around here, like that guy with Mona, eww."

"So how old is he?"

"I don't know, like in his twenties or whatever. It's weird, though, like I definitely notice girls like us attract a certain kind of guy. Usually *gaijin*, the occasional Japanese guy but not often."

"Girls like us?"

"*Ha-fu.* You know, we are kinda Japanese but a little more exotic. Like we're kinda Asian but we're more Western culturally. The crossover is easier maybe? It's really desirable to be with a mixed girl here. I get asked all the time about modeling but Dad is super against it."

"It is? It's desirable?"

"Yeah, I think so. Why, what's it like back in Philly? I guess it's different to here?" For the first time since Kit had met Amy, she paused to wait for Kit's response.

"It's really different and less international. People grow up there and live there for their whole lives. Take my mom, for example, she was born there and she never left. My dad didn't either. It's not like you and Ryo, you have two parents who are from different countries. I can't imagine what that is like. I only know growing up in Philly."

"Do you wish it wasn't that way?" Amy asked. The simplicity of her question made Kit hesitate. Did she?

"I don't know." Kit paused and looked at Amy, who was no longer waiting for her response. "So does your mom know about this new guy? Like do you talk to her about this stuff," Kit asked, knowing the answer.

"Oh my god no, can you imagine? The drama? Mom is all about acting respectably. You know, the whole saving face thing, right? That's a big thing here in Japan. And you know, Ryo, I love my brother but he is like a golden boy—he can't do anything wrong. He's captain of all the teams, he's going to Berkeley in the fall, he's their pride and joy," she said with sudden energy. Kit didn't say anything.

KIT WOULD LATER learn that Yuriko's entire existence hinged on living an elegant, refined, respectable life. This applied to everything, from how she maintained her weight at the very same fifty kilos for twenty years of her marriage. Even with the two pregnancies, she managed to rein everything back within two months of giving birth. She watched her weight, she watched her sun exposure, and she watched her children. She had always planned to be the wife of a great man, and when she met Rick, a young diplomat in Tokyo, on track to be a future ambassador, she could picture herself with him, hosting cocktail parties at a grand official residence, and that was what mattered, that she could envision it as a place she belonged. The children were brought up as liberal American kids, which had pushed her far beyond her comfort zone, and nothing had prepared her for the resistance and disobedience she faced in Amy. But if Yuriko closed her eyes and ears to the little things, she could still talk about them for what they were: smart, good-looking, charming citizens of the world.

CHAPTER SEVENTEEN

Kit

Tokyo, July 2015

Kit had not spoken to Sabrina since she had arrived in Tokyo. They'd tried to call each other but hadn't connected. Sabrina left comments and Likes on Instagram, and sometimes they'd have quick exchanges on WhatsApp just before Kit fell asleep. The inadequacy she felt around Amy made her miss Sabrina all the more. She longed for the familiarity of her old friendship, one that required little to no effort, where she knew exactly where she stood, always. During her first week in Tokyo, Kit had woken up every night to check her phone.

> Just going to my shift, I'll try you later.
> What did you eat today? Tell me.
> Met any cute guys? It's hot and boring here.

Kit walked down to the kitchen in a morose mood. It had been two days now since her night out with Amy and Ryo. When Ryo had collected her from Bar Zero Zero, and she left Amy to meet her date, Kit was disappointed to find him accompanied by his friends. She found herself sitting two or more seats away from him for the remainder of the night. There hadn't been an opportunity to spend any time with Ryo.

Two weeks into her summer of self-discovery, Kit missed her best friend: for selfish and selfless reasons. She missed Sabrina's constant company. The way she provided solidarity with a mere look. Sabrina gave her a boldness she realized she needed, at least to sustain that veneer when underneath she felt like she was unraveling. Instead, here, she was exposed and had to find her own way. When she was around Amy, Kit felt on edge, although she suspected that most of the time Amy didn't know herself what she would do next.

It felt strange to Kit that Sabrina's life was moving along and Kit had no idea where she was headed. They had done everything together. She wanted to know what show Sabrina was watching, who she hated at the country club, what Lee Lee had ranted about lately. Kit wanted to sit outside and talk about nothing and everything. She simply missed Sabrina.

She was interrupted by another message notification. "Honey, send us a picture. I'm with Grandma and we want to see your face." She flicked away her mother's text.

"Have a great day, Kit!" Yuriko called before the front door clicked shut, and she realized she was alone with Linda, the Filipino housekeeper who had made her breakfast and was in the utility room doing laundry. Amy would be asleep for hours still, and she had heard Ryo leave the house with his father earlier that morning.

Kit refreshed her email and saw an email from Sabrina, almost as if she were thinking of Kit too. She smiled as she sat down to her breakfast to read it.

MY OTHER HEART

Hey Kitso,

Oh my god, I miss you girl. This has been a weird summer already without you. I thought I'd write an email, long form, because then I won't forget all the things I wanna say. It's better in one place.

How are you? I wanna hear all about what's happening in Tokyo.

I ended up taking the job at the country club and started my internship. The woman I'm working for is totally badass. Her hair is like Edna Mode. Remember her daaaahling? She's totally pottymouthed and does amazing things for the Asian community in Philly. Anyway, it's cool working with her.

So at the club, I have to work with that Tommy Bryant. You probably don't remember him but he was in ninth grade Geography with us and we were always creeped out by him. He is a creep, and he definitely has some weird Asian girl fetish. There is another girl whose Mom runs the Chinese restaurant down in Mount Airy, do you remember her? Connie Lau, she was in pre-K with us and then she ended up going to the charter school instead of staying at CHA. Anyway, she started working the same shifts as him in the pool clubhouse so he's creeping out on her. I think they might even be dating now.

What have you been doing with your days? What is it like there? Is it hot? And how about the food? Have you been eating sushi? Tell me more about this guy! Have you made other friends? Will you travel out of Tokyo?

It's been kind of boring during the break. Maybe I should have made more effort to make friends at high school, lol, but I guess it's too late now!

What do you think about going down the shore one last time when you're back? I know we only have like two weeks before college starts, but we could for a bit if your parents let us? Isn't it so great we don't have to do any studying this summer? My mom is telling me to get ahead for college, but I literally can't. So I'm reading a ton instead. For once, we have a clean slate. Last year's grades don't matter, we don't have any baggage with any teachers. We're starting afresh. I can't believe it. Did I tell you I've been thinking I might opt for this other college I had an offer for? It's so late now, and I have to try to get financial aid. But Penn State said they would let me defer. I haven't made up my mind yet.

I've heard rumors of some kind of party happening before we all go off to college. I can't remember where. It would be kind of cool to go before everyone leaves Philly. I think you're back by then. I don't wanna go to something like that if you're not there.

Did you hear from Dave? I know he is weird about you guys. I could see you were upset, it must have been tough for you, and you never wanted to talk about it but anyway. I think it's this high school hierarchy that gets in the way of things that could happen, you know? But it shouldn't right? Anyway. I don't know why, but I get this feeling that

this new guy you mentioned could be something. Maybe
by the time you read this, you're having a steamy romance
with him.

Anyway, Xiao Pengyou. I'm missing you! Send news.
Lotsa love, Sabrina

Sabrina had always written in the exact same way that she spoke. And now, 6,754 miles away, this long email made Kit smile. She could hear Linda vacuuming upstairs in the bedrooms and the distant hum of cars and traffic a few streets away. She went to the refrigerator to search for more food. She found some string cheese with Japanese writing on the packaging and broke off a stick. She looked down at her shorts and tucked her T-shirt into the waistline. The reality of Sabrina not traveling to China crept up on Kit again. She knew that Sabrina was stuck in Chestnut Hill all summer, but it was an idea and image rather than a reality that she pictured, her friend working at the country club, earning money for college. Kit's summer had been promptly arranged the moment she asked for it. Her parents had flirted with the idea of Kit getting a part-time job, earning some money to go, but Kit had quickly extinguished this: *I can't take a job when I have so much studying to do before graduation, Mom. Do you want me to flunk out?* She knew that Sally and Terry wouldn't sacrifice her grades for a lesson in principles.

Wasn't it Sabrina's harebrained idea at the beginning of the final semester to find out more about their own so-called roots? Kit thought about calling Sabrina. But she rationalized that her friend sounded perfectly happy in her message. It was easier for Kit to believe that Sabrina was fine with the way things had turned out. It was the middle of the night back home, and Sabrina wouldn't be able to call her back anyway. She told herself to try later and forgot about it almost instantly.

AFTER BREAKFAST, KIT walked through the neighborhood around the embassy. The summer heat hadn't risen yet, and the morning was still in its dewy beginnings. It was becoming her favorite time of day—it was still her own before anyone could claim part of it. Kit headed past the underground sign and picked up her pace. Tiny beads of sweat started to form on her upper lip. She crossed the broad six lanes of traffic, followed a footpath, and watched as queues of cars snaked through the city, moving slowly around the moat of the Imperial Palace. The path turned into a more wooded dirt track that went up into the park. She could see the tips of the castle's pavilion over the trees. Ryo had said he walked their dog there sometimes, and Kit hoped to bump into him.

When she came to the clearing to find the vast rolling lawns that hugged the Imperial Palace's periphery, she immediately recognized the Buchanans' German shepherd, Genji, bounding and gnawing playfully with a corgi. Genji saw her and ran up to her, jumping at her, and she scratched him behind the ears. He then bored of her and ran back to his playmate who stood with legs splayed, waiting to be chased. Kit remained crouched down and watched him as he jumped alongside an enthusiastic labradoodle. She knew Ryo would be nearby but couldn't bring herself to look for him.

"Hey, Kit." It was Ryo's voice, behind her.

She arranged her face before standing up and turning to him. She tried to appear surprised. He jogged to her over the wet grass, and she felt the flicker of dew on her ankles.

"You walk here?"

"Once before, yeah," she lied. "I didn't realize this is where you walked Genji."

"When one of us gets up in time. It's never Amy, as you might have guessed. I've always been an early riser, even during summer break. I'm gonna miss the guy when I head off to college, so I'm kinda making the most of him. How are things? Haven't seen you for a few days. You been able to get out to see everything you want to?"

"Yeah, I guess so. I'm working my way through my hit list."

"I'm sorry I haven't been a great host until now, I've been catching up with all my buddies before college starts in the fall. I will be better, I promise."

"Oh don't worry. It must be super weird having me, some stranger, staying in your house. I don't want to get in your way." Her cheeks started to color from embarrassment, but she tried to hold his gaze.

"Nah, we've done that sort of thing before. We get sent off by my folks to old friends in this place and that, and you just need to turn on the charm, right? And be polite and then they just kind of let you do what you want. Isn't that what you're doing?" He winked at her and cocked his head to the side.

A couple her parents' age waved to Ryo, calling something out in Japanese. Ryo turned, took his glasses off, and bowed as he responded in Japanese.

"Are you feeling awkward with us?" he asked as he switched his attention back to her.

"No, I don't think I do. It's just like I'm subletting a room or whatever, isn't it?"

"Right. Sure. I guess I never thought of it that way. Well, some of us are going out tomorrow night and you should come out too. It'll be way more fun than the last time. So come along."

"I don't know, I guess . . ."

"Leave it with me, okay? *Shinpai shinaide*. That means don't worry about it."

"Okay, sure. How's Amy? I haven't seen her the last couple days."

"Good, I think. I haven't seen her either. She's seeing some guy I think. Her summer romance probably. I didn't like that bar I picked you up from the other night, Bar Zero Zero? I know Amy likes to go there with Mona, but I get a weird, seedy vibe from there. I've told her. Don't go there again, okay?"

"Okay." She felt a rush of pleasure at the thought of him looking out for her safety.

"Oh yeah, have you been to the fish market yet?"

"No, I haven't. I'm kind of nervous to go alone."

"No no, we'll go. It's best to go after you're out one night. And then you can see the awesome auctions and eat the best sushi for breakfast. The food is nothing like you've ever tasted. Are you good with sushi?"

"I think so."

"All right, I gotta go. See you tomorrow." He kissed her on both cheeks and she mistimed the turn of her face. He laughed and ran in the other direction, whistling for Genji, who charged after him, jumping up in the air with joy.

The monks walked out slowly to the front of the shrine, acknowledging the visitors with a quick bow of the head. They shuffled in socked feet, soundless, across the floorboards. Their heads were shaved, shining beneath the glint of the metal bell above them. The sun's beams were almost blinding as they bounced off the bell in strobes like lasers. Kit washed her hands in the water barrel at the foot of the stone steps. She ran the cool water over her wrists a few times over, had to stop herself from splashing her hot face with it, and walked up to stand under the arched shrine front. She gathered the coins from her pockets. Their worth was still unclear to her, but she threw them into the rectangular box, clapped her hands, and felt droplets flick back into her face. She looked around to see if she had splashed anyone else. What was she praying for? For Ryo to message her? For Dave to realize she was gone? For college to start, but nothing to change? To find out about her birth mother? What was she hoping to find in Tokyo?

∽

Just as he had said he would, the next day, Ryo arranged the evening and her tour of the Toyosu Fish Market. He warned his parents they wouldn't be home until morning. She wondered whether the Buchanans would tell her mother about her staying out all night with their son. It seemed like something Sally should know.

But this time it was different. Kit was by Ryo's side all night, and the friends he'd invited along were always at their periphery—or so it seemed. He was attentive in the same way he was in his own home the night of the party. When they sat down at a table in the bar, he wiped down the surface of the table and pulled the chair out for her to sit on. Small plates of food were ordered and put in the middle of the table, but she had no appetite. Sabrina would have said *Your heart is full, Kitso.*

The music was loud but Ryo took care of ordering and always leaned in to speak in her ear. When he returned with drinks, she watched the effect he had on the people around him. She thought she saw most women cast a furtive glance toward him. It made the hairs on her neck spring up when he touched her arm or playfully threw his arm around her. He was her host and maybe something more.

By 3:00 a.m., Amy had still not joined them.

"She's probably just fallen asleep. She looked so tired this morning," he said, glancing at his Tag Heuer watch. "Another drink?"

Kit had already asked Ryo's friend what his name was twice and forgotten it again, so she couldn't ask anymore, but the girl was Donna. Kit could remember this because Donna had taken a visceral dislike to her. She was slight, with wavy, shoulder-length hair and a small button nose. She drank a lot, always ordered the same vodka soda with ice and lemon, and swirled her straw in the liquid, lifting it and sucking on the end while staring at Ryo. When Ryo would touch Kit's arm during a story, she sucked on the straw for longer, eyes open, shifting from curiosity to the colder edges of a glare. Donna giggled with her hand over her mouth when Ryo or his friend whose name Kit couldn't remember joked, but Donna's eyes stayed still and cold whenever Kit spoke. Her responses to Kit's questions were single words and were never reciprocated with another question. *It's your turn now to ask something*, Kit thought as she looked at Donna with expectation and then gave up.

"We're gonna go to this last bar, then we'll head to the market, okay? I'm going to get some cigarettes. Come with me?" Ryo said to Kit. She nodded and accepted his hand when he reached for hers.

The streetlights outside the club were still bright, and she needed to squint to get used to the light. His grip on her hand was firm, and she felt him leading her with purpose toward the convenience store. Kit worried that her palms were getting sweaty.

"You okay there?" he asked.

"I'm fine. It's just the lights. The bar is so dark, you know?" Kit could taste the vodka in the back of her throat and the sweetness of the Coke starting to turn bitter. She was conscious of the alcohol on her breath.

"Do you have any gum?" she asked.

"Sure. Here." He passed her a packet with his other hand. He always seemed to be chewing gum, and even though he'd been smoking Mild Sevens, she could faintly smell the aftershave on his clothes.

"Let's get a Pocari Sweat or something. It helps you hydrate," he said.

They crossed the road, and she wondered whether the girls who passed, giggling as they looked at him, assumed she was with him. She pulled her blouse up at the front and wished she'd worn a better bra, not this plain white one.

The electric bell sounded as they walked into the convenience store, and she heard the welcome announcement in Japanese over the intercom.

"I love these stores so much. All these cute snacks, they're just full of so many weird and wonderful things," she said, hovering around the busy packaging of the sweet section.

"Oh man, you have to try these. They're the best," he said and picked up a packet of candy with HI-CHEW written across the pink and purple packaging.

"You like candy?" she asked, surprised.

"Oh yeah, and Japanese candy is the best, seriously. Although I love Reese's Pieces too."

"I should have brought you some."

"Well, we can gorge on them when I'm there for college and we meet up, 'kay?" He was paying at the counter, and the girl behind the cashier stared at both of them.

"Deal," Kit replied quietly and wished she knew what to say. But her mind was blank.

She thought of their friendship extending beyond the summer and tried to picture him in Chestnut Hill. What would Sabrina say if she saw Ryo? His dark eyes, the way his biceps bulged out of the polo he wore, the collar flicked up. He was so different from any boy they had known at CHA. His hands were dry, nails perfectly clean and short, and sun-tanned. She thought of them on her body for a moment and felt herself clench her thighs.

She followed him out of the store, looking at the packet of sweets he'd handed her, and as they walked across the street, he held her hand again. His jeans hung by his hip bones, and she wanted to find him too short. She searched for something to repulse her, to make her distant and de-tached from him in some way. But she found nothing.

He ordered shots back at the bar where his friends were waiting for them. She licked the salt off her hand and threw it back, sucking on the lemon for as long as possible to clear away the taste of cheap tequila. She danced and sweated through her blouse, her makeup melted away. They walked out of the club at four in the morning into a dark night. Ryo, his two friends, Donna, and Kit walked through the deserted streets. Kit looked up at the windows of what must have been apartments and thought of the people sleeping inside. Her feet hurt as they walked and walked, and she swigged at her bottle of water. Soon, the others were ahead of them on the broad boulevards of Minami Azabu. Ryo pulled her back and put his hands around her face. His mouth was soft against hers; the mint and his aftershave lingered in her own mouth. His tongue pressed into her mouth, gently at first, then more insistent. She allowed herself to lean into his chest. She felt herself rising above, looking down on herself with him; it didn't matter who was there, who walked past. There were only the two of them at that moment. He kissed her mouth again, his hands on her collarbones, her face.

"I had to do it before we get to the market." He kissed her hand, and she followed.

~ ✺ ~

CHAPTER EIGHTEEN

Sabrina

Philadelphia, July 2015

Before Sabrina started spending time with Dave, every time she thought of Kit in Tokyo, she got a bitter taste in her mouth. For most of her life, she'd looked on as Kit traveled abroad, to places she only saw through her friend's posts on social media. Sabrina had left Philadelphia only a handful of times. In January of her senior year, she went to Connecticut with her mother so Lee Lee could collect her used car and license. Pennsylvania State wouldn't issue a license to Lee Lee, who was undocumented, but Connecticut would. It was a short trip, and Sabrina tasted the small joy of having a parent who could drive her places finally, just like her friends.

One summer in eighth grade, Mr. and Mrs. Herzog had invited her to join them at Disneyland in California. She had begged her mother for weeks to let her go. Sabrina had offered to take on every chore she could think of, but her mother wouldn't budge. So Sabrina watched as Kit invited Casey to join her instead. It was weeks into the first semester of ninth grade before they would stop talking about the malls in California, the surfing on the beach, the rides at Disneyland, and how they stayed up late every night eating Twizzlers and Milk Duds.

Sabrina knew that Casey stepping in as her replacement gave Sally and Terry Herzog some relief. During the elementary school years, they refused to acknowledge Sabrina and Kit's friendship; their fear of the friendship was visceral. Sabrina never forgot Sally Herzog's wide-open eyes, mouth ajar when she arrived to collect Kit after the first day of second grade. Her eyes fell on Sabrina and Kit holding hands as they skipped out of class.

It's totally fascinating how they were just drawn together. They must feel comfort, you know? Ms. Cuthbert had said to Sally, smiling at the two girls.

I think they see themselves as the same. I really do, Ms. Cuthbert continued, as Kit jumped up and down in front of Sally, asking if Sabrina could come to play. *Another time, sweetheart. We're busy today, remember.* Once, Kit pressed on. *Her mom won't mind; she's never back until late because she works. Let's bring Rina home, we can do a carpet picnic, pleeeease, Mommy. We can even work on our homework. We won't even make a mess, Mommy.*

Sally widened her eyes and looked at Kit, begging her to stop. But Kit wouldn't. That was the thing about Kit in those days at elementary school; she always took it too far. *Sweetheart, I think Sabrina is probably busy in the afternoons with her chores and homework. We'll get her to come another time.* Sally had said this to nobody in particular, least of all Kit, her face a twisted expression of sympathy and pain.

Since that afternoon, Sabrina noticed that she was never invited to Kit's house after school. Meanwhile, Casey Steinham, Avery Thompson, and Kaitlyn Jones always went over for playdates. She watched the huddle of mothers standing in front of the school's front doors, their light hair glinting in the afternoon sunshine, their long cashmere camel coats wrapped tightly around them, in a closed circle. She walked past them to the school bus and watched as Kit ran with Casey to her mother's car, holding hands.

They would all be home before Sabrina had even left Germantown Avenue. She always imagined them drinking hot cocoa in front of a roaring fireplace, the mothers laughing and playing with their girls. Sabrina would walk down the uneven pavement of Roxborough Avenue to her house on Dexter Street. The house was cold, except when summer arrived—and then it became airless and stifling with heat. She walked up the stairs, too high for her short legs. She threw her bag down on the floor, reminding herself to pick it up before her mama returned. Kit had probably unpacked hers already, or maybe Mrs. Herzog had done it for her and hung it up in a boot room. She searched the fridge for leftovers, something she could heat up from the miscellaneous boxes that held dumplings, noodles, or rice. And then, in the dark, she spooned the food into her mouth and watched *The Simpsons*. She always got home in time for *The Simpsons*.

Kit wasn't allowed to watch that show. And sometimes, when they were at school, the older kids would joke and shout *Eat my shorts!* Sabrina would smile slyly and join in with her encyclopedic knowledge of Homer, Bart, and Lisa. It gave her instant popularity points, and Kit looked on as though they were speaking in a different language. But none of these victories lasted more than a few minutes.

Sabrina had almost forgotten about the way Sally Herzog winced every time Kit would beg her to invite Sabrina over. Those memories of feeling displaced around Kit and her family during the early years of the friendship had almost completely faded until she saw Mrs. Harrison in the parking lot of the country club dropping Dave off for a tennis game. Mrs. Harrison had that same frown and wince that Mrs. Herzog had worn all those years ago, as Dave's mother looked at her and tried to work out what the relationship was between her son and this girl in the staff polo shirt. She looked at Dave, who was watching a group of country club campers passing in their matching shorts and T-shirts, dirty from the day's activities.

"Oh Sabrina, it's you again. David, honey, you didn't say you were meeting *Sabrina.*"

"Hi there, Mrs. Harrison," she replied.

"How are you, dear?" she asked, not waiting for a response. "David, I'll see you home sometime later, okay? Remember I have my book club tonight."

"Sure, Mom." He started walking away, toward the club; Sabrina felt unsure what to do, to follow him or stay.

Maybe Dave didn't hear his mother reminding him of her plans that night because he had walked too far ahead. Maybe he was looking out to see if anyone would see him hanging out with Sabrina. Maybe he didn't notice the strain in his mother's voice. Maybe she always sounded that way. Maybe he didn't notice any of it, because he had the bluest eyes and golden hair, kissed by the sun, and nobody ever questioned Dave Harrison.

"You know, Sabrina, you should come over anytime. Dave, you should ask her more." She called out to her son who lingered by the road now. "We have this wonderful girl who works for us," Mrs. Harrison explained, using her hands; her nails were painted crimson, and her gold charm bracelet jangled. "I'd love you to tell me what you think of her cooking."

Sabrina imagined for a moment how Mrs. Harrison must see her, standing before her, dust on her sneakers, her polo shirt crumpled, with the faded print of her country club uniform logo. Her hair was frizzy, and her nose was too small to hold up her glasses, designed for high-bridged American noses. And then she thought about what Eva Kim would make of this situation. The sniffy white woman from Society Hill, telling the smart Ivy League college–bound (or so she hoped) Asian girl to talk to the housekeeper about cooking. She could almost hear Eva's voice rising to supersonic levels in her dismay. But Sabrina said nothing; she remembered Eva's words about the power of silence. Sabrina understood now that her silence and tight smile could make Mrs. Harrison uncomfortable. There *was* power in that. It might not make her question what she said today, but it planted a small seed of doubt about herself in her mind. Sabrina glanced at Dave, who was looking at his phone and, Sabrina realized, waiting for her before he headed into the club. She wondered if Mrs. Harrison could smell the garlic Lee Lee used in her cooking the night before. She had sprayed Sea Breeze all over her skin before leaving the club in case she bumped into Dave.

Sabrina said nothing, and nodded, and wished she had the gumption of Eva Kim. But Sabrina wasn't ready to fight. She would be one day, but not yet. Instead, she smiled weakly at Mrs. Harrison.

What did Sabrina Chen know about cooking? She had barely even left Pennsylvania.

CHAPTER NINETEEN

Mimi

Ho Chi Minh City, January 2015–July 2015

Four. Four was the number of times Mimi *almost* got back to America since she lost Ngan. The first time was just a year after she had returned to Saigon, before she had met Toan, before she started to come back to herself. The agency her sister had used to get their jobs in America had closed down—their previous contact said that US Immigration Services had become more stringent in allowing entry and gave them another name to try. The new agency agreed to try to find Mimi another placement at a price, but two weeks before she was due to board her flight back to New Jersey, Immigration Services discovered that this new company was issuing false documents and it had to disappear fast. They took all her money, and she never heard from them again. The second time, after three years, Mimi had saved almost enough money for a flight: every salary, every tip, living in the most modest room, taking every extra shift on offer, and eating the cheapest food she could find. She was just three million dong away from being able to buy her ticket, when her sister called her crying.

"They're going to take our home. The loan sharks . . . we just can't pay it back." Cam's wet sobs echoed through the phone lines. "What about the boys? We'll be begging on the streets, the shame of it . . ." Mimi knew then that she would be giving all her money to her sister to pay off her husband's gambling debts. She would have to start again.

The third time was when her first expat employer, her first American madame, had asked her to come back to California with them. But just three weeks before her flight, her husband had lost his job, and she was told they wouldn't be needing Mimi anymore, but not to worry, they would find her a position with a nice Western family.

The fourth time, she had tucked the money for a ticket inside her jeans pocket as she rode her motorbike through District 3. She was going to buy her ticket from the travel agent, but she was stopped by a police officer, who searched her and took every last note. She hadn't even told Toan she had the money saved, he just assumed her tears were from the sadness about Ngan, which he accepted was a waterfall of grief that stopped and started on any given day.

And this time, five, she didn't even need the money. Providence brought all the pieces together.

⁓

Mimi's eye lingered on the pile of bedding Toan put on a stool in the corner of their living room. Her day began as Toan's ended. He was working night shifts at the InterContinental hotel in District 1 as a security guard after loan sharks had taken over his driver's agency.

Their living room was a mess of boxes filled with items from her old employers: a toaster, though they only ate *banh mi* (she planned to sell it in the market), a pair of cycling cleats (they didn't own a bicycle), a blender (she preferred to hand press her juice). Eleven dresses that were four sizes too big so that the necklines fell off her slight shoulders. For over a year, she'd planned to take them to the tailor. *It's always easier to make something smaller,* she had explained to Toan.

Mimi noticed that Toan was starting to put on weight, around his stomach mostly, and now his jawline had softened. She wasn't surprised, since he sat all night in front of a security monitor at the hotel. Toan told her he walked around the floors twice a night, but Mimi suspected he spent a lot of time smoking outside, based on the smell of stale cigarettes on his clothes. She pictured him sleeping at his desk and eating whatever the room service staff gave him from the leftover tray.

"The smell gets everywhere," she complained, leaning on the doorway as Toan batted away the morning mosquitoes. He stood outside to undress in the courtyard, putting his nicotine-stained shirt in a basket, and tutted.

Mimi put a plate of pomelo, dragon fruit, and watermelon in front of him, telling him to fill up before she offered him any meat, noodles, or rice.

"You are so regimented, my little general," he complained, his eyelids drooping as he forked the fruit into his mouth.

She rubbed his shoulder, and he squeezed her hand. He would go to sleep after she'd left.

Mimi left the house by seven and rode her motorbike across three districts. She joined the snaking traffic through the newly laid roads of Saigon. She loved to drive through District 1. She mentally waved to the statue of Uncle Ho in the city square, passed the twisted orange turrets of Notre Dame Cathedral. The city was alive: shop stalls opened, vendors shouted as they argued over prices, workers slurped their morning *Bùn Bô Hue* on the street corners, and the smell of freshly baked *banh mi* was in the air. She stopped at her favorite *Café Sua Da* stall and watched the black liquid being poured into the cup. A swirl of condensed milk snaked its way through the ice cubes that only the locals could stomach without getting sick, then went straight into her marrow, fuel for the day.

The sign above the iron gates of the BP Compound in Thao Dien, Ho Chi Minh City, read CÁI KHÓ LÓ CÁI KHAN. And every time Mimi drove through this entrance, she shook her head. "Adversity is the mother of all wisdom," the sign said. Her mind always returned to her child when she saw the sign, back to that moment seventeen years ago when she couldn't see Ngan anymore in the Philadelphia airport. Mimi was not wiser. Losing her child at an airport and never seeing her again was one of the greatest adversities a mother could endure. To not know whether her child was dead or alive for seventeen years and still be living herself. This was adversity, surely? Mimi was not wise, no. Her grief was a giant boulder at the bottom of her soul that she could not move, no matter how hard she pushed.

The irony of this sign was not lost on her. What did adversity look like to those living within the walls of Vietnam's most prestigious foreigners' compound? What did these people know of hardship? Their tables overflowed with food. They had drivers, maids, and gardeners to serve their every need, and still they complained, snapped at their staff, shouted at their children, and drank away their sorrows. Their adversity, she recognized, may have been to be far from family and friends in a foreign land. But money could take away the bitter taste of loneliness.

The compound was made up of four roads, each with six sprawling houses: twenty-four houses, varied in size, forming a tidy grid. The houses on the outer edge were the most modest. There were no swimming pools, only courtyards instead of gardens. The residences closest to the river were the grandest, with six or seven bedrooms and with swimming pools, and were usually home to the foreigners with the most important jobs. Many worked for international companies she had never heard of.

The lawns were manicured, and the palm trees swayed in the infrequent breezes that ran up from the Saigon River. During the rainy season, security guards barricaded the entrance to the compound with sandbags and pushed the gushing water back into the streets. Those working for the compound used any means necessary to avoid inconveniencing their pampered residents.

The houses were white when residents moved in, freshly painted for each new arrival until the walls and garden fences started to blacken along the edges from the rain and mold. A tar-like trickle dripped down the once-white walls, an assault by the city's relentless heat and rain. The Vietnamese said you were always wet in Saigon, either from the humidity or the rain.

The architecture of the houses was a nod to the French, the last colonists. They were built on brand-new foundations, a new world. There were vast, sprawling lawns guarded by sleepy security men. Delicate, hot-pink bougainvillea–laden branches hung over the high brick walls that offered privacy to the residents. These bright pink flowers and leaves were favored by the poisonous tree snakes, who had a venom so deadly it could kill a dog or a child. Most Vietnamese knew that dense trees and bushes meant more mosquitoes, frogs, snakes, and whatever else the jungle would throw out. But on the BP Compound, this was all part of living in the jungle, and part of living like a *king* in the jungle.

Just outside the gates, the rich fragrance of cinnamon and star anise filled the air, from simmering cauldrons of chicken stock for hundreds of bowls of *pho* about to be served to hungry workers. Hawkers peeled back the delicate skin of mangoes to reveal the sunshine flesh on top of their precious and short-lived commodity. The heady smell lingered, but it would turn sickly in a matter of hours, as the mangoes began to rot.

Two years after meeting Toan, Mimi had left the Paradise Hotel and taken a position in a private home as their "helper," a maid. Toan's employer's boss was looking for someone to work for his family, and she went for the interview. Mimi was a natural when it came to working in a private home. She was industrious, professional, quiet, and could disappear when tensions arose.

She never forgot that she held one of the most coveted jobs a country girl from northern Vietnam could hope for. Her employers were wealthy Westerners, and everybody knew that foreigners made the best employers.

Mimi referred to all of her madames by the country they had come from. But Madame New Zealand had been her favorite. She had spoken to Mimi like a human being, asked about her family and her views. She was the only one who knew about Ngan. She had paid Mimi an entire two months' salary when Mimi got dengue fever and ended up in the hospital for six weeks. After the third week, Madame New Zealand came to visit her with food and offered to pay for her medical fees at a private clinic. Mimi had refused but never forgotten it.

Then Madame New Zealand fell pregnant, and Mimi couldn't stand the thought of caring for someone else's baby. So she moved on, pretending she had to go care for an elderly relative. But not before Madame New Zealand helped her search for records of adopted children in Philadelphia who might fit Ngan's description. *It's a start*, she had told Mimi. And for years, until she finally returned to America, Mimi treasured the yellow legal pad paper that Madame New Zealand had started for her. It was kept in a special box beside her bed. Every few nights she would take it out, carefully unfolding it and examining the names. One day Toan brought a computer home, and she would look up these names, in the way that Madame New Zealand had showed her, and see the images of the girls listed after carefully typing in their names and the words *Philadelphia, Pennsylvania*.

Next was Madame Australia, who was Mimi's first alcoholic employer. There had been strict rules about no vacuuming when Madame Australia was asleep late into the morning, which Mimi hated because she liked her work to be done in a particular order. Floors first, then bathrooms, laundry, and then cooking for the day. She once tried to suggest that Madame Australia try a *pho* for her hangovers, but acknowledging the condition had tainted their relationship, and afterward Mimi learned to mind her own business.

Some nights, when Mimi was asked to babysit Madame Australia's children, she would giggle into her phone to Toan as she watched Madame Australia stumble through the garden. She wobbled and struggled to get a foothold on the uneven paving stones, faltering with her arms spread out like wings to gain balance.

But not all the jobs had been good for Mimi. In her second position on the compound, she had ended up with a couple with no children, but their extended family often visited with babies, and she was asked to look after them. Most of the time, these Western children looked so different from her Ngan that she could separate her missing daughter from her charges, but there were moments when their fleshy arms would reach around her, or their cheeks would press against her own, and she would close her eyes and imagine her baby.

Ngan would be a teenager now. Mimi tried to imagine Ngan's life somewhere in America, where her house didn't flood when it rained, where she could ride in a car with air-conditioning, somewhere without dengue-spreading mosquitoes. To Mimi, she was always a living, thriving child, because the alternative was too horrific to bear. She daydreamed about a privileged life for Ngan, where she might even be the daughter of a woman like one of these madames she worked for. She might even have a helper of her own.

Still, Mimi knew how fortunate she was. And the way these foreign women had treated her in her own country was far better than what other helpers endured doing similar jobs for wealthy Vietnamese families. The helpers knew which nationalities made the best employers. The British were polite, and Australians and New Zealanders were relaxed with less formality. French and Germans were clear about what they wanted, but it was hard to become accustomed to cooking their food. She was told the Japanese could be awkward because one never knew what they wanted. Nobody said no, and when they said sorry, they meant *you are sorry*.

Vietnamese women married to white men were the worst and to be avoided. Tales of a madame hitting and kicking her maids were not uncommon.

Top of the pile were the Americans. An American madame guaranteed a comfortable working life. They were riddled with guilt for having help, and at the beginning, they spent most of their time apologizing and thanking a disproportionate amount for any menial task completed. But no matter where the madames were from, they eventually became accustomed to having everything done for them. They were fast learners.

Mimi had been working for this particular Madame America for almost two years. They were a kindhearted, alcoholic couple from Dallas, Texas, who lived at 18 Orchid Avenue, empty nesters who hosted brunches that continued all day long and offered Mimi hefty overtime rates for working Sundays so they could drink their jugs of cocktails and wine while Mimi ensured their house was pristine for Monday morning.

But in the same way that all her previous madames had left, she spotted the telltale signs of her employers' relocation: posts on social media to sell items they didn't want to take home, moving companies and their sweaty reps arriving at their doors with clipboards. She would have to start asking around for any new families looking for a helper. The girls at the apartments in their matching *ao dais* were usually the first ones to know. She didn't want to leave this fancy compound yet.

Mimi was left in charge of watching over their belongings being packed up by throngs of young men, professional packers. As she stood over Madame America's expensive handbags during a packing day, she thought she saw a young man who looked just like Ngan's father, Lam, though he had Americanized himself and called himself Lenny.

Lenny was just a boy she made a mistake with one night, a boy whose handsome face and pale brown eyes, sweet words, and promise of love, charmed her between shifts at Mimi's uncle's textile factory.

One mistake, and her sister's big plans to start a *Café Sua Da* empire in downtown Philadelphia were dashed. Within six weeks, Mimi's complexion was green and her body shape changed dramatically. Cam knew she was pregnant before even Mimi did and presented her with four pregnancy tests one night when they got home. *You need to know, so we can prepare ourselves.*

When they saw the two lines, they knew then that they had to get home. Lenny had disappeared when news started to spread that Mimi was expecting a baby. Uncle Huan, who had sponsored their visas as a favor to their mother, said they were better off finding work back home, and he had done enough helping them to come to America, he wasn't about to start offering all the factory workers at his textile business maternity pay. Mimi couldn't wait to get home to her Vietnam.

Now, all she wanted was to return to America. As she watched the boxes loaded onto thirty-foot-deep containers headed for the shipping yard, she imagined herself climbing into one bound for America. She would find her way back there and search for her daughter. Search for this lost part of her. She spent years arguing with Toan over when they would return to Philadelphia and retrace her steps. He was adamant that she should never return there. That the pain of not finding Ngan would be too much to repair.

— ∞ —

After the packers left, Mimi rode home through the wet, humid streets of Thao Dien. A dense river of riders wore full-body ponchos branded with a logo she didn't know. Hers read P&G, though it never occurred to her to find out what this meant. Hawkers cycled slowly in the same lanes wearing traditional Vietnamese hats instead of bike helmets. When the rain came in hard, the streets overflowed with brown water, the river running through the ditches and out onto the roads. Enormous Toyota Land Cruisers transporting expats through the city drove down the roads creating waves through the flooded streets. Food carts were submerged, with sellers storing bags of perishables as high as possible on top of their glass shelving units that usually stored their food. On nights when the rain came horizontally, Mimi saw rats swimming upstream, looking for anything to gorge on. But that night, there was no river of rain, just the soft gush of moving water as motorbike wheels moved through big puddles. Everyone rushed to get home for the family meal.

✦ ✦ ✦

EARLIER THAT DAY, Madame America had planted a seed of hope in Mimi's mind. A seed that grew quickly and powerfully. "I would love it if you came back with us for six months, to help us get settled back into life. Troy can help with the visas. What do you think? We live on the East Coast of America, in a place called New Jersey. Of course we'd cover all the expenses and even give you a raise." As the roots bedded down, a tree of hope started to bloom.

Mimi knew this much. Philadelphia was next to New Jersey.

Act Three

CHAPTER TWENTY

Sabrina

Philadelphia, July 2015

The first time Sabrina realized her mother was a liar was when she was ten. Kit and Kaitlyn had just returned from their Christmas holidays with tales of starfish on Caribbean white beaches. Sabrina had boasted in a fit of jealousy that her mother was taking her away to the tropics over the midterm break, and they had teased her that she had probably never been to the airport, probably didn't have a suitcase, probably didn't even have a passport.

Sabrina sat at the kitchen table that night sharpening her pencils. She asked Lee Lee, "Mama, where is my passport, I want to take it to school tomorrow." Since leaving school that day, all she could think of was how she could prove those girls wrong.

"Why do you need your passport at school? You're not getting on a plane," Lee Lee asked as she put dry plates and glasses away.

"I just want to prove I have one to some of the girls at school. I do, right?"

"*Ai-ya*, I don't know where it is right now. Now finish your homework. You're going to be so late going to bed."

Her mother went to the sink. Sabrina thought how Lee Lee always looked tired; her skin was sallow, her eyes dragged down by dark rings around them, and her hair had become peppered with little wiry white strands.

Sabrina doodled along the margins of her notebook after finishing all the math she had been set that afternoon. She watched Lee Lee wearily climb the stairs to the bathroom. *Time for myself. Do not disturb*, she said. Sabrina crept up behind her; she knew which stairs made the most noise and tiptoed from one quiet step to another, making her body as light as possible. She went straight to her mother's bedside table, where all her important things were kept: a jade pendant given to her by her *nai nai*, a small photograph of her family with somber faces in front of a Buddha on a mountain, their hands raised flat to appear as though they held the sun in their palms, and two pieces of paper with Chinese characters she couldn't read with a faded red stamp that had the star she recognized from the flag of China. But it was only Lee Lee's Chinese passport. There was nothing there that looked like it could be Sabrina's passport. Nothing that bore her name or photograph.

"You shouldn't be snooping in my things." Her mother's tone was terse.

Sabrina looked up and closed the drawer fast.

"I really wanted to show my friends my passport."

"That doesn't matter, you should not be in my things."

"But Mama, I want to show them they're not the only ones who can do things, I wanted to show them I am just like them."

"We'll get you one later, Sabrina."

"You just said you already had one though." Sabrina watched her mother carefully. Lee Lee's eyes stared down at the drawer, not at Sabrina's face.

She pressed again.

"I either have one or don't. Which one is it, Mama?"

Sabrina readied herself for her mother's temper to fly. But Lee Lee didn't raise her voice.

"I know, I made a mistake. I thought we had one. I thought I applied a few years ago but I must have forgotten. We will do it. Now go to sleep, I'm tired." Lee Lee turned to go to the other side of the bedroom, toward the chest of drawers, and picked up the tub of Ponds and unscrewed the top.

Sabrina said nothing and walked out of her mother's bedroom and into her own. That was the first night she chose to be alone. She did not want to lie beside Lee Lee and have her hair stroked until she fell asleep. She didn't want to tell her about every event that had taken place in her classroom that day. Or what Kit had said about Casey or what she hoped she might get for her birthday next month. She lay on her bed, her covers too soft from lack of washing, and she closed her eyes. That night, Sabrina fell asleep in her clothes, and when she woke the next day, her mother had already left for work. She rushed to catch the bus, and as she dragged her bag behind her, laden with library books to return, she remembered that she hadn't brushed her teeth. On her way to school, she worried someone would say something about her breath.

When she walked into the classroom, she looked down at her uniform skirt and noticed a stain from the previous week's lunch.

"Hey, Rina! Sit here next to me!" called Kit, and she patted the seat beside her. Kit always found the part of the classroom where everyone gathered, while Sabrina had always been drawn to the periphery.

In that instant, Sabrina became truly part of Kit's world. Kit never asked Sabrina about her passport again. Sabrina would always think it was because her friend saw the sadness in her eyes. Maybe Kit had felt bad that day when she and Kaitlyn had teased her about her passport.

Maybe Kit hadn't felt anything at all, and just moved on through the fickle trains of thoughts that ten-year-olds had. Maybe that moment in the playground had meant nothing to Kit at all.

~⚬~

The second time Sabrina caught her mother lying was during the Chestnut Hill Academy International Day, when she was twelve years old. The Chinese families had been asked to host the China stand. Mr. Haines had been a chemistry teacher for almost twelve years before he was promoted to Head of Middle School. He wore a green Eddie Bauer fleece every day, zipped up over his stomach, which protruded over the waistline of his trousers more each year, and a matching green bow tie that Sabrina suspected was a clip-on.

"We'll call it the Far East Asia region stall, okay, Ms. Chen?"

He also referred to each student by the prefix of Mr. or Ms.

Lee Lee Chen had one of those faces that expressed every emotion that passed through her, as plain as a traffic light changing color. She arrived late, and her hair had been blown loose by the wind. Her purple coat was frayed, the zipper broken.

"Ah, Mrs. Chen! What a pleasure to finally meet you! *Ni hao ma!*" Mr. Haines said, hands together like a Thai statue, bowing deeply. "I'm the famous Mr. Barry Haines. I'm so honored you could make it."

Lee Lee looked at him, a smile twitching at her mouth.

Sabrina begged her mother with her eyes. *Don't say anything. Leave it.*

"Mr. Haines, you are not as tall as you look in your picture," she said, her lips a flat, rigid line across her face. This was her mother's way of clenching her fists to prepare for a fight. Insult his stature first.

"Well, yes, photographs can be deceiving, I know . . ."

"And you look older. In the photo in the yearbook, you look young, but now I see you have very little hair left at the back there." She pointed to the crown of his head.

Sabrina tried to look away, to spare him one pair of eyes at least.

He took a breath, upright again, his face starting to color as he touched the crown of his head as if to check whether she had done something to his hair.

"Like I said, it's good to meet you, Mrs. Chen. Sabrina is one of our superstars. Do you have some extended family here in America?"

"Yes, I have some aunties on the West Coast."

"We do?" Sabrina asked.

Mrs. Chen ignored her daughter and continued instead to talk to Mr. Haines.

Her mother spent the rest of the afternoon explaining to everyone who came to the stall the difference between Tainan, China, Korea, and Japan—the oppressors, imperialists, freedom fighters, and traitor Chiang Kai Shek. How Hong Kong wasn't really China at all but an island full of British slave owners, and the island of Tainan was where drinking snake's blood was believed to give sacred powers—but how this was really a Chinese tradition, not in fact Taiwanese, as they claimed.

Standing at the stall, Sabrina leaned away from her mother, creating as much distance between them as possible. Why had Lee Lee said she had family here when Sabrina was almost certain that it wasn't true? But now a strange feeling of doubt crept into her.

Sabrina wished that Lee Lee hadn't come that day. She usually felt this way when her mother came to school events. Anything that involved sitting in silence through a performance was fine, as long as there wasn't any audience participation. Lee Lee Chen couldn't reliably judge when to hoot and when to stay quiet. Lee Lee was too proud of her origins and heritage to miss any opportunity for a monologue about the best country in the world. *We are the inventors of everything. Everything came from China originally. I tell you, if you like moo-shu from your Chinese takeout, we make the best. The garbage you eat here is not moo-shu. You should come to my house next time, I will show you.* She stood right in front of people, too close, never breaking eye contact. Eye contact was essential to Lee Lee Chen. *Then they know your position. You must always look them in the eye. And show them you won't budge.*

As Sabrina got older, she learned to keep things from Lee Lee too. School events she wanted to avoid, the times she stole liquor from Mr. Herzog's cabinet with Kit, the feelings she had for Dave Harrison, Snapchat and Instagram accounts she set up on her phone, the offer from Princeton.

⁓

One especially hot Wednesday afternoon that summer, Eva drew up a chair beside Sabrina, jolting her out of her work.

"Something you need to know about me, kid, I don't do elephants in the room."

Sabrina looked up as Eva Kim said this. Eva had moved to her desk, with no noise or fanfare, standing before her in the same black shift dress she wore every day. Sabrina wondered how many of these hung in her closet.

"Let's just get this conversation out of the way now, shall we?" Eva asked as she sat down.

Sabrina swallowed what felt like a large stone in a single gulp.

"The undocumented thing . . . you always knew about it?" Eva asked.

Sabrina didn't know whether to look at Eva Kim or not. She felt shame wash over her. She shook her head and felt like the armor she had so carefully constructed around her would disintegrate into ash. She was reminded of the time she saw a dead animal on the road. She wanted to look away from the mess.

Sabrina never asked herself if she had really believed that her mother had just forgotten to apply all those years ago. It was a memory she had filed away with no intention of revisiting. There had been no mention of the passport again until a few months ago, when Sabrina had talked about her summer trip to China. The trip that would never happen.

"No, I didn't." She shook her head. "I didn't have a passport, but my mom never told me about the rest of it—a lot of Americans don't have passports, right?"

"How? What I mean is, how could you not know? You didn't have situations where you needed to travel and present your ID?"

Sabrina looked at Eva Kim and smiled faintly as the very same thoughts passed through her mind. Why did Lee Lee not simply tell her the truth?

"I guess because we didn't have a lot. I rarely had to present any documentation. In fact, I don't think I remember one time when I did. If that makes sense."

"Driving?"

Sabrina shook her head.

"You take the bus?"

"Yeah. And we never traveled anywhere because we don't have money to go on vacation. We don't have insurance because we don't have any money. I just figured everything came down to our financial situation."

"But you wanted to travel to China. How were you planning on doing that this summer?"

"Mom told me she had already put my passport application through, that she had gone to the Chinese embassy. All of it. I don't speak or read Chinese so I figured she had it all under control."

Eva nodded. "Can I ask a question? It might make you uncomfortable . . ."

"Sure."

"Do you think she was going to get you that passport legitimately at the Chinese embassy? Or was she getting creative and getting it through less traditional ways?"

"I really don't know. She could have been getting it illegally, but maybe she just didn't do anything. I think it would have scared her to do anything."

Sabrina noticed her voice had quietened to almost a whisper, as though she didn't want the walls to hear.

"How did you find out for sure? Or have you found out for sure?" Sabrina didn't answer for a moment, because even she didn't have proof. Not yet. But she knew that if she tried to find out, the truth would be there in plain sight and there would be no way to go back.

"If you suspect this to be the case, why did you plan to travel?" Eva asked.

"I guess I held on to a bit of hope that maybe she really had done this for me—applied for my passport. That's what I'd hoped." Sabrina surprised herself with the truth.

"How do you feel now that you know this? About your undocumented status?"

Sabrina didn't answer Eva.

"Do you blame her?"

"No! God no." She protested louder than she had meant to.

Eva Kim looked at Sabrina with surprise.

"A lot of kids your age wouldn't be so forgiving."

"I'm not saying I'm not upset. I am. But I guess I haven't really looked at what this means for me yet. Things are a bit harder for me."

"Things to do with your future?"

"Yes."

~∽~

After lunch, Sabrina ran her hand over her keyboard. She pressed save on the research she had started to gather on vaccination rights for immigrants in Pennsylvania. Sabrina wanted to impress Eva in the purest way possible: through diligence and proactivity. These were qualities that she suspected (rightly) that Eva Kim valued.

Most adults Sabrina had met, and they were usually parents from her school, asked her questions that skirted around the very things that made her different from *their* children: the money she didn't have, when her mother had come to the United States, and what life was like at home. Sometimes she felt an insurmountable interest from adults about how Chinese it was, how different it really was in her household. She could see people calculating the information they could extract: Were you born here, Sabrina? How many jobs does your mother have? Your mother must be so proud of you and the opportunities you've created for yourself.

But Eva Kim didn't do that. Eva Kim got straight to the point and asked the questions that would make everyone else uncomfortable. But they were the questions that mattered.

"So in your opinion, Chen. Do you feel like this new revelation leaves you completely fucked in terms of college and jobs?"

"I guess I do feel a bit like that, yes."

"So we need to do something about that then, don't we?"

Sabrina expected her to say more, but instead Eva simply looked down and started to type on her computer again.

A FEW DAYS LATER, Eva stood in front of Sabrina's desk.

"I've been thinking about your situation. Maybe we need to get some ideas together." Eva waved a pink folder toward her.

The pink folder she waved around was Eva's latest case for a Thai woman who was only four years older than Sabrina. Achara had come to work for a family who had sponsored her visa. But when the visa had run out, she didn't return home as she should have, and instead took a job at a nail parlor. She was fine until she found herself in the salon alone one night with a faulty circuit that caught fire after she had turned on the UV sanitization unit for the utensils. Achara suffered from third-degree burns all over her arms, but with no papers, and no money, she had no access to health care.

So Achara found Eva. Until Sabrina had started her work with Eva Kim, she had not realized how desperate some people were. That they barely had the basic things to live, let alone an education or a home. It was only when Sabrina started to see what Eva did for each of her clients that she realized how terrifying life could be. There were women who had been trafficked as sex workers, families who had been separated over their precarious immigration status. And to Sabrina, some of their situations started to resemble Lee Lee's, and even her own.

"You mean a plan? For me?" Sabrina ventured.

"You're adorable for thinking I have a plan. How can I have a plan before I see the lay of the land. I never have a plan," Eva added.

"Really?"

"You're surprised to hear this?"

Sabrina looked around at the scattered folders and chaos in the office and smiled.

"I can't always have a plan, kid. And if there's one thing I've learned in my work, it's that human beings are unpredictable, and we are ultimately just reacting to the actions of others, right? I mean, take your situation for example. I'm guessing you sure as shit didn't plan for this?"

"No. I mean, I do try to plan for everything. My mother plans, well, day-to-day things, anyway. Even the time she leaves the house to get the exact bus to avoid the exact traffic and you know, the rest."

"Maybe that makes her feel in control," Eva suggested.

"Of what? I mean, given my latest revelation about my status and everything else, I now realize just how much she doesn't have control. But I guess she tries to control some things . . . Me." Sabrina laughed in a way that sounded hollow.

"Oh yeah? Tell me about that?"

Sabrina felt her shoulders closing in, her chin dipping down.

Eva waited until Sabrina was ready to speak—another thing that Sabrina wasn't used to. Most people would take her silence to mean they could talk over her, their opinions mattered more than hers. Not Eva.

"I think she wants *me* to be a certain way, and I don't know that I always live up to the ideal, you know?"

"What ideal is that, Chen?"

"The good Asian girl. You know, I get good grades, I don't sleep around. I do as I'm told. I respect the family honor. But sometimes I say stuff that she deems disrespectful. I don't always fall in line."

"Honey, this is 2015, you are not fucking Mulan, and there is no honor to defend except how you honor yourself. Plus, you are a product of an American education. It's different for you."

"But that's not really true, though, is it, growing up in our culture . . ."

"Listen, you have this one life, and you're in a time now where you are trying to find your feet, and it's going to take some time to find them, maybe years. And now we have this new challenge ahead of us. You know, with life, sometimes it's good, sometimes it really fucking sucks. But I'll tell you one thing I've learned, and it's something I always come back to, this whole living up to expectations and feeling invisible is also about who we are in our core. We can change that to a point, because nothing stays the same, but it's a matter of how much we're willing to be controlled from the outside, and how invisible we are willing to be. I wish when I was your age I'd known that everything passes. You feel bad right now because you like a boy and you don't know how he feels? Or you feel bad right now because you don't know which college you want to go to? And in your case we have the great uncertainty of whether we can get you those precious papers, right? Things change on a dime. Am I promising you that you're going to go skipping into the sunset and live happily ever after while everyone accepts you with open arms? That nobody ever makes you feel small because you're different, or because you were brought up with less than some? No, but I think you'll find the people you want to be around, the people who inspire you, the places you feel accepted, and you'll start to care a lot less. You're going to make it, Chen. Time will be your friend. Everything is fucking temporary. The good and the bad, none of it is forever. And if nothing else, just wait."

Sabrina said nothing. When she was around Eva Kim, she felt she could be patient with herself and allow herself to feel the things she had pressed down to the pits of her being but that were starting to bubble up.

CHAPTER TWENTY-ONE

Mimi

Newark Liberty International Airport, July 2015

A woman standing beside Mimi at the baggage carousel was talking loudly.

"This airport is a zoo. You should have seen the immigration lines. It was nuts, so many people, so much noise. I felt like a refugee, for Chrissake."

Mimi had erased almost everything about America from her memory until this point. She had waited three hours in the immigration line to be interrogated by the officer behind the desk. She presented the officer with a dense folder containing form after form. The woman didn't smile. She peered at Mimi through the glass with suspicion, and Mimi was overcome with that familiar feeling of wanting to be invisible again.

"Welcome to America," the officer said with the robotic tone of constant repetition.

"Thank you, Madame," Mimi answered.

Newark airport was both entirely different and just the same as the Philadelphia airport. The smell of confined air and windows that did not open were just as suffocating as she remembered. A glass prison where nobody could enter or be free of without their papers.

The airport carpet was worn from luggage being dragged across it. She watched as overtired children sat amid their parents' disheveled hand luggage. It struck Mimi that this would have been her and Ngan all those years ago. Ngan, playing under her seat. Ngan, screeching for another snack, Ngan demanding to be held, Ngan's hand holding on to her ankle. Ngan, gone.

She arrived in America this time, seventeen years later, with no belief that anything might go her way. This time she was armed with knowing what the worst possible thing felt like. Losing Ngan, having no means to fight to bring her back. She had looked the nightmare in the face, and it had already happened to her. Nothing could be worse than that. So she firmly believed that it was her providence to fight every battle from here on, because it would be easier than anything that had already happened. And she might just find Ngan. Her child could be anywhere. Yes, she could be in a different state, a different country by now. But there was also a small possibility that she could be within arm's reach, and Mimi found herself looking at every young woman at the baggage claim belt who was what would have been Ngan's age now, eighteen. She knew she'd recognize Ngan instantly. She instinctively followed her, pulling her suitcase along behind her, trying to imagine what her Ngan would look like now.

Mimi stepped outside and was surprised to be met with a gust of hot summer air. In her memory, America was cold. But today, outside the arrivals hall of Newark airport, she was hit by a wave of heat. Her sweatshirt immediately felt heavy, and she wanted to take it off. She stood still and looked around until she spotted Madame America, waving at her from beside a bright blue car. Sir America sat behind the wheel, scrolling through his phone.

Madame America hugged Mimi, and she felt herself freeze in her employer's embrace. She didn't want to get into the car yet. Mimi wanted to get a sense of her bearings, to understand where she was in relation to where she might start looking for Ngan, but there was no time. She sat quietly in the back of the car, running her hand over the fabric of the seats. The air-conditioning chilled her face. She already missed Toan. She looked out and watched families embrace—families that looked nothing like her own but had missed each other, loved each other. She scanned their faces until they became blurs ahead of her, and she tried to imagine how it would feel and look if it were her and her daughter, Ngan, outside the airport embracing after so long away. How would she feel to hold Ngan, her daughter all grown up, in her arms again?

CHAPTER TWENTY-TWO

Kit

Tokyo, July 2015

A few weeks into their friendship, Kit realized that Amy was always late, unlike Ryo, who always stood waiting for her with a broad smile on his face at whatever place they had agreed to meet. This was a new dynamic for Kit, who was used to Sabrina waiting for her—there was an unspoken law of friendship that the person who waits was always more invested than the late arrival.

Amy didn't wear a watch. *It's too stressful, those pings and being controlled by time.* Which meant that she was always late—by at least half an hour, if not more. Kit almost expected her to say that "time is just a construct"— but she wasn't sure yet of how philosophical Amy actually was.

So she sat, waiting for Amy in the American Club reception, the recreational club where Amy often chose to meet, so she could *sneak off for a pedicure and put it on my parents' tab.* She finally realized how Sabrina felt every time she met her at the country club, where she was forced to wait in the reception area before she was signed in and allowed on the premises. When they met for lunch, she always ordered the same thing: a taco salad, finely shredded lettuce, tomatoes, jalapeños, and chicken in a bowl made of crispy taco shell that she left untouched, and a Coke Zero. She also always ordered the same thing for Kit.

Kit sighed and looked at her watch. Twenty-eight minutes late. She shook her leg impatiently and began to scroll her phone. She opened up Sabrina's Instagram and wrote a message to her. *Hey Rina, miss you. Hope you're not too sad about China. Been thinking about you.* For a moment, she hesitated before sending it. She thought about all the times she had been late to meet Sabrina, and pressed send. She typed Ryo's name into the search window. She found his account and saw he had posted a picture of Genji with his tongue hanging out of his mouth and a comment in Japanese she couldn't read. There would always be parts of him she could never reach. A part of his mind that would think in Japanese, his life in this country where she felt so foreign. Perhaps she was *ha-fu* like Amy had said, but she had not been raised in the same way as Ryo and his sister. Kit's world was confined to the familiarity of Chestnut Hill, where nobody even knew what that word *ha-fu* meant.

Amy's arrival was always unpredictable: either silently appearing from the shadows or announcing herself with the most ceremony she could muster. Today it was the latter. The word *bloodsucker* ran through Kit's mind.

"Oh, honey, I'm sorry, I was totally distracted and lost track of time. You know me."

She kissed the air around Kit's cheeks.

"It's okay. Where are you coming from?"

"I was at Christian's."

Kit paused for a moment, certain that the older music teacher Amy had met up with at the bar was called Sean. She couldn't adjust her face in time, but Amy didn't seem to notice, or maybe she didn't care.

"Hold this for a second, will you, while I sign us in." Amy handed her bag to Kit. Amy signed at the desk and walked straight to the entrance without reclaiming her bag. The door closed on Kit's shoulder as she tried to balance Amy's bag, her own bag, and her water bottle in her arms.

"Christian?" Kit called after her as she followed her through to the café. "I thought it was Sean? At the bar? Christian, as in Ryo's friend?"

Amy flung herself noisily into a booth and scanned the restaurant.

"Yeah, things got kinda complicated."

Amy ordered for both of them. Kit didn't like Coke Zero; she preferred water. She tried to say as much, but Amy's attention had already moved on.

Kit looked around. There was a depressing lull in the air. Hushed voices, a canteen-like echo of plates and glasses being moved around. She understood now why Amy liked to go there—her parents paid the bill, and there was nobody she knew, no young people to impress, the older members eating there midweek were meaningless on Amy's social radar.

"So I think Ryo has planned this trip to Kyoto. I heard him talking to Christian last night. Guys are not good at these things, you know? Like, they don't think about numbers. Whether it will be even. Boys never seem to think that way, that someone might be left out or whatever."

Kit realized that to Amy, having a place within the group dynamic was of great significance to her, while Kit's only concern was whether she had a place beside Ryo.

When lunch arrived, Amy began to explain that last summer she had been involved with Christian, Ryo's best friend. A fling, she called it. Ryo had been away, staying with their uncle and aunt in California for three weeks. Kit wondered what he might have been doing in California during that break, who he had been spending time with. She hated the thought of him on a beach beside another girl. Amy explained how she had had sex with Christian and lied to him about it being her first time. "I lost my virginity in tenth grade to Paul Lehman, I think I was fifteen or something. He was a senior. I was so into him. I'd sneak off in the afternoons to the gym when I was supposed to be in my singing lessons, and he'd fuck me on the mats in the storeroom."

Kit was shocked to hear Amy describe her first time like this. The aggressiveness of the words. There was no romance, as though it were something that had to be endured. She still promised herself that her first time would mean something, and felt a relief that she still held on to her first time as something sacred.

"I had no idea what I was doing, most of the time he just guided my hand down there, it was kinda gross, I guess. But also, like, it wasn't pleasurable for me."

Kit couldn't disguise her surprise, and wondered whether Amy was saying all this for dramatic effect. When she was around Amy, she teetered between nervous fear of what she would do next and excitement at being around someone so different from anyone she had ever known. She felt this with both Ryo and Amy, that their world was so far and foreign from the one she had grown up in. It made her miss home.

"Did you love him?"

"Christian? No way. But I was super into him, so I just went along with it all. But I guess that's not very sexually empowered of me or whatever. I think he got bored of me, it only lasted a month, but we never told Ryo about it and I made him swear all of it to secrecy."

Kit thought about Dave. Maybe he had used the same words as Amy: *We keep this between us, okay?*

"I'm glad I got it over with. So I knew what to expect with a guy."

"And that was . . ."

"A couple of other guys, and then Christian."

Kit's eyes widened for a moment, her brain couldn't catch up. She wondered how many guys Amy had been with—and if this was all true. She wanted to grab her hand and ask her if that was what she really wanted.

"Can I ask you something, Amy?" Kit didn't wait for a response. "Don't you want to love them? Like, isn't it better when you're with a guy in that way, if you love them?"

Kit readied herself for Amy to laugh at her or brush off her question.

"Maybe, but it's not how it has been for me so far."

They were silent again. The only sound was Amy's taco shell being snapped off in her fingers as she looked away into the room full of people she didn't care about.

"Christian is pretty sensitive, but I don't know how he'd feel if he knew about Sean. Or that I'd been dating other guys. I mean, we haven't had the talk yet about whether we're exclusive. But I don't think he loves me either."

"Do you love him?" Kit asked, her voice coming out in a whisper. She realized that she sounded childish. All this talk about love.

Amy shook her head, confused. "God no."

"So you're not going to keep it going with Christian, then?" Kit asked.

"I mean, probably not. I don't know. But I am definitely not looking for anything serious with him. What about you, honey? You're not hungry?"

Kit hadn't touched her salad. She didn't know why. And she didn't tell Amy about her feelings toward Ryo, or that anything had happened between them at all.

CHAPTER TWENTY-THREE

Sabrina

Philadelphia, July 2015

S abrina checked her phone too often. She tried to set rules for herself. She turned her phone off completely before turning the lights out at night, but twenty minutes later, she turned it on again. She looked up Dave in her contacts on WhatsApp to see if he was online. She checked her Snapchat to see if he had posted, then Instagram. She spent every spare moment between her shifts, chores, and sleep refreshing her feed. When she got up in the night to go to the bathroom, she reached for her phone in her drawer and could not stop herself from checking again. She worked out the average time it took him to reply to her messages based on the exchanges they'd had so far. It was ninety-four minutes. This was longer than she wanted. If she had her way, his average time would be a single minute, just enough time for him to compose the perfect response. She was getting better at the messages she wrote too. Sometimes she was even proud of her tone.

When it took him almost a whole evening to respond, she felt a black mood descend, a cloud she could not shake. If she was tired, she would get to the point of tears until she heard that heartening ping on her phone. She changed her notifications, so he had his own sound. He was busy, she told herself, although she knew this was just opening the door to the far more disturbing question of what he was busy with. Was he messaging a girl? Or worse, was he doing nothing and simply looking at her message with no desire to respond? This thought caused the black cloud to thunder and rain over her until she heard the reassuring ping again. His messages were brief but warm, sometimes an emoji she stared at, trying to find its meaning.

The best nights were after they had seen each other that day. They would message for hours, and sometimes she would realize it was already one in the morning and they were still talking. Then she couldn't wait to see him again. And until she did, she thought of only that, the excitement rising in her as the hour drew nearer.

To Sabrina's surprise, Dave Harrison was a good listener. He took in everything she said, carefully considering her words and turning them over in his mind. She stared at his face in those moments, studying his features: his mouth, his nose, the way his hair fell over his eyes. He was interested in what she had to say. It was intoxicating. This came as a surprise to Sabrina because of how Kit described him. She expected Dave to be distracted, that his only reason to spend time with Sabrina was because nobody else was there. Kit always presented him as a "user." Someone who was just waiting for a better offer. But this was not how he made Sabrina feel. Mr. Hargreaves, her English teacher in senior year, who was British, once told the class that they were *always on send*. She liked this phrasing, and the way he said this in his British accent. Sometimes she tried to mimic it in front of the mirror. She sounded ridiculous. On the other hand, Dave had perfected his British accent and always shouted out to her as she left his house *Toodle-oo, jolly good, tallyho*. She never looked back as he called after her, but her smile spread wide over her face, and by the time she reached the end of the street, her smile felt like it would burst out of her cheeks.

"I WILL SAY this . . ." Dave always started conversations this way when he wanted to make an observation about Sabrina.

She examined her nails as they sat on the Philadelphia Museum of Art steps. There was just enough cloud and breeze to keep them there comfortably for a while. She listened to the rustling branches with her eyes closed. The clouds darkened on the horizon. The rain was coming.

"You are not at all how you seemed at school," said Dave.

"Oh yeah?" She kept her eye on the clouds, trying to work out when the weather would shift.

"No. You are a straight talker, Chen."

She loved when he called her that. Out of his mouth, her surname, which she had loathed most of her life, had a sweetness that trilled in the air like birdsong.

"I think leaving school, graduation, it made me feel different."

"Meaning?"

"Meaning I felt like I was always waiting for a chance to speak. . . . There were a lot of competing voices in high school. It's kind of hard to be heard over them. Everyone's talking at once."

"I guess when you put it like that, I probably wasn't heard much either. People *were* loud."

"Ummm, I don't think it's the same thing. Being you is different from being me," she said with a sharpness she regretted.

"Why, because I'm theoretically popular?"

"Yeah, that and you're white, and you come from the *right* family."

"Oh come on," he said, "you really feel that way?"

"People treat you differently. I don't just mean the kids in the class, I mean teachers too. Friends, parents, even Kit. You're immediately on the *inside* and I'm not. Just like Kit. Kit is a Herzog, so she's in the fold, though she can play at the edges too."

"You really think so? I mean, my best friend is Manish Agarwal. You think he feels that way too?"

"Maybe a little . . . but he's also rich. His dad is a professor at Penn, isn't he? And works at Microsoft."

"So it's what, down to money?"

"Listen, there are always going to be people on the inside and those on the outside. But at a school like CHA, after a certain age, you start to notice. The kids who have their beach houses down the shore. When they go on school trips to Europe. I'm guessing the reason you're there is that someone in your family owns a house or some business in Chestnut Hill, right? So it doesn't matter that you live in a brownstone in Society Hill, you still get a spot at the school? Look at the cars in the parking lot. You ever notice how those school buses are kinda empty? There is an invisible line that exists between those who have money and those who don't. That line gets more visible when you throw in minority parents, or a less-educated family background. My mom is working class. She works as a janitor in a public school, a real public school, and sometimes takes a second job doing overnight shifts at a motel to work at the reception desk. She is not stupid. She's smart, she's just not educated. And she is not from here. And we have no money, except for just enough to pay the bills, to buy discounted food, and sometimes, when she feels real wild, she might take me to Target and treat me to something. So yeah, I am on the outside for all the reasons above. So it's different for me. In the Venn diagram of high school differentiators, I'm on the opposite side from you."

Dave paused and took in her words.

"I didn't know."

"How could you know though?"

"By looking." He finally said, "And I'm sorry that I didn't."

⁓

Dave was nothing like his mother, nor the image Sabrina had of him from Kit's descriptions. They took a walk together through the Wissahickon one early morning before her shift was due to start. Summer was exploding around them, gigantic trees weighed down, branches abundant with leaves, and magnolias hung heavy as the silky pink-edged petals scattered the well-trodden earth. The flowers popped out, pinks and violets. Some were weeds, Sabrina knew from the yard work she did at home, but they were still beautiful, and they still persevered, pressing through. They walked past an elderly man with a cane and two slow-moving Labradors. One of them pushed his wet nose into Sabrina's hand as he rubbed his body along her legs.

"Dogs like you, hey?"

"What makes you say that?" she asked, a smile on her lips.

"Can tell. It's a good thing."

"You don't have a dog?"

"We did, Gordon. He was my best friend growing up. Always had my back when Brad would beat the shit out of me."

"He did that?"

"Who, Brad? Yeah, always. He's kind of an asshole. Don't know if you noticed."

"I noticed," she said quietly.

The sound of their steps over the path became louder, and she heard her breath shorten as they walked up the hill, back toward the school parking lot. She noticed his white tennis sneakers bore a mark from the dirt path. In the distance, they saw a deer quietly nibbling on the branches and buds. They stood beside each other, just the rise and fall of their breath moving between them as they watched her, the doe.

"Can I ask you something? And I mean this totally from just wanting to know more about you. So your family are from China, right? That's your ethnicity?" Dave asked as they reached a narrow road that split the vast green expanse of the country club golf course behind the parking lot and main entrance.

Sabrina paused and smiled at the way he asked her. There was a thoughtfulness in it.

"Well, yeah, insofar as my blood. But I'm kinda fake Chinese, because I've been here in Philadelphia all my life and my Mandarin sucks."

"Faux Chinese," he said and smiled. There was an immediate intimacy when he teased her, and the fact that she couldn't go and visit her real ancestral home over the summer felt less and less disappointing.

"Better than my family."

"What fake are you? Fake Irish?"

"Nah, we're like phonies, you know? Like, look at all of us at CHA. All the money goes into whatever it is the parents think is useful. Most of our parents can still afford to send their kids to a private school but insist on calling themselves real or whatever because they have us all attending this fake public school. I mean, do you think low-income families who can't afford to even eat properly care that we have the council advocating for gluten-free pasta? If you think about it . . ."

"Do you think about it?" Sabrina asked.

"I do, yeah. I mean, don't get me wrong, I'm still as bad. I'm the one eating the gluten-free pasta, I'm the one going on the school trips to Europe, while attending a public school I can attend because of my mom's rental property off Germantown Avenue. My parents have made my life pretty comfortable, and I guess as a result I am not aware of the challenges other people have to face."

"Whoa . . ."

"What?"

"I just never knew you were aware."

"Yeah? You thought I just cruised along and took it all? But I do, so I'm kind of even worse than the rest. I take it all and I hate myself for it. Because I'm not really standing up to say no thanks. You know?"

"I would probably be the same way if I had everything you had."

"What do you mean?"

"Well, you go to a public school in the fanciest district of Philadelphia, and you live in a brownstone in Society Hill. You know about Asian American issues but not really, you're just a voyeur. I know you did your history paper on Vietnam and the war and immigration rights, but how can you really know about the Vietnamese or the Chinese or any of us Asian American minorities really? There are hardly any of us at CHA."

"I thought that Asian Americans were the fastest-growing group in America."

"Is that what you really think, Dave? What do you really know about the Chinese in America? Like seriously. You are in your own comfortable bubble here." She heard her voice sharpening at the edges.

"Whoa, burn, Chen . . . What is that statistic about the Chinese population in America today?"

"I think you mean Chinese restaurants, Harrison."

He laughed and a silence fell between them, interrupted by the sound of car horns turning the corner up to Lincoln Drive. She couldn't leave it alone though.

"You know the truth is that school is predominantly Caucasian with just a sprinkling of African American students. And I'm not talking the

African American community from North Philly, which is just a fifteen-minute drive away. And as for me, and being Chinese, well, in all honesty I don't have a clue. Because I'm a phony too. I'm Chinese but I don't know what it is to be anything but Lee Lee Chen's daughter, or whoever I was at school."

The words tumbled out of her from a place she didn't know had started to grow. Among the dusty folders of Eva Kim's office, it sounded like Eva's voice, but it wasn't. It might have been her own.

CHAPTER TWENTY-FOUR

Kit

Tokyo, July 2015

K it liked who she was when she was around Ryo. He knew about everything. He wasn't fazed by the fact that she was younger than him but treated her as though she were his peer. They were only a year apart, but he had lived already, in comparison to her small existence in Chestnut Hill. He had traveled for a year before college already. The night they had kissed, they walked hand in hand on the deserted streets and he'd told her, "I don't know when I'll have the chance again to be so carefree. I'll want to get a job at the right place when I graduate. And I want to see more, participate in more, to witness life and places and not just talk about things in theory but know I've had experiences that are real."

Ryo had plans. And he never answered anyone with *I don't know, man.* The way the boys back home did.

In the first few days since kissing Ryo, Kit was nervous. She woke up early and listened for any signs of him moving around the house. She wanted to appear nonchalant even though she wasn't. But the moment he saw her, he went straight to her, and any doubt she had of his feelings evaporated before her eyes.

A routine started to form. In the mornings Ryo waited for her and made her coffee when she came down the stairs, then invited her to join him to walk the dog in the park. Ryo made her feel none of the agony she used to feel around Dave, waiting for him to glance at her across a crowded cafeteria. And with this open reassurance of Ryo's feelings for her, confidence emerged in Kit once again.

"But surely you have some other girls you are interested in, girls who are sniffing around," she said one afternoon as they walked to his favorite café in Shibuya. Kit laughed as she said this, but it was not a joke.

"There are always girls sniffing around, Katherine. Just like there are always boys sniffing around." He took her hand.

"Interesting." She had never said this before, in response to anything before. A Ryo-ism.

Ryo ordered the coffees in Japanese, still holding her hand. She drank her iced coffee black now, just like Ryo did. At first she had found the taste bitter, but now the thought of a milky caramel frappuccino repulsed her.

"The thing is, you're stuck with me. Until you don't want to be. It's pretty simple," he said with a smile.

He wanted to see her, so he told her so, and sought her out. *Want to watch a film? Come join me for a swim. Let's go and get a bite.* When she was out and she messaged him, he responded to her almost immediately. He actively made plans for them. *Come and try some kaki-gori, it's the best on a hot day.*

Ryo was thoughtful, so she didn't have to second-guess, she completely lost her appetite, and her chest was beating with such violence all the time, as though a hummingbird were trapped inside her rib cage. She was infatuated with him.

She loved that Ryo knew about everything. He had an opinion about the election year, the state of Japan's economy, about macros in proteins and carbohydrates, about copyright laws in the music industry, about the gender pay gap, about racial identity as a third-culture kid, about plant-based diets and the latest album from Drake. She felt out of her depth in his company, but at the same time managed to appear to know what he was talking about, even if it involved rushing to the bathroom and searching her phone for a summary of whatever the topic of conversation was. He prompted her to listen to podcasts she had never heard of, even though she would stop them midway and put on sappy songs that inflated her feelings for him instead.

When she listened to him speaking, she felt pride swell inside her—though she was uncertain of exactly why. Was she proud to be on his arm? Or was it pride in him as a person? She watched him handle his sister with care. Kit suspected that she would like Ryo even if they were just friends. It wasn't just his looks and athleticism, although this set him apart from anyone she had ever met before. He was inarguably desirable, and *she* was the one he chose. And this made her want to be the best version of herself.

⁓

Parents were not supposed to have favorites, but Yuriko and Rick Buchanan did. What surprised Kit, though, was Amy's acceptance of her parents' preferences.

The more time she spent in their home, the more she started to see the intricate family dynamic. At the center, the eye of the swirling storm, was Amy. Kit observed that Rick Buchanan practiced neutrality by hiding behind the wall of his work to excuse him from any real engagement in family discussions where she was involved. Ryo, on the other hand, stayed quiet when his sister announced herself and her latest ideas, with a smile on his face that she would look to for reassurance, and occasionally Kit caught Mr. Buchanan and his son exchange a look to say *Here she goes again*. Ryo managed to hold a position that was a fine balance between being an adult and being her greatest ally.

Ryo occasionally teased Amy, but Kit could see that he protected her most of the time, finding ways to swiftly divert his mother's attention from Amy when tempers started to rise. Yuriko's shoulders would tighten when her youngest child was present. Her eyes squeezed at the edges when she looked at her daughter, the way a person without children looked at a toddler having a tantrum in the middle of a crowded store. Amy was like a faulty alarm, set to go off at any time without warning, with no possibility of deactivation. Her unpredictability and whimsy vexed Yuriko. The moment Amy arrived, Yuriko's voice changed.

Must you sit that way, Amy?

Are you not going to say hello to us?

Really, why do you always have to draw attention to yourself?

The more Amy acted out—and this, Kit realized, was a daily thing with Amy—the more Yuriko became preoccupied with the order in the house. Amy's instinct for order was as underdeveloped as Yuriko's need for hygiene and harmony was overdeveloped. Kit learned over the days she spent at the house that Ryo and Amy's mother had a highly sensitive sense of smell. Kit watched Yuriko walk into a room and take a deep breath through her nose. Kit could only smell whatever ornate bouquet of flowers was displayed in the hall. Sometimes a scent of cooking would escape from the kitchen, but it was always agreeable—never too tantalizing or invasive, but just enough to alert curiosity from the appetite. Kit also learned that Yuriko ran her hand over the furniture in order to check for dust. On one occasion she saw Yuriko through the kitchen doors, sniffing the marble top of the kitchen island. She glanced at Ryo, who was too absorbed in his phone arranging something for them to do later that night.

I'm sorry, Linda-san, but I can still smell it, it's damp, it's something. Maybe it's the cloth? Please get some of the bleach and spray and then wipe away with hot water. Right away, please, Linda-san.

Kit tried to imagine Yuriko in Chestnut Hill, walking alongside her on Germantown Avenue to the Weavers Way Co-op for groceries. Would she even eat the food there? She tried to imagine her at a parent-teacher conference, how the other parents would act toward her. What would Mrs. Harrison say to her at a family barbecue? What would Sabrina think of her? Would she seem glamorous or would the other parents at CHA talk to her in a raised voice the way they sometimes did to Mrs. Chen? But Yuriko was on a different plane than Lee Lee, and even her own mother, Sally. Yuriko would do everything she could to fit in. She tried to imagine what it would be like to have a mother like Yuriko, and how nobody would ask her where she was from if they were walking together. She shook away the uneasy sense of disloyalty to Sally. She would never tell Sally any of this.

"You're just different from the girls I knew in high school here, you know?" Ryo said one afternoon as they walked through the Pachinko arcade in Shinjuku. The noisy balls echoed all around her.

"In what way?" Kit felt giddiness rise in her, the promise of a compliment, reassurance of his feelings in the air.

"I've just never met anyone like you. You're not trying to be anything. Like, you're you. There's not a prissy kind of pretense at coyness. I don't feel like you play games. And we can talk about real things."

For a moment Kit's face froze in a smile, as she thought about the pretense of indifference she had put on for almost a year toward Dave. The way she felt herself put on her "Kit-ness" before stepping out to meet Ryo each time. She wished right down in her belly that what he said was true. She also felt a small pang of hurt as she longed for him to tell her she was the most beautiful girl he had ever been with, even if it wasn't true.

"You couldn't talk about real things with girls before?"

"Not like I can with you. We have so much expat privilege here. And most of the girls I know, I don't feel like they've come from the real world."

"I guess you can't get more real than Philly." She laughed. "And Tokyo feels really really far away from that," she heard herself say, although the words felt a little like a lie in her mouth.

She knew she was exciting to Ryo exactly because of the things that felt so ordinary to her. For once, it wasn't her origin story or her ambiguous ethnicity that piqued a person's interest. The picture she painted of her home was of an America that seemed so pedestrian to her. He just didn't know it. The vast vistas of land, everything that was big and a little bland at times, including the cars, the food, the houses, even the highways. She talked about the parties on the beach during summer breaks, and the family trip to Los Angeles, as though it were a regular occurrence and not something that happened four years ago, when she sulked in a hotel room for most of it because she was bored and embarrassed following her parents around Hollywood Boulevard.

Ryo had interests that were different from the boys back home. He read books, he visited museums. She learned during the second week at his house that he went to a boxing club on Tuesday and Thursday nights. She wanted to go and watch, but didn't dare ask. She couldn't imagine him punching someone's face. Sometimes he came back with a bruise on his shoulder.

"Have you ever been hit in the face?" she asked.

"No, I'm good at defending myself. Everything happens from the waist down in boxing," he explained, "that's probably the most important lesson I ever learned there. Not how to throw a punch. I know it sounds weird, but I feel like it's kind of a reflection of life too. It's not the things on the outside, the punch, it's the things happening underneath that count."

He didn't look like a person who acted on impulse, but to her, boxing seemed so violent, so rash.

"The training and everything I do stops me from acting out of panic. I'm on autopilot—I know what to do to avoid the punch and put myself in the best position. And striking first, that's important too. It's hard because you have to control your emotions. Getting hit in the face, you're going to get upset. But you have to push it down and keep moving forward, to stay in the moment. Man, I sound like an ass."

But he didn't. He sounded smart. He sounded measured. He sounded like someone who made cautious, considered decisions. Someone she could trust in an emergency.

Three and a half weeks after Kit arrived in Tokyo, the Buchanans threw their annual midsummer party. She was not prepared for the effect Ryo's mother wearing the traditional pale blue and delicate *yukata* would have on her. She greeted Kit with a bow, hands together, her thumbs lightly hooked together in front of her body, and when she raised her arm to gesture guests into the house, the swooping sleeve of the robes floated against a breeze that rushed through the doorway. Her steps were small, weightless, and silent beneath the swathes of fabric wrapped tight around her body, and when she turned around, the flourished finish of the knot against the back of her obi-belt looked like the sudden blossoming of a flower. Everything was tucked in and restrained except the final burst of this knot.

Kit felt big-boned and clumsy next to Yuriko's tiny frame and intricate kimono. The paper lanterns that swayed in the garden took on a yellow tinge and blurred in the distance. Frosted glasses of beer were passed around by Linda, who smiled passively. Yuriko placed her small, birdlike hand on Kit's shoulder, and she felt the warmth of acceptance flood through her.

"Katherine-chan, *youkoso*, welcome," she said, bowing and revealing a lacquer comb that was placed in the ribbons of her hair.

Kit bowed in response and tried to think of how far she should bend her head, recalling a documentary that explained the direct relation of the depth of bow and social status. Her green floral dress that she always reserved for special occasions back home felt ordinary and plain. She pushed her hands deep into the pockets, her favorite thing about the dress, and rubbed her leg through the fabric.

"Ryo and Amy are somewhere around here. Make yourself at home. Try the food, have a drink, enjoy yourself. Ryo is planning a Kyoto trip for you all, I believe. You will love it."

"You look beautiful, Mrs. Buchanan."

"Oh thank you. You are always so charming, Katherine. I keep saying this, but you really must call me Yuriko, please."

"Sure, Yuriko." Kit felt her cheeks color. "We always say Missus or Miss back home." She heard herself unable to pronounce the *r*—or was it an *l*—in Yuriko's name. For Ryo and Amy it rolled off their tongues, but when she said it, heavy with a foreigner's accent, it sounded forced and so clumsy to her ear. But Yuriko politely ignored her mispronunciation and smiled.

"Well, no need here. Please, make yourself at home, Katherine."

Yuriko guided her out toward the lawn and then vanished through the entrance without a sound. Kit started to walk toward the garden to seek out Ryo but turned to watch Yuriko expertly meet every guest, offering refreshments. She would look up and signal to Linda with a carefully lacquered hand. Once she caught Linda's attention, Yuriko then tilted her head toward a tray that needed to be taken away or a guest who needed a drink.

She saw Ryo dressed in a white shirt with chinos, no shoes, as he spoke to an older couple, a blond man and a Japanese woman with dyed platinum hair. Kit stood on the periphery of his eyesight. They could have been her parents, she thought.

Kit watched Amy standing against a wall wearing a tank top with thin straps that revealed her stomach and showed a neon yellow bra strap slipping down her shoulder, engrossed by the numerous insistent pings from her phone. As Kit approached her, Amy then put her finger up to Kit, *just a second, honey,* and prowled the edges of the outside bar with her face scrunched up over her phone. Kit wondered who she was messaging. There was a gentle hum created by the guests talking, but there was no breeze, and the air felt like it was closing in on her, like she couldn't take in a deep breath. She heard an American woman with a Midwestern accent greet Yuriko. "Oh my, you are so beautiful, Mrs. Buchanan, oh Japanese women are so elegant. We visited Hong Kong before coming over here and the traditional dresses there are so intricate and wonderful too. What are they called? I can't remember. This is exquisite." Yuriko nodded, her lips pursed, and said thank you. Only Kit could see the sharp minuscule breath she took in as she looked away from her guests.

Kit saw Amy signal the other maid from across the room. Kit sipped her drink and watched the girl, dressed in a blush-pink uniform that was made up of a ruffled apron and skirt and fell at an unflattering length blow her knees. Amy used the same hand gesture her mother used, fingers flipping inward to call her over.

To Kit, Yuriko had become an almost mythical creature, a movie star she watched from a distance. The way her clothes hung from her thin shoulders, her protruding collarbones and milky white skin. Her hair was black with a glossy shine and her eyes were always open and alert to everything that happened around her. Her gestures were deliberate and elegant, and she never spoke over a certain volume. Yuriko looked to her children with a pride that Kit recognized in her own mother's eyes.

CHAPTER TWENTY-FIVE

Mimi

Philadelphia, July 2015

To Mimi, America was a dark, unspeakable tumor in the pit of her stomach. Every good thing that had happened there before she lost her child was forever stained by the moment she realized Ngan had disappeared. She hated the smell of the dirt that seeped from concrete sidewalks and the garbage that oozed out of the trash barrels. It wasn't the same as the mountains of garbage in Saigon—somehow it was worse here, filthier. There were no fragrant flowers, trees, or fruits that could compensate for the stench that sat in her throat as she walked along the streets, past forgotten dumpsters.

The only redeeming thing about this country was that the days were longer during the summer. Every weekend Mimi would take a bus to Philadelphia and return to parts of the city she knew. She searched for clues about the girls listed on the piece of paper Madame New Zealand had made for her. She walked around the stores where she thought young girls who would be Ngan's age would go, she stood outside the fast-food restaurants to see if there were any faces she might recognize. At the end of the day she watched the sun set over the Schuylkill River on the land around the city in the blistering July heat. As she looked down at the water's curves, she turned and saw the sun setting behind her, the sky in front becoming pink and soft, then slightly blue again, as though it could not stop its beauty, then the land closest to the setting sun would get dark, almost black against the orange line of the horizon. For a moment, she could be anywhere, and the land softened, the outline of the buildings and the sky lingering, then finally dark as the sparkling lights came on. Her soul quietened for those moments, and Mimi didn't hate it there so much. She started to see it as a place that might have some answers about her daughter, or maybe even bring her back.

WITHIN A MONTH Mimi had transformed Madame America's enormous house and created a well-ordered, spotless home. Mimi had never seen houses like this in Vietnam. The cooking stove in the kitchen was of such enormous proportions she wondered how many people she would cook for there, she could have fit inside the refrigerator three times over comfortably. And for some unknown reason they had three cars parked in their driveway. Why did they need three cars when only two of the family could drive? The amount of food in their pantry was more than anything she had seen in any home. Because of the cooler climate, things did not spoil, unlike the food at home, where she would have to study packets of grains with great vigilance to make sure there were no weevils in them. She placed everything in the pantry in height order and came back to find Madame America had moved things around. Mimi nodded and arranged things according to how her new employer preferred. The words weren't necessary sometimes; Mimi always understood the things that were left unsaid.

She tended to the neglected yard with feverish energy, weeding and trimming overgrown hedges and sweeping away debris from the ground. She accompanied Madame America to the grocery store, where she sat quietly in the passenger seat and took in all her surroundings. She was introduced to gardeners, pool guys, acquaintances in the store as though Mimi were a member of the family, and Madame America started referring to her as "the housekeeper" and not "the helper" the way she had back in Saigon.

Every Sunday Madame America told her to relax, and soon she offered Mimi Saturdays off as well, unless she had guests over. By the fourth week, Mimi took the bus from New Jersey to Philadelphia's Center City and found a café with free wi-fi to call Toan. She had promised to call him every fortnight on her Sundays off.

"How is the madame?" Toan asked. She could hear the radio playing a Vietnamese pop song, he was in the driver's waiting room waiting for Sir Jin. The old driving company had reregistered under a new name and Toan had gotten the call. She pictured the smoke in the air, the other drivers lying down with their feet on the tables and chairs.

"She's okay. She acts guilty for asking me to do things here—not like at home. She'll change her tune soon."

"They always do."

"Yeah. Are you waiting for Sir Jin again?"

"Always, this guy, I don't know what he's doing with these hookers, but he likes to spend a long time in there."

"Have you been eating properly?"

"What about you? All that junk there?"

"It's terrible food. And my madame, they eat so badly here. She asks me to cook when people come over. But when nobody is visiting, if you could see the stuff they have. This horrible stinking thing, Macs and cheese, they call it. Disgusting. Dried-up orange stuff smells like vomit."

Toan laughed. A silence fell between them. She could hear the radio in the background again.

"Be careful, my little general," he said quietly, and she knew he meant it.

"Anyway, don't know how long Sir Jin is planning to stay here." He continued, "I think I heard the driver's agency talking about him moving. I hope next time I get an Australian or even better, a Danish Sir. You know I told you my friend Liem had a Danish Sir, he doesn't even call him Sir. Can you imagine?"

"Don't get any ideas, just take the money and keep your mouth shut."

"Yeah yeah, I know, I know. I've been eating *Bùn Bô Hue* almost every night. It's the easiest thing."

She thought of him sitting alone at the stalls they loved to go to, and she felt a sadness creep in. His voice made him sound so close. He could have been in the same city, on the same street. That was how close he sounded.

"Look after yourself. I'll try again in a couple of weeks," she said, eager to finish before her resilience wore down further.

"Wait wait, you haven't told me about the job yet. How is it? What's the house like?"

"It's big, not as big as those houses on the compound. It's different. The city is filthy. You can't imagine it."

"Have you thought about what you're going to do?"

Of course she had. She thought about it every time she saw a child who might be Ngan. Every time she pulled out her crumpled list with the name of the adopted Asian girls they had found in the Philadelphia news stories online. And then she had to check herself because, by now, Ngan would be grown up. She would be eighteen years old. She had already looked up five of the girls on her list.

"Why do you think anything will be different this time around?" Toan asked.

Mimi was silent. Why did she need to answer him again? Somewhere inside lived a shoot of hope that she had not culled. She allowed it to grow when a moment of happiness appeared in her life, like a mulchy patch of earth that she nourished overnight. This root was stubborn. It took hold.

After the line had gone dead, she sent him a message. *I love you.* And walked back to the station. She walked and walked straight down Market Street from 30th Street Station all the way to City Hall.

She walked through the streets toward Reading Terminal Market, weaving between the throng of weekend shoppers and small groups of people huddled over standing tables scooping forkfuls of jerk chicken and rice into their mouths. Mimi stopped before the cake stalls and stared at the enormous sponge cakes with pink icing and sprinkles. She watched as shoppers ate half a cake and threw the rest into the garbage. *Two dollars of cake,* she thought to herself. Mimi remembered her time in Philadelphia before; after the lunchtime rush, she always walked into the market at four in the afternoon as some of the stalls started to clear up. She was given discounted loaves from the Amish stalls. The girls in their stiff white aprons and hairnets would pass her a loaf, never breaking their flat expressions, lips firmly closed. Her big spend every week went on a tin of condensed milk for her *Café Sua Da.*

CHAPTER TWENTY-SIX

Sabrina

Philadelphia, July 2015

K id, things are always fucked, this is one certainty in life," Eva said, handing Sabrina another pile of pink case folders. Sabrina had created a master Excel spreadsheet for all the cases new, old, and active that Eva worked across, and they called it "the Nerve Center." Sabrina had created wide columns outlining each case: dates, actions, challenges, appeals, further appeals, and rarely, the outcomes of just a few that conceded defeat and were labeled closed. Eva did not like to lose. Sabrina began to see problems that were once theoretical words on a page as realities when she studied profile pictures of the people who depended on Eva, and some she met in person when they came to the office. They were dealing with deportation, no health care, groundless evictions.

"The people who have nothing get zero help, and the people who have everything hold on to all their everything. I'm generalizing, of course. America is also home to some of the greatest philanthropists in the world. But you see what I'm trying to say."

Sabrina thought she saw, but at the same time, she had a mother who worked every hour of every day given her, and still ended up having to buy her food from the discount aisle and clean bathrooms for a living. Lee Lee had no help. She had the kind of job her CHA school friends would have either laughed about or looked away with uncomfortable embarrassment, *for Sabrina*, not themselves for their inability to recognize just how lucky they were.

"How often do you get through though? Like, how often can you make a *real* difference?"

Eva took her glasses off and smiled at Sabrina.

"Kid, I'm a Rottweiler. I can't perform miracles—some cases are hopeless. Let's take this one. The Wdjadjas. Got here on legit visas, overstayed. They have a kid who is really smart. But now we have a battle because we gotta find a way to help him stay here to have his education, even if his parents may be deported."

Sabrina felt the temperature of her entire body rise.

"But I'll fight to the end. And you'd be surprised how far you can get when someone's willing to fight for you. Sometimes it's all you need, actually. A person who's willing to fight for you. Also, I am real good at getting people to do stuff—stuff they didn't think they wanted to do."

"How? I mean, how would you do it?"

"Get this kid to stay?"

Sabrina nodded.

Eva paused and Sabrina stopped typing into her spreadsheet. She pressed save, just to be safe.

"People rarely understand another person's situation when it's presented to them on a piece of paper. Or if it's someone they can't relate to—someone so far removed from their own reality and life. You have to get good at telling the story so that the person listening is invested, so they see *a case become a living, breathing person.* Life is full of coincidences, and you'd be surprised how many people will find a small thread that relates to them, and the walls come down. Isn't there some Chinese saying, 'No coincidence, no story'?" She made quotation marks with her fingers. "That coincidence can be the lifeline."

Sabrina was silent.

"There's something else you want to ask me, Chen. Go ahead."

Sabrina didn't speak. She didn't want to ask.

Eva Kim did not continue to look at Sabrina when she saw that she was uncomfortable. She respected her emotional state. It was one of the things Sabrina liked most about her. It must have come from years of speaking to people who had suffered trauma, Eva only pressed when there was a willingness to give her the information.

"I don't blame my mom for the choices she's made. She has had a tough life. I really love my mom, even if it's a little hard to see that sometimes."

"No, kid, it isn't. I can see you love her. We just don't say these things, right? It's just not how we do things in the East is it? It's certainly not the way I communicated with my very conservative Christian Korean mother. I'm guessing maybe that is the case for you too. It's not all hugs and *I'm so proud of you, honey*, all the time?"

Sabrina laughed, she couldn't even imagine Lee Lee's mouth forming the shapes required to say those words.

"It's funny how suddenly it all changes when you get to a certain age. Like, I used to hug my mom. I used to share her bed. I mean I probably shared her bed for longer than most white kids do with their moms. I don't know if my friend Kit ever shared a bed with Mrs. Herzog."

"Right, we definitely have this weird contradiction, right? Like we sleep with our moms but we don't show them affection. We don't talk about love, everything is about duty and respecting the elders. But duty and respect are just different forms of love. And you can't have love without respect; they coexist. Do I make sense?"

"Yeah, exactly. But also, I feel like the respect thing holds me back from being able to tell her what I really want sometimes. And that, along with the fact that I just don't want to think about things that aren't possible."

"Like what?"

"Like going to Princeton."

Eva took off her glasses and folded them neatly beside her desk.

"Right, like going to Princeton. Exactly."

Sabrina nodded. "Well, I *had* an offer in April."

"Why didn't you take it?"

"How could I possibly afford that? I don't even know why I applied."

"With financial aid."

Sabrina snorted. And regretted it immediately.

"Well, I never thought I'd get anywhere on that front. I missed the deadline. I guess I was just a realist about it. There are a lot of other kids with better grades even than me, and I think it would have been tough. And now I have another problem, you know, so it's an even more impossible idea."

"Yes, I know, you are undocumented. There are ways, kid. Ways we can get around it. But now we have the problem of getting your place back at Princeton. You haven't even put up a fight yet. Can't give up yet."

"I don't know, Ms. Kim . . ."

"Eva."

"Eva, I don't know. I don't know that my mom could deal with it all, and I would have to move away. And well, it's a lot. Plus, in real terms, I don't even know that they would give me my place back. I'm sure they've given it away."

"Never say never. I still know some people over there," she said, smiling.

"It feels like a huge leap."

"I think it would be, yes. Great things are a leap. But also, it would be cri-mi-nal"—Eva wrapped her lips around every syllable dramatically—"if you left it hanging and didn't give it a good old college try. . . . Ya see what I did there?"

Sabrina laughed. Sometimes Eva made her feel like she *could* do anything. That the invisible borders that had always kept her inside were just faded lines of paint on the sidewalk that she could leap over at any moment.

"But that means I gotta understand the whole picture too. Your mom, her situation. All of it. You understand what I mean, right?"

"I just don't know if my mom will talk. It's never been something we really talked about, honestly."

"Well, like I said, you never know what I might have in common with her. Bring her by next week. No coincidence, no story."

CHAPTER TWENTY-SEVEN

Lee Lee

Philadelphia, Winter 1996

I t was the end of the winter of 1996 when Lee Lee arrived in America. She had just turned twenty-one and had taken a huge debt, beyond her imagination, from a snakehead in Chengdu to get there. When she arrived that February, she carried all her belongings in one small bag that she taped up at the edges to secure the holes. And she was met with a wind of such ferociously icy air it felt like she had been smacked hard in the face. Nineteen years later, Lee Lee still could not get used to the way the days darkened and shortened in the winter months, as though she would be swallowed up into the darkness. In China, every sunset was at the same time. Here the night came too quickly during the winter months, or threatened its invasion all day with the dark clouds.

But she grew accustomed to other things—the way she accepted the flooding season in her hometown. She accepted the icy winds that froze the skin on her face, the permanent drip that threatened to drop off the end of her nose. She accepted the shocking gust of air that almost knocked her over as the subway raced beneath her. She accepted the homeless men she saw warming themselves on top of the manholes that sometimes released a push of warm air in winter. She accepted the way that people would look through her. She accepted being spoken to loudly, slowly. And she accepted not understanding what was going on around her.

She learned to walk fast among the people who rushed past her on the pavement. She kept an eye on who was ahead of her when she entered a new neighborhood; sometimes there were clusters of men she knew she shouldn't walk past. She was not pretty, or someone who drew attention to herself when she entered a room. She was thankful for that when she wanted to be invisible to them. Unlike in Chengdu, in Philadelphia she could cross the road with ease, the lights told her when to go, when to stop. It was the first thing she noticed about America. Signs everywhere, to tell you what you could and could not do. No Parking. No Turns. No Loitering. No Dumping. No Smoking. The green man flashed and screeched to tell you to walk. There was no room for error. You had to do what the signs said. Especially somebody like her.

Smiling did not come naturally to Lee Lee, her demeanor was always strained, as though she were on the verge of having to fight something, someone. The little softness she had within her heart hardened over the years. She was healthy, her body was strong, there was a stubborn will in her that kept her moving forward. But fate was not kind, it was so un-kind, in fact, that when she was faced with periods of peace, she was overcome by foreboding. Her father died in a mining accident when she was five. She lost a cousin to the floods during the rainy season just seven years before. She knew what it was to feel real hunger in her body, from days of cavernous emptiness in the pit of her stomach.

In Philadelphia she was alarmed to find a place that felt even less hos-pitable than the vast, growing metropolis of Chengdu. A city full of strangers was unkind, but she was terrified in a city full of strangers speaking a language she didn't understand. At night she lay on a creaking bed in her allocated dormitory, where the snakehead gangsters who smuggled her through, who seemed even more sinister than the ones back home, had taken her on her first day. She felt that familiar emptiness in her gut, and shivered as an unrelenting cold she had never known before loomed over her as night fell and bore into her bones. In the same room were twelve other women who watched her with wary suspicion and kept to themselves. She longed for kindness, even though she knew how to scramble in the earth to stand on her feet. Back home, she always knew she could find comfort with her mother, who was everything to her. They only had each other left, everyone else was gone. Here she had no such source for warmth. She had never, according to anyone who knew her, been a person who made friends easily. Even in her own language, in her hometown, she couldn't break down the walls that needed dismantling to create human connection. Instead, she stood on the periphery, waiting to be invited in.

Three months after Lee Lee had arrived in Philadelphia, she met the man she later agreed to marry. He was a tall and wiry twenty-eight-year-old from Fujian province, named Daming. And he had a green card, though she did not know this at the time. He was the first person who spoke to her in the hallway outside her dormitory, waiting to use the bathroom one night. He had a job at a chain restaurant in the shopping mall. She was instantly impressed by his confidence and how he seemed to know everyone in the dormitory. It was his fifth year in Philadelphia. He had started out in New Jersey, and now he finally felt like he was going to achieve the American dream, he told her. As she came to know him better, she realized that Daming's familiarity was offered freely with no discrimination to anyone he passed, even if people didn't respond. His air of confidence began to seem stuck on, with old tape and glue that had lost its stickiness, and would come apart the moment you looked too closely. Lee Lee also realized that Daming, too, was longing for kindness, and understood then why it was providence that they found each other.

"Once we make enough money, we can bring our families here, buy a house out in the suburbs. We'll have a garden with a fence around it. Then we keep growing our fortune. Maybe we can make investments, Lee Lee. We can grow an empire. Our little world. This is the country where hard work pays off." He said this every night as he rubbed his feet on the creaky rocking chair he had claimed from the junkyard for his room. The more he said it, the less believable it became, only Lee Lee kept that to herself.

But Lee Lee did dare to imagine the house that he was describing, and how she would look standing in the doorway of a place like that, with her own children running around.

"You are an optimist." She laughed, but deep inside the darkest crevices of her soul, she allowed the shoots of hope grow a little. She realized when she was with Daming, she was a little bit of an optimist too.

She didn't love him. Lee Lee didn't know what it was to be in love with a man. But she knew what it was to be lonely. Until he had greeted her, befriended her, it had been days, even weeks since anyone had spoken to her. She lived in a dormitory full of women. She was surrounded by other people, but she had never felt so alone as she did every night when she heard the sighing, the whispering, the crying from the other girls. Eventually they all started to form their friendships and bonds, and she watched as the Chinese girls created their own group, but there was no space for a strange, hard-faced woman from a tiny village in Szechuan. The hours she had to spend in the dormitory stretched out before her; she hated being there. And then, there was Daming, and suddenly she did not feel like an invisible shadow that took up a bed. So she found herself following him, like a sad stray dog, abandoned on the side of the street, faced with momentary kindness from a stranger. *This might be someone for me,* she thought to herself.

Daming was more affable than Lee Lee by nature, but once the initial greetings passed he was strange, awkward, and often said the wrong thing. His ears and eyes were not attuned to the small openings people offered to create the bonds of a relationship. But Lee Lee did not care, because she too was awkward and could not make friends. What she was not prepared for, was the effect the news of her marriage would have on her mother at home.

"Finally you can start a family. Bring a child into the world. Now I understand why you had to go to America, your fortune was continuing our family name, this way our bloodline can keep going into the next generation. And think of all the opportunities this child will have there."

"Mama, we are not even married yet, we're not planning on a family right away," she said, but in her usually empty stomach there was a cluster of butterflies flapping their wings at the thought of a child.

Daming was earning good money at the restaurant now and he had paid back his debts years before they met. So he supported Lee Lee in paying back her debts too, and they quickly moved out of the dormitory full of strangers who shouldn't have been there.

"Once we're all paid off, we'll get married in City Hall. *Ai-ya,* we could not sound more American, could we? City Hall! And then we will get you the green card too. Legal, my sweet plum." He said this after every payment they made.

Each day Daming woke before dawn and spent ninety minutes on three different SEPTA buses to reach the mall for work. He spent the morning preparing his workstation, hunched over the counter chopping vegetables. Then from eleven o'clock, he spent the rest of the day standing over an open flame and pan frying, deep frying, steaming. The food was Pan-Asian, but everything was cooked in dirty oil and tasted the same, which was why he never brought it home, he told Lee Lee. His ankles swelled from standing all day long. At seven o'clock every night he would plunge his hands into the washer, then move to cleaning up, where he scrubbed the cooker with a sponge afterward, rubbing away at the oil that would not fade. Then he would take the same buses home, which sometimes took two hours because of the canceled routes and diversions late at night. *Oh it's good to be back, home is my castle,* he said. *We taste the sweetness later. I promise you, my sweet plum.* Lee Lee always waited up for him, no matter how late his buses were. She waited to hear the rusty turn of his key in the door before she would murmur good night and turn over and go to sleep.

But one day Daming didn't come home. That night, there was no turning of the key, nor his soft padded footsteps through the room after washing his face in the bathroom down the hall. The door remained closed, and she stared at it all night. She sent him text messages in the dark. She never once put on the light, because if she did, his absence might suddenly be real. She went to the pay phone and dialed his work number over and over again. Nobody answered. The sun rose the next morning and her heart thundered hard as the orange glow of the dawn pushed through the broken blinds. What could have happened? No answer, no news. Had he left her? Without a word of explanation? Finally, an American voice picked up the phone and she heard the word *hospital.*

By the time she reached Temple University Hospital, he was gone. He had had a sudden heart attack on the third and final bus on the way home. He was only four stops away, that was all Lee Lee could think.

What had caused it? A hereditary heart condition that was apparently extremely rare. Had he had issues with his cholesterol? a translator asked. But she couldn't answer, because she didn't know. She knew nothing about Daming's health. Nothing about his family history. Nothing about his past conditions, not even whether he had been well that morning or not. She hadn't even spoken to him before he left for work. What did she know? Nothing.

AFTER THE DEATH was official, his body was given up for medical research. What else could she do? She didn't have the money for a funeral, she could not send him back to his family, the family she had never met. They weren't even married. She could not bring herself to tell her mother that her husband-to-be had died. Between the grief and shock, Lee Lee knew she wouldn't find anybody else. It had been a miracle that she had found Daming, and this shame was like a stone in her mouth that meant she couldn't say the words, *He died, Mama, the man I was going to marry is dead.*

In moments of stark, brutal honesty, days after he died, she had regrets she was ashamed of feeling. He had been sponsored by his workplace, a green card in place. If they had just married sooner, she would have one too. They had not consummated their relationship, there was no child in her womb. Instead, she was left empty, no companion, and her insides began to ache. How could she be the daughter she was expected to be?

The one blessing Daming had passed to her in his untimely death was money. Money that Lee Lee did not know he had while he was alive. He had saved almost thirty thousand dollars, which she found in a box under a broken floorboard in their room. She came upon it by chance when she dropped the coins from her pocket one night after work, and saw it drop through a hole big enough for her fingers to slide in and dislodge the plank. She kept the money under the floorboard just as Daming had, and every night she counted the notes, organizing them by value, into neat perfect piles of hundred-dollar bills, ten-dollar bills, single-dollar bills, all scattered around the room.

Every week, her mother would call and ask, *Any news? The baby?*

She did not care about the marriage, she only cared about a baby. And Lee Lee could not bring herself to say that she was alone again, without hope of finding a future with someone, without the possibility of bringing news of a child to her mother, who wanted nothing more than the family line to continue. So Lee Lee sat alone in this room with her thirty thousand dollars, with her grief.

She searched the internet on the desktop computers at her local library obsessively. *Adoption for undocumented immigrants, fertility treatment for immigrants.*

But every time she came to the cost or the documents required, she was met with a bureaucratic wall so thick and high, blocking her way, that her neck started to ache. It was impossible, no matter how much she saved, or what path she tried to imagine, without a green card. She watched some of the girls from the dorm transformed in high heels and makeup. They walked down the street, a flash of recognition between them. Lee Lee heard later they had married Americans, found boyfriends. She knew she wasn't the type of woman that men looked at. If only Daming was still alive, she would have had her baby. But now, she was just alone.

So instead, every week when she spoke to her mother, she lied. *Not yet Mama. As soon as I have news, I'll tell you. We're building our nest egg.*

Lee Lee took on two jobs, cleaning at night, and then the day shifts clearing the canteen at the airport. She worked and worked and worked. She didn't touch the money under the floor, she only added to it.

She waited, she lived on nothing. She waited and waited. There was never enough for the treatment, or the adoption papers. But her debt was paid.

Her mother still asked, the shame in her voice rising, *Why are you waiting so long? Is it him? What is wrong with you both? Don't you know that this is all that matters in life? A family? To continue our line?*

Lee Lee could not stand to speak to her anymore. Her lies had continued for so long that when she spoke to her mother on the phone, it was as if Daming really *was* alive; she almost believed it herself. In the room, sitting behind her. He was there with her, equally complacent and accountable for their childlessness. A ghost who bore half the weight of this familial duty.

Be patient, Mama, she said, *I know we will have our baby. The time will come.*

CHAPTER TWENTY-EIGHT

Kit

Tokyo, August 2015

Kit was due to leave Tokyo in just a couple of weeks, so Ryo organized a trip for her to Kyoto with a great gang, which ended up being Christian, Amy, and two other friends of Ryo's from high school, Ken and Edward, who Kit barely spoke to. Kit had already visited the giant Buddha in the small seaside town of Kamakura, at Yuriko's insistence. She had gone to a sumo match at Kokugikan Sumo Arena with Ryo, surrounded by passionate, sweaty middle-aged Japanese men shouting at the otherworldly, fleshy fighters wrestling in the ring.

Kit was beside herself with nerves as the overnight trip to Kyoto drew near. Her legs felt wobbly as she boarded the train; she sat quietly and watched the view whooshing past her as she tried not to listen to Ryo and his friends discussing everything they had done that summer. Edward had been having an affair with a married woman, and Ken was working as a photographer's assistant. Her hands shook as she pulled her suitcase to the check-in desk of the hotel. The young man of indistinguishable age with floppy orange-dyed hair kept bowing and apologizing, *Sorry, one more time, please spell*. He had never heard of Philadelphia.

Kit became distracted and self-conscious. She felt the heat of embarrassment rush over her like an unexpected wave and her face became hot and red.

"Everything okay?" Ryo asked, turning away from his friends.

"Yup, all good thanks," she replied through a sigh and wrote out P-H-I-L-A-D-E-L-P-H-I-A on a scrap of paper for the desk worker.

Her room had twin beds, and Kit set her bag in the corner and sat on her bed. She was sharing with Amy, who followed her in, threw her bag on the floor, and immediately lay down, clasped her hands on her stomach, and closed her eyes with a loud sigh.

It was the first time she had seen Amy in a week, but Amy barely spoke to her—or anyone for that matter—on the bullet train from Tokyo. She'd been getting home late and sleeping until the late afternoon, and Kit could see from the dark circles under Yuriko's eyes that she'd been waiting up for her too. Kit wondered who she'd been out with every night.

"Hey, are you okay? You hardly said a word on the train."

"Yeah, I'm just tired. My mom's on my back about college, and guy problems on top of it," she said dismissively, eyes still closed.

Kit had heard Amy and Yuriko arguing the last few nights. Their raised voices vibrated through the walls. They shouted in Japanese, so she didn't know what they said, but felt like she understood as Yuriko's voice trilled with a sharpness she never revealed in company.

"Wanna talk?" Kit asked.

Amy said nothing, and Kit waited until she began to feel awkward.

"Were your parents on your case about college? Like, did you ever consider not going?" Amy finally asked as Kit started to unpack her bag.

"I never considered not going to college. But my parents did get on my case when I wasn't studying hard enough. It's not my bag all the time, you know?"

"What is your bag?" Amy asked.

Kit was surprised, since Amy never asked questions.

"I guess, my friendships, social life. I'm not super academic. My grades are fine, but I'm not very hardworking."

"I know what you mean. Kind of. I'm the same in a way." Amy sighed.

"Are you? Well, what's your bag, Amy? What are you interested in?"

Amy rubbed her eyes with both fists, and Kit saw black kohl smudge across her knuckles.

Amy suddenly laughed. "You know, I don't know why I said that earlier, I actually do okay at school. My grades are good. But I am not interested in going to a fancy college like my brother. I do better than Ryo. I know, you can't believe it, right? And that drives my mom totally crazy."

Kit was stunned by this new information. In her mind, Amy's reckless behavior with older men over the summer had led her to assume that school and grades were not important to Amy.

"Yeah, it drives my mom crazy that I could go to an even better college than my brother and yet I am showing zero interest or willingness. *What about Harvard, Amy-chan? MIT? Oxbridge?* But maybe it just won't suit me, you know? I might just prefer to go straight to work or something. Anyway." She paused and yawned. Kit had to stifle her own impulse to yawn too. "I'm so tired. I'm going to have a little sleep."

Amy sat up and grabbed an eye mask out of her backpack and pulled it over her eyes. Kit sat completely still for a few moments and stared at Amy. In that moment, she just looked like someone who was lost and exhausted. A child who didn't know when she'd reached her limits. Kit recognized it, because she too could be this way.

She stood up and walked quietly to the window that overlooked the city, a vast spread of gray and white low-rise buildings that seemed unremarkable. This was Kyoto? But then as she looked again, beyond the buildings and peppered in between were the ornate tops of shrines and pagodas. She wanted to get out. It was midday, and her stomach grumbled and told her it was time to eat.

She could hear Amy's breathing had slowed and her stomach moved up and down as she slept. She let out a quiet snore. Kit moved slowly toward the door and closed it behind her with a padded click. She walked down the hall and heard Ryo's muffled laugh through the walls. She hovered by his room, changed her mind, and turned to leave as the door suddenly opened.

"Hey, we were just coming for you guys," Ryo said, his hair wet from the shower. He wore the hotel slippers, basketball shorts, and a T-shirt.

"Oh hey, I was going to go out, get some food."

"We're going to get some soba. Come with?" he said, pushing past Christian as he locked the door.

"Where's Amy?" Christian asked.

"Asleep, she seemed tired," Kit said, pinching the neckline of her shirt.

"You guys go ahead," Christian mumbled and disappeared back into the room before they could persuade him to come. Kit looked back as Ryo led her down the stairs and saw that Christian had reemerged from his room and was walking barefoot to her and Amy's room.

Ryo opened the door for her and put his hand around her wrist as he pulled her alongside him. "Where do you want to go first?"

She shrugged, smiled, and let him lead her. She didn't care where they went; she felt as though joy would burst out of her.

They walked in silence down the street, and before the bus arrived, he kissed her hand. There was a strange sphere around her when she was with him; she felt like the world was still and nothing outside this very moment mattered. It was like she was two people. She was always two people—split into two halves that wouldn't fit: one part Kit Herzog, one part the adopted girl. But with Ryo, the two pieces that were always floating apart came together: Philly Kit, and Tokyo Kit. She might be whole.

They walked around the glittering lake surrounding *Kinkakuji* where the golden walls of the temple sparkled over the surface of the pond, and when the sun hit the water and reflections danced against Ryo's face, its impossible beauty rippled through her. She felt as though she weren't actually there, but dreaming. They slurped soba noodles, after they watched the soba master pull and knead and cut and pull and knead and cut in front them, never once getting a speck on his crisp white uniform. They jumped back onto a bus to *Ryoan-ji* and sat on the steps in silence, their knees touching, while they watched tourists walk in and out of the shrine. But the heady silence set off a strange hysteria between them. It started with Kit clumsily tripping over her own feet as she walked to the edge of the garden; she gasped, and her face flushed. Ryo grimaced but his eyes were laughing, and as they looked at each other the silence became bigger. Some of the other tourists tutted, which only gave Ryo an even broader smile. Kit started to shake from the back of her throat down to her stomach, a giggle threatening to escape her mouth. Her eyes began to well up with hot tears of laughter, and Ryo kept his eyes on her, biting his lip, trying to hide his smile. They stood up noisily and rushed out, eliciting disapproving looks.

The day was slowing, the sun falling lower, and there was a pink blanket over the rooftops. The cicadas' humming quietened as they climbed up the hill toward *Kiyomizu-dera*. The stairs to the deck surrounding the main shrine were at a very steep gradient, and went on and on. Her thighs began to burn, but she tried to keep up with Ryo, who skipped two steps at a time. *Show-off.*

They watched the sun go down, and the lights of the city took over from the day. There were two girls, dressed in kimonos, purple and red obis around their waists. She watched the small, delicate steps they took as they tottered carefully over the uneven floorboards. Kit thought of Yuriko at the midsummer party dressed in her *yukata*.

"I don't want to go back," Ryo said suddenly as he leaned over the ledge, keeping his eye on the horizon.

"I know what you mean, it's amazing here." She sighed and let herself lean against his shoulder, emboldened by their day.

"No, I mean, I don't want to go back to the hotel, to everyone, I just want us to have some alone time before we join up with them again. I don't want to think about the fall, about you going back to Philly, about what's coming next. I just want to stay here now, like this."

"Me too."

"I guess Amy probably knows about us by now. I haven't said anything because she seems to be going through one of her moments right now. Unless you already told her."

Kit said nothing and shook her head.

"She can be weird. I love my sister, but I don't always know how she's going to react to things. She can be impulsive, passionate maybe. She'll think I took you away from her or something. Or maybe even that you're taking *me* away from her, when it's our last summer together as a family. You never know, that's the thing about Amy."

"I'm an only child, so I can't really relate."

"Do you wish you had siblings? Do you *feel* like an only child? If that makes sense?"

"I did when I was younger. I envied my friends who had brothers and sisters to play with. But now, I want to do my own thing at home. I'm happy to be solo. I guess the fact that I'm adopted is the thing that makes me feel different. Like when you look at my parents, it's so clear that they're not my biological parents, and I feel like they want to talk about it, but they also really, really don't." Kit didn't understand the boundaries around this subject at all. It was simultaneously a shiny object she wanted to hold so desperately but was also terrified of breaking.

"Yeah, I can see its totally different—being adopted. I couldn't even begin to understand it because I don't have the experience, and never will, not from your side anyway. I'm sorry if that sounded insensitive. I just mean, it's not the biggest thing I see about you. In fact, if you hadn't told me, I wouldn't even know it. It must feel like a big part of you though."

It did.

Ryo continued, "When I met you, I figured you were just another *ha-fu* kid, or something. A third-culture kid, you know what I'm saying, right? My parents never mentioned it either. Dad just said his friend from high school's daughter was coming to stay. "

Kit nodded slowly and tried to imagine how Ryo must have seen her that first day at the party. She remembered again how beyond her own years he had seemed when they first met.

"Do you talk to your parents about *everything?*" she asked.

"Some things, yeah. My dad is pretty good at listening. He gets it. He has a fairly laid-back attitude. My mom can be a little rigid. There is definitely a culture clash at home. But it's mainly Amy culture versus Mom culture."

"I hope you don't mind me saying, but I find your mom super glamorous and inspiring." She felt she was being too earnest, she could hear it in her voice, but she wanted him to know.

"You do? That's a bit weird to hear. But yeah, my mom is cool. To me, anyway. But with Amy, she's kind of explosive. When Mom's conservative Japanese side comes out, Amy seems to do the exact opposite of what my mom wants. They both rile each other up. The more one does one thing, the more the other does the opposite. And it's kind of weird. It shows in a way that they're both kind of cut from the same cloth, you know?"

Kit didn't know. She didn't know at all what kind of cloth she was cut from, really.

⁓

After the trip to Kyoto, Kit's head was full of Ryo and all the things she wanted to do with him. He was the only thing she thought about. She also felt her face flushing a bright pink at unexpected moments as she thought about sex. In fact, the thought of pressing up against him occupied most of the hours of her day. The world around her was telling her to "go on and just do it." The music in the bars on '90s night sang about sex. Shinjuku, with its red flashing lights, where she searched for the best bowl of ramen in the city, was littered with "Love Hotels," rooms hired out by the hour for clandestine lovers to meet. On the way back from Tokyo, she sat beside Amy on the train, rows away from the boys, as she whispered to Kit, full of details about the things she did with Christian while Kit went out with Ryo and his friends.

The more time she spent with Ryo, the more she wanted her relationship with him to move forward, but the Kyoto trip had not given them enough opportunities to be alone. Instead, they spent most of it doing the touristy things that she was meant to do in Japan. Whether it was Ryo who distracted her or not, she had yet to find the Japanese-ness of herself, or whether there was any at all. There were only fourteen days left before she returned to Philadelphia. How many hours did she have left with Ryo before she went home?

A disappointment sank into her stomach when she saw "Mom cell," rather than "Ryo Buchanan" flash up on the screen.

"Hey, Mom," she said quickly, sitting up against the headboard.

"Hey, Sugarlump. How are you? How is it all going over there?"

"Oh fine. Everything's fine. How are you?"

"You know. Same old. It's a hot one. I guess it is there too. I saw on CNN. I've been watching the international news and weather segment since you left."

"Yeah. It's hot. But everyone has air con. Just like at home. Fewer bugs though."

"So tell me what you've been doing."

Kit tried to concentrate, but she wanted to hang up. What if Ryo called?

"Well, I went to Kyoto with the Buchanan kids. And it was really great. Really interesting."

"Oh you did? What are those kids like? And how are Rick and Yuriko?"

"Good. They're good. I dunno. I don't see them all that much. They seem really busy. But they have been really nice to me. I guess I've spoken to Yuriko just a little bit more."

"You have? What do you talk about?"

"What do you mean? Stuff about Japan, I guess, like where I should go sight-see, you know?"

She could hear her mother getting impatient on the phone, holding it back.

"Mom, can I ask you something?"

"Of course, honey, shoot."

"It's about, well, my adoption."

The line was silent. Kit hadn't planned this conversation before she answered the phone. The words started to pour from her mouth before she could scoop them back up.

"It's just, I guess I'm not totally sure what I was expecting to find here. Or how I was expecting to feel."

"I understand. But I'm glad you are having this experience out there. Like you wanted to." Kit could hear her mother's voice slowing down.

Kit said nothing. She wanted her mother to speak again, since she wasn't ready to say what she wanted to say.

"No matter how you feel right now in this moment, to have traveled across the world and experienced a completely new culture is a wonderful thing." Sally's words felt empty to Kit. She felt herself losing her patience.

"So, I'm thinking about getting in touch with my birth mom, or parents, when I get back? I mean, are you open to that?"

The line was silent again, and Kit could only hear her mother breathing.

"Where has this come from, honey?" Sally finally asked.

"Well, I was talking to Amy, you know Rick and Yuriko's daughter. I know it's a closed adoption, but there are ways to get around this stuff. We could get an intermediary, I can appeal for the release of the records. I can contact the agency you adopted me through. Maybe even ask Mr. Buchanan to help, because he has an official role with the government. I don't know." As Kit said this, she felt a momentary pleasure when she said *intermediary*. A week ago, she and Amy had lain side by side to research her rights to finding her birth parents. *My Dad always says, information is power.*

Sally sighed on the other end of the phone.

"Look, we should talk about it all together as a family when you're back. Dad and I will support any decision you make. We always want the best for you. You're about to start college. That's a big deal. You need a clear head, and my reservation is that if you start digging into this *now*, it might just take away from this really important moment in your life. Starting your future. Do you know what I'm trying to say?"

"Sure. But maybe it's because I'm about to start this next stage that I want to figure it out. Like a clean slate, you know? So, Mom, if I want to look into it, you're not going to stand in my way?"

Sally didn't respond.

"Is there something you know about them, about her, that you're not telling me?"

"No, honey, I'm just wary."

"Of what?"

"Wary of what this will bring into your life, what you will gain out of it. I'm just trying to protect you."

Kit said nothing. She wanted to snap back that it was her choice, that it wasn't up to her parents now that she was going to be an adult. She wanted to say that it wasn't fair that her mother was not encouraging her to explore the very essence of who she was. But instead, her throat caught on the words, and she let the tears that started to fall form a wet patch on her T-shirt.

"Let's talk about this properly when you're home. Life isn't always as neat and tidy as the movies."

"So you just assume that it all has to be bad? That I was just unwanted and thrown away? That they were bad people?"

"No, that's not what I said."

"Or do you know that, Mom? And you're just not telling me?"

"We have always been honest with you about how you came to us, Kit. Always."

Kit said nothing. She listened to her mother take deep breaths, and she let the silence continue. The gulf widened between them.

Finally, Kit croaked a response. "I'll call you soon, okay?"

"Are you all right? I'm sorry this conversation has upset you."

"I'm fine, I gotta get ready for dinner. Bye." She hung up before she could hear her mother's response.

Kit cried and cried until the skin on her face felt tight with salty tears and her eyes ached as they opened. Was her mother keeping something from her about her birth mother's identity? What was it about Kit that was so easy to give up? In that moment, she hated everyone who knew exactly where they were from. She envied everybody whose life wasn't peppered with unknowns. She resented Sabrina, and how clear she was on where she was from. Lee Lee had immigrated from China, and that was where Sabrina wanted to travel. Amy, Ryo, and all the other *ha-fu* friends of theirs she had met in Tokyo all knew their origin stories. And Dave, with his born-and-bred-in-Pennsylvania bloodlines. The magnitude of her unknowns felt like the greatest injustice in the world.

A FEW DAYS later Yuriko invited Kit to an *ikebana* class she held for the American-British Society, and to her own surprise, Kit accepted. She watched Yuriko work deftly at the stalks of the flowers on the countertop. The sharp needle points of the *kenzan*, where the flowers and stems were placed to stand them upright, in its dark metallic slate color made a stark contrast to the bright green of the stems.

"Now you try," she said, shifting to the side to allow Kit to move in front of the arrangement.

She tried to carefully push a lily into the base, but it snapped and folded over.

"Oh no." Kit sighed.

Yuriko encouraged her. "Try again," she said, and Kit could feel Yuriko's eyes on her.

Kit picked up another stem; it felt thicker, sturdier. She pressed it carefully into the center of the pad of spikes.

"That's it." Yuriko smiled. "You've got it now."

Kit beamed with pride and stood back to see her creation. It looked sparse and incomplete.

"Is that right?"

"Not yet. But it's a start. Think about what would work with this. Take your time."

When the class was over, Yuriko walked around the room and said goodbye to the ladies who had attended her class. Kit was still lost in the positioning of the stems.

"Why don't you come next week to join the ladies I teach? I have to get ready for my lunch appointment. But Ryo will be back any minute."

"Great idea," said Ryo, who came into the room at that moment. "Hey, Ma, Dad said you're going in like twenty minutes."

"Oh, okay. Bye, Katherine. I'll see you soon. Bye-bye, Ryo-kun." She ruffled her son's hair and left.

She watched as Ryo bent down to examine the *ikebana*.

"This is so lady-who-lunches of you." He smiled and threw a handful of peanuts in his mouth. She could smell the earthy nutty smell in the air.

"I think the ones your mom does are amazing," she said, looking at the finished dish Yuriko had left. A single white flower was sheltered by the perfect curve of a stem of delicate leaves. Her hand hovered over it, without touching it. The intricate balance, the fragile placement, just a change in the wind might topple it over.

"All these bowls of flowers look the same to me," Ryo said, poking a leaf that looked as though it would snap at its stem. Kit drew a quick breath, willing it not to fall or snap.

"This is the one I made." She walked toward her stand and he followed.

"You're an *ikebana* protégée now! God, Mom has been trying to lure Amy into this stuff for years."

"Where is Amy?" Kit asked, looking back through the door as she listened to the clip-clopping sound of Yuriko's heels walking across the entrance hall.

He pulled her up the stairs.

"Out with some friends."

He began to kiss her at the top of the landing and she pulled away.

"Let's go to your room?" she asked.

He suddenly became more hesitant, pausing before his doorway, asking a silent question: *Are you sure?*

She nodded and pressed on, closing the door behind them. They fumbled their clothes off in his immaculate room. Kit took her own T-shirt off, proud of the tan lines from her bikini on her chest. He ran his lips along her collarbone and the hair on her arms stood up.

He asked her aloud this time, breathless. "We don't have to. We can wait."

She said, "No, we can't."

CHAPTER TWENTY-NINE

Mimi

Philadelphia, August 2015

Mimi never told Toan about the list. She sat in the Dunkin' Donuts on Walnut Street and stared at the faded yellow legal pad paper that Madame New Zealand had started for her. She had traced over the writing so many times to prevent the names from fading. *A place to start*, she had called it. Mimi never forgot her kindness, the days she had spent at her computer searching public records and newspapers in Philadelphia for the names of adopted Asian girls who would have been Ngan's age.

All of this would have terrified Toan, whose only real motives in life were to keep Mimi safe and his belly full. There was safety for Toan in knowing there was an endless expanse of a country that she would never get to. He thought it would protect her from more pain.

There were hurdles at every turn: her funds were limited, her time was limited, and there were many dead ends. Mimi could not tell Toan about the seven names she had already crossed off her list. She could not tell him about the woman at the Social Services office who shouted at her through the glass barrier, "You gotta learn to speak properly. I don't understand what you're saying."

Nor the terrible cold she caught standing in the rain watching the house of the fifth girl on the list to see if she might recognize Ngan's face. She worked through cold sweats in her madame's basement the following day as she cleared out the cobwebs for their new wine cellar installation.

She wondered what Toan would say about the third name on the list, Rachel Wu. She was listed in the *Philadelphia Inquirer* as an adopted Asian American, thought to be of Vietnamese descent, who had been named "Young Musician of the Year" in 2010. Mimi spent her third week's wages on a ticket to see her perform at the Kimmel Center. She had never been to a concert. The stage was made of mahogany wood and encircled by red velvet chairs. People looked down from tiers that were built up like a stairway. Mimi sat at the back but had a clear view of all the performers. There was only the echo of shuffling paper, programs that were being put away as the huge hall fell silent. A woman with hair so black it was almost blue, tied away from her face in an unforgiving bun that pulled on her hairline, walked onto the stage.

The woman, Rachel Wu, swept her skirt back and nestled a cello between her knees. It rested against her neck and shoulder like she was cradling a child to sleep in her arms. Her slim fingers pressed against the neck of the instrument, and she drew her right arm up before she closed her eyes and began to move bow against strings. As the deep comforting notes rose to her ears, they reached every part of Mimi's body. A tingling ran through her veins, and the hairs on her arms stood up, her skin pimpling as the melody rose and fell. But the deeper notes sank into the deepest part of Mimi, where she had buried her happiness so many years ago, stirring it up. In that moment, the sadness that had eaten away at her faded. She no longer languished. It all became immaterial for the two and a half minutes of music. Hope had sprung again, and it was Rachel Wu who had given it to her. Thousands of tears had run down Mimi's shirt, and she felt a smile beaming from her face. This was not Ngan; no, she was too old, at least ten years older than her girl would have been. But Mimi never regretted the week's pay nor the time she spent traveling to and from the Kimmel Center that day. When the lights went up and the last person had left her section, she stared down at the empty orchestra seats as the lighting staff started to pull lengthy black wires into neat loops around their arms. She found a program on a chair beside her, folded it in half, and slipped it into her bag. The music she had heard that day was Bach's Cello Suite No. 1 in G Major, and she searched for the song on her cell phone as she walked out of the concert hall.

Once she returned home, she sat on the small bed that Madame America had bought her. She placed her headphones in her ears and listened to the opening notes of the piece. If she closed her eyes, she could feel the swift wind of the ocean envelop her. The cello suite began with her careful steps in the sand, her feet sinking deeper than she expected. The sun glistened over the water, and the sea air rushed through her lungs. She felt the heat on her hair and skin. And there was another gust of wind against her body. She started to walk faster, the sand hardened beneath her feet, and the waves kissed her toes. The notes rose and rose as the water rushed over her feet. Each note of the cello's deep baritone pushed her forward, and she felt the occasional splash of salt water on her lips. The waves and music began to resonate in unison, the burst of crashing water, a surprise between the rise and fall of the melody.

The music was every good moment she'd encountered in her life, the moment she held her daughter in her arms, the moment Toan had kissed her, the first mouthful of her mother's cooking when she had returned home, the lovers she wished to forget and remember, her sister, her father, the enemies she saw off . . . it was everything that had happened that made her heart soar in that piece of music. She felt the beauty in life again in the brief two and a half minutes as the music played.

Mimi fell asleep that night with her clothes on. The following morning, she woke before the house began to stir, unfolded the yellow legal note paper, and carefully crossed out Rachel Wu's name. There were just three names left on her list. Amy Tang in Bryn Mawr. Jennifer Thanh in Fort Washington. Katherine Herzog in Chestnut Hill.

Act
Four

CHAPTER THIRTY

Sabrina

Philadelphia, August 2015

They were halfway through the film, and Dave didn't seem to notice their knees touching. Sabrina wanted to move. Her leg had started to tingle, and her back ached, but if she moved, they would no longer be touching. Even worse, he might notice that she hadn't moved, that she had stayed there.

"So . . . Kit gets back this week?" Dave asked, throwing a handful of popcorn into his mouth.

Heat flushed through her chest and face. He hadn't asked about Kit for weeks.

"Yeah, I think she gets back like tomorrow or the day after."

"Did you hear from her while she was away?" He glanced at her for a moment, then went back to watching the movie, a car chase through a shipping dock screeched on the screen.

"A few messages, yeah. You?"

Dave passed her the bowl of popcorn, and Sabrina took a handful.

"Nah, we didn't keep in touch."

"Did you want to?"

"I'm good," he said. She could tell he was lying. Sabrina could always tell when people lied. Kit had obvious tells. Dave, less so. She noticed he scratched the back of his head when he was uncomfortable with the topic. She watched him rub the crown of his head.

When the film ended and the credits rolled, Dave jumped off the sofa fast enough that he may have not noticed that their knees had been touching at all.

"So, do you want to go out this weekend? I think some of my friends are having a party over in Ambler. One of the big houses. You know the ones I mean? The McMansions? My mom hates them. Says they're new money."

"Whose party is it? I mean, am I invited?"

"Sure you're invited. We can just go together," Dave said as he threw the small basketball through the hoop and missed.

Sabrina knew it didn't occur to Dave that an official invitation felt necessary to her. Sabrina also knew that Dave would know what to wear, when to arrive, and what to bring to a party like this. She didn't. Kit had sometimes gone out, especially when her other Chestnut Hill friends would invite her, but Sabrina's mother had always been strict about curfews. She had accepted, without question, that this was a part of high school she simply wouldn't experience.

"Okay."

"So how about I pick you up at your place?"

Sabrina stared at Dave for a moment. Her thoughts rushed through her head, pushing one after the next out. *No, that won't work. No, he won't believe me. But then I can't turn up alone.*

"Manayunk, right?"

"Yeah."

Sabrina walked slowly up the stairs behind Dave and heard him greet

Jona at the top of the stairs. "Oh, hey, Jona. Don't worry, I can turn everything off. See you in the morning."

"Hey, if Kit is back by this weekend, you want me to ask her to come to the party?" Sabrina asked, squeezing her foot into her Vans.

"I don't know. I feel like it's our thing. Maybe the next one," he said as he opened the door for her. "So I'll see ya on Saturday. Call you before." He stood at the entrance to watch her walk down the street. He always did, and she wondered whether it was something he did for Kit too.

~⚬~

Sabrina's first high school party was also her last. Stuart McKluskie's house in Ambler was the biggest home she had ever stepped foot in. The driveway was vast, and the lawn out front that hugged it seemingly had no purpose at all, but it was bigger than the entire square footage of her house. She looked at familiar faces from high school, most of whom glanced at her and showed no recognition in return. There were Jeeps parked in the driveway, music blasting from the house, with the doors wide open. In the distance she saw other houses that looked either abandoned or closed up for the summer.

"Stuart doesn't have neighbors?" Sabrina asked, skipping to keep up with Dave.

"Think they're away for the summer."

Sabrina questioned herself. Was he walking fast because he didn't want to be seen with her?

"Is that what rich people do? Close up their whole house for the summer? Just switch from one to another? Kit and her parents were always down the shore for the whole summer."

Dave didn't answer.

They walked into the kitchen, and she saw his group of friends standing at the marble kitchen island setting up a triangle of red cups. There were bottles everywhere around the sink, several of which were on their sides, the sticky liquid already staining the white tops. Pizza boxes lay stacked on the floor in the corner where she imagined the trash was hidden inside the kitchen unit. Who was going to clean up in the morning? Sabrina imagined Stuart McKluskie's mom had a team of girls to help in the house.

Beyond the kitchen and into the open-plan living room area was a huge double-height window that looked out at the yard. In the middle of the enormous lawn was a swimming pool where people were jumping into the water. A seating area with a mounted TV was blasting a ball game. There was a fully stocked bar in the corner and a barbecue with a huge dining table outside as well. Sabrina tried to imagine what a family dinner looked like. How Stuart must have felt, walking into a home like this every day. It was the same displaced feeling she had at Dave's house, and to an extent Kit's too. She fiddled with the waistline of her shorts and pulled at the T-shirt she had tucked into them. She wished she had worn something else.

Stuart greeted Dave with a high five and looked beyond him at Sabrina. She saw his eyes take her in and look back at Dave, tilt his head and raise his brows in question.

"This is unexpected," he said.

Sabrina didn't know Stuart well enough to read the exact undertone of what he said.

"Hey, thanks for letting me come along," she said, forcing a smile that did not hide her deep fear that she would be asked to leave.

"Sure, open house! Let me get you guys a drink." Stuart knocked his shoulder into Dave's and Sabrina saw something had sparked between the two boys. She looked away and watched the silhouettes in the house writhing and jumping to the deep bass that blasted out of the built-in speakers.

She wanted to tell Dave that this house was like a castle, but she knew better. Stuart passed her a drink and she held it in both hands. A girl she vaguely recognized from her drama class jumped into the swimming pool fully clothed, and Sabrina decided in that moment she wouldn't drink that night.

SABRINA HAD GONE to the bathroom in the pool house, which took much longer than she had expected because of a long line. By the time she came back, Dave had started a fight with Stuart. She couldn't hear what they said to each other over the music, but she saw spittle fly from Dave's mouth as his face colored red. She tried to get to the front of the crowd gathering around them. In that moment, everything started to slow down, and she watched with horror as Stuart pulled his freckled arm and fist back and lunged toward Dave's beautiful face. She didn't know what they fought over, nor what could even make Dave so angry. He was always so placid and kind.

A bright stream of blood trickled down Dave's nose. He wiped it away with his arm, and now the red streak was spread over his pale blue shirt. He took a swing, hitting Stuart in the face. Sabrina watched his head swerve back and pink spit fly out of his mouth. She tried to shout for him to stop, but her voice was padded down by noise from the crowd gathered around them. Some cheered, some shouted loud *oooohs*. She called his name again, but he didn't look back at her. Finally, two boys broke them up after what felt like a never-ending fight. Dave had taken three more punches, including one in the ribs, and Stuart had blood pouring from both nostrils. Dave shook himself free and rushed out of the room.

Sabrina tried to follow him, angling herself sideways to squeeze past the sweaty bodies, but a crowd blocked her way. She watched Dave walk out the front door and tried to keep her eye on him as his figure moved further away from her into the dark night.

She finally made it outside and ran down the driveway to find Dave opening his car door.

Was he about to leave without her?

He turned back, looked at Sabrina, and gestured with his head for her to get in. Relief swept over her. He was waiting for her.

"Let's go."

Her happiness was mixed with a tinge of shame. That she was there, alone with him again. He had chosen her. They drove through the dark back roads of Lower Gwynedd.

"Hey, have I still got that liquor bottle behind your seat? I took it from my dad's bar."

"Your dad has a bar?" Sabrina asked and regretted it immediately.

"You can pour some coke into the bottle, it won't be so gross if we drink it mixed."

Sabrina put the bottle between her knees and patiently tapped the top of the Coke can.

"What are you doing? Just open it," he snapped.

Sabrina paused.

"We're not drinking this now. You're not drinking this now. You're driving."

"I know that, Sabrina, I just want a drink when we stop, all right?" His breathing was heavy.

"Are we not going to talk about what happened back there?" Sabrina asked while carefully examining the bottle to determine how much was left.

"Why do we need to?"

"Because you're upset. You just got into a fight."

He didn't say anything. He drove with his jaw set tight and stared ahead at the road. When they stopped at a light, he was silent, and she waited until he was ready to speak.

"Well, we're not going to drink tonight on top of everything else," she finally said. She regretted it the instant it came out of her mouth, knowing he would be angry with her.

"God, Sabrina, come on. I just want to get back to the city and blow off some steam. I got into a stupid fight over you and I want a drink. Are you with me or not?"

Over her? She hadn't seen the argument. Only the punching. Was it that Dave had shown up to the party with the janitor's kid? The Chinese dork? Sabrina said nothing. She didn't want to know.

"You got into a fight over me?" she finally asked. She had always hated Stuart, but Dave Harrison had punched him in her defense. The insult didn't sting as much knowing this part.

"He's a dumbass and said something about you. I couldn't stand it. I lost my temper. He deserved it. Are you happy now? We discussed it. Now are you going to hang with me or you want me to drop you home?" he asked, but he already knew the answer, because Sabrina had already screwed the top back on securely.

"I'm not going to drink with you, if that's what you mean."

"Rina," he pleaded and glanced at her but turned quickly back to the road.

"No, Dave. It's not happening. But I will hang with you. I don't think you need to drink either to be totally honest. You're high on life already." She smiled. He sighed heavily.

"This has been a real crappy night."

"Yeah, and it will get crappier if you wake up with a huge hangover after drinking some, what is this anyway?" *Crappier.* The word felt strange in her mouth. She raised the bottle to examine it. "Vermouth? You were going to get crazy drunk on vermouth?"

"I don't know."

Dave shook his head and started to laugh. She looked at his knuckles, which were red and swollen from the fight.

"You want some ice from the store? We can stop?"

"No, let's just keep driving."

The radio started to play a song she liked. She mouthed the words and repeated the song over and over.

"I love this song," she said and turned the volume up. It was an old Hootie & the Blowfish song. She knew, like Eva Kim knew, that sometimes people didn't want to talk about the biggest thing when the smallest thing would do. The biggest thing and smallest thing could exist side by side.

Dave listened, and as the song faded, he laughed again.

"What?"

"Nothing, it's just such an old song."

"I love old songs." She leaned back and closed her eyes.

"You're something," he said. "I've never met anyone like you before, Rina." Then he opened up Spotify on his iPhone, and they listened to the song again.

Rina, she whispered in her head to herself, and her heart soared up to the sky, wings flapping hard, pushing to heights it had never known until now. *Rina.*

CHAPTER THIRTY-ONE

Kit

Tokyo, August 2015

Kit had talked to Sabrina once about how love was thinking of that person the moment you woke and last thing at night.

"Yeah but if that's really true, then that means that I love Mr. Hargreaves and this assignment on Thomas Hardy more than anything in the world, so there is no real science behind that." Sabrina had laughed.

SHE DID WAKE and think of Ryo first thing, and every other moment she spent with him and away from him. When she lay beside him in his bed when everyone in the household was out, she loved to listen to Ryo's breathing as he slept. His back went up and down slowly with every inhale and exhale, the fine, almost invisible hairs on his shoulders, golden from the sun. She looked around his room, the shelves with trophies, and walls with no pictures.

In a week she would be home. Back to walking along Germantown

Avenue to the ice cream parlor with Sabrina. They might drive down to the shore for a weekend, or watch the sun go down from her treehouse as they talked into the darkness. Soon, the summer would be over and college would start. She wouldn't know anyone—not really. A blank slate.

She wondered what Sabrina was doing. It had been over a week now since they had exchanged messages. She couldn't remember the last time so many days had passed without contact with her best friend. Her imagination wandered further and further away from Ryo, like smoke that curled up from a forgotten burning cigar.

Five days before Kit left Tokyo, she sat with Ryo at the dining table; the whole family was out and Linda was at the store. Their legs were entwined under the table.

Kit rubbed a swollen mosquito bite on her leg and scratched at the top with her index finger. It had begun to bleed.

"What have you done there?" Ryo asked. He folded a napkin from the center of the table and pressed it on her leg. His hand was dry and cool. They looked like the napkins her mother bought for parties or at Christmas.

"So when will I see you after you leave?" He didn't look at her as he asked.

"I don't know. I mean, will you head out to the East Coast at all? I do go out west sometimes too. And our parents are friends, so . . ."

"Here's a thought. Just something that came to me last night. Should I come out before the fall? Check out Penn? Keep my options open? There are some good schools out east, right? A transfer isn't impossible."

She didn't respond to him. She was afraid of how her voice might croak, giving away the feelings that surged inside her, feelings she couldn't quite name. Her heart was expanding, with the reassurance of love returned, rather than the contraction she always felt with Dave.

"Wow. I guess I should be offended." He sighed. His neck started to color.

"No, no, no." She grabbed his hand and squeezed it hard. "I just didn't want to talk about what happens next."

"Why not?"

"Because I didn't know how you felt, and well, this . . . I assumed was a summer fling. Not your first or last."

He laughed. She waited for a response, hoping for an answer.

"This is different."

She giggled awkwardly and regretted it when she saw the flicker of hurt cross his face.

"It's understandable you're laughing at me. But really—I wouldn't consider such a huge thing like changing my college choice if I didn't feel like we had something really special." Something close to pleading passed through his face. Then it disappeared.

"But what if . . . what if this doesn't last? What are your parents going to say? And then you've moved to another college and city and your plans have changed for something that didn't work out."

"I'm not making any big moves yet. I'm just looking at options, and transferring is one of them. How do we know if we don't give something a try?"

Two DAYS LATER, Ryo told his father during a squash game that he wanted to visit Penn before the fall, in case he wanted to transfer. When Kit walked into the dining room that night, Rick neither smiled nor frowned but sat at the head of the table and glanced at her before returning his gaze to his son. Yuriko scrolled through her phone to look up university rankings, and Amy's expression was surly. Ryo looked at Kit and smiled, nodding his head toward the empty seat beside him, but her feet were welded to the ground.

"I can't believe you're just going to transfer like that. You can't. It's not that easy," Amy snapped.

"Actually, it *is* pretty easy. I mean, I have checked and there really isn't a payout as long as I transfer within the minimum time frame, and if I release the spot within the first semester, it won't cost us much. Providing I get a place at Penn, of course. The programs at Penn are really fantastic, and some would even argue that it's a better university for my interests."

Rick nodded, taking in his son's announcement. Kit wondered if this was worse than him shouting. Kit's father had never been the disciplinarian. Instead, he disappeared when conflict threatened. Rick struck her as a different type of father altogether. As she sat at their family table, she could hear the sound of Linda through the doors washing dishes, and she wanted to escape into the kitchen with her. Kit suspected Ryo's father gave the impression of calm and safety but that he might later snap in a single movement.

"Why Penn, Ryo? You've never mentioned it before. The only East Coast colleges you were interested in were Harvard and Columbia. Is it because you two are . . ." Rick looked at Kit for a moment and nodded toward her.

Amy stared at her father, reeling him in.

"I've been thinking all summer. And it's the one that has some of the programs I'm really interested in. And the business majors are great too."

"Katherine, my dear, would you mind terribly just letting us have a moment?" This time Rick looked at her again and Kit felt herself want to shrink into her chair. His eyes were cold.

"Oh, of course, yes, I'll head up. I'm sorry," Kit said, pushing her chair back loudly and cringing at the thought of the scratch it might leave on the wooden floors. At the same time she thought, *I want to go home.*

"No, don't. Stay." Ryo grabbed her hand. Kit looked at him, pleading for him to let her go. "I told Dad earlier this afternoon and we just told Mom and Amy." She felt his grip loosen over her hand.

"You need to talk this out with your family. I'll see you tomorrow," she said quietly. Rick forced a stiff smile and nodded.

"Thank you for understanding." Kit smiled uncomfortably, and quickly fled the room. She couldn't make out what Rick was saying as he spoke to his son in a hushed voice.

"ARE YOU GUYS serious right now?" Amy's voice carried down the hall, however, as she slammed her fists onto the table. The glasses rattled.

Kit could hear their voices rising as she climbed the stairs. Ryo talked calmly to his father. He argued his point, with no edge of frenzied emotion to his voice.

"You're just going to throw away your place at Berkeley for *her?*" Amy's voice traveled up the stairs again.

The truth was, Ryo *wasn't* throwing away his place for her, but he wanted it to be an option. Kit knew this about him, he liked to have choices. And it was easier for Kit to accept this than to think he was turning his life upside down just for her. That would have been too much, even for her.

This was the difference between them. Ryo Buchanan, she was starting to realize, took chances because most of the time, or *all* the time, things worked out for him. For Kit, the path to the next day was more muddled. It never occurred to her that she might sail effortlessly, with perfect winds and conditions, through the waters. To Kit, risks meant a borderlessness she had feared her whole life. This wasn't her mother's interpretation of boundaries—Kit often heard her mother say to her father, "Kit's the kind of child who needs firm boundaries"—this was about limits she could set for her own abilities, for how far she was willing to travel, how far she was willing to look beyond the safety of the only home she knew.

But she hadn't found a place where she felt she belonged yet, nor had she really found the courage to venture out by herself. Not really. Even here, everywhere she looked, she had the soft, safe padding of her mother's arrangements. Sometimes it brought a profound fatigue and melancholy, a longing for a life she ought to have the nerve to live.

For Ryo, it was different. As far as Ryo Buchanan was concerned, everything was for the taking. Privilege did that, being *ha-fu* in Japan did that, and having a father who was an ambassador did that. He didn't have to stay within the confines of a small world he had grown up in, because he had already broken out of it *while* he was growing up. He'd already joined the wider world.

⁂

The following day, Rick and Yuriko called Sally from their bedroom, not knowing that Kit stood outside Ryo's bedroom door and listened to her mother's voice on speakerphone.

"We have some concerns," Rick said.

Kit knew that this was the type of phrase that would send her mother into a frenzy. She swallowed, a mixed lump of relief and fear. Rick was managing her mother.

"Can you even hear anything?" Ryo whispered to Kit from the bed.

"Ryo and Kit, it seems, well Ryo has decided he wants to visit some colleges on the East Coast, with the possibility of transferring. I don't know exactly how much of it will actually happen . . . he made all the changes himself and looks like he wants to visit before September. So we may be coming to Pennsylvania."

Kit could hear her mother's silence. It lasted too long to put up any pretense of happiness at this news.

"I think it's because of this relationship they've begun. I am a little concerned, but I'm trying to avoid placing any firm brakes in case things just fade out."

Kit didn't look at Ryo as she heard this. He was on his computer looking something up. She felt affronted at the parents' lack of belief in their blossoming love. But somewhere in the deep recesses of Kit's mind, she was also terrified of what this would do to her carefully laid plans for college. She was grateful to Rick Buchanan for delivering the news of Ryo's interest in transferring instead of having to tell Sally herself. It saved Kit from another argument with her. She also knew that her mother would be afraid of losing control.

While Sally and Rick continued to make arrangements, Kit started to think about looking for her birth mother, and how Sally would deal with the news of Ryo transferring, and the cocoon of safety on Gravers Lane started to feel like it was made of fragile, thin glass. A little mishandling could leave her whole life shattered on the floor. Kit had built a fence around her story and the parts she didn't want to explore or discuss, and she was starting to realize how the people in her life—her parents, Sabrina—respected it. Kit realized that she wasn't so sure she wanted to know, even though all this time she had acted as though she did. Because she would lose control. The truth was, she was always going to be different, unlike Ryo, Amy, Sabrina, or any of the other children she had grown up with in Chestnut Hill. She would always have her origin story, whatever that was.

CHAPTER THIRTY-TWO

Mimi

Philadelphia, August 2015

To Mimi, Ngan was always Ngan, her Vietnamese child. The fact that her daughter was most likely to be American still unsettled her in ways she couldn't fathom. Ngan probably spoke like all these white people who dismissed her, chewed their words at the end. Perhaps Ngan would even dismiss her were they to come face-to-face—a thought Mimi pushed away immediately.

Mimi read the article again from the local newspaper in a Philadelphia suburb, a review of a high school theater production and a girl from Chestnut Hill. Could it be her Ngan? Who had written this article? Mimi's hope was sparking inside of her again. A faint flame was trying to attach itself to kindling. Why would it be her? Why here? She tried to manage her expectations. Mimi swirled the thoughts around her mouth, a foreign liquid she'd not tasted in years, bringing back a tidal wave of memories. She knew this taste.

If Mimi had learned anything from life so far, it was that inexplicable things happened. Coincidences that could not be blamed on anything that existed within the realms of science—good and bad. Her mother had died the very same day Ngan was born, an impossible tying of loose ends that she had no real hand in. These lives that had meant everything to her came full circle in a neat symphony, but in truth, it was just a huge coincidence.

She pulled out the worn, faded photograph of Ngan as a baby and placed it neatly beside the old newspaper article that Madame New Zealand had printed out for her all those years ago. Mimi had carefully preserved it in a manila envelope. Once she came face-to-face with her own child, no matter how long they'd been apart, she would recognize her, wouldn't she? A mother was sure. Those beautiful dark brown eyes she remembered when her daughter had cried for something. How could she forget? It was still the same memory, the same image she cherished, but sometimes her mind would wander, and she would question how well she could recall *all* the details. So many years had passed, and she had lost the privilege of holding her daughter, of watching her grow. A mother's memory of seeing her run for the first time, hearing her mimic a phrase that sounded impossibly grown up, watching her tie her shoes, brush her hair, hold back tears from a sudden self-consciousness that set in. This was what it was to be a mother, after all—to see your child's transformation, to hold her beside you, and stare at her in the wilderness as she grew into a full-length shadow that came to life, becoming her own living being, slowly separating from her mother—and no matter how hard you grasped at her, she evaded you, was running to the next thing while you faded into the background. Only for Mimi, she never had her moment in the foreground, at least not long enough to bear any significance. This was a thought she couldn't seem to push from her mind. No matter how much she reached out to touch her daughter, she was out of reach. Because her child was gone.

—⁓—

It had taken Mimi almost two hours to get to Chestnut Hill. The train routes had been canceled as it was a Sunday, and she had to change buses twice. She looked out the window as they drove up the winding road along the river, restaurants on boats that must have been lit up with lights at night, but she only saw the empty ramps that led on and off the road. She stared out at the stairwell and sandy warm stones that made up the Philadelphia Museum of Art. She wondered whether Ngan had ever stepped foot in there. Westerners always talked about museums, and she wondered whether she would ever go there herself, maybe one day, with Ngan. Once she left the city, the bus tumbled along the potholed roads that led up to North Philadelphia. The buildings were lower, the houses boarded up. Mimi glanced at an upstairs window and her eyes met an older Black woman's staring back at her, her face weathered with lines, the kind of brow that was permanently knotted.

And just like a dream, suddenly the bumps were from the cobbled streets of British architecture instead of forgotten roads, and the gentrified main street of Mount Airy began. There were more trees with branches full of lush green leaves. A chalkboard outside a fancy deli read "Try our signature wine cooler for the dog days of summer" in an elaborate curly cursive script. Fairy lights were strung among the branches of the trees, and Mimi tried to imagine what it might look like at night.

Mimi stepped off the bus outside the Chestnut Hill Coffee Co. and breathed in the scent of roasted beans, knowing the taste would only disappoint her. A fleeting image of Saigon came to her. It was too quiet here. There was no deafening assault of motorbike horns or angry shouts between hawkers and rooster crows. There was only the sound of children chattering to their parents, churchgoers walking down the street, and cars silently driving past.

MIMI PULLED OUT the newspaper article she had carefully folded and tucked into her wallet. The folds were so old now that some of the writing had faded away into the creases.

> Katherine Herzog is a junior high schooler at Chestnut Hill Academy, starring in their Winter Showcase of Jane Austen's *Sense and Sensibility*. She plays Lucy Steele, the love rival to the main character, Elinor Dashwood. Katherine's performance is a refreshing interpretation of a traditionally unlikable character—but her charisma on stage leaves the audience torn over who to root for. The *Chestnut Hill Inquirer* has its eyes on this rising star, who is sure to be doing great things in her future . . . onstage and off.

"Excuse me, ma'am," a woman's voice interrupted Mimi, and she stepped out of her way quickly. She could have been the same age as Mimi. She had thin strawberry-blond hair tied up in a ponytail. There was a slow, deliberate pace in how this woman walked, and as Mimi stood beneath the shade of the awning by the hardware store, she realized that everyone around here carried themselves with the same unhurried, languid comfort. The sun was shining, and the smell of fried onions occasionally escaped the Tavern a few yards away. She could hear the leaves rustling as the breeze pushed along the avenue. Two men dressed in polo shirts turned up at the collar and shorts and sneakers talked and laughed. A silent wealth pervaded the air here. It did not smell this way in most of Center City Philadelphia or New Jersey except for Essex County, where her Madame America lived. She waited for the light to change at the pedestrian crossing and saw a group of teenagers sitting on a bench outside a frozen yogurt store. They could have been Ngan's age. The two boys had broad shoulders and floppy hair, and the girls wore denim shorts and high-top sneakers. The girls' hair swayed with the breeze, so much hair hanging carefree down their backs. Mimi had never had that type of hair. It was always short, sensible, and thin. Could they be friends with her Ngan? She thought about how Ngan's hair might be. Was it like her own or thick and glossy like these American girls'?

Mimi took out her map. She had scribbled down the address on the back. A sweat patch formed under her sweatshirt as the sun bore down on her. She picked up her pace. It was already afternoon, and she had to be back in Essex County by nightfall.

The pavement on Gravers Lane was uneven. She counted the house numbers on her left and saw that she would soon be at 51. She stood opposite the house and looked at the driveway through the open gate. The house was old, with a grandeur that shouted out at her *We have money, don't forget to wipe your feet.* It was a different type of money from Madame America's, whose house was full of small, expensive decorative objects. A menagerie of things Mimi always feared she might break, the cost of which would come off her monthly paycheck.

This house was sure of itself. It didn't need ornaments; its stature was enough. The garden was full of blooming flowers, heading toward the end of their summer glory. A hydrangea bush heavy with blue flowers bounced in the breeze near the front door. She looked through the painted fence around the huge garden; it was a garden that was loved and cared for. She saw a swing under a vast thick tree and a metal spiral staircase leading up to a treehouse. Fairy lights hung in the branches, now abandoned, and an old weathered bucket on a rope. Mimi tried to imagine her, a girl giddy with excitement in this secret hideout with her friends. She tried to imagine the house at night, lights on in the windows, the family meals, the bed she slept in, and the couch she sat on. The gravel started to crunch as a car came down the driveway, and Mimi began to walk away. She kept walking past the house and the next house until she reached the bus stop. Five buses passed. She sat and felt a stain of sadness spread its way into her chest, a new sorrow she hadn't known until now. Could this be her Ngan? If it was her child, had her daughter had a happy life without her? A happier life than she might have lived in Saigon with almost nothing, but with her real mother? What then?

CHAPTER THIRTY-THREE

Sabrina

Mount Airy, August 2015

D ave always wanted to meet in the same place, at Snak's Coffee House toward Mount Airy. Sabrina learned that he liked to know what was coming—Dave didn't like surprises. Sometimes Sabrina would suggest they try a place she read about downtown, in a different neighborhood, but he liked this one and always sat at the same table, which was, in Sabrina's opinion, too close to the bathrooms.

Snak's was usually full, except for a brief time between two and three in the afternoon. A line of regulars who she started to recognize chatted among themselves. The loaves of bread behind the counter were displayed with proud precision, and she would stare at the shiny gleam over the cinnamon buns. A wiry Australian man sometimes served her, and wore a lopsided name tag that read *Matt*. He joked with her sometimes, but Sabrina had felt awkward talking to him. She stopped standing by the counter where he served the baked goods. Eventually, he made a tight, unfriendly smile, and she returned it before heading through the coffee shop to find Dave.

He sat in his usual spot, his back to the front windows and doors of the café, hunched over a book, the remains of a croissant on his plate. Dave liked to fold his napkin and tuck it underneath the side of his plate. She liked this. When she was in kindergarten and right the way up to second grade, she had hated the way Kit scrunched up her napkin, grabbing it with her messy fingers when she ate. The stains stared back at Sabrina, and she wondered how this ever cleaned anything. Sabrina wanted to fold the napkin neatly and pass it back to Kit.

She pushed the seat in front of Dave with her foot and put her bag on the floor. The thud announced her arrival, and he looked up.

"Hey, I'm sorry I'm late."

"You're fine." Dave made a half smile. Was it fine? Was *he* fine? She was still learning about him. And thanks to his mother, Sabrina had come to learn a great deal about Dave in the weeks they had spent together so far.

Mrs. Harrison liked to remind everyone, including Sabrina, that Dave was born in New York. The Harrisons had moved to Philadelphia soon after the boys were born.

They looked like the perfect family, but Dave hated his brother, Brad, though he never said those exact words. Sabrina knew this about him. A part of Dave judged his brother because popularity and athleticism were enough for him. Sabrina knew this about Dave because she felt the same way when she tried to imagine what it would have been like to be Dave. This was something she did for everyone she cared for: to imagine how their clothes would feel, how they felt walking into a room, how they slept at night, and what made them smile from the inside out. So Sabrina could guess how Dave saw his brother. Some would have put it down to sibling rivalry, jealousy from the less popular, less boisterous brother. But Sabrina did know how this felt, because every day since she had known Kit, she was the lesser one. But now, the inequality between them no longer seemed so vast. Sometimes, she felt an overwhelming swell of joy, knowing that there were some heights Kit would never reach. And one of them was knowing Dave the way she knew him. Kit probably didn't know that Dave only read physical books. That he loved Hemingway and daydreamed of going to Les Deux Magots in Paris to write all day and drink red wine from a carafe. That he daydreamed about what he would do with his life when he finally got to leave Philadelphia. Sabrina knew that Dave hated milk and would never have any in his coffee or tea, that his favorite show was still *The Sopranos,* and his favorite character was actually Carmela Soprano and not Tony or any of the mob. She knew he had been in therapy for most of his high school life since he found his grandfather dead in the hallway one summer at the end of middle school. And that he preferred his father to his mother, but actually, he had loved his grandfather most. She knew him so well that she protected all of this as though it were the most tiny precious quail's egg in her palm, and she wanted to keep it from everyone.

The other thing she loved about Dave was that he asked her the best questions.

What's the most embarrassing account you follow on Instagram?

Would you rather be eaten by a snake or a great white shark?

What would you buy Billie Eilish for her birthday? Dave knew she loved Billie Eilish.

What is the best Prince song of all time? "Purple Rain"?

Are you a good gift giver?

What's your death row meal?

Would you rather own five snoring pugs or three yappy Jack Russell terriers?

She watched him swirl the coffee in his cup. The black liquid had left a stain halfway down the cup, and she knew he'd already been there for some time.

"What's up? No tennis today?"

"Nah, wasn't feeling it. How was your day?"

This was another thing she noticed about Dave. He really listened. He didn't ask questions with the motive of answering them himself the way Kit did.

"It was fine, regular."

"A regular Sabrina Chen day." He smiled.

"So I've been thinking . . ."

"Uh-oh . . ."

"Yeah, I've been thinking maybe I need to tell Kit we've been hanging out. When I see her, you know?"

Dave didn't move, but his expression changed for a millisecond around the eyes.

"I don't think she's gonna like that." He looked away from Sabrina as he spoke.

"Probably not, but she will like it even less if she finds out and we never told her."

Dave rolled his eyes. She waited, but he said nothing.

"What is it between you both? I never ask, because I'm trying not to intrude, but what happened?" She asked as though it had just occurred to her.

"I don't really wanna talk about it," he said quietly.

"Why not?"

"Because I'm not proud of how I acted. Because I was kind of a dick to Kit."

"Why? Because she wasn't popular and you were ashamed?"

"No!" He looked hurt at her suggestion—and she felt a deep shame spread through her—to have given him so little benefit of the doubt.

"That's what you think of me?" A redness rose to the surface of his skin, and his lips pursed.

She regretted saying it.

"I didn't know what to think. Kit would barely talk about it with me. I just knew when she was upset or angry. That was all, I never knew why."

The bell rang again at the door as the last of the remaining customers left. That quiet hour.

"You wanna know what it was with Kit and me? And this is me being totally honest. Because what I'm going to say makes me sound like a real asshole. Maybe you won't wanna be my friend afterward."

"I doubt that," she whispered, but he heard her.

She wanted to reach out to hold his hand, a way to tell him that it was all right. She wouldn't pass judgment on him. But she wasn't entirely sure she wouldn't.

"I didn't really like *her*, so much. Like, she was pretty and all, but her personality. And it was weird because we're kinda tied outside of school, right? Our parents know each other. I never thought she took it so seriously with me. I thought, actually, she just kind of used me a bit too. I knew she liked Brad, but he would never give her the time of day. And so, one time we were all drinkin' down at the shore."

"I remember . . ."

"What?"

"I remember. I was staying with Kit that time when you guys first . . ."

"Oh yeah . . ."

"You don't remember."

Dave paused, his eyes searching beyond her again, and then he shrugged and shook his head. This hurt her more than having to hear about his feelings toward Kit. It hurt her most that even though she always knew it, she had been invisible back then.

"It was different, Rina. I didn't know you then—we didn't know each other, really."

This was a truth.

"So? Why did you keep it going with Kit if you didn't like her?"

"I guess because I found her pretty. But I didn't wanna spend time with her outside of fooling around. And somehow, that's how it ended up being between us."

"So what you're saying is, you treated her that way because she let you? That seems a little convenient, don't you think?" She couldn't hide the disappointment from her voice.

"I don't know, I guess. I'm not saying this to excuse myself. But I wasn't good to her. I knew she liked me, and I just let her carry on. And now I feel bad about it. But I know if I talk to her about it, it will be a whole thing, and I just want to leave it behind. Because it's all finished now and we're all going our separate ways after the summer and it will just be easier to make a clean break. Somehow with Kit, it's always drama. I don't want a big thing. I'm not looking for a big dramatic moment. I want quiet. I like it quiet. And she's not quiet. Am I making sense?"

Sabrina nodded. She understood him better now.

She could have berated him in that moment. She thought about what Eva Kim would say: *This is toxic masculinity, Chen. Run for your life.*

But the outrage evaporated. This was one of many things she decided to let Dave get away with: convincing himself that Kit pushed him away. She knew that Dave had just done what he wanted with Kit, and Kit's feelings were too big to push back. He had ignored her in the cafeteria, in the library. They had fooled around in his den at home, with that heady scent of lilies from the hallway creeping down the stairs. She didn't remind him of the times that Kit would cry in the bathroom stalls when he had passed her in the hallway and ignored her.

"I know what you mean about being quiet," she said.

So instead, Sabrina chose to believe her version of the truth. That she wasn't invisible all those years, that Dave had felt Sabrina's shadow somehow. And that all this time they had just been moving toward this, their inevitable friendship.

CHAPTER THIRTY-FOUR

Kit

Tokyo, August 2015

He called her Katherine. Not Kit, Katherine. And when Kit was alone with Ryo, when his eyes were on her, his hand on her knee, she was Katherine. Kit, who felt the tone of her skin and her almond eyes would invite long stares from passersby back on the cobbled streets of Chestnut Hill. Kit, who drowned her body in oversize Champion sweatshirts. She was no longer Kit, whom Dave Harrison couldn't acknowledge in public but met in the dark corners of the school library. With Ryo, they were two *ha-fus* who made a whole. Did it work like that, she wondered? With Ryo, she knew he might not remain hers for long, once he started college and realized his infinite possibilities stretched beyond the borders of Roppongi and 1-Chome in Tokyo. She wondered that she might never feel like Katherine again once the plane took off from Haneda Airport. But for this last hour before her journey home to Philadelphia, she felt like Katherine.

"Katherine, I love you," he whispered. The air between them was heavy, the seams of their connection were so visible to her eye. But somewhere in the deeper recesses of her heart, she knew it wouldn't last. It thrilled and repelled her to hear him say it.

She looked at the curve of muscle on his arms that reminded her of those Italian statues of the Greek gods, the neat knuckles on his hands that sat on her bare thigh. But now she was with him. She had captivated him. But she also knew she did not belong with the gods like him.

She allowed herself to imagine him with the girls of his past, and her chest would tighten. How could she, Kit, be enough for him? It did not occur to Kit that her infatuation with Ryo might not be universal. One day she would understand that each person's preferences were different. But this would not be clear to her for many years yet.

"I love you too," she said back, her voice quiet as a mouse. If she didn't say it loudly, it wouldn't hold her down, she could run away from it if it all became too much. She glanced up at the clock again. Just twenty minutes now until her ride to the airport. A tear fell down her cheek, and more began to follow. She was swallowed up with what felt like sorrow, but she fought the feeling of relief too. Everything was happening so fast: college, Ryo, her distance from Sabrina.

"I'll be jumping on a plane to Philly in no time."

She nodded. And sniffed loudly, a giant, noisy mess of mucus up her nasal passage.

"So sexy." He smiled and wiped away the tears that had soaked her cheek. "So many tears."

She laughed, afraid more mucus would find its way out of her nose, and covered it with her hand.

She felt drained, emotions swirling around her in that room. Her last week in Tokyo had passed like a dream. Since they had come clean about their relationship with each other and then to his family and hers, they had spent every waking minute together.

✦ ✦ ✦

SHE HAD CALLED her mother the night before. She anticipated disapproval, but instead, she was met with curiosity.

"So, honey, Rick has told me all about you and Ryo. What's he like?"

"Uh, what do you mean, Mom? What's he told you?" she asked, knowing the answer after overhearing their call.

"Well, he called me, you know how we're old friends. And he mentioned that you guys had gotten involved and that Ryo was coming to look at Penn before the fall semester starts. I just want to know what he's like, sweetie. You've never introduced me to any of your boyfriends before." Did her secret fumbles with Dave mean that he was her boyfriend?

"He's great, Mom. You're going to love him. He's smart and polite."

"He sounds wonderful. And I remember from years ago, Rick sending us photos of him. He's pretty handsome, if I remember?"

"Yeah, he is. He's *ha-fu*, like me. That's the word they use here. You know, when people have like a white parent and a Japanese one. I guess it applies to anyone part Asian, or it could just be if you're Japanese? I should check. But yeah, isn't that funny? We're two *ha-fus*."

She listened to her mother's silence for a moment down the phone line, a quick intake of breath. Kit waited, knowing her mother wanted to say something else, but instead, she cut her short.

"I can't wait for Sabrina to meet him too."

"I bet. Oh, I bumped into her at the country club with Judy the other week."

"You did? With Judy? Working there, right?"

"She's been working there all summer. At the clubhouse between the tennis courts and the swimming pool."

"Oh yeah, I knew she took the job there. She's still working now?"

"I don't know, darling, I just know I've seen her a couple times. Working there and then sometimes with David."

"Oh right. I didn't know they'd been hanging out so much," she mumbled.

"We can't wait until you're home. Dad's going to put the grill on, and we can just enjoy the last few weeks of summer. I'm sure you'll want to see your friends and get everything ready before . . ."

Kit listened, but Sally had stopped talking, and the words just hung there in midair.

"Before college? Yeah, I'm looking forward to being home too. Although I'll miss Ryo, of course."

It didn't occur to her then that her mother had been away from her for more than a month and that her mother had missed her every moment of every day, with the prospect of college ahead. It didn't occur to her that her mother's heart was breaking every time Kit spoke about the future. Every time she brushed aside the suggestion of time together as a family. One day it would occur to Kit. But not for many years yet.

AMY WALKED INTO Ryo's room without knocking, and leaned against the doorway. Her nail polish was chipped and her hair was messed up, pulled to one side in a matted ponytail. She looked like she had just woken up.

Kit felt herself tense and tried to stand up from the bed, but Ryo pressed down on her knee. *You don't need to get up. We have nothing to hide,* the gentle pressure said.

"So, this is the long goodbye, is it?" Amy rubbed the sleep from her eyes.

"Dude, it's like two in the afternoon. Where were you last night?" Ryo said, throwing a cushion at his sister.

"Out." She batted the cushion away.

"Okay, so we need to talk. You've been so shady all summer," Ryo said, his tone playful, but Kit could detect concern bubbling beneath.

Kit watched Amy's expression, which revealed nothing. Her eyes were dull, complexion paler than Kit had last seen her, making the dark circles under the smudged eyeliner look ghostly. She had been out most nights since the Kyoto trip, and once she had found out about Ryo and Kit's relationship, she had stopped lingering around Kit's bedroom and inviting her out. Kit wondered who Amy had been seeing—was it the music teacher from the bar? Was it Christian? Or was it someone new?

Kit looked at Amy and knew she needed help. She needed a friend, a real friend. But in the last fifteen minutes she had in Tokyo before she headed to the airport, Kit could barely be that friend. And the bare-knuckle truth of it was she was greedy for her last few minutes with Ryo. She wanted his touch, his kiss, to remember each other right there, and to feel enveloped in the scent of his Eternity aftershave, which smelled completely different on him than on anyone else. She wanted Amy to leave because she didn't want the alarmingly altered look of this girl to soil this moment.

Amy must have read her thoughts, or Kit liked to imagine she had.

"Safe travels, Kit. Come back and visit, okay?" Amy came in and wrapped her arms around Kit's neck. Kit got a waft of old cigarette smoke in Amy's hair.

"Look after yourself, Amy. Maybe I'll see you in Philly?"

Amy looked down at her, a tight smile spread across her lips again.

"Sure. Yeah, of course. You guys might be in the same college together supposedly."

Supposedly.

She walked out of the room, waving as she left.

Before she could consider her own motives, Kit got up and followed Amy.

"Hey, hold on," she said and reached for Amy's arm.

When Amy turned to look at Kit, there was a sadness in her eyes that Kit saw for the first time. It occurred to Kit then that Amy would be losing her protector when Ryo headed off to college. She wasn't the same as her brother, she didn't have endless plans for a year of traveling and working. Instead, she was now trapped in a cycle of bad choices: older guys she was seeing behind her brother's back, anything that drew her parents' attention. And she was too addicted to the attention, good or bad.

"What's up?" Amy said.

"That wasn't a real goodbye. Here," Kit said, and opened her arms to Amy, holding her small, bony frame. She didn't remember her being so thin. "I wanted to give you a proper hug. I will miss you, Amy Buchanan, and it was so great to meet you this summer." For a moment, Kit felt Amy shake before her body relaxed into hers. "You come see me anytime, okay? And let me know what you get up to. I'm excited for your plans for college next year too, and to hear about your year off. And if you ever want to talk or anything, I'm just a message away," Kit said, feeling like a sister figure to this girl she hardly knew.

"Thanks." It was all Amy could say at first. Then Kit saw her draw a breath and a masklike smile land on her face again. "You knock 'em dead at college, okay. See you around." And before Kit could respond to the phony optimism, Amy had turned and closed the door to her bedroom behind her.

When she returned to Ryo, his expression was unreadable.

"Is everything okay?" Kit asked, touching his face. He pulled away instinctively, and she drew her hand back.

There had barely been an exchange between them, but Amy had taken whatever she could from that room. The last moments they had clutched together were gone.

"Let's walk in the garden until your car comes," he offered and jumped off the bed.

Kit wondered how she would kiss him goodbye, the kind of kiss she wanted him to remember, the kind that would make him soar above, out of his body, the way hers had that night in Roppongi. But the promise of their final embrace and kiss evaporated like early morning mist when the car arrived early and the Buchanans stood by to wave off their house-guest.

CHAPTER THIRTY-FIVE

Sabrina

Philadelphia, August 2015

The bus route from Manayunk to Chestnut Hill was almost entirely straight. Aside from a few turns through the Roxborough district, past a famous cheesesteak restaurant, Dalessandro's, there were no more turns. Sabrina liked to sit by the window up front and listen to her music on her headphones as loud as she could. Sometimes when she pulled them off for a moment, she realized how loud the music was. Today she was playing the Doors. Dave was obsessed with Jim Morrison and had made her watch the biopic with Val Kilmer. Her favorite song was "Love Her Madly." And she imagined this was how Dave Harrison might feel about her one day.

The opening sounds of thunder and rain began as the electric piano riffs of "Riders on the Storm" started, and she thought about how the song felt strange, played in daylight. Lee Lee hated this type of rock 'n' roll and suggested that she return to her Whitney Houston or *even that Beyoncé gyrating is better.* Sabrina felt like she was rising outside of herself. That she was finally a woman, that she would take a shot at Princeton.

We go all out, kid, Eva had assured her. And now Sabrina was on her way to meet a boy who was actually smart and handsome. And it didn't matter to him that she had to apply for full funding for college or that she worked at the country club where his family held a life-term membership, and his grandparents too.

Since Stuart McKluskie's party, she had been battling with a decision. If Dave cared enough about her to punch a guy, he must feel something for her. Something meaningful *had* started to grow between them.

Sabrina couldn't talk to anyone about Dave, not even Kit. In fact, Kit and Sabrina had started to lose touch, they had barely texted each other. As Sabrina understood it, Kit had Ryo, and she didn't yet know that Sabrina had Dave. And her feelings were escalating by the day. She would feel a desolate sadness overwhelm her when she hadn't spoken to him. When he arrived at the country club, she saw him in her peripheral vision, but she waited, heart in mouth, until he walked over to her. Everything she did led to seeing him. But why had he not kissed her? Why had they not moved their relationship forward? She wouldn't even stop him from putting his hand up her shirt. She would let him. She felt daring and confident with him, though she sat on the periphery of this recklessness because nothing had happened between them. It was the fear of what could happen to her if she turned to him and he rejected her that stopped her from acting. Because somewhere inside, she knew that if he was too embarrassed to own up to his fumbling with Kit during senior year, he would never own up to the undocumented Asian girl who worked in the clubhouse all summer in a stained uniform. She saw him sometimes, sitting with friends, and he smiled at her, a hand raised in a wave. But he never asked her to join them. At first, she thought it was the protocol of the club. After all, there was a dress code for the bar. But soon, she suspected it was her and not the rules they kept to. She thought she might love Dave, but her feelings were ferocious; they scared her. But she also hated him a little for being the coward he was.

SABRINA'S OTHER GREAT fear was that Dave would see Kit, and he would fall immediately under her spell again. Kit and Sabrina had hardly been in touch in the last three weeks, but when Kit finally messaged to say she was back home and to invite her over, Sabrina knew that the tectonic plates of their friendship had already shifted too far. Something had changed for both of them over the summer. The bus tumbled up the cobbled streets of Germantown Avenue and Sabrina prepared to get off at her usual stop before the left turn that would take her down to the country club. It wasn't time for her shift yet, but Dave might be there by now.

❧

"Your toes look so cute with that color on them," Sabrina said, sitting beside Kit, barefoot on the wall facing Gravers Lane by the Herzog garden.

"Oh thanks. Yeah, my friend, Amy, out there, she took me to have them done. They had these cool nail bars. Maybe we should start a tradition doing this too?"

"Sure." Sabrina knew she would never go to a manicurist. She would never pay someone to do something that she could do herself. She could hear her mother's voice in the inner recesses of her brain. A song on a loop she could not turn off.

"So how has it been? Your summer?" Kit asked.

"Oh it's been okay. I mean, I was disappointed not to go away, but it's been fine. The job at the country club has been fine. And this internship I did all summer was actually awesome. The lady I work for is incredible." She paused and added, "And I've been hanging out with Dave a bit."

"Yeah, we saw Mrs. Harrison yesterday. She mentioned. How is he?"

"He's cool. I mean, nice. You know. So tell me more about Tokyo, come on. You've hardly said anything about it yet."

"Oh it was so amazing. I mean, it's like, so different than here. It's super busy but quiet. It's super modern but then people are kind of old-fashioned. The food is awesome."

"And this guy?"

"Oh yes, Ryo."

Kit pronounced his name in a way that Sabrina had never heard, ly-o. Short and sharp, *Lyō*.

"What's he like?"

"He's gorgeous. Like so hot. He's half Japanese, half American. He's about, I guess, Dave's height. Real tanned. He speaks Japanese, totally fluently. Like a Japanese person, but he's American, you know? Like, he grew up all around the world, but goes to an American high school there. Well, he did. And now he's coming out here before college starts, to check out Penn. I don't know, we're talking about trying a long-distance thing maybe to start."

"What? He is? So you guys are like a thing? Going into college?"

"Yeah, we're going to try. He's got a place in Berkeley now but is going to look at Penn in case he wants to transfer later this year. So, we'll see, I guess, if we want to be together."

"That's huge, Kit. Does your mom know?"

"Yeah, she knows. They're kind of being weird and not talking about it. But he's coming over with his dad, like soon. I really liked his parents too. Like, I *connected* with them, you know?"

"And did you, you know? With Ryo?"

Kit nodded, her mouth crooked in an awkward smile. But there was no superiority or showing off in how she delivered this news. Sabrina would have preferred Kit to gloat in the way the old Kit would have. Then she would know how to handle her. But this reserved version of Kit left Sabrina feeling like an animal cornered. Was Kit about to turn on her? She felt unsure and frozen.

"Yeah, we did, I don't know. It's pretty serious," Kit said, not looking at Sabrina as she spoke.

"Wow. Do you like, love him?"

Kit shrugged and looked down at her toes. Sabrina wondered if she was admiring her own pedicure. Sabrina's thoughts went straight to Dave. How will he feel when he learns this? Would Dave and Ryo meet? It was likely they would.

"Rina," Kit said, breaking Sabrina's swirl of emotions. "If I ask you something, will you answer me honestly?"

Sabrina looked at her, tilted her head, and nodded. But the inside of her stomach was falling. She knew what was coming.

"Did Dave talk about me when I was gone?" It wasn't what she was expecting Kit to ask. And yet, of course, Kit wanted to know about herself before anything else.

"Yeah he did. But nothing that is worth reporting, you know? Like, he asked if you'd been in touch."

"He asked if I'd been in touch?"

"Yes. He also just said things in passing. But never things that were like, interesting or anything."

"Right. I guess I understand. He's probably been seeing someone over the break."

"I don't know. He didn't seem to be with anyone when I hung out with him."

Kit was silent, and Sabrina thought about asking another question about Tokyo but stopped. She wanted to change the subject. She was not ready to tell Kit about her friendship with Dave. She was not prepared to own up to the evenings they spent together talking about everything they were afraid of in college the next year. She was not ready to tell Kit about how Dave judged his mother for how she treated the Asian woman who worked in their house and felt embarrassed by it. She was not prepared to tell Kit that Dave didn't know about Ryo, at least not from her. And she was not prepared to tell Kit that she was seeing Dave that afternoon after his tennis tournament down at the club. They were going for a drive up to the Morris Arboretum. She wanted to keep him for herself just a little longer.

"I can't wait for you to meet Ryo. You'll love him, Rina."

"Yeah? You have any pictures of him?"

"I do, we took this in a booth in Shibuya. It's this cool part of Tokyo. Loads of shopping and restaurants. It's the famous crossing, you ever see a picture of that place?"

Sabrina shook her head and watched her friend flick through her phone.

The picture was bleached out with a heavy filter, the way Kit had started to take pictures since she left for Tokyo. Ryo draped his arm around Kit's neck. Sabrina hadn't imagined his hair so dark, his skin so tanned. She swiped across the photos slowly, zooming in on his face. In the final shot, they kissed, and he held her face in his hands, his fingers around her jaw and neck.

"Wow. He is so cute. And he's eighteen? He looks like a man."

"I guess he is a man. In a way? He's super smart too. He's only one year older."

"Yeah? He's so, like, chiseled."

Sabrina tried to imagine what it would be like to kiss a boy who looked like Ryo. There were certain people she didn't even dare to look at directly. She felt like her eyes would hurt, like when she looked directly at the sun. Kit was never this way, she believed she deserved everything, unlike Sabrina.

But this summer, something had changed, and Sabrina found a way to shine and allow her true self to emerge from the shadows. Kit was never really an outsider like Sabrina, but Dave's inability to acknowledge her in public would have left her with wounds and cuts to her pride. Kit never had a problem standing up and being seen when her name was called. Sabrina knew that deep inside of Kit, a part of her wanted to be looked at. And only a person who wanted to be seen could be with a boy who looked like this. Because Ryo was what Kit and Sabrina used to describe as "devastatingly handsome."

Sabrina lied to Kit and left the house on Gravers Lane early.

I gotta go check on my shifts and get some work down to Eva before the end of the day.

Sabrina rushed to the club and waited for Dave in the parking lot.

She watched the entrance from beside his car. She was playing the Indigo Girls a little louder than usual on her headphones. She mouthed along to the songs, not letting her voice emerge.

She wondered if Kit still listened to this album after years of them exchanging playlists. Did she keep them? There were so many things she had wanted to ask Kit, but an invisible wall had slowly built up between them while they'd been apart. The thread of friendship was frayed so dangerously thin now, it threatened to snap at any moment. And now she knew she had to see Dave—to tell him the truth about how she felt about him, before he saw Kit again, before everything that had happened over the summer moved firmly into the past.

He came out the door, talking to another boy. They both wore backpacks slung over one shoulder, racket handles sticking out behind them, their hair wet from the locker room. Dave had seen her, and she heard herself sigh as he said his goodbyes, pointed toward Sabrina, and ran over to his car.

"Hey, I didn't know you were working today."

"I wasn't. I thought I'd come say hi."

"Cool. I don't think I'm going to have time for our drive. I have to head home soon, we have people coming over for dinner—it's so boring. Shall we do something tomorrow?"

Sabrina wondered if it was Kit and her parents who were coming over.

THEY WALKED ALONG the path that split the golf course from the club. Lee Lee always made a comment every time they drove past the club on the way out of Chestnut Hill. *If only you knew how lucky you are. We never had this in China. In China, it's all concrete. Your exercise is all done together on the concrete playground, and you follow the instructions. These Americans and their fancy clubs, all these facilities, all these fields and gyms, just for your health and well-being. None of it is necessary. They don't know how lucky they are.*

"So I went to see Kit earlier," Sabrina said and regretted it instantly.

"Oh yeah? So she's back?"

"Yeah, she got back yesterday, I think." She had started now, and there was no going back.

"Did she have a good time?"

"I think so. She met a guy. He's actually coming to visit." Sabrina watched Dave's face carefully. How he responded now would determine what she said next.

"Oh yeah? I think my mom mentioned something."

"So how do you feel?"

"About what?" His voice became tense.

"About her with this guy. I mean, I hear he is like really amazing and stuff and that they're going to try to do some long-distance thing."

"Wow. That's pretty intense. After what? I don't know how long she's been gone. Two weeks?" He knew how long she had been gone. He had told her yesterday that it had been six weeks since they had seen Kit.

"Longer. Do you feel weird hearing about her?"

"Nope, not really. We're all heading off, it's a new start."

"Yeah, I guess."

They walked the path that looped all the way back around to the club. They had stopped talking. Sabrina wanted to say that she was happy Kit had found someone else. That she and Dave had become friends. She wanted to say that she was happy that he got in a fight over her at the party the other night. She wanted to tell him that this friendship between them meant she had had the best summer of her life. She wanted to tell him that seeing him meant everything to her.

"Hey, Dave, we're friends, right?" She tried to suck down a breath, but something blocked her throat.

"What? Yeah, of course."

"So, we're not, I don't know, anything else."

"You mean us? Like you and me?"

"Yeah, is that so crazy?"

Dave was quiet, and Sabrina knew the silence meant what she wanted to hear least. She knew that he didn't feel the same way. But now he would have to let her down gently, and he might not be her friend anymore, and she felt herself starting to choke on the tears that closed her throat.

"It's not crazy, but it's also not what I would want. I think our friendship is too important." He was serious, the most serious she had ever seen him. His eyes were pained, as though he were on the precipice of pleading with her.

"Oh, sure. Okay."

"This is not some brush-off, Rina. I mean this." He stopped to look at her when he spoke to her. "I want us to be friends. I *need* us to be friends. This has become real important to me."

"I understand. It's cool. We are friends."

"Yeah, but now I don't want it to be awkward. I want to keep hanging out with you. To keep going to the movies, to keep having you nag me about not doing stupid stuff when I drink."

Sabrina snorted, but the pain started to seep into her. To her surprise, instead of tears, she felt a raging fire erupt in her chest. Just like Kit, he wanted everything on his terms. What about what was important to her?

"So what you're saying is you want a babysitter. For when you're not out fucking girls you actually *want* to be with?"

Dave was shocked when she swore. She was too. She didn't know where it had come from. She felt outside her body, like someone else had taken over her brain.

"That's not fair."

"Isn't it?"

"No, it's not. I didn't mean it like that, and you know it. You mean a lot to me, Sabrina." He tried to hold her hand. And she just let her arm hang there. Her eyes had started to fill with tears, and she hated herself.

She couldn't say anything. She was afraid she would choke up, and he would know how sad she was, knowing he didn't feel the same way.

"Is it because of her? Because she has moved on with some new guy. Some super fancy Japanese American hot dude who looks like a movie star. Because you're out of the picture now."

"It's not because of her."

"Then why? I'm just not pretty enough? I'm not as pretty as her. I'm too Chinese for you?"

"Jesus, Sabrina. No." He was getting red around the neck. They stood awkwardly as a gust of wind came up onto the raised path overlooking the field.

"Well, what is it then?"

"I just don't feel that way, okay? I can't force that. I'd be lying. And I want to be your friend. I want to *stay* your friend."

She didn't reply. Her lip stuck out, she felt ugly, and her eyes were red from the tears she kept trying to push away. She wanted to run back to Kit's and pretend none of this had happened. Maybe steal a bottle of wine from the Herzogs' cellar. She wanted to be anywhere but there, standing in front of Dave, who wouldn't look away. She wanted to scream *Don't look at me.*

"You better go," Sabrina replied and started to walk ahead of him. Before this conversation, she would have worried about how she looked to him, walking ahead of him. The shape of her legs in the shorts she wore. Not then.

They walked in silence back to the parking lot.

"Sabrina." She heard her name called and turned to see Sally Herzog talking to someone at the club entrance.

Sabrina forced a smile, but she could see from Sally's knitted brows that she wasn't fooling her.

"Are you okay?" Sabrina saw Sally's eyes travel beyond Sabrina and land on Dave. There was a look of understanding, Sally could see they were no longer just high school acquaintances. And now Kit would know. Mrs. Herzog would tell her daughter how she had walked in on something, just like Lee Lee would have told Sabrina if she had walked in on something that had passed between two teenagers she knew.

"Yes, thank you, Mrs. Herzog. I'm great."

"Hi, David," she called out.

Dave waved. "Hey, Mrs. Herzog." He smiled. He was better than her at pretending. She wondered whether, to him, nothing *had* passed, whether, in fact, none of it even mattered to him. Meanwhile, she wanted to lie in bed and cry for days.

"Kit's here too, we came down to pick up some takeout. Hold on." She walked into the club again.

Sabrina wanted to run. Dave looked at her, silent, asking *What should I do?*

"I'm going, you just tell them I had to leave, okay? So it's not weird or anything."

Sabrina nodded and pushed the tears away from her eyes. There was a wet streak over her hand that she wiped behind her.

Kit walked out with Sally. Kit's hair was down, her eyes soft from the jet lag. Sabrina watched as Kit looked at her and then beyond her at Dave in his Jeep. She saw the pieces come together in Kit's mind. She waved her hand to Dave, and he turned his engine off.

Sabrina felt welded to the ground. Mrs. Herzog had gone inside. Now it was just the three of them in the empty parking lot, the orange sun lowering over them.

"Hey, were you leaving?" Kit asked Dave.

"My parents have this thing tonight. I gotta get back. Hey, so how was the trip? You had a good time?"

"Yeah, I did. Sabrina, I didn't realize you were coming down to the club. You should have said, I would have given you a ride."

"Oh yeah, sorry, I just realized on my way to the bus that I had forgotten something, that was all." Sabrina turned her head, trying not to look at her friend. She worried that if she looked directly into Kit's eyes, Kit might see the real extent of her feelings—everything she was trying to bury now, everything that had happened that summer that wasn't actually real. In the end, it was just fiction she had dreamed up.

"What's going on, guys? Did something happen?" Kit asked Dave the question, and Sabrina watched him scratch the back of his head.

"We just had an argument about something," Sabrina replied, an edge in her voice she couldn't hide.

Kit's eyes asked for more.

"It's nothing," Dave mumbled.

"What about?"

"About you," Sabrina heard herself say.

"Really? What about me?" Kit was combative now. Her hand rested on her hip, and her eyes had hardened.

Dave looked at Sabrina and she could see his thoughts working hard to find something to say in response.

"I accused him of still having feelings for you," Sabrina said. Her mouth kept moving ahead of her thoughts. A banner that said DESIST waved through her brain.

"What? And what does that have to do with you, Rina?"

Dave said nothing and stared back at Sabrina. *What are you doing?*

"Well, it kind of does actually. Because I like Dave, and you like Ryo now, and Dave, it seems, still likes you. And here we all are. A shit show."

"Sabrina," Kit said, her mouth mimicking Dave's, open and shocked.

"Yeah I know, it's so shocking for Sabrina to say this stuff. It's so shocking that good little Sabrina swears and says *shit* or *fuck* or *asshole.* But here I am. This is such bullshit. Kit, I know Dave was a dick to you, but you didn't have to keep going back for more. I'm glad you and this new guy found each other because you're so much more than that. And Dave, don't' tell me you're surprised. You must have known I felt this way all summer. Why didn't you just put me out of my misery earlier?"

Sabrina turned her back on them both and walked out to the road as fast as she could. She took out her headphones and pressed play. They probably didn't say anything to stop her. Her mouth curved like she was going to smile or cry. She was caught in a sun-shower, where the skies opened while the sun still shone through, neither here nor there. A thin line between love and hate, Lee Lee used to say. You could hate the people you loved the most. The sun could fight through a storm.

Act
Five

CHAPTER THIRTY-SIX

Sally

Philadelphia, 2012

In the winter of 2012, Kit changed completely. Sally could see that adolescence had arrived. Kit loved her friend Sabrina fiercely, but social struggles at school began: lunchtime politics, whether she was invited to birthday parties or not. Kit ambushed her mother with her pent-up rage after school.

Every afternoon as Sally waited in the school pickup line, she played Bonnie Raitt softly in the background to calm her nerves. What mood would her daughter be in today? She hated this feeling of dread; she shouldn't be feeling this way every day her daughter returned home. *Today will be different. Today she'll be in a better mood and we'll do something nice together, have a mother-daughter conversation that Kit can store within her core memories,* Sally told herself. But those days rarely came. Instead, she studied Kit's body language and facial expressions carefully as she broke out of the middle school doors to properly arm herself against whatever wrath Kit needed to expel.

"Mom, we need to talk about periods," Kit declared as she slumped into the car one Tuesday afternoon.

Was it happening? Had it begun? She had talked to Kit a little about sex, but somehow she felt out of place doing it. Was it because they weren't bound by blood? Or did every mother feel this way?

"Has yours started, honey? You know I don't ask because I know you'll tell me if it does." Sally didn't know this at all.

Kit rolled her eyes. Another new habit.

"No, I haven't. But Sabrina just told me hers had started. And a bunch of the other girls in my class, they all got theirs like last year."

Sally always worried about Kit's development, physically and emotionally. She had taken her to Macy's for her first training bra. But she had noticed that her friends' daughters all needed one several years before Kit. She talked to her doctor. Everything was genetic when it came to development. And what did Sally know about Kit's genes? Nothing more than a few lines written on a document Terry had locked away. Her thoughts started to spiral. Why had she not started to menstruate? Would it affect her fertility later down the line? Was it a signal of some other underlying issue with her reproductive organs that Sally needed to look into?

"Well, I think everyone just starts in their own time. No need to worry about it. I'm not," she lied.

"It's kind of weird, everyone else having theirs, and not being able to talk about it. Like, what does it feel like? When you have it? Some of my friends say it hurts." Sally tried to look at Kit's expression as she asked the questions, but her daughter spoke into the window of the passenger seat.

"Some people experience cramps, that's right."

"When did you get yours?"

"Around your age, I'd say."

Neither of them spoke, and the air grew heavy. What did it matter when Sally got hers? It had no bearing on Kit. She wanted urgently to get in front of the computer and type in question after question to further expand her fear.

KIT FORGOT ABOUT the conversation the moment she returned home and locked herself up in her bedroom. Meanwhile, Sally went to her desk and surprised herself. She wrote an email to the adoption agency to request more information on the health of Kit's biological parents. It was a gut reaction as her mind swirled around the most dire, desperate scenarios. She never looked at the best case; it was always the worst. This way she could be fully prepared emotionally to face whatever problems might come. Only the problems never came. Instead, she just had a wealth of knowledge of what *might* happen. And a deep ocean of fatigue that swept over her. She needed to know what Kit's genetic fate was. It was imperative as her mother that she know who her biological mother was and how it might change the course of Kit's life.

She couldn't talk to anyone about her decision, including Terry. Though once she had sent the email she realized that the agency could reply to him too. It was a small risk, but one she rationalized taking. For the following three days, Sally observed Kit carefully. Every movement, and whenever she could get close enough, she would try to look at her with a clinical eye. That weekend Sally knew Kit's bowel movements, when her energy spiked in the morning and fell into a sleepy afternoon lull. She observed with forensic detail Kit's concentration ebb and flow as she tried to sit down and do her homework. She studied the small mounds that had emerged on Kit's chest. Were they symmetrical? Were they developing at the expected rate? She googled "relation between breast development and fertility in teens." And then looked back again at

Kit's silhouette, tilting her head to study her body shape further. Kit had learned to walk in a way that swung her hips from side to side.

"What are you doing, Mom? You're giving me that weird look again," Kit snapped.

Sally was jolted out of her internalized analysis and sat upright.

"Oh sorry, honey, I was miles away."

"Miles away where?" Kit asked. She crossed her arms over her body, her eyes hard and cold. Sometimes, Sally could see a different woman in her daughter. The woman who she was becoming. Her whole face was changing. She was still Kit, but a small feature, something in her expression, was different. Was it the way her eyes moved, the way her brows knitted? Or was it the way her lips pursed a certain way? This was a woman Sally didn't know.

"Just thinking about things. Are you feeling all right? You're not coming down with anything? It's so cold out and everyone seems to be getting strep right now."

"Yup, I'm fine," Kit said and turned on the heel of her fluffy slipper and stomped up the stairs.

Sally missed the younger Kit. She went from being a child who would never stop talking—who talked so much in fact that Sally's brain would hurt after spending an intense hour with her on Sunday when they went for their weekly playground and hot cocoa—to being almost completely silent overnight. Kit would talk in a breathless monologue about every interaction that had happened that week. She commanded Sally to *ask me more questions, Mommy!* Until they ended up arguing over how the nuance of conversation came down to a reciprocal discussion: one person asked a question, the other person would inquire after the other. That was good manners.

When Kit was little, she would cover Sally's face with kisses and squeeze her mother so hard as she hugged her. It was the kind of smothering physical contact that Sally wanted to get away from, and when she had that thought she felt an intense guilt sweep through her. But nobody prepared her for the fact that one day the tap of claustrophobic affection would just dry up. One day Kit woke up and no longer wanted to snuggle, or give herself over to her mother for free examination, whether it was a hand on the brow for a fever or to look at a scratch on her knee. She no longer wanted her mother in her bathroom so they could talk while she bathed and showered. She no longer wanted her mother to stay in her bed with her as she fell asleep in her arms. Instead, Kit became what seemed to be independent and aloof overnight. She was guarded about her body, and Sally always suspected it was because somewhere in the back of Kit's mind she always remembered that at the beginning, they were strangers. She wanted to know what the other girls were doing at home, but she never asked her other mom friends. She never talked about the adoption to anyone, not even Terry.

One thing Sally had learned about other mothers was that they loved to say, "Oh, you know how it is," as they shared their parenting struggles. But Sally didn't know. She didn't know because she didn't even know what it was like to have a baby growing inside her. Now, the pain of this emptiness had subsided almost completely; instead, there was an anxiety that nothing was holding her child to her. There was no invisible thread like the remnants of the umbilical cord that would keep her connected through adolescence and adulthood.

For Sally and Kit, everything was newly formed: their bond, connection, and need for each other. It was painstakingly rooted in the paperwork that allowed them to be a family. Only through these sheets of addendums and clauses could they be held together, like a paper ring chain that could snap if pulled too hard. There was no blood, DNA samples, or facial traits that attached Kit to her.

Each stage of motherhood so far was like this for Sally. She walked around the buried land mines, holding her breath for fear of taking a wrong step. Life flowed on and demanded reactions from her, demanded discomfort, discipline, and boundaries. Like all her normal, biological parental peers, she had to guide Kit. But there was no luxury of imagining Kit as herself with more opportunities. Sally was not entitled to the phrase *She's just like I was at that age*, because Kit was probably just like someone else, a complete stranger. She could only imagine what life might have been like for Kit if she hadn't been adopted by them. This was something Sally had never thought of. Her heart ached too much to think of what might have become of this baby, left with nobody to fend for her. It was an unspeakable image, the same theoretical devastation she felt when she imagined Kit falling from the playground climbing frame or tumbling down the stairs of her home. This made her know her maternal love was real, the fear part, anyway.

As FEBRUARY ROLLED into March that year, Kit did not bring up her period again. Or much of anything else to Sally. In fact, the stubborn snow stayed on the ground despite the first shoots of spring emerging through the ground, and the winter felt like it would never end. To Sally, the frost was like Kit's newfound silence toward her. Meanwhile, Sally fell deeper and deeper into a spiral of research about adopted children, their unexpected health issues and birth mothers reappearing in their lives. Her Google search history was a battlefield of her imagined worst-case scenarios: *Does a hereditary condition give an adopted minor rights to connect with her birth mother without adult consent? Can an adopted minor choose to leave her adoptive parents?*

"What are you up to in here, hon?" Terry said as he put a coffee on the coaster beside her computer monitor. She had already heard his scuffling footsteps in the kitchen. She knew her husband's tone. This was a greeting, and he wasn't expecting a response.

"Does Kit seem a little, I don't know, off to you lately?"

"What do you mean, hon?"

At some point, and Sally couldn't remember exactly when, Terry had taken to calling her "hon." She hated it.

"I just worry she's not developing fully, physically, I mean."

Terry shifted his weight uncomfortably. Sally knew her husband well enough by now to see she'd launched him outside the protective sphere of his comfort zone.

"Aww, Sal, she seems to be doing all right to me. She's taller than I thought she'd be."

He was always so literal. She fought the urge to sigh heavily. Instead she ignored his response and continued.

"I'm talking about her development as a young woman. She mentioned to me that some of the girls in her class, actually, she said *all* of them were starting to menstruate. And . . ."

"Whoa, Sal . . ." Terry said, standing back as though Sally had punched him.

Sally stared at her husband and blinked.

"Anyway, I am worried that she hasn't started to menstruate. And if she's developing at the rate she should be. Do her breasts seem a normal size to you?"

"Sal, I'm very uncomfortable right now. This seems like your territory to me. I'm the build-the-treehouse guy. The take-her-to-soccer-practice guy, put-some-burgers-on-the-grill guy. I'm not the talk-about-all-the-girl-stuff dad. You know this." He laughed, but she could see a shine of sweat form on his forehead.

Sally had always taken Kit to soccer practice, in fact she wondered whether Terry even knew that Kit was no longer on the soccer team, and now trying out for the basketball team instead.

"Terry, this isn't an *optional* activity. You're her father. I'm her mother. We are both *here*, no matter the topic. If we had a son, and I thought he was masturbating too often, yes, I would feel uncomfortable to talk about it but I would still talk about it. I wouldn't just say 'Oh no, honey, I'm in the pot-roast department, you have to take this on'!" Her voice rose higher and higher, after the words she hadn't planned tumbled out of her mouth. "We have a young woman who is developing in our house. She is going to have her period soon, she is going to grow breasts. At some point, she will start having intercourse. . . ."

"All right," he shouted suddenly. "That's enough for one day. I don't know what's got into you today."

Sally's face flushed to a shade that felt close to crimson red. She was furious as she stared at her husband. Had he become shorter when she wasn't looking?

Sally took a deep breath and closed her eyes. She half suspected him to have left, taking the first opportunity to run away, but he stood there, a pained expression on his face.

"Terry. I worry about her. We don't have the luxury of knowing her family medical history. We are totally in the dark. We don't know if she has some genetic susceptibility to something. We don't know if things run in the family, we don't know anything."

"We know enough. We know the mother was young. We know she was healthy. Kit came to us healthy. We go to our annual doctor visits. She runs, she sleeps, she eats. I don't know what's got into your head about this not developing properly thing, but she is developing, Sal. We just don't see it all the time because she's right in front of us. One day we're going to blink and she's going to be a full-grown adult. I think you might be blowing this out of proportion a bit."

Sally stopped listening as her mind started to walk through the conversation she planned to have with the adoption agency. Three weeks had passed since she had emailed them.

A WEEK LATER, Sally didn't know yet that Kit's period had arrived, in just the same fashion she had heard the other girls describe it. An inconvenient moment between classes when she went to the bathroom and had to whisper in Sabrina's ear in the hallway to ask for a sanitary towel. That same day, Sally was sitting in the waiting room of the True Hearts Adoption Agency, after receiving a response to her email. She had prepared her questions, doctor's notes, and her need to know more. She felt confident that she might be able to get more information from them.

It was just an office in a building, a high-rise in Center City, nestled among accountants, finance brokers, and recruitment agents. Finally, she heard her name called out and a woman in her fifties, perhaps, stood in front of her. Her ash-blond hair was swept back into a loose bun that sat at the back of her neck. Sally noticed a smudge of brown eyeliner gathered under her eye and a fleck of coffee stain on her blouse.

Helena Driscoll had worked on Kit's case twelve years ago, she told Sally on the phone, and she remembered it clearly. She had met Terry but not Sally at the time of Kit's adoption. The case worker who had visited them in Gravers Lane was retired now. Helena offered Sally a seat and placed a tray with stacked water tumblers on the small coffee table.

Yes, Kit's adoption was still closed with no status change. Helena explained that Sally's health concerns were absolutely understandable and wanted to offer some reassurance of the state of health of Kit's biological mother, at least at the time of adoption.

Sally wanted more.

"I want to put your mind at ease, Mrs. Herzog, I can absolutely understand you want all the knowledge you can get in order to prepare yourself for Kit and the life she has ahead of her. Sounds like you're a wonderful parent."

"Well, we do our best. Do you have children?"

"I do, yes."

The silence spread between them again. Sally wanted her to speak up, to tell her everything she knew about Kit. Everything she could remember. But she had to press gently.

"I'm sure you already know the basic information. The age of the mother, the ethnicity," Helena said.

"Perhaps you can give me everything you can again, something might feel helpful, I guess."

WHEN SALLY GOT home that afternoon, she was surprised to find Kit had skipped her after-school club and sat under a blanket in front of the TV.

"Hey, what are you doing here, kiddo? I thought you had an extra study period on Wednesdays."

Kit shrugged and muted the TV.

"Is Dad here?" she asked.

"I think he's out salting the stairs for tomorrow's snow."

"I got my period today," she said quickly and bit her lip.

"Oh wow, honey." Sally felt an enormous sigh escape her as she spoke, "Big day for you."

"Yeah, it was like, right between my math class and phys ed. I got a pass from the nurse. Because I didn't have anything, you know, to take care of it."

"I have a bunch of things I prepared for you. Just in case it arrived."

"You do?" Kit's eyes widened.

"Sure, just in case. Let me go and get them while Dad's out. He'll be awhile," Sally said and smiled with relief as she took the staircase two steps a time.

Helena Driscoll had told her nothing new earlier that day. She knew that Kit's father had likely been American. She knew that her mother had willingly given Kit up, she knew that the ethnicity was likely to be East Asian, but when Sally had pressed her about specific parts of Asia, she detected a momentary doubt in Mrs. Driscoll's tone. Maybe it wasn't completely certain that the mother had been Korean or Japanese. She had learned that Kit had been a very small baby, smaller than they had expected. She didn't know what the mother's legal status was, nor whether she was even legally allowed to put her child up for adoption if she was struggling with her immigration status. Helena Driscoll wouldn't answer any of those questions. Sally would look that up later. She told herself it would be another question she'd fire into Google later. But she never did.

CHAPTER THIRTY-SEVEN

Sabrina

Philadelphia, August 2015

Sabrina had never received multiple messages from a boy. Not even when she had started her friendship with Dave at the beginning of the summer. The only two people who really ever messaged her were Lee Lee and Kit. But this summer, her circle had grown. She heard from Eva Kim sometimes, who sent her funny videos from YouTube and links to newspaper articles about Asian hate crimes.

Now, she found herself opening her phone in the morning to seventeen messages from Dave Harrison. At first, she felt a snap of happiness, the same rush she had felt all summer at the sight of his name. And then as her eyes grew accustomed to the morning light, an enormous sadness exploded in her heart as she remembered what had happened between them. That he had not returned her feelings, that her heart was broken.

She stared at the alert on the home screen, *17 new messages*. She turned her phone face down again and rolled over and curled herself up into a ball. She had another twenty minutes before she would have to get up for her shift at the club. She wanted to speak to Eva Kim, not her mother, not her friend Kit, who had just returned aglow with the rosy hue of a summer of love, a reciprocated love, and whom she had also shouted at in front of the club. She would have to explain herself. She couldn't bring herself to do it yet. But now, the only person's voice she wanted to hear was Eva Kim's. She wanted to hear her swear and call Dave a *fucking douchebag*.

Sabrina reached underneath her mattress and looked at the envelope from Princeton. The soft padding under her hand gave her comfort; inside there was a promise of escape. Eva had made some calls, as she promised she would. She had been holding on to the envelope for three days now, as though it were a fine, delicate, fragile piece of glass so thin that the tiniest mishandling would cause it to shatter in her fingertips, into a thousand piercing shards. She would accept her place, and take the financial aid that was offered to her. This much she had agreed with Eva. This much she owed herself for how hard she had worked. She told herself this, but it was Eva's voice that actually said the words. It would be some time yet until it was her own voice saying it or believing it.

SABRINA SHOWERED, BRUSHED her hair, dressed herself in the same uniform she had worn every day that summer. There was a stain on the hem of her T-shirt she tried to ignore; it was always the teas and the sodas that splashed her clothes as she cleared things away in the clubhouse. She felt tired as she brushed her teeth and stared at her reflection in the mirror. Her eyes were puffy, with dark circles underneath that took on a bluish tinge. She didn't open any of Dave's messages, even though she wanted to see what he had to say.

When Sabrina arrived at work, the heat and sun of the day felt like a dusty haze that settled over everything, the summer apocalypse. Everything felt magnified and slow. She wiped down the tables in the clubhouse, she tuned out the noise the children made as they rushed in for the Sprites and cookies. She ignored the caps and wristbands that were thrown around among them. She ignored the call from Lee Lee, and the message asking Sabrina to collect her eczema cream from the CVS pharmacy on her way home. She ignored the three missed calls from Kit as she sat on a bench overlooking the soccer fields staring at the tuna fish sandwich that became warm and flaccid in her hands. It was easier to be numb. She wanted to feel nothing. She wanted to erase everything that had happened between her and Dave this past summer. She wished she'd never responded to his first message.

A message from Kit: Rina, pick up. I just want to talk.

She stared at the message. Kit was typing again. I can see you're online.

Sabrina smiled. No matter how angry she felt at Kit for any given time, her love for their friendship sometimes leaked out of her, like a dripping faucet that couldn't be stopped. It was always there.

I'm sorry I shouted at you, you got caught in the crossfire.
And I'm sorry for other things.

Sabrina finally replied.

You don't need to be sorry. I'm just checking
you're ok.

Sabrina started to cry again. She didn't expect her friend to be kind. She expected Kit to be angry at how everything had unraveled between Dave and her. But instead, Kit's attention was elsewhere now. She didn't trust that Kit would forget Dave entirely after so long, but maybe Ryo had changed things? For the second time in Sabrina's life, she wanted a

343

drink. She wanted to buy a bottle of wine and drink it alone and fall asleep and feel nothing for the next few days. The day dragged by.

⁓

"Kid, you look like the saddest person I've ever seen. Not a young woman who's about to start Princeton with full funding."

Sabrina hadn't noticed Eva looking at her. She was staring out the window, the filthy window in Eva's office had a small circle of glass that was still clear enough so she could make out the clock tower and the time: 4:53 p.m.

She tried to smile and a small croak escaped her mouth but no words. *You are not going to cry in front of Eva Kim.*

"I have a bit on my mind, that's all," she finally managed.

"Something to do with a boy, I'm guessing?"

"Yeah, I know. It's pretty dumb, but yeah, it's a boy."

Eva nodded and didn't say anything. Sabrina watched her pause and take her glasses off. She was shocked to find that Eva Kim was in fact quite pretty. Her nose was small and perfectly in scale with the rest of her features, the small apples of her cheeks were high and held a pinky natural flush to them (Sabrina assumed Eva Kim did not wear a scrap of makeup), and her eyes were large, doe-like even, deep dark brown, with long lashes.

"Is that stupid? To be upset about a boy? I don't know. There are a lot stupider things in my opinion. You wanna talk about it?"

Sabrina shifted in her seat. She was uncomfortable. "I have a feeling you're going to make me. And I know what you're going to say."

"I bet you don't. Try me," Eva said with a crooked smile.

"You're going to say I shouldn't be wasting my time and energy being upset about a boy when I have this bright future ahead of me. And that I'm better than that boy, and I shouldn't waste my tears."

"All these things are true. They are. And while I wholeheartedly stand by my view that some people are total garbage, I don't know this boy you are talking about, and he might be the most amazing kid in the world. But also, your feelings are true and we need to fucking deal with them if we're going to get you to do any kind of useful work for me. And you cannot start this big bright future you have ahead of you with a heart broken into a thousand pieces. You're about to go to my alma mater, and I cannot have you let me down by not living up to the inflated picture I painted of you to the dean of admissions to get you that golden ticket. Shocking as this might seem, I do know a thing or two about love and relationships."

Sabrina only ever pictured Eva Kim in three places: her office, the corner store, and the hotdog stand across the street.

"You do? I guess you must see a lot from all these cases, right? Families, couples torn apart and stuff," Sabrina said quietly.

"Well yeah, I mean you see your fair share of broken hearts and also in our work we see families and couples under pressure, relationships put to the test in extreme circumstances, right? But I also have some experience with relationships myself. I *am* engaged, after all."

"You *are?!*" Sabrina blurted out, unable to hide the disbelief from her voice in time.

"I know, hard to believe, right? This cynic taking a chance on love. But yes, I am engaged to be married, to a man I legitimately love. The man is not certifiably insane, and we are planning to tie the knot in his hometown up in Connecticut in the fall. I'm even planning to wear a white dress."

"I didn't mean . . . what I mean is . . ."

"No offense taken. Now come on. Tell me what's going on."

Sabrina explained. As she started to speak, the words tumbled out of her. She told Eva everything, right from the beginning of summer, when she first felt Dave notice her. The unexpected interaction in the library, how they started to message each other every night, until it began to feel strange when they didn't wish each other good night before one of them went to sleep. She told her how she had hidden the friendship from her mother, who just *wouldn't get it*, and the pain she felt every time she thought about Dave and his relationship with her best friend. She felt a shock of shame shoot through her as she explained Dave and Kit's history together. But it passed as Eva listened and nodded, her big eyes watching Sabrina carefully as she spoke.

"So in a nutshell, you always had it bad for this boy who was hooking up with your best friend, who by the way, I need to add, sounds like a bit of an asshole to me—but that's by the by—and now you guys became close with what sounds like a real genuine friendship but you feel *all the things* for him, and he has friend-zoned you. Correct?"

"Correct," Sabrina whispered.

"Love is really tough, Chen. In fact, it downright fucking sucks. I don't know what to tell you. I mean, don't think for a second that my guy and I just found each other and bang, we lived happily ever after. I kissed a series of frogs, you might say. Actually, toads would be more accurate. And teenage first love, it's the hardest."

Sabrina felt a tear trickle down her face. She wanted to stop, but she couldn't. It had started now.

"This Dave character, I mean, he was a little punk to your friend, I think we can both agree on that. But it sounds like he's trying to salvage something between the two of you. Whatever it is you guys found this summer is important to him. Sounds like he couldn't give a shit about his relationship with your buddy, though, but whatever he has with you, he might just treasure it. So the ball's in your court. Do you want to cherish it too? Is the dent in your pride worth taking in exchange for a friendship that might just last longer than any little flash-in-the-pan romance pre-college, anyway? Or were you planning on some kind of arranged high school marriage kind of thing with him and do we need to involve your moms in this?"

Sabrina laughed. It was the first time her tear-soaked skin had felt the stretch of a smile pull on the sides of her mouth in a while. It felt good.

"I care about the friendship. It matters to me," she said finally.

Eva Kim nodded. Then she slowly cleaned the lens of her glasses with a tissue on her desk.

"Well, then. You know what to do. Sometimes the pain is just what you need to realize how important something is to you." She placed her glasses back on and tapped the keyboard to her computer again to bring the monitor back to life.

Eva Kim typed on her computer for a while, and then suddenly took her glasses off and looked at Sabrina again.

"There are going to be more Daves, Sabrina. He will always mean something to you because he's your first. But you have a lot to offer the world. And one day some guy is going to see the whole of you. And you will find yourself fitting with him, able to be the exact person you are striving to be because he accepts and sees you for exactly the wonderful person that you are. That person is going to be the smartest person you've ever met in your life, after me, of course. And maybe Dave will still be in your life then. Maybe he'll be watching in the wings, wishing he hadn't blown it with you that day in the parking lot of that stupid uppity country club you're working at. Or maybe it will be the kick in the ass he needed to actually realize what he's missing out on. Or maybe you will have lost touch by then and you'll just look back on him and say to yourself *What the hell was I thinking? He was such a wet rag.* But when you meet that person, you'll feel like you want to fly straight out of whatever self-limiting cage you've built around yourself. And here's the real shocker. That person, might even be *you* . . . you just haven't met this version of yourself yet."

"You think I'm in a cage?"

"I think you *think* you need to keep yourself small, and that you *only deserve* certain things. You deserve everything and more than the next person. But you'll get there. Now stop moping around and get on with your work." Eva snapped with laughter and pointed to the computer in front of Sabrina.

After work Sabrina walked and walked, all the way up to the bus stop and beyond, and into the Wissahickon Valley Park. The river rushed past her, and she felt the warmth of the day settle on her bare arms. The clouds floated along the wide blue horizon she saw beyond the trees, as she looped out of the forest and around toward the rolling groomed greens of the golf course near the country club. She passed the grand houses that led up to her old school. Another five messages from Dave. She opened none of them, she couldn't bear to see what he didn't say.

"What is wrong with you, Sabrina, you are acting so strange lately. No energy, your face, look at it," Lee Lee snapped the following day at breakfast.

"I'm fine, Mom. Really."

"You don't look fine. You are slouching into the chair. Sit up straight. I don't know what's happened but come on, pull yourself up."

Sabrina wanted to tell her mother what had happened, she wanted to cry into her mother's arms like she did when she was a child. But she knew how Lee Lee would react if she admitted to feeling this magnitude of emotion as the result of a boy.

How can you cry over a boy? Nobody is worth those tears. Don't embarrass yourself, she would say.

So instead, Sabrina swallowed down the bitterness that threatened to escape her mouth.

"I'm just tired, I'll be fine. See you tonight," she said and walked out of her house.

DAVE SAT ON the cement bumper of his usual parking space facing the club. He stood as soon as he saw her walk up from her bus stop.

"Hey."

She stared through him and didn't change her expression. He slowed his pace to hers, and their steps were in unison. She felt the same momentary flutter she did at the party when he was waiting for her after the fight.

"I don't want to talk, Dave," she finally said, without turning to him.

"We have to talk, Rina."

Her silence weighed down the air between them. He tried to take her hand in his.

"I'm not leaving until you talk to me."

"Maybe I don't care that much. Maybe we're about to head off to college and I can just forget this all ever happened. Maybe you're forgettable to me." She hated the way her voice sounded.

"Maybe I am. But I care a lot."

She didn't say anything. She wanted him to stop talking. The words he said made her want to cry more. She hardened her mouth, a stiff line across her face, but she felt the tears come to her eyes, and they began to fall down her cheeks. *Stupid, stupid tears.*

Dave waited. His eyes were always the same. He stopped to listen to her. He took in everything she said and listened to everything she didn't say. He waited for her to speak. It was her turn. She couldn't hide from him anymore.

"It hurts," she said finally. "I hate that it hurts."

"I hate that too, Rina."

"Really though? Do you even care about that? Look how you were to Kit. You didn't care about hurting her."

He nodded and she felt his gaze on her face.

"You're right, I didn't care that much with Kit. I was too selfish to care about how I treated Kit."

"So how is that any different with me? You just don't like me enough in *that* way, you just don't want to do the things you did with her."

"I'm sorry, but I don't want to do those things with you. But I do love you as a friend, and I really, really care about our friendship. This is pure to me. When I think of how I acted toward Kit all that time and admitting it to you, I felt so ashamed. But I feel like it would be worse for me to lie. Because it matters what you think about me, Rina. And I want to be here for you. You can have a friendship that is full of love too, right? I want to see you take on the world and jump into the future you have with college and everything else. I'm excited to be here with you. I don't want to mess this all up. Isn't that worth more than a little summer fling or whatever?"

She held on to his words. They managed to hurt and soothe her at the same time.

"I just wish you thought of me like a girlfriend too, I guess."

"I know, but I can't force it. And my hope is that this makes for something that lasts. I don't know if that's better or not, but I'm starting to think it could be."

She turned to him finally, and he stood in front of her and opened his arms. She stood stiff against him and let him hug her. The tears started to pour now, a cascade of salty warm drops falling from her eyes. She wanted to let out a loud sob. His T-shirt got soaked through.

When she pulled away, he laughed. "This is my favorite T-shirt."

CHAPTER THIRTY-EIGHT

Kit

Chestnut Hill, August 2015

It was the loveliest August day. The southern wind that blew through the Herzog yard brought wisps of scent from every other blooming, voluptuous garden that hugged the edges of Gravers Lane. This was how Kit would always remember summer. The swing that Terry built for her swayed gently, the scent of charred meat on the grill, and freshly cut vegetables that Sally had grown being prepared in the kitchen. The breeze was warm and reassuring, and shadows were yet to settle over the flat grassy lawn. Kit laid out her blanket and set down her bottle of water, which started to sweat and left a wet patch on the fabric. Every summer before today, she waited for Sabrina's shadow announcing her arrival as she stood at the edge of Kit's favorite picnic blanket. They'd lie next to each other, talk all day, scroll their phones, listen to music, and laugh. Today it was Ryo's shadow that blocked the sun as she watched the bees fight over the dahlias' nectar.

Kit's body was finally back on Philadelphia time. She had never been to a place as far as Tokyo, had never been in love with someone who returned the same feeling, and had never felt so distant from her best friend, Sabrina.

"Air smells different here," Ryo said. It had already been four days since he had arrived in Philadelphia with his father, and she couldn't get used to the sight of him in her hometown, in her house.

The dense earth beneath the blanket absorbed the soft thud of him sitting beside her.

Something about him being there gave him a different shape—she couldn't quite understand it. When they walked up to Germantown Avenue for a frozen yogurt, he looked different among the white Americans on the high street. He didn't look as tall, his skin a shade or two darker than the boys from high school. His accent jarred a little. It sounded different, the nuance of how he'd say things. *Hey, man . . . Mr. Herzog,* he never said "sir," like the boys she'd grown up with. The bold confidence he had with adults she had marveled at in Tokyo felt strange here. She saw Terry bristle and Sally watch him carefully as her mouth curled up in an unnatural smile. But when these thoughts started to creep into her mind, Kit pushed them away quickly and kissed him urgently when they were alone. The kisses would make these niggling feelings go away, she told herself.

"You're nervous about me meeting your friends?"

"Well, things are a bit weird right now with Sabrina and me so . . ."

"I'm sure you'll be okay. You guys have been friends forever, right?"

"Yeah, maybe."

"I'm going to check in on Dad and your folks."

She watched him jump up, light on his feet, and run up the steps.

───❧───

Kit walked into the kitchen to help her mother set up the table outside and heard Sally talking to someone at the front door.

"I don't think you have the right house." Kit stood in the hallway and listened. Sally's voice was strained, and she rubbed her neck with her fingers.

"Hey, Mom, what's going on? Is Sabrina here? I told her to stop by to meet Ryo."

Nobody answered.

A small, thin Asian woman was standing before her mother. She clutched a piece of paper, torn from a yellow legal pad with faded, tiny, illegible handwriting. Kit's eyes rested on the woman's hands, which were small and bony, neat, compact fine fingers and short nails. Her nailbeds were pale and bitten around the edges. These were working hands, she could see from the creased, roughness of her skin. This woman's hands reminded her of Patrice, the janitor at CHA, who always smiled and closed the door quietly whenever she found Kit crying by the bathroom stalls.

"Nothing, love, you can go back out."

"No, I come to see her," the thin woman said quickly.

"Me?" Kit asked. Fear started to circle around her. She didn't know where it came from.

The woman's eyes bulged, taking in every part of Kit's face.

Kit felt herself color up from the neck and wanted to hide from these prying eyes.

"This is Katherine . . . adopted in 1998 . . . yes?"

Kit looked up at Sally again, her father had appeared, and she stepped back into the crook of his arm that was stretched out and leaning against the doorframe.

"How can I help you, Miss . . ."

"Mimi, my name Mimi Truang," she said in a clipped voice that reminded Kit of Mrs. Chen. "I want to meet your Katherine, I have question for you. For her."

Her mother was thinking of what to say; she could hear the cogs in Sally's brain slowly rotating. How to answer this woman's direct questions—what did she want? Kit glanced back at the garden and felt grateful that Ryo was busy with his father at the bottom of the garden, that he didn't have to see this.

"Ms. . . . Mimi. You look distressed, can I bring you a glass of water?" Sally offered.

Mimi's brow was wet, a film of dampness over her. The pores on her skin were visible, speckled almost, and Kit's eyes moved back down to her hands again. She felt her father's arm behind her, the cotton fabric of his T-shirt against her bare shoulder. She leaned back further, away from the woman.

"Yes, please, Madame. Water." Mimi looked around the boot room. Kit thought the woman might want to sit down. But nobody said anything. This strange woman with a piece of crumbled paper in her hand, where Kit could make out the "ath" in Katherine and "zog" in Herzog.

Nobody said a word as Sally entered the kitchen and began to run the tap. Kit heard the water running; her mother cooled the water first before filling a glass. When Sally returned, her hand shook as she handed over the plastic tumbler, which was only three-quarters full. Water splashed onto the toe of Mimi's right sneaker. Kit stared at the soak mark on the blue fabric of her shoe.

Mimi drank down the water, her eyes closed tight as she drank, and Kit wondered what she would do next. She took a deep gulp of air and spoke again, her words clipped and unsure.

"My baby, many years ago, she go from under my chair, in airport. Only one year old, Madame. I look, and gone. She very small small."

Kit found it hard to swallow. She looked back again and saw through the living room window that Ryo and his father were standing on the deck outside, out of earshot.

"Nobody help me at the airport, Madame, Sir. I alone. I try, I cry, nobody come. My baby Ngan. Her name Ngan. Gone."

Kit said the name in her head. She willed her mouth to stay rigid, not giving away her attempt to put her mouth around the unfamiliar sound. Ng-an. The *an* was sharp, staccato.

She stared back at Mimi, whose eyes flickered back and forth from Sally's face to hers.

"I fly back my Vietnam, but I sleeping, Madame, I sleeping because they give me the medicine, and I cannot do anything. My Ngan, she gone . . ." When she said *My Ngan*, she raised her hand toward Kit. Kit immediately turned her face away and looked to the ground.

The only sound in the room was the birdsong that came in through the open windows. A car drove past on the road outside their driveway.

Sally cleared her throat. "This is truly terrible, Miss. . . . Mimi, really, I cannot imagine. But . . ."

"So I come . . ." Mimi spoke faster; there was a breathless urgency as her chest rose up and down quickly. "I come from my Vietnam, so many years gone now. I ask my madame in my Vietnam, she help me to find my child here in Philadelphia. I try to find the children, my baby." Again, her hand was held out again toward Kit. She moved further back into her father's arms.

"This is all terrible, Mimi. What a terrible thing to have happened. But I can't see how *we* can help."

Mimi opened her mouth to speak again, but nothing came out. Her eyes only looked at Kit, and for the first time, Kit stared back at her. There was a familiarity to her face she couldn't place, and she began to shake. A car pulled up outside, and she recognized the green top of Dave's Jeep Cherokee. She recognized the music, the Rolling Stones. The music was cut off. Sabrina's voice drifted in, riding along the breeze that blew in through the screen window.

"I'll take the dish. You get the door." A familiarity between them Kit hadn't heard before.

THEY WALKED UP the steps from the driveway, and as Sabrina moved to push the doorbell, her eyes fixed on Kit's, then glanced at Sally, and then to the back of Mimi's head. Sabrina stopped. Their eyes locked, and Kit felt herself trying to warn Sabrina: *Run*. Kit glanced back at Mimi, and for a moment, she saw the same eyes that were a round, large, deep dark brown and that creased into their cheekbones when Sabrina smiled, it took over her whole face, she imagined Mimi's would too, and the square line of their jaws that rounded at the cheeks were identical, and even the way the hair fell with waves around their temples. Only Mimi looked tired, exhausted, beaten up even. Kit's eyes returned to Mimi, who turned toward the door, and in a moment, everyone in the room stood still. Sabrina looked at Mimi through the screen door that separated her from everyone inside.

Kit watched as they stared at each other. One sees the other in their future, and the other recognizes a ghost from their past.

The sound of a bowl smashing on the ground, the loud crashing of the china that shattered into shards as if it were one of their lives that had been picked up and thrown upon the ground pulled Kit out of this moment that had unfurled in slow motion before her. Sabrina crouched down and saw a small cut appear on her hand.

"Rina . . ." Dave said in a whisper.

"Ngan . . ." Mimi's breath was heavy, her deep sigh vibrated through the room. It was a breath full of fear, relief, sorrow, and bitterness, with only the smallest edge of sweet joy at its periphery. Mimi's piece of paper fell to the ground, and Kit moved forward and released herself from the shield of Terry's arm.

But in her best friend, she saw only terror. Sally had rushed to get a towel for Sabrina. Kit watched Sabrina turn to Dave, reaching out to him to hold his hand and then she took the car keys from his fingers.

"Rina!" Kit said louder than she wanted to. But Sabrina didn't look back, she rushed down the stairs back to the driveway, tripped over the final one and almost flew headfirst into the ground, but she steadied herself. She slammed the door to Dave's car. The Jeep reversed suddenly, and Kit heard Dave shout out to Sabrina. The tires crunched across the driveway. The screen door slammed again and Mimi rushed out to follow Sabrina. The plastic tumbler fell from her hand. A pool of water started to soak the yellow paper she had been holding. Kit picked it up to see a series of names, hers included, with crosses through them and writing in a language she didn't understand. There was no Sabrina Chen on the list. She felt her mother's arm around her shoulder, and she leaned back into the warmth of her body. It was hot, but she wanted more. There was a cold rush going through her. She wanted to shiver.

"Oh, my sweet girl," Sally said as she stroked her daughter's hair, and Kit felt herself shaking. What had just happened? Her brain had not caught up with the fear and relief she had felt in these eternal minutes. They stretched out like a torturous slow-motion video where her life's dreams hovered over the ground, ready to shatter, and were saved just before impact. But Sabrina . . . what did this mean for Sabrina? Was this woman her mother? Kit saw Mimi Truang's face in her friend's. Anybody could see that Mimi Truang was Sabrina's mother. And her thoughts went to her friend, mangled with the relief and guilt she felt that this was not how her search ended, but where Sabrina's world as she knew it fell apart.

CHAPTER THIRTY-NINE

Sabrina

Chestnut Hill, August 2015

An awful thing happened at the Herzogs' when Mimi Truang appeared at their door that humid August afternoon.

All Sabrina could think about was getting away. She wanted to put as much distance as possible between herself and this woman. She didn't know where she wanted to go. And she didn't know how to drive. But she had to remove herself. The music blasted out of the speaker at a volume that assaulted her eardrums as she turned on the ignition. She could hardly remember the things that Dave had taught her during those few driving lessons he had given her on those empty roads. She put her foot on the brake, she released the hand brake. Then she stepped on the accelerator without taking her foot off the brake. The car made a strange noise and jolted forward and then stopped. Sabrina could see Mimi behind the car. She needed to get to Lee Lee. She needed to get to Eva Kim. She needed to get to somebody who could tell her what to do. She saw Dave running in the rearview mirror. Where was that woman who had the same face as her?

She shifted the car into drive and prepared to steer herself out. But when she pressed down on the accelerator, she went the wrong way. She felt her body jerk forward against the wheel as she reversed. She felt a thud against the back of the car. The thud was muffled and deafening—it sounded like it was coming through her headphones. But after that she could hear nothing, just the mumble of Dave's voice, and the leaves and birds among the trees that lined this house on Gravers Lane.

Had she backed into something she hadn't seen? She couldn't remember seeing a boulder as she drove out. She couldn't remember ever seeing a boulder in all the times she had come in and out of the Herzog drive-way. *What was that?* she thought to herself, and saw Dave sprint faster down the driveway, and then he was out of view as he reached the car and squatted down to the ground. A cold sensation ran through her stomach, and she felt like her bowels might give way. Where was Mimi? She hadn't caught up with the car, had she? She stared into the rearview mirror, at the oak trees and their branches swaying slowly in the breeze. She wanted to scream out *WHERE IS SHE?*

Sabrina turned off the ignition. This is what she recalled. For the rest of her life, this moment came to her in fragments. She couldn't always arrange them in the order in which they happened. The shape of Mimi's body as she lay on the ground. The look in Dave's eyes as she stepped out of the car. The smell of the hot summer day in the air that lingered. The memory of what happened on the driveway at the Herzogs' appeared out of nowhere like flashes of a freak storm in the distance for the rest of her life. But as time passed, she wasn't swept away by the howling winds and began see those moments with glimmers of clarity.

Sabrina had driven Dave's Jeep into this stranger who had appeared at the Herzogs' front door.

This was the end of her world as she knew it. She was at the edge of her most terrifying dream, staring down a sheer vertical precipice. She found Dave kneeling beside this small bird of a woman. This woman was lying on the ground, her shoulders slumped against the stone wall, and a dark terror swirled violently inside Sabrina's stomach.

Was Mimi dead?

She could be.

Did she hit her head?

A concussion?

What had she done?

What should she do now?

The initial fear of who this woman was evaporated the moment she saw her on the ground.

Sabrina stared at the body. She couldn't move. She felt the blood draining from her own face.

Dave was beside Mimi, his finger pressed down on her wrist, checking her pulse.

"Her pulse? Is she?" she heard herself ask Dave. She felt her body starting to move toward them.

Yes, she has a pulse; she's breathing. She's conscious. Good, thought Sabrina, yes. She put aside her fear for a moment and the rational part of her brain took over. Here was a woman who had been hit by a car. She needed attention. She might have a concussion. They needed a doctor. Sabrina had always been good in a crisis, Lee Lee had always told her that. And then she could hear the same words that swept her into a black terror again, like a silent sea monster who came to the surface of the violent riptides. *Ngan, my Ngan.* The way Mimi said the name, Sabrina couldn't get her mouth around it, the nasal sound of the letters clicking in Mimi's throat. It could have been the most foreign-sounding name she had ever heard in her life. In that moment, it was the most alien, most terrifying sound. Somewhere inside of Sabrina, even years later, she blamed Kit, and her return from her summer away from everything.

This woman had come to Kit's house, and now she lay on the ground with her eyes darting around, while she and Dave frantically tried to figure out what to do next as her life started to disintegrate at a pace she had no control over.

Sabrina noticed Ryo and his father were standing by, with expressions of concern over their handsome faces, arms reached out to Mimi, to her. Mr. Buchanan crouched beside Mimi, and Sabrina felt Ryo's hand on her shoulder.

"We should call an ambulance. Or I can drive us to the ER. I'll call 911," Ryo said.

"No, that'll take too long, it's close, the hospital is right there. Can we move her?" she heard herself say again.

"I'll take her, it's faster," Dave said.

"Is her head okay, Sir? Mr. Buchanan? How can we check? Is there a way to know now? Can we move her? Or should we wait?" Her own voice again.

"Her head. There's no blood. I don't see anything, she's alert," Rick said, holding Mimi's hand.

Ryo stood, his head moving back and forth between Sabrina and Mimi. He turned to his father for direction. He looked as though he were ready to start a race, ready to do whatever he was ordered to do. Sabrina looked at him for the first time and saw kindness in his eyes, rushing to help two women he had never met. He ran back to the house to get ice.

Sabrina looked back and saw two figures huddled against each other by the house. Kit and her mother. Sabrina wondered where Mr. Herzog was. She couldn't see the expression on Kit's face. She turned back to Mimi. She looked alert, and her eyes stared back at Sabrina, taking her in. Sabrina crouched down beside her and Dave.

"I think she's okay," he whispered to her. His hands shook.

"Ma'am," Sabrina said it, and stopped. "Mimi . . . Miss, are you hurt?"

Mimi took Sabrina's hand and squeezed. She nodded, tears in her eyes.

Terry Herzog appeared as Ryo disappeared into the house with Kit. "Is she hurt?" Terry demanded from halfway down the drive.

The afternoon sunlight had started to dance in golden-dappled droplets on the gravel path and lawn.

"Her foot is a little swollen, maybe a sprain," Mr. Buchanan responded, now crouched by Mimi's side.

"How many fingers am I holding up?" Terry Herzog asked and thrust his short fingers in front of Mimi's bewildered eyes. *Three.* Mimi said nothing, but her eyes stared back at Sabrina.

"Now Rick, I'm sure you understand my concerns here, and they are of course with this woman's welfare, but you know I'm a belt and buckle kinda guy. I need to ensure there is no room for damages, lawsuits. I know it's . . ."

"Not now, Terry." Rick's words cut through Terry's like a cleaver. A blunt silence fell between them.

"I hear you. But these things need to be covered up front. In my years practicing law . . ."

"That's enough. We need to get this woman to a hospital."

Ryo reappeared alone, pressed the ice against Mimi's foot and told her kindly to keep it in place. He stood and started to examine the car and mumbled to his father in Japanese as Mr. Buchanan spoke to Mimi in English in a hushed, slow, deliberate tone so she would understand what he said. "You're going to be fine, Miss. We will get a doctor."

"I'll drive," Dave said. Sabrina heard the distant rattling of keys.

Mimi's shoe had fallen off, and Sabrina noticed blood—a small stain soaked through the flesh-colored pop sock. It was the kind that Lee Lee wore. And every day when she returned home, she'd sit back in her La-Z-Boy, rubbing the soles of her feet, flexing her toes back and forth. Dave helped Mimi up and lifted her into the rear passenger seat and buckled her seat belt. He carried her as though she weighed nothing. This fragile woman with the same face as her own.

"Are you okay?" Dave asked. She felt his cool fingertips grasp her forearm as she clicked her seat belt. Nobody had asked after her yet, and she was quickly jolted out of her haze.

She nodded and exhaled. "Is your car okay?" she asked, even though she knew it didn't matter.

"Sabrina, who cares. Are *you* okay?"

"I don't know," she said. She looked at the woman in the back seat. "I just don't know."

Mimi looked worse when they arrived at the emergency room. Her face was gray and clammy. Her eyes barely shifted from Sabrina's face. Sabrina could see the resemblance between them. The soft curve of their cheeks. The way their top lips dipped and created a pink petal-like shape. Sabrina's hair fell in exactly the same way over her shoulders. She couldn't erase the resemblance from her mind. It cut through her with savage violence. She pulled her fingers up to her mouth, seeking a loose piece of skin to chew, then cupped her nose and cheek as if somehow covering the features would make the resemblance disappear.

Her thoughts were interrupted by a woman in the waiting room retching into a bucket. "Someone, please help me," she pleaded while expelling whatever was in her stomach. The acrid smell reached Sabrina's nose, and she covered her face again with her sleeve.

The receptionist sucked and clicked her tongue as she looked at her cell phone, typing a message noisily with her acrylic nails tapping against the screen.

"Excuse me, ma'am. We have a woman here who needs to be examined right away," Dave said.

The woman looked beyond Dave, and her eyes settled on Mimi.

"Ma'am, what seems to be the problem?" she asked. There was a lag in her speech, as though she couldn't find the motivation to get to the end of her sentence. The name tag on the lapel of her shirt hung precariously.

Mimi was fully alert now, but she hadn't spoken since falling.

"She fell. Possibly hit her head—and there is a cut or something on her foot," Dave offered.

"Does she not speak English, son?" She slowed her speech, said, "Do-you-understand-me-ma'am?" and Sabrina felt a sudden anger flare the way it would when people shouted and slowed their speech to Lee Lee. She looked at Mimi, searching for a reaction, and at that moment, she could see this was how she expected to be spoken to. As though she were hard of hearing, the expectation was that she wouldn't understand and what a generous act of charity it was that they slowed their speech to help her along. But Mimi was resigned—unlike Lee Lee, who still demanded not to be treated as though she were an imbecile. Mimi was accepting, while for Lee Lee, an offensive stance was always the best strategy.

Sabrina looked around and saw Mr. Buchanan rush through the automatic doors with Ryo beside him. She wondered when the Herzogs were coming. Mr. Herzog said he was getting his car. She messaged Kit. *Is your dad coming?*

The message was delivered but not read.

She started to send a message to Eva Kim. She would know what to do.

She wished she could talk to Dave without Mimi there. She didn't know how much English Mimi understood.

"Ngan . . ." Mimi's voice ventured, and Sabrina felt that cold terror sweep through her again.

"Ma'am, this is Sabrina," Dave said in a voice that was laced with kindness.

Mimi nodded and looked at Sabrina again.

Sabrina opened her mouth but no sound came out. She wanted to reassure this woman, who looked so bewildered and lost. She tried to find the same kindness as Dave, but nothing came out of her mouth. The words just disappeared into a fine mist.

Kit never replied to Sabrina's message, and Terry Herzog never appeared. Mr. Buchanan paid Mimi's medical bill and remained with Dave and Sabrina, who finally had a moment to sit alone while Mimi was examined for a concussion, taken for an MRI, X-ray, and finally given a support bandage for her swollen ankle.

Eva Kim arrived. She stood with Ryo and Mr. Buchanan, where they spoke in hushed voices.

"I'm gonna need a hot minute to get my head around everything, kid. But don't worry. We are going to get through this together."

It was all Eva could say as she put her arm around Sabrina.

Later, Sabrina sat beside Dave in his car in the parking lot as Eva Kim spoke to Mimi in the waiting room.

"Rina . . ."

"Don't ask me anything, Dave. I don't know anything, I don't know any more than you."

"But . . . do you . . . is it . . ."

"Do I see it? Of course I see it." Her body felt an unlocking as she said the words. They were out. It was better to have them out.

"I do too."

Hot tears started to fall down Sabrina's face. And before she knew it, she couldn't properly catch her breath. She felt his arm around her shoulder and leaned into him. His hand stroked her hair.

"Hey, just breathe through your nose, and out through your mouth. We'll figure this out. We will."

CHAPTER FORTY

Lee Lee and Sabrina

Philadelphia, August 2015

Even years later, Lee Lee Chen insisted that taking the baby that day at the airport was fate. That all she did was give kindness and love to a child who had been left behind and would have faced a miserable life otherwise. Lee Lee had raised her, clothed her, fed her. She had taken responsibility for this abandoned baby. What would Sabrina's life have been like if she hadn't rescued her from the airport floor that day? A life of destitution in a deportation center in Philadelphia, or worse, falling into the system as an orphan, into foster care. Lee Lee had provided a stable home and a privileged education. She couldn't admit even to herself that it had actually been about serving Lee Lee's own needs, about her own sense of failure to give her mother a grandchild, to make a success of America. Her familial duty.

Lee Lee had felt the emptiness in her body, the loneliness without Daming. And then this baby appeared and suddenly there was an opening. An opening for more to Lee Lee's life. She was no longer alone.

The invisibility she struggled against was the very thing that allowed her to find Sabrina. No one even glanced at her twice as she clocked out of her shift at the airport with a baby in her arms.

Over the years, nobody stopped to take in the difference in their features, the difference in the shape of their eyes, the way her hair fell differently, she didn't have the same square jaw, her skin tone ever so slightly different than her mother's. Nobody asked why Sabrina looked nothing like her mother. After all, China was a big place, someone from northern China looked completely different from another from the southern provinces. Lee Lee still asserted that her own mother would have known immediately. But would she? She would have been so relieved at the news of an expected baby, she might have just ignored the differences altogether. She had never met Daming after all; she could have just said he was from a southern province of Yunnan or Guangxi, just across the border from Vietnam. *Maybe the next one will be a little boy,* Lee Lee's mother had cooed on the phone when Lee Lee told her the good news, and that she had named her baby Sabrina.

As her daughter grew up at this nice fancy school, nobody questioned it, because nobody really looked there either. When she walked out of that airport, Lee Lee never imagined she'd get this far.

—✦—

Five days after Sabrina met Mimi Truang on Gravers Lane, she sat in a Dunkin' Donuts with Eva Kim and Lee Lee and felt true heartbreak for the first time. The exquisite pain was not from her unrequited love for Dave Harrison, but from her mother, a woman who had pretended to be her mother. As she understood the complete hopelessness of Lee Lee's situation, her heart shattered.

"My *xiao haizi* . . ."

"Don't call me that, I'm not your child."

"You are my Sabrina. Oh but you are."

Sabrina stared at her mother. Lee Lee's eyes were sunken, and her slight frame looked frail and weak. Nobody knew yet what would happen, whether Lee Lee Chen would be deported or if she would face charges for everything she had done. Sabrina could not stand to know the truth yet. But she knew that beneath her sorrow, she cared for this woman, whoever she was.

Since the afternoon that had changed everything, she had been staying with Eva Kim.

"Are you eating?" Sabrina asked.

"A little."

"What?"

"Rice, I eat rice."

Lee Lee's skin had a yellow tinge, especially around her nose and jaw. Jaundice maybe. She remembered looking it up once when Kit was convinced she had it.

"Have you been to work?"

"No, *xiao haizi*, Ms. Eva Kim told me to wait. So I listen to her."

All the strength and fight that Sabrina had always known from her mother was gone. She was a shell of a person. Eva Kim returned and placed three bottles of water on the table and a box of donuts that nobody touched.

"Mrs. Chen," she said, "we really don't have a lot of options. The worst-case scenario is that you get charged with kidnapping. If you're found guilty, you'll be put in a maximum security prison for a long, long time. It could be the remainder of your life, and they may even send you home to serve this sentence. I know you are a tough lady, but I think we can all agree that we do not want that. Agreed?"

Lee Lee, who had been leaning forward to catch every word that Eva said as though she might lose something precious if she missed anything, now nodded furiously.

Sabrina looked down at her hands. She couldn't bear to look at her mother's face.

"A translator and I have been talking to Mimi Truang. Your biological mother," she said to Sabrina. "Right now, she only wants to reconnect with you. That was her sole purpose in coming here. She also doesn't want to stand in the way of your future. She has been very clear about that. She hasn't talked about pressing charges. I'm sorry, we need to get that part out of the way. And it's something we have to talk about. But I think there is a way for us to exercise some damage control."

Sabrina sighed. Such mercy from this stranger.

"Lee Lee, you got here illegally. Your status has always been illegal. You know as well as I do how small communities can be. I'm not saying the Herzogs or anyone in their immediate circle will tell the authorities, but it takes just one person to say something to someone who *would*, and then word starts to travel. The undocumented part is one thing, the abduction of a child . . ." Eva paused and looked at Sabrina. "Well, I've already spelled it out. The best thing you can do, Mrs. Chen, if you agree to it, is to turn yourself in to be deported, but you will be able to live freely back home. But you will never be able to enter the United States again."

Lee Lee's eyes widened and Sabrina took in Eva's words. *Never be able to enter the United States again.*

"*Never?*"

"Never. I'm sorry. That will be nonnegotiable."

Lee Lee nodded, and then she looked at Sabrina. "And what about my *xiao haizi?* What about my girl?"

"I'm working on that. I'm doing everything I can."

There were tears in Lee Lee's eyes now.

❧

The overalls that Lee Lee had to wear in the Pennsylvania Detention Center swallowed her up. She had lost more weight in the week since she had been taken away.

"Do they let you out?" Sabrina asked, fighting back tears.

"They let me walk around. There is a yard. I go there sometimes. To breathe some fresh air. We're waiting. Your friend Eva says I might be able to get back to China soon. Maybe . . . we see."

"Are you scared?"

"I'm not scared. You know me. I am strong. I'm big dragon and you're the little dragon, remember."

A weak smile pulled at the edges of Lee Lee's mouth. Sabrina couldn't smile. She wanted to show her mother she would be all right. But she couldn't pretend—she didn't know if she would be.

"Are people, are they . . . do they threaten you?"

Lee Lee looked at her and tilted her head. She didn't know the word . . . or did she?

"Do the people here say they will do bad things do you?"

Lee Lee smiled and shook her head, but Sabrina wasn't sure if she believed her.

"Now tell me, *xiao haizi*. What did you decide about college? Did you get the funding? I see Eva! God bless you, Eva!" she shouted through the glass to Eva, who came in and sat behind Sabrina. Her support.

Eva had been with Sabrina every day, and had hardly left her side. It was only a matter of time before people found out what Lee Lee had done. Eva said they had to get ahead of it and take control immediately. They waited to hear what would happen to Lee Lee, and then to make a case for Sabrina's status, forging a path to legal citizenship in the only world she had ever known.

"Hey, Mrs. Chen. How you holdin' up in there?"

Eva Kim never slowed her speech or changed her tone when she spoke to Lee Lee. She spoke to everyone in the exact same way. And Sabrina loved her for it.

"Oh, I'm a survivor, Eva Kim. Always okay." Lee Lee forced a smile. Sabrina felt the fracture in her heart deepen as she looked at her mother's face.

"So, I've been doing some research, and I am going to be totally honest with you both."

Sabrina smiled. When would Eva Kim ever tell them half-truths?

"For you, kid, I made an application for DACA, the Deferred Action for Childhood Arrivals. You can stay with me, if that's okay with you, as we figure this thing out. You will be able to stay in this country. On the documentation side, I'm confident we can eventually get you a green card and naturalization, but it will all take a bit of time. All right? We just have to be patient and get everything together."

Lee Lee nodded, and Sabrina could see her mother taking in the words. Sabrina would stay with Eva Kim, but would she ever see Lee Lee again?

"So, my girl, she will still go to college?"

"Yes, she will go to Princeton and get her degree."

"And she is safe? She can stay here in America? Nobody will come for her? Nobody will send her away? She can have the papers?"

"Yes, Mrs. Chen. I will make sure of it. Sabrina's future is secure."

"What if something happens? Who will she go to?"

"She will come to me."

"You adopt her?" Lee Lee's eyes widened.

"No. She's a legal adult now. But I will be there for her, in any capacity she needs as an adult, as a friend. I'll be her emergency contact, I'll be her legal counsel, I'll even have her at Christmas if she doesn't have other plans. She's stuck with me. Okay with you, kid?"

Sabrina couldn't speak. She never expected so much from Eva Kim, and she had nothing left in her heart in that moment.

"I think, Mrs. Chen, we can both agree that you raised one hell of a young woman here, who is probably ten times the adult that you or I are." Eva put her arm around Sabrina and squeezed her close and Sabrina's eyes welled up. Her face was quickly soaked with tears that would not stop.

She felt her mother's eyes on her.

"This is all that matters," Lee Lee said quietly and placed her hand on the glass pane between them. "This is the best way." Sabrina raised her hand and placed it against the thick glass that separated them, meeting her mother's palm.

EVERYTHING HAD BEEN arranged swiftly in the weeks following their meeting at Dunkin'. Donuts. Lee Lee cried with gratitude when she saw Eva Kim. Sabrina had never seen her mother cry until Mimi Truang came back into their lives. Now she cried every time they saw each other.

The day Lee Lee was taken away to the detention center, she grasped at Eva's hands and sobbed *God bless you, Eva Kim, bless you bless you.* With each declaration of thanks, another piece of Sabrina's heart broke away. She watched her mother being driven away in a state vehicle, her eyes fixed on the silhouette of Lee Lee's head in the window until the car disappeared around the corner of Ridge Avenue toward Kelly Drive.

Sabrina wondered if she would ever be able to go back to seeing her mother the way she did before any of this. Would she be able to love her in the same way?

Sabrina's life was falling apart, but for the first time she could remember, somebody was taking care of the things that felt beyond her capabilities. She had placed her full trust in Eva Kim's hands. *You leave it with me. Out of all this mess, we are going to get you a passport, a green card, and you will get your degree if it's the last thing we do. Hell, I'm even going to personally take you down to that dump of a DMV to get you a license.*

In the week before Lee Lee's departure for China, Sabrina continued going to her jobs at the country club and at Eva Kim's office. One afternoon she overheard two women talking about Sally Herzog in the clubhouse. She hadn't shown up for her usual ladies' tennis clinic because she was away at the shore for the final two weeks of August. *How strange to go away before the end-of-summer party. Everybody's back in town to show off their suntans. Maybe it's because their daughter is starting college?*

That afternoon, as Sabrina sat on the bus on the way back to Eva Kim's apartment, she messaged Kit.

> SABRINA: Hey, I heard you went away or something. The shore?

Almost immediately, a response came back.

> KIT: Hey Rina, yeah, I'm sorry I haven't been in touch. We've been busy prepping for college. And I didn't know if you wanted to be left alone or not with everything that happened. Ryo's family are still here too, so we brought everyone down to the shore for the rest of the summer break.

Sabrina felt a pain in her chest that rose up to her throat. Was it Kit's idea to get away or was it her parents'? Maybe they just wanted as much distance as possible from her, from all the mess on their doorstep that day. Another message alert.

KIT: I hope you're OK. I can't imagine everything you've gone
  through.

Sabrina stared at the words, but she didn't know what she expected from her friend. It wasn't this. So she sent the easiest response she could bear to write.

SABRINA: I'll get there.

ON THE DAY before Lee Lee was deported, Sabrina went to see her mother and sat with her at a table, supervised by security officials. They held hands, and Sabrina could see the white in her mother's knuckles. They were told they had one minute left.

Sabrina could hardly speak as she felt Lee Lee's arms hold her so tight, like never before. And when she pulled away and looked at the pools of tears in her mother's eyes, she couldn't stop herself from asking.

"Why did you do it, Mom . . . Why?" Her heart throbbed inside her chest.

Lee Lee answered, "Because I had to. You needed me. And I needed you."

CHAPTER FORTY-ONE

Lee Lee

Philadelphia International Airport, May 18, 1998

The day Lee Lee took Sabrina, she did not yet know that it would be her last day alone. Lee Lee woke up to her alarm at four o'clock and swung herself off her mattress in one motion. It took her a moment to remember it was a Monday—just an early shift, a half day.

Her commute was always the same. The same bus from South Philadelphia. The same older woman who drove the bus. But she never looked up at Lee Lee, who paid with single coins, in spite of the irritated line that formed behind her. One week, Lee Lee had decided to count how many times the bus driver ignored her, but after four days in a row, she stopped counting. She heard her from the middle of the bus. *Hey, sugar, what you got for me today? Oh it's gonna rain cats and dogs later. God bless you, honey.* But the words were always for someone else.

Lee Lee always sat in the middle. It was easier to get off at her stop that way. She dreaded when larger men sat beside her and she was forced to raise her voice to ask them to move aside. But mostly, nobody took that seat, and she stared out at the low-rise houses and the graffiti and watched the world outside as the bus tumbled its way to the airport.

Before the sun rose fully, Lee Lee paused to stare out the window as the orange and pink skies transformed everything into a thing of beauty. A young mother stopped beside her, clutching at the neck of her child's T-shirt. The boy rushed toward everything.

"Just won't stop moving, this kid," she mumbled to nobody in particular, but it could have been to Lee Lee, as the woman forced a smile.

Lee Lee watched the boy climbing up onto the chairs and climbing back down again. An immense pleasure and satisfaction spread across his face, and he laughed as he clambered up and down. The mother held him lightly by his dimpled elbow.

Children were everywhere she looked. She couldn't get away from them. Daming had died almost six months ago. She didn't know whether she grieved for him or for the life they had planned to have. Lee Lee still hadn't told her mother that he was gone, and she continued to ask after a child, her admonitions increasing with every call. Lee Lee knew she was being a coward, she knew she needed to tell her that the man she had planned to start a life with was gone, but she did not want to admit that she had failed. She woke every morning to notice that any evidence of his existence was fading. She felt invisible and forgotten, and wondered whether Daming had ever loved her, or whether, like her, he was just lonely.

Hurry up, Lee Lee. Don't wait around like these Western women. Just get on with starting your family.

We all have a duty to continue our line.

You could even have two children, you're not here, after all.

She let her mother's hope for a child continue to grow over the phone lines.

✦ ✦ ✦

IT WASN'T JUST the family expectations. Lee Lee knew she was too sharp, she lacked a softness that many women had. She had no delicate vulnerability, no need to be cared for, or saved by a man. She liked to be in control. Daming would take her orders and shuffle a few steps behind, that was in his nature. But now he was gone, she wouldn't find anyone else like him.

That morning, she walked into the staff canteen and saw that Tanya from Sbarro had taken Lee Lee's usual seat in the far corner by the window. A small knot of anger rose up inside her chest. It was Lee Lee's seat, didn't Tanya know this? Lee Lee considered sitting at the same table, but the thought evaporated fast. She turned to find another table and heard the squeak of her left sneaker with every step she took. The noise was deafening in her head until she sat down, close to the bathrooms. She was hungry. The staff breakfast was a burrito. She stared at the congealed egg that had started to glisten on her plate. She felt the hunger pull at her insides. She longed for rice. Clean white rice and green vegetables, cooked in garlic and chili. She closed her eyes and took a large bite of her burrito. The red sauce with its sickly sweetness clung to the insides of her mouth. And a large drop of green mush fell onto her plate. The wet heaviness of the sauce splashed onto the table in specks. She wiped the table with the thin napkin. There were tiny wet dots on her gray uniform. Her eyes darted up to see if anyone had seen the piece of food fall onto the table. But nobody saw. Nobody was looking.

THE BABY WAS not crying. Her eyes were round and shiny. When the baby looked up at Lee Lee, she expected the child to cry or crawl away, but instead she held her gaze. Lee Lee stepped away from the carts she had collected and walked toward the chubby hand that reached outward and found herself meeting her small fingers with her own. Lee Lee looked around Gate D12 to see where the child's mother was. But there was nobody. The gates were closed and there wasn't a single person there. She always went to the empty gates at the end of her shift to return abandoned carts for any coins she could claim. She watched the passengers in the distance walking quickly toward their gates and heard the siren of the buggies carrying those who needed physical help fading on the opposite side of the terminal.

"Where's your family?" she heard herself coo. But the child just looked up at her. Sitting, legs open on the floor in front of a five-seater bench.

The child held Lee Lee's finger in her hand, and something burst inside of her. A dam that held back her sadness from the last year began to overflow. She pulled her finger from the child's grasp and looked around. She was just twenty or so steps away from the staff door that would take her to her locker. She slowly started to move away from the child. But the child laughed and began to follow. A game. A few more steps, and the child's deft hands and knees on the ground carried her in pursuit of her new friend. Lee Lee finally reached the staff exit and looked around her. It was still a few hours until any passengers would come to this gate. She pushed the door open, and the child looked at Lee Lee. The child seemed to immediately accept her, and a small part of Lee Lee's heart broke away, a small piece that would always belong to this child.

She knelt down and picked the baby up as she passed the threshold into the staff area, which was empty after lunch. In the distance she heard crying—a woman wailing. She glanced back and saw a small crowd of people. But she didn't turn back with the child. The baby wrapped herself around Lee Lee's waist, a movement that felt natural, and her small legs instinctively squeezed, as though she and the baby were two pieces of a puzzle that were suddenly fitting together after so much time searching. The child played with the end of Lee Lee's limp ponytail, and she wished she had washed her hair the night before. A crumb from the child's fingers balanced among the strands. She decided she must be a girl because of the leggings—but it was only hours later when she knew for certain. Lee Lee stood in front of her locker and took out her bag. The child's weight started to strain her arm. She looked down into the round shiny eyes that smiled at her. Lee Lee wrapped her arm tighter around the child and threw her bag over the other shoulder. She walked out of the room, putting her time sheet into the wall-mounted shelf. She looked ahead, eyes straight as she walked out of the terminal, toward the bus stop, and then past the bus stop. She walked and walked, as the child sat on her hip and laughed. Her arm burned from the pain of carrying her, but she walked. Finally, Lee Lee sat down at a different stop from her regular one and waited to see if she would recognize the bus driver who pulled up.

CHAPTER FORTY-TWO

Mimi

Ho Chi Minh City, November 2015

Toan looked at his wife with expectation every morning. *He's waiting for me to break down,* Mimi thought to herself. Perhaps he was. But a strange peace had come over her since she finally saw Ngan. Now her fear was replaced by a melancholy resignation. After everything that passed that day, she was forced to recognize that her Ngan was a woman who had grown up without her, her mother. She was American, and things that seemed so far from the realms of possibility were within arm's reach for her. They lived in different worlds that might never have crossed, except for this thread that bound them together, the thread she could never let go of, that drew them back together. Mimi had finally found her beautiful daughter, and she wept constantly afterward, but they were tears of bittersweet joy that only a parent could understand. She ate the bitterness, so that only sweetness would await her child.

Toan, on the other hand, tiptoed around her with the same delicate care he might offer a small bird with a broken wing. He searched her expression every morning. She expected him to stop after the first few weeks following her return to Saigon; instead, the weeks stretched into months. She finally found a job back on the compound with a Scandinavian family who had just arrived in Saigon. There were two young children, but she didn't feel the same pain around children as she had before.

And so Toan and Mimi's existence resumed.

As Christmas drew near and the rainy season began, she thought of Ngan more and more. A message appeared on Mimi's phone on a stormy day as she scrubbed the bathroom floors for her madame.

Mimi, it's me, Sabrina. I wondered how you've been?

A small shoot of hope sprang through the dark, damp earth.

"Look at this, Toan, look what my girl sent."

He peered into the phone and chewed his lip.

"I want to reply. Maybe she will come to visit?"

Toan returned the phone to her.

"You don't think she will?"

"Maybe yes." He smiled.

Mimi felt annoyed. She wanted more from him. But she didn't ask. She knew her husband by now. His mind was somewhere else. She could see it in his eyes.

MIMI'S DAYS BLURRED into one long stretch of waiting. She waited for the water deliveries for her madame. She waited for Toan to collect her from the compound on Fridays, on his motorbike. She waited for the rains to stop so she could clear the gardens. She waited for Sabrina to send her more messages. And sometimes, she was rewarded for her patience. Sabrina would message, and Mimi's heart would soar.

✦ ✦ ✦

TOAN HAD STARTED to act strangely. There were small signs at first. Returning home late, forgetfulness. One day he came home wearing someone else's shoes from the driver's room, and she knew something was wrong.

But for Mimi, his sudden lack of interest in food set off the cogs in her frontal lobe. Instead of looking at his wife expectantly with a wry smile on his lips an hour before mealtimes, he was engrossed with his phone. Sometimes he woke before her, and she kept her eyes closed and pretended to be asleep. As he rolled over, she could see the faint glow of his phone in the dark room as he scrolled and tapped. She watched him put the phone away in his pocket, the weight of it pulling down on his tracksuit. He pulled it back out in less than a minute, checking again, scrolling. His incessant checking increased as evening drew on.

Mimi watched him leave for work on his motorbike, and a morose dread settled like a dark rain cloud blocking the light. She knew her husband well enough to know it would never be another woman. Instead, she suspected he was going to ask his mother to come live with them, as so many men did as their mothers grew older. Mother and son were plotting together. Mimi's duty as a wife to Toan would now mean she had to look after the elderly parent. Their time together, the two of them in their peaceful existence in her crazy Saigon was coming to an end. There would be another body in the house, watching and criticizing all the time.

Mimi had never pictured her life being this way. She had always wanted a large family, poor but happy. She imagined her children, and they always looked just like Ngan.

One morning she woke up and had had enough.

"When are you going to tell me the truth?"

A look of surprise passed over his face.

"The truth?"

"Yes. The truth, Toan. When are you going to tell me that your mother is coming to live with us? You're just like all the others, bringing your mother to watch over me, criticize me."

Tears started to glisten in Mimi's eyes. She fought them back and held her mouth in a stiff line.

"What? My mother?"

For a moment, a wave of doubt passed through her. He looked shocked, then amused at her suggestion. It suddenly occurred to her that she might be wrong. Maybe it was even worse—a sickness he was hiding from her.

"You are hiding it from me. Don't you know I know? Tell me the truth, Toan."

She wrenched her fingers, squeezing and twisting them as she stared into her husband's face and willed him to confess.

"You think I'm bringing my crazy mother to live with us?"

"Well, how else do you explain your behavior? You've been so strange. Checking your phone all the time. Forgetful. You even lost your appetite."

He smiled, and she felt the anger inside her rise up her throat.

"How can you laugh at me? This is cruel of you."

He moved to sit beside her, and the chair made a loud noise as he dragged it across the floor. He reached for her hands, cupping her clenched fists in his hand.

"How could you think I would do such a thing to you? When I am the luckiest man. I am so happy in our little paradise here together. My little general."

She snorted. "What nonsense, I'm damaged, and you took pity."

"One day you will see what I see."

Her tears began to fall, and her whole face was soaked in no time, a sob escaping from her mouth.

He waited for the heaving to stop and reached for the tissue box on the table.

Mimi wiped her face and patted down the wet pool of tears that had soaked her T-shirt.

"I have been speaking with Ngan, Sabrina. I never know what to call her. In my mind she is Ngan. We wanted to surprise you."

CHAPTER FORTY-THREE

Sabrina

Ho Chi Minh City, December 2015

The light over the city took on an astonishing pink that Sabrina had never seen before. Everything before the moment she arrived in Saigon suddenly seemed muted, and now she was seeing in Technicolor. She drank everything in. The buildings rose up before her, and cranes interrupted the horizon, but beyond that, she could still see the green land, palms, and a jungle.

There was a quiet beauty in the veins that ran through the city, slow-moving motorbikes all finding their own ways, splitting, adapting, giving way. The city was a living, pulsing beast that grew higher and broader overnight. The vista of this city could have been her home. She watched figures walking along the streets, hawkers pulling their carts, and she tried to imagine their lives. How do they greet their children when they return from work? What do they talk about? Do they hold each other?

Her phone pinged in her hand.

DAVE: You arrived? How is it?

She turned off her phone and put it in her backpack. She had read on a travel blog that this was the best time of day. Dusk in Vietnam was the magic hour. It filled her with joy, the familiar joy she'd felt when she walked along the country club at the end of her shift in summer, as the skies burst with colors they'd been hiding all day long, the light giving up one last fight before the darkness came. But here, she didn't know what lay ahead of her. She could only see the possibility.

LATER, WHEN SABRINA looked back on the months before she decided to visit Mimi, she would remember very little. The distance grew between her and Kit after college began. In truth, she hadn't tried very hard to hold on to the friendship, and eventually Kit's messages went from daily to weekly to one every couple of weeks or more. She could see from Kit's Instagram that she was doing what all freshmen at college do, going to parties and joining societies at Penn. She was happy for her friend—this part she did remember. And one day she looked at Kit's most recent story and saw a blond boy she was snuggled up to in the picture. They held each other; he wore a cap backward and she wore a beanie, and she recognized the backdrop of the Snak's Coffee House in Mount Airy. *Drinking in that hot chocolate goodness with my love on the first day of winter,* read the caption.

She thought about the last time she had seen Kit. They met downtown, across the street from Kit's dorm at Penn during Kit's midterm break. They were only an hour apart, but it was the first time they had seen each other since college had started.

"You look so different, Rina," Kit said they sat in the diner on Vine Street.

"Well, I cut my hair?" Sabrina offered, pulling at the ends of her blunt shoulder-length cut. She still felt a brief pang of surprise when she saw the flicker of blond at the tips. Lee Lee would have hated it. *You look like a punk girl, drug addict, rock 'n' roller,* she would have tutted. But she knew that Kit wasn't talking about her hair.

"It looks good."

"How's school?"

"Yeah, it's good . . . Ryo and I are taking a break." Kit said the last part fast.

Sabrina listened and waited. Kit's fingernails were short and raw. They looked as though they had been bitten recently.

"You want to talk about it?" Sabrina asked finally.

"Not really. Tell me your news."

Sabrina waited, because when Kit said she didn't want to talk about things, she often didn't mean it.

Finally, Kit sat back and took a deep breath.

"I don't know what it was, I think we were just kind of drunk on Tokyo and that final summer before college. When he started at Berkeley, and we started this whole traveling back and forth to see each other, all the FaceTime calls, the messages, it just . . . I don't know . . . we were so different. Like, he is so *so* outgoing. And yeah, I know, I'm kind of sociable too, but I don't want to join all the societies or go to every party and I'm not even sure I want to be part of that whole sorority, fraternity scene, which I guess he's into. He wants to be part of everything and be active and involved all the time, like all these groups in college. He goes to these rallies, and he's always trying to enlist new members. He's always like, *participating,* that's what he calls it. I get it. I'm part of that too, but you know how I am, I'm not a joiner, we always used to say that, remember?" She half smiled at Sabrina, waiting for acknowledgment. "And I know I have a responsibility to my fellow mixed-race, *ha-fu* students. Like getting rid of the labels of being half, it kind of implies we're not enough, and how we're seen in Japanese society too. But I just . . . I don't know, it's kinda a lot with him. And sometimes I felt like judged by him or something for not being more vocal about my beliefs. And I don't know if I felt *good* with him. And to be honest, I don't know what I do feel about everything because I still don't exactly know who I am and stuff. Because I'm kind of confused and I need to figure myself out a bit too. I don't know that we really *belonged* together, you know?"

Sabrina tried to think of any moment that Kit took responsibility for anything.

Kit's eyes were bloodshot, her face drawn, and her skin had lost its golden glow after the summer. Sabrina suspected it was a combination of late nights, drinking, and whatever had passed between her and Ryo.

"Are you guys still friends?"

"Yeah, sure. I mean we kinda message sometimes. But less and less. I think he's met someone new, you know? How could he not, right? Look at him. And I've been hanging out with some of the guys from high school. Nothing serious."

Sabrina took a sip from her Sprite and studied Kit's face.

"Did you find a way to contact your birth mother in the end?" Sabrina asked, knowing the answer already.

Kit looked away from her friend and Sabrina could see the thoughts churning in her mind before she opened her mouth.

"Mom and I are still talking about it. I'm thinking about getting an intermediary, to see if I can reach her that way. I guess it was such a long time ago she gave me up, right? So I guess I need to think on that and decide. It's a big decision, and I'm not sure yet . . . I mean, she probably has this life now and all. But you know, what if it's this big anticlimax and it just causes these problems between Mom and me? I mean, it was a closed adoption for a reason. And so, I don't know, I'm trying to think before I act on this one. For once in my life . . ." She laughed. Sabrina could hear the words that Sally Herzog would have said to her daughter, but beneath it all was a fear that she had not seen in Kit before.

"That's tough. I'm sorry. But it sounds like you're being really smart about how you're taking this forward. Like, you know what you want to do, and you're thinking about all your options." Sabrina said this because she knew it was what Kit would want to hear and what she needed to hear from her friend, the same blind support Sabrina always gave her.

Kit smiled and said nothing, and finally asked about Dave.

Sabrina explained that they were still in touch, that the friendship withstood everything, but to her surprise Kit didn't look annoyed. She had expected her to be, but maybe her friend was letting her have this, after everything.

"It's kind of funny you guys ended up getting so close."

"I know, right? I never expected it," Sabrina replied.

Kit smiled, but there was no malice. "You know, I think before everything I would have felt kind of pissed that he chose to be your friend over me. But I mean this totally, hand on heart, I don't feel pissed at all . . . in case you thought I was. And it kind of makes sense you guys being close. There's something that just fits better, even as friends. You guys like the same stuff, those old bands you love. You're both kinda quiet."

"That's nice, Kit. I'm happy to hear it. As long as you're happy. I'm sure you have guys lining up for you."

There was another silence, they came more often now, and Sabrina felt the space between them expand again.

"What about you? What are your plans?" Kit asked, straightening in her chair.

"Well, quite a few things are happening, I guess. I'm finishing up my jobs soon. I accepted my place at Princeton last week. So yeah, this year is my year off, I guess." Sabrina finally added, "After everything with my mom and Mimi, Eva helped me with the legalities of staying here in the United States, keeping my place at Princeton. She also made me realize that maybe I need to try to understand things a little better. Get to know my birth mother. And in time, I'll go and visit Lee Lee. It's weird calling her that because she's still my mom. We're in touch now. I couldn't talk to her for a while but we're working through that now. It's just, I have to adapt to how things turned out, you know?"

"Is it weird? Knowing everything you do now about your mom, well, not your mom, but you know . . ."

"Of course. I feel like I might have always suspected something . . . or maybe that's just the power of seeing things in retrospect. I keep calling her Mom—Lee Lee, I mean. Because she *was* my mom, she *is* my mom . . . but how I see everything now is different."

"Kinda . . . but not really."

"All this time you have this idea about yourself. Like, for example, your Japanese roots, right? And then imagine you find out that actually you are not at all from Japan, but somewhere totally different, like Vietnam like me, or somewhere?"

For a brief, barely detectable moment, Sabrina noticed Kit's lips pursed before she rearranged her face back to an expressionless state. But Sabrina couldn't leave it alone. "How do you think you'd feel about that?"

"What do you mean?"

"How do you think you'd feel, finding out after all this time that you weren't from Tokyo, or Japan, or whatever. What if you were from a super poor developing country, like me? What if your biological mom had nothing? Like Mimi, like my mom. What if she was desperate too?"

"Why would she have nothing? I mean, I know that she's from Japan. It says on that document, you know? The one about her nonidentifiable traits, remember?"

Sabrina knew that wasn't exactly what it said on the document but she couldn't bring herself to point it out. "That's not the point I'm trying to make."

"What is your point?" Kit's voice had beome sharper again. Sabrina knew that tone, and by now Sabrina knew it wasn't her, it was never her that angered Kit. It was something inside of Kit that blew up, because she couldn't find peace in herself, she didn't like the sum of her parts.

"My point is, that we believe what we want to about ourselves."

Kit rattled the ice in her cup with her straw and said, "Maybe."

She had not told Kit of her plans to go to Vietnam. She could not unsee the look of relief on Kit's face that day when she'd realized that it was Sabrina who was, in fact, Mimi's lost daughter. Something between them snapped in that moment. It wasn't malicious. She was just happy it wasn't her. Because Kit was happy exactly where she was: the big house, her fancy exotic origins left unscathed. It wasn't personal—anybody would be horrified to know they were a baby who had been taken in an airport. But Sabrina also saw something else in Kit's relief, the discomfort with Ryo, as time passed. It was all too far from her world on Gravers Lane. There was almost too much *ha-fu* with Ryo, and Kit was only comfortable with the suggestion of her Japanese-ness, as long as it wasn't too much. Kit was a Herzog in her marrow, while Sabrina was a Chen, and now she was also a Truang.

The things that Kit feared most were getting too far away from the safety of her borders, while Sabrina's greatest fear was losing the only mother she had known, Lee Lee. And that had already happened.

Even though the blood that ran through her was not Lee Lee's, their bond would never be broken. There had been too much love, in whatever form Lee Lee had chosen to show it, the long hours she worked to provide for her daughter, the stern pressure she put on her to study hard, even in the *baozi* she made for her. She was always eating the bitterness to give Sabrina everything. Lee Lee always endured. And now Sabrina had Mimi, a mother she had never known, from a place she had never been to. She wondered what kind of mother Mimi might have been.

The only thing she remembered with total clarity after that August day in the Herzog driveway was Dave's hand on her arm. He was the only one who saw at that moment how her life might fall apart when she recognized herself in Mimi's face. He didn't let go. He stayed with her in the hospital. He drove her back to her house and waited in his car for her as she confronted her mother. He took her to the detention center whenever she visited Lee Lee. He came to the Coalition office with her when Eva Kim was working on getting her a passport and green card. He sat with Eva Kim and pushed Sabrina to take her place in Princeton the following year. He was the first person she called when she decided with Eva that she would visit Mimi to find out the truth about herself. And Dave was beside her, never altering the hand of friendship he offered her, keeping all the pieces of her from shattering on the ground.

Now Sabrina stood alone. A hopefulness and wholeheartedness filled her. She looked out over Saigon. Mimi never said Ho Chi Minh City. She always said *My Saigon*. Sabrina was in the city where her birth mother had lived without her for her entire life. She wanted to know this woman she had this invisible connection to. This woman who loved her so much that she never gave up searching for seventeen years. She hoped the surprise she had planned with Toan through broken messages would come off. Sabrina's flight had landed so late. She would call Toan in the morning. She wanted a moment to take it all in before she opened the door to this part of herself. She felt a tenderness for Dave—his determination to keep their friendship even when he had broken her heart. She understood now it was just a different way to be loved. This was the wilderness . . . and she felt exhilaration and fear run through her as she realized she was out there, all by herself. Finally, she was finding her place in the world. She took her phone out again and started to type to Dave. I've arrived . . .

ACKNOWLEDGMENTS

This book has taken several years to come into being. And there were many that contributed to the work you see you here.

To my agent, Sheila Crowley, the most supportive, wonderful agent an author could wish for. Thank you for believing in me, and my work. For always putting up with my wobbles and always in the front row to support me. Many, many years ago when I was clutching at my *Writers' & Artists' Yearbook* and searching through literary agents, my dream was always to be signed at Curtis Brown, and look at me now.

To my incredible publishers at Hutchinson Heinemann. Thank you to Helen Conford and Ailah Ahmed, who believed in this novel immediately and gave me a chance I could only dream of. I can truly say I love spending time with you both, and I'm so grateful for the care you have given this work. Thank you Venetia Butterfield for always knowing exactly what to say.

To Alice Dewing, who works tirelessly to promote the book, and Ania Gordon for your infectious cheer and joy and gently pushing me along.

To Pamela Dorman, who has steered me on course in every way. What a rock star.

To the great Marie Michels. I couldn't have asked for a more wonderful editor, and I love your straight-talking notes and incredible eye.

To Deborah Sun de la Cruz for your sensitivity and work on this book, and for being the most amazing sounding board throughout.

To Abby Parsons at Curtis Brown Creative, who was a huge early supporter of my work and gently pushed me to finish the manuscript and keep challenging myself to get it just right before it went on submission.

To Anna Davis, Lisa O'Donnell, Andrew Michael Hurley, and Nikita Lalwani at Curtis Brown Creative, who were key to pushing the story forward in the early stages. I always remember Nikita's words, "You have to cannibalize your own work to create the very best version of it." It's something that really stuck with me.

To my CBC course mates who took the time to look at the very early pages of my work, I'm so grateful for your patient, kind words and feedback.

Thank you to Emily Harvey, Ann Curvis, and Ceara Elliot at Cornerstone.

At Pamela Dorman Books and Penguin Random House US, thank you to Brian Tart, Andrea Schulz, Patrick Nolan, and Kate Stark. To Tricia Conley, Tess Espinoza, Nick Michal, Diandra Alvarado. To Sharon Gonzalez, Jason Ramirez, Lynn Buckley, Claire Vaccaro.

Thank you to the amazing publicity and marketing team: Mary Stone, Raven Ross, Rebecca Marsh, Sara Delozier. The sales team: Andy Dudley and Rachel Obenschain.

Thank you to Jane Cavolina for your incredibly sensitive notes and needle-sharp knowledge of downtown Philadelphia geography.

To Nanna Arnadottir, my greatest cheerleader—you've seen the good, the bad, and the ugly—without you, there would be no book, truly. And all of this started on those dusty streets of Thao Dien, as we tapped away at our laptops in Mekong Merchant while sipping on Café Sua Da.

Thanks to Kat Crane, the very best of tennis buddies, supporters, and wholly invested first civilian reader. Our hikes around Dempsey Hill and up and down Bukit Timah Hill were the best backdrops for talking about every aspect of life, including this book.

To Claire Warren, my gorgeous Alves, for always supporting me. To Julia Atwood, who is the Queen of pep talks—when the doubt starts to creep in you always deliver and how I miss our sacred date nights.

To Marisol and John, for all your support over the years.

If Kit and Sabrina showed me anything, it's that friendships are often the very essence of belonging. I have been lucky enough to be blessed with the very best of friends who have quickly become like family around the world. My darling Katherine Neathercoat, Anya Gardiner, Natalie von Hurter, Katy Rickards, Eliza Paige. From Chestnut Hill to Singapore, thanks to Diana Bellonby, where we searched high and low for the perfect location to work, Breeny Kim, Georgia Day, Mel Fernandez, Lynne Taylor, and Caroline Brill.

To my parents, who gave me the kind of life that showed me the world and left me questioning—and a willingness to find out. My mother for her love of literature that she passed to me. To my father for his love of a good story and its soundtrack, the backbone of it all, really. Everything (including every idea I have) starts with a playlist. And my sister Kirsty Kelly for witnessing the teen angst firsthand (that may have come through in some of these pages) and still sticking around!

To my husband, James. I have wanted to be a published author since we met twenty-five years ago. And you never stopped believing in me, and always telling me to get my ass in the chair. Thank you for everything.

And finally, to Maya Skye Strenner, my brave, thoughtful girl who is full of gumption. She too has traveled the world with us and finds a different shaped place to belong every time. She busts open my world, takes me well beyond the boundaries of my comfort zones, and makes me want to be a better person who doesn't shy away from getting into the arena . . . just like her.